With One Kiss

A Novel

Carol Ann Iaciofano

This is a love story, I love baseball. A long time ago, I spent days with my dad learning about baseball so that when I went to a professional game I would know what was going on. I cherish those days. Those memories are ones that will always stay in my heart ♥

I dedicate this book to my friend Rhonda, you know who you are — I didn't forget the little people— for giving me an experience I had never had before. A love for baseball! Thank you for encouraging my passion for baseball. I have had many favorite baseball players through the years, but a few will always stay in my heart for the kindness I saw them show towards fans and teammates both on and off the field. They were inspiring.

Crystal Bella Steele can't believe that Cody Parker is on the same flight that she is on. As he walks down the isle of the plane heads turn. Crystal doesn't have to turn her head to watch him. He is walking right to her. A woman on the other side of the isle nods at Cody and smiles. She is very flirty with him until the guy next to her says who he is. She looks at him again and says as Cody Parker walks by that he is a washed up has been baseball player. Crystal looks down at her phone and then back up at Cody and says how stupid the woman is. Crystal and him lock eyes and she smiles at him.

She looks at her iPad and snaps the case closed tossing it in her purse and closes her eyes. Cody watches Crystal and sees her head drop forward. A pilot walks down the isle and asks Cody if he would take care of Crystal if there was anything wrong. Without hesitation, Cody agrees and sits next to Crystal. After he gets comfortable in the seat, she takes his arm and snuggles against him.

Cody gets off the plane and goes to the baggage carousel. He looks all around the air port for Crystal. He briefly sees her pushing her wheelchair as fast as she can through the air port. As he boards a second flight, he looks at all the passengers as he passes by and his heart flutters when he sees Crystal yet again. She again is busy on her phone. When she finishes she throws it in her purse and again closes her eyes. He takes the seat next to her and again she takes his arm and snuggles against him. Cody loses her yet again.

He heads to a resort in Fort Lauderdale, Florida. He is going there to be a part of his cousin's wedding party. He thinks to himself that if he is fortunate enough to see Crystal Bella Steele again, he plans on taking her in his arms and kissing her.

Crystal enters the lobby and Cody can't take his eyes off of her. His cousin's soon-to-be husband dares Cody to kiss any woman he sees. Tyler, the soon-to-be husband, tells Cody to live up to his nickname Lover Boy and kiss any woman he thought was pretty. Crystal crosses his path and smiles at Cody. Cody watches her check in and when she turns to leave the lobby, he gets closer to her. Before she can get away, Cody walks over to her, puts his hands around the back of Crystal's head and kisses her. He knows that he has met the love of his life with just this one kiss. He kisses her again. He wants to kiss her forever.

Chapter One

"Crystal, I need you to call me as soon as you get this. I am looking at a picture of you on Facebook and…. just call me. You look stunning. It's your mother."

I laugh when I listen to her message. I know that she has seen a picture of me on Facebook getting kissed by a stranger. Well he isn't a stranger to me. I know a lot about him. He doesn't know anything about me. My mother is constantly on her iPad scrolling through my pictures on Facebook. The only thing is that I never posted this picture. I was tagged in the picture.

My phone rings. I pick it up and groan. "Hi Beth."

"What the hell, Crystal? What are you doing?"

"I am working. I was checking into the resort after being delayed by two flights that were late. I had a needless layover in the Atlanta airport. When I finally landed in Fort Lauderdale, the car that was supposed to be at the airport was not. They provided transportation for me. I almost got knocked out of my wheelchair."

"Ok. Ok. But what is with the guy kissing you?"

"I have no idea. I never saw him before. He is a guest in the resort." I have seen him before. I should have said that I was never in the same hotel lobby with him before.

"Why was he kissing you?" She asks almost in a yell.

Why wouldn't he kiss me? What's wrong with me? What is my boss saying? I feel like I want to reach through my phone and choke this woman. Sometimes she is extremely insensitive.

"Crystal? Are you listening to me?"

Um…. Did she ask me something?

"Crystal?" She snaps loudly.

"Beth, I am listening to you."

"That's not what I asked."

"What did you ask?"

"Are you alright to do the job?"

"Why wouldn't I do my job. If I was going to quit, it would have been when you had me on a plane flying to Orlando that was routed to Ohio first. Then I flew to Atlanta and had a three hour layover. I then flew to Fort Lauderdale and now I have to drive three hours to get to Orlando to come back to the office to get my stuff so I can come back to the job in Fort Lauderdale." I want to throw my phone. I want to scream.

"Why are you yelling?" A male's voice asks.

I spin around so fast and I look at the second bed that is in my room. I look at a half naked man looking at me. His eyes are bright.

"Beth, I have to call you back!" I say. I end the call and gawk at this stranger who is not a stranger at all. I know him. I have known him a long time and have loved him since—

"What are you doing in my room?" He asks.

"Who the hell are you? And why are you in my room?" I know who he is. I am curious why he is in my room. I get my purse and rush to the door.

He hops out of bed and stands in front of me. "Who are you?"

"You first?" I say.

"My name is Cody." Somehow I think you know exactly who I am. He doesn't say.

"Cody, what the hell are you doing in my room?"

"I am part of the bridal party."

"Are you the groom? Oh god! That would be just my fucking luck."

He looks at me and smiles. His smile is big, it reaches his eyes. He laughs. "I am not the groom. I don't even like the groom."

"Then why the hell are you in the wedding party?"

"I am the man of honor." He runs his fingers through his hair. When he raises his arm, his muscles flex. My heart skips a beat. Cody is the most handsome man I have ever seen.

"Is that a thing?" I ask teasing. In my line of work that is a thing. It doesn't happen often, but occasionally it does.

"It is a thing." He says.

"Is it?" I ask him.

""Who are you?" He asks me.

"I am Crystal." I look at him. "Are you Cody Parker?" I know that he is Cody Parker and my inner child just did cartwheels and fainted with excitement. Cody Parker!

He steps back and looks at me. "You know who I am?"

I look at him and smile. "Doesn't everyone know who you are?"

He walks over to the bed and sits. He is still half naked. He is wearing nothing but boxer shorts. I don't stare, but I don't take my eyes off of him either. He puts his feet on the bed and hugs his knees. He lowers his head.

"Are you alright?" I ask him.

"What are you doing in my room?" He looks at me.

"This is my room." I tell him.

"Lets go to the front desk and find out what the hell is going on."

"I agree to that." I look at him. "You need to put some clothes on."

He gets a big grin on his face. His smile once again reaches his eyes. "You don't like what you see?" He has an arrogance to him. Some people would be turned off by it, I am turned on by it.

"I didn't say that." I am a fan of Cody Parker. I have been for a long time. I have dreamed of this exact encounter. Well not this exact encounter because this is better than I ever could have dreamed.

His cell phone rings. He looks around the room. His pants are in a heap on the floor. His shirt is on the floor. He leans over the side of the bed and digs the phone out of his pants pocket. "Hello. I am heading to the pool now." He stands and pulls his pants on. He walks into the bathroom and closes the door. The toilet flushes and then water from the sink runs. He opens the door and sticks his head out the door. "Do you know where the soap is?"

"Its on the little dish on the back of the sink." I tell him.

"How is that you know who I am?"

"I follow sports."

"I haven't played in years."

"You made an impression." I tell him. I take my phone from the table. I take the room key and leave the room.

Its ten minutes until eight and I have to be in a banquet room at eight. I will be there all day for a seminar that I don't want to be at. I push my wheelchair up to the automatic doors of the lobby. The doors open and I am blasted by a gush of cold air. It feels so good, I stay in the entry for an extra moment.

"Crystal?" A lanky guy asks walking over to me.

"Yes."

"First and foremost, let me apologize for all that you had to go through to get here." The grin on his face doesn't reflect the words coming from his mouth.

"Thank you. I appreciate you saying that." I look at him. "What is your name?"

"Lee."

I extend my hand to shake his hand. He extends his hand. "Its nice to meet you." I know this weasel. Well, actually the one time I met him he was younger. He wants my job.

"Let me show you where we will be for the next three days."

I smile. I look around. "What room is it?"

"The Pelican Suite." Lee says.

"I will be right there. I have to take care of something quickly."

"Oh sure." He says. "Can I get you a coffee and something to eat?"

"Coffee? Yes thank you. Dark roast with cream." I tell him. "Thank you." I say again.

He walks away.

I turn and approach the front desk. "Sir." I say to the guy behind the counter.

"Can I help you?" He has a very welcoming tone.

"My name is Crystal Steele. I am staying in room two-forty-eight."

"Yes. Is there a problem with the room?"

"Not at all, but one. I am supposed to be in that room by myself. When I woke up this morning, there was another person in the other bed. The only problem is, I don't know him."

"Let me check." He looks at the screen that is built into the desk top. His face glows blue from the lights when the screen changes. "I have right here that you are staying in room two-forty-eight."

"Yes." I say. "I checked in alone."

"No, you checked in with Cody Parker."

Cody walks over and puts his hand on my shoulder. "Are you telling people that you don't know me again?" He winks at me. He leans close and kisses the side of my neck.

"Sir, I did not check in with Cody Parker."

"I am sorry for the error. The problem is there are no other rooms available."

"What happened to his room?" I ask.

"He is booked in room two-forty-eight." The guy behind the counter says.

"Well that's wrong. That's my room."

Lee walks over. "Crystal, we need to get started."

I roll my eyes. "Get started, I will be right there."

"Your coffee will be cold if you don't come quickly."

"I only drink cold coffee." I say.

Cody looks at me. "Who the hell drinks cold coffee?"

"The same person who apparently is sharing a room with you."

A beautiful woman walks over just as I am saying that. She looks at Cody. "Lover boy! Oh my god, you kill me. When did you meet her?"

I look at the clerk behind the desk, "If another room becomes available, can you move him into it?"

"Why am I moving rooms?"

"It's the only disabled room we have on the first level available." The clerk says. He looks at me and says. "Right now there are no other rooms available."

The beautiful woman looks at Cody. "Lover boy, you never stop."

"Jillian, cut the crap." Cody snaps at her.

Lee stomps his foot. I look at him and glare. "Is there a problem?" I ask him.

"You are lead, you need to greet everyone."

"As lead, I am telling you to go greet everyone. I will be there in a minute."

Lee is so lanky he looks like a skeleton wearing a suit. If I wasn't so mad at his attitude, I would let my laughter bubble up. I know its wrong, but who the hell does this guy think he is?

Jillian looks at me. "How do you know my cousin?"

Cody walks over. "We woke up in the same room."

"You woke up in bed together?" Jillian asks.

"No." Cody and I say at the same time.

I leave the area and go in search of the Pelican Suite. Just before I put my hand on the handle to open the door, Jillian runs up to me. "Wait!" She says.

I look at her.

"You are the one running the seminar?"

"Yes." I say.

"Beth Greene was supposed to run the seminar."

"I know." I tell her. "I work with her."

"Will she be coming?"

"I am here so that she doesn't have to be." I say.

She looks at me. She looks me up and down. She makes me feel like I am part of the wall and she is looking at a spot on it. "Ok. Well. I am paying for her services and I expected her to be here."

"Jillian, everything will run the way that you expect it to because she has trained me to do the job just as she would do the job. Yes. I put my own spin on things, but generally you are going to get the same service." I say and square my shoulders to sit taller. I trained Beth and I do do all the work. She takes all the credit.

"There are pictures of you kissing my cousin." She says.

My phone rings loudly just as my ears hum loudly. I am angry. I answer my phone. "Hi Beth."

"I am not happy." She says.

"Why?"

"Lee called me and told me that you're not cooperating."

I am tired. I have been on four planes that were needless flights. I had just finished a job for her in Indiana. I was supposed to fly directly back to Orlando. That didn't happen. "Beth, you are not here. You don't know what happened."

"I am on my way, you can get your stuff and go. You are done."

"I am sorry. Did you fire me over the phone?"

"Yes." She yells loudly.

I throw my phone into my purse. "Bitch!" I yell. I turn quickly and rush to return to the lobby. I go to the room and gather my stuff.

Cody is no where in site. I leave a note for him. All in bubbly girly style with hearts and everything.

Cody Parker-

Best wishes to you. I know that you are wonderful. I felt it in the kiss we shared. I will remember it my whole life.

Crystal

I enter the lobby and return to the desk. I look at the same clerk. "Thank you for everything, it seems that my services are required somewhere else." I hand the key back to him. I give him my credit card and let him charge it.

I push my wheelchair out the front doors and set my bag down that I have over my legs.

Cody runs over. "What's going on?"

"I am at the wrong place." I say. I cover up for Beth. I don't want anyone to know that I have been fired because of Lee whom I don't know and Cody Parker's cousin.

A guy walks over to me. "Crystal?"

"That's me." I say.

"Your car is here."

"Oh perfect." I say.

"We are sorry for the delay."

"No worries." I tell him.

"We parked it in the first spot." He says.

I look across the parking lot. "Thank you so much." I don't look at either man standing next to me. I pick my bag up from the floor. I balance it on my lap and push my wheelchair across the parking lot. I put the key in the trunk and open it. It springs open immediately. I put my bags in the trunk and then grab the dog leash that I use to close the trunk. I toss the leash inside just before it slams closed.

I get in the driver's seat and fold my wheelchair. I take a remote in my hand and push the button to open the contraption on top of my car. When it opens, a swing like device drops down. I stick the metal piece under the seat of the wheelchair and then push the up button on the remote. Once it closes, I close my door and put the car in reverse. I pull out of the spot and leave the parking lot.

Lee comes running out. "Where the hell is she going?"

Cody looks at him. "She said she was in the wrong place."

Lee looks at Cody and the other guy standing there. "Did Beth fire her?"

"Fire her?" Cody asks.

Jillian runs out from the lobby. "Did any of you see Crystal?"

Lee paces the driveway. He runs his hands over his face. "I think Beth fired her."

"I hope it wasn't because of me." Jillian tries to act innocent.

Cody looks at her. "Did you know that she was going to get fired?"

"She is not supposed to kiss her clients."

"She kissed a client?" Lee asks.

"She threw herself at my cousin last night. Then she brought him back to her room."

Cody looks at her. "Jillian, that didn't happen. When she was checking in last night, I kissed her. We were drinking and Tyler dared me to kiss a pretty girl. She was the only one I saw." He ruffles his hair. "As for her taking me back to her room, that didn't happen. There was a mixup and we were put in the same room."

"A mixup my ass. We are her clients."

"You are — were one of her clients. I am just a guest of yours." Cody says.

Cody walks into the resort and continues through to the back doors. He walks out of them and walks to his room. He walks in the room and puts the key on the table. He sees my note. He picks it up and reads it over and over.

He looks around the room to see if I have left anything behind. On the nightstand between the two beds is a pair of earrings. He picks them up and holds them in his hands. He steps back. He looks around the room again and sees something sticking out from under the bed. He walks over to the bed that I slept in the night before. He squats down and reaches under the bed. He pulls out a light brown teddy bear with an outie belly button. He stands and holds it up to look at it.

"She left both of us behind." He says to the bear. He walks over to his bed and puts the bear between the two pillows. "Maybe she will miss you." He says to the bear.

There is a knock on the door. "Hey man, its me." Tyler calls out to Cody.

Cody opens the door. He is still holding the earrings in his hand.

"Cody, I thought that phase was over." Tyler says with a big smile on his face. His smile doesn't reach his eyes.

"Very funny."

"I came to show you something." He takes his phone out of his pocket. He accesses his videos and pushes play. "Watch." He says. He looks around the room. "Cute teddy bear." He walks over and picks it up. "I haven't ever seen a teddy bear with a belly button."

"She left it. I don't think she knows she left it. It was under the bed."

"What else is under the bed?" Tyler asks with a wicked grin on his face.

"I didn't think to look." Cody says honestly. He still has my earrings in his hand. "Diamonds and garnets. These are expensive."

"You need to watch."

Cody sits at the table. He holds Tyler's phone up and watches the video. I enter the lobby with all my bags. I am at the counter. When I turn my wheelchair to leave the area, Cody grabs me and kisses me. He curls his hand around my head as he deepens the kiss. He then wraps his other arm around me and holds me to him. The kiss lasts a long time. Cody breaks the kiss and then kisses me again. He notices that he appears to recognize that he has found something that he has been looking for his whole life.

"Cody, if I wasn't marrying your cousin, I would be a jealous guy watching you kiss her like that. If I was your cousin, I would have her fired."

"She did." Cody says.

"What? I was joking."

"Beth is coming to take over."

"Will you be ok with Beth being here?"

"Tyler, I hate Beth."

"So what's this girl's name?"

"Crystal."

"Crystal what?"

"I don't know. She knew who I am." He looks at the earrings in his hand.

"Cody, every woman on the planet with a pulse knows who you are."

"That's not true." Cody says.

"Come on, man. We don't call you lover boy for nothing."

"Come on, that was a long fucking time ago."

"Where did she go?" Tyler asks.

"I don't know. She got in a red Mustang and drove away."

"She was the passenger?"

"Tyler, I just said that she drove away."

"Go after her."

"I wouldn't know where to look for her." Cody takes the note and reads it again.

"What's that?"

He holds it out to Tyler. Tyler takes it and reads it. "Cody, you have to find her."

"Jillian would kill me if I miss your wedding."

Chapter Two

I put my bags on the bed. I am in another new place. It's a cute little cookie cutter house. I push my wheelchair from one room to the next. I return to the bedroom and open my duffle. My teddy bear should be on top. I look inside and pull all of the contents out. I open up the small tote that reads —Kiss My Lips. I dig inside for my earrings.

"Shit!" I say. "I left them at the fucking hotel."

I leave my new room and go to the front door. I open the door. I push my wheelchair down the wide driveway. I get in my car and drive back to the resort. I pull into the lot. This is the last place that I want to be.

The earrings were a gift from my mom for my graduation from college and the bear was a gift from my dad. I haven't spoken to him in three years, but I go no where without that bear. Its my favorite thing in the world.

My dad remarried and his current wife is good to him, but she doesn't like me or my two sisters. I am the middle child. My step-mother has two boys of her own. They are great. They treat my sisters and I like we are their real sisters. And not just siblings through marriage.

My phone rings just as I am about to enter the lobby. I take it out of my purse. I smile. "Hi Brandon."

"Hi." He says.

"What's going on?"

"I just got a Facebook notification."

"So how does that concern me?"

"You were tagged in it."

I smile bigger. He can't see me smile. "I am tagged in a lot of posts on Facebook."

"Not a lot of them where you are being kissed by Cody Parker."

"You saw that?"

"Crystal, the whole world saw it." Brandon laughs.

"I am not going to apologize." I say.

"I wouldn't want you to. Just be careful. He's a player."

"I will. I love you." I tell him.

"I love you too. Kyle will be back in town at the end of next week. Lets plan that the five of us have dinner."

"You call everyone and set it up, I will be there." I put my phone back in my purse. I enter the lobby.

Beth is sitting on a decorative bench. She looks as sweet as a porcelain doll. I know better. She doesn't see me. I look around the lobby. There is no way I can get to the front counter without her seeing me.

Cody walks over, he takes my hand. He walks off in the opposite direction. He never lets go of my hand. I look at him. He grins. He walks back to the room. He sticks his key in the door and it turns green. He opens the door and holds it while I go in the room.

"I was wondering how I was going to get in touch with you." He says.

"I just came back for my earrings and the bear."

"I heard you on the phone. Do you have someone in your life?"

I laugh. "You heard me on the phone with my brother."

"Your family saw the pictures of us?"

"I am sure they did." I look at the bear that now sits between his pillows on the freshly made bed. "I will be out of here as soon as I get what I came for."

"No. I want you to stay." Cody says. His phone buzzes to life in his pocket. He takes it out and looks at it. Then he puts it back in his pocket.

"You are here for your cousin's wedding. My boss is here to make sure that everything goes well. Oh wait— former boss."

"Why did she fire you?"

"I am sure that the paperwork that she needs to fill out for the termination will state what the reasons were. Over the phone she just told me I was fired."

"Be my plus one." He is serious. He stands close to me and steps closer taking me in his arms and kisses me just as he did last night.

I could get lost in his kisses. I want to get lost in his kisses. I put my hands on his chest. "Cody, I can't." I want to. I would be his plus one for the rest of my life. It would be a dream come true. Some people dislike him right off the bat, I fell in love with him right off the bat. Cody Parker kissed me. We shared this very room. I am on cloud nine.

He sits on the bed and takes my hand pulling me closer to him. "I want to be honest with you. I have a nickname. They call me lover boy."

"I know that." I say.

"Beth and I have history."

"I know that. She has pictures of you all over the office. One of them is in a heart frame. On the frame it reads – FUTURE Mrs. Parker. She has a Barbie and Ken in a shadow box and on the glass it reads – until death do us part."

"Oh boy. Tell me you are kidding."

I take my phone out of my purse and hand it to him. "Click on the photos."

He looks at my phone. "Does she know that you took these?"

"No. I took them to show my sisters and my mom."

"I am sorry." Cody says seriously.

"For what?"

"Kissing you."

"Please don't be. I will never be sorry that you kissed me like that. Ever." I look at my watch for no reason at all. "I should go."

"Stay." He says.

"You have stuff to do for the wedding."

"I know. I want you to be my plus one."

There is a knock on his door. "Cody, its Beth. I was hoping we could chat." She sounds all flirty even with the door separating her and us.

Cody gets up and walks into the bathroom. He brings me with him.

She knocks on the door again. "Cody! I am going to call your phone. Someone said that they saw you come back to the room. Cody! Come on. We were friends once."

His phone vibrates in his pocket.

"Cody! You said that we could talk. Come on, I came all this way to be with you. Lover Boy!" She says 'lover boy' in a seductive way. "Where are you? Your cousin promised that you would take me as your plus one."

I take my phone and text the front desk. When I checked in last night they gave me a link to text the front desk. I check to see if its still working and it is.

Me: I am a guest in room 248 and there is someone outside the door banging on it and yelling. I feel threatened.

Front Desk: We will send security immediately

"They are going to send security." I whisper to him.

"When they usher her away, we should get out of here."

"I will go. You have to stay." I tell him.

"Will I see you again?" He says the words like we have been together our whole lives.

"I don't know." I say.

Cody's phone rings. He fishes it out of his pocket. "Hello." He says.

"Cody, what the hell is going on?" Jillian asks.

"I came back to the room to take a nap."

"Are you ok?" She sounds concerned.

"I think I am still hung over from last night. I wanted to rest up before the rehearsal dinner. Beth is outside the room banging on the door. You told her that she is my plus one?"

"No. I told her that you didn't have a plus one."

"Jillian, I have a plus one."

"I didn't know."

"You didn't ask."

"I should have assumed, you always have a different girl." She says rudely.

I hear what she is saying. I watch him tense up. I put my hand in his hand and link our fingers. He looks down at our hands and squeezes our fingers together. A jolt of electricity pulses through me. I think he feels it too.

"Jillian, that was a long time ago."

"What do you call last night?" She asks him.

I close my eyes. A dream come true. One that I have wanted to come true since I watched him pitch his first ball at a professional ballgame when he wasn't even a professional yet.

Cody bends and kisses the top of my head.

"What do you call last night?" She asks again.

"Ask Tyler."

"Cody! I am asking you. What the hell do you call last night?"

"The best moment of my life." He finally says.

I look up at him and can't help but smile.

Cody ends the call and walks back into the room. He sits at the table and spreads his legs and pulls me close kissing me. There is so much heat in his kiss. There is a hungry feel to it.

His phone rings again. I pull back. "What?" He snaps at his cousin.

"Cody, what are you doing?" Jillian asks.

"What is the problem?" He asks.

"Is someone with you?"

"I am in my room."

"I am coming there."

"No." He says.

"Why are you hiding?"

"Jillian, I have a hangover." He says.

I know that's not true because he doesn't drink. He hasn't for years.

"Don't forget, we need you at three."

"I will be there." He says.

I take my earrings and stick them in my ears. I take my teddy bear and I leave the room. Its after three in the afternoon. I leave the resort for a second time. I get in my car and drive away.

I pull into my new driveway. I park my car and get out of it. I go in the house. I go straight to my bedroom and put the teddy bear on the shelf. I take the earrings out of my earlobes and put them in the jewelry box I keep them in.

I open the refrigerator and take out cold-cuts that Brandon and Ashley got for me for when I came to my new house there would be food in the refrigerator. I smile brightly as I make a sandwich. I sit at the lowered counter and eat it. I take my phone and call my mom. I put her on speaker.

She answers the phone happily. "Where have you been?"

"Where do I start?"

"First. How are you?"

"Oh my god, I am on cloud nine." I laugh.

"Do you know him?"

"Mom, everyone knows him. Or knows of him."

"Yes, but do you know him?"

"I want to know him better." I tell her what I do know of him. He used to be a professional baseball player. He was a pitcher. Cody Parker also played any position that he was put in. He could play with precision. He played in college and went to the pros two years into his college career. He played only two seasons. He had gone out with a model to dinner, they were mugged and the guys who were caught not far from the crime used a baseball bat and beat Cody Parker up. The model wasn't hurt. She had set it up. She didn't want it to be as bad as it was. She got arrested too.

"Wow, that's some story."

"They call him lover boy still. He had a reputation. Mom, I have never been kissed like that before. I don't know that I will ever meet a man who will kiss me like that again."

"Are you going to see him again?"

"He wanted me to stay."

"Why didn't you stay?"

"Reality hit." I say.

"What does that mean?"

"Beth fired me. His cousin is the bride that Beth's company is organizing so it all goes perfectly."

"Why didn't you stay?" she asks again. "It was your company."

"I don't know."

"You should go find him."

"Mom, the whole world knows where he is."

"The whole world doesn't want him. You do." She says knowing me.

I hear a car pull into my driveway. "Mom, let me call you back."

"Of course. I love you."

"I love you too." I go to the door and look out. "What? How does he know where I live?" I go outside. "Cody? What are you doing here?"

He stands in my driveway just looking at me. "You live in a she shed?" He looks at my little house.

I laugh. "I live alone. How big does the house have to be? Would you like to come in?"

"Yes." He says.

"How did you know where to find me?"

"I looked you up. I found out that you just invested in property. You just moved here?"

"I did just move here."

"Did you see this house before you bought it?"

"Come in. You will see that it's bigger inside. Come on in." I turn around and go back in the house. He comes in with me.

He looks at my half eaten sandwich. He picks up the half that is on the plate. He takes a bite of it. "That's really good."

I laugh. "Feel free to eat the rest of it." I open the refrigerator and take out a bottle of water. I hand it to him. "What are you doing here?"

"Come back with me and be my plus one." Cody stands in front of me and kisses me.

"Cody, you don't know anything about me." I breathe in his cologne, shampoo and sunscreen. I so want to be his plus one.

"So tell me about you."

"Where do I start?"

"Where ever you want." He says.

I look around my new home. "Are you comfortable?"

"Yes. Tell me something about you."

"Ask me questions?"

"Where are you from?"

"Fort Lauderdale. I was born here. I moved to Orlando to go to school. And now I am back."

"What did you go to school for?"

"I was on a full ride for academics."

"For what?" He asks. He stands up and walks around. "Can I look around?"

"Of course."

"You don't have anything that tells anything about you." Cody says.

"Cody, I just got the keys to my new house in the mail three days ago."

He walks over and sees a box that is labeled pictures. "Can I open this?"

"Yes."

He looks at me. "Do you have a knife?"

"Are you only going to use it on the boxes?" I ask laughing.

"Yes." He says and smiles.

"I am sorry that you were mugged and can't play baseball anymore."

He sits on the floor and looks up at me. "Thank you." He says. He puts his hand on his shoulder of his throwing arm.

"Does your arm still hurt?"

"Nope. You first. I am here to get to know you."

"Were you always a pitcher?" I ask him handing him a knife.

He looks at me. "You know baseball?"

"Why wouldn't I know baseball?"

My phone rings. I take it off the counter and look at it.

"You can answer."

"Its my dad."

"Answer."

"I haven't spoken to him in a while. He must have seen the videos on Facebook. I am sure that my step-mother couldn't wait to show it to him."

Cody slices through the tape. There is another layer of tape. "Why so much tape?" He asks.

I laugh. "I got carried away."

My phone rings again. I roll my eyes.

"Crystal, answer the phone." Cody says. "What's the worst that could happen?"

"You don't know my dad."

"I have only known you since yesterday, but I would tell him he is missing out on knowing a treasure."

I can't help but smile. "Thank you for saying that."

"I mean it." He says. He gets on his knees and takes my phone. He slides it to accept the call. He puts it on speaker. "Say hello." He says softly.

I look at him and my smile is gone. "Hello."

"Crystal? Hi. How are you?" Dad says with joy in his voice.

"Hi dad. I am good. How are you?"

"I heard from your brothers that you are back in my neck of the woods."

I roll my eyes. "I just moved back."

"I saw you on Facebook."

I look at Cody. "Here we go." I say softly.

"What?" Dad asks.

"What did you see on Facebook?"

"You found a great guy." He says about Cody.

Cody sits back on his feet. He takes my hand. "Talk to him." He says softly.

Dad clears his throat. "Crystal?"

"Yes."

"How did you two meet?"

I look at Cody. "We were on the same flight from Indiana together. He was across the isle from where I was." That is true. He never saw me. I didn't know if he did or not.

"I did fly from Indiana." He says softly.

"I know." I say.

"You know what?" Dad asks.

"Oh nothing. I am just trying to get my wheelchair unstuck."

He laughs. His laughter fills my house. "Where are you stuck?"

"Between a coffee table and the couch." I say. I smile.

"You don't have a coffee table." Cody says softly. He kisses me on the chin. Then he sits on the floor again and opens the box. He takes the pictures out one by one and studies them.

The one on top is me at a baseball game holding Cody Parker's jersey and I have a big bright smile on my face. He holds it up and looks at me. I try to turn away from him but he sticks his feet in between my wheels.

Dad clears his throat again. "Well, I would like to welcome you back in town. Can you go to dinner tonight?"

Cody looks at me and waits for my answer.

"I would love that. I am going to a rehearsal dinner."

"Oh how wonderful. You are going to a celebration to welcome you back to the area."

"Actually, its for my job." I say.

"So you did it?"

"I did what?"

"Became a wedding planner?"

"I am a personal assistant for a wedding planner." I say.

"What happened to your company?"

I close my eyes. "How did you know about my company?"

"Your sisters and brothers filled me in over the years."

"Of course they did. Actually Beth, my boss, bought my company."

Cody unwraps another picture. It's a family photo of me with my mom, sisters and step-brothers. My mom saw how well we all bonded and she took them into her heart like they were two of her own children. They love her. They call her mom.

In the photo everyone is wearing black accept my sister Kelsey. She is in a red dress. Cody looks at the picture and points to Kyle.

"You know him?" He asks.

I nod my head.

"How do you know him?"

"Dad, can you hold on just a second. I need to reach something." I say.

"Listen, I will not allow you to be a stranger any longer. Do you hear me?"

"Yes."

"Have fun at the wedding. Dance with the guests."

"That's not why I am going." I say.

"I know." He laughs. "I love you."

I am caught off guard. I get a pain in my chest. I choke. "I love you too." I say.

"I will call you in a few days."

"When Kyle gets back in town, we are all going to get together. You should come."

"Joanne too?"

I roll my eyes. I know that this is not what Brandon was planning. "If you think its best." I say trying to swallow the knot in my throat.

"Let me talk to the boys." He says. "Just so you know, I am so proud of you."

"Thank you."

"Give me your address so I can send you flowers."

"Two-forty-eight Gulfport Street." Is the only thing I get out.

"You live in one of my bungalows." Dad says.

"What?" I ask.

"I was the developer for Gulfport. I know the address. I know the community. How did you find out about it?"

"Ashley and Brandon brought me here when I said I was moving back. I didn't see any other place. I fell in love. It's the house that I dreamed of my whole life." I tell him.

I hear his breath catch. "I love you. I will talk to you soon."

"I love you too." I say.

I feel goosebumps prickle on my skin. I call Brandon. He answers right away. "Why would you take me to one of dad's developments?"

"What?" He asks.

"Come on. Don't play stupid. Did Kyle know? Did Kelsey know too. God! Why wouldn't you tell me?"

"We didn't want you to say no right off the bat."

"I might not have." I say.

"Crystal. Come on. You know you would have. How did you even find out?"

"He called me."

"He did?"

"He loves me. Your mother doesn't."

"Right I forget that part." He laughs. "Do you need help moving in?"

"I am still waiting for the rest of my stuff to get here."

"When will that be?"

"Next week. Wednesday or Thursday. When will Kyle be back?" I ask.

"Next Friday."

"Dad wants to join us for dinner."

"Does he want my mom to go too?"

"Listen, you talk to him about it. You all decide. Don't let me get ambushed."

"I will text you. Want to go to dinner?" He asks. "Ash and I are going to dinner."

"I am grossed out." I mock a gagging noise. Brandon and Ashley are dating each other. They love each other.

He laughs. "I love you."

"Me too. Hug her for me. On Second thought — don't."

He laughs again. "We will be in touch."

"Me too."

"Oh wait, mom says she needs to talk to you."

"I spoke to her." I hold my phone out. "Bye." I say loudly and disconnect the call.

Cody looks at me. "How do you know Kyle?"

"He's my step-brother."

"He was my roommate."

"He didn't tell me."

"Beth really bought you out?"

"She did."

"And she fired you?"

"She did."

"So you went to school to be a wedding planner?" He asks.

I laugh. "No. I went to school to be a sports commentator."

"Really?"

"Yes."

"So how did you find yourself planning weddings?"

I laugh. "I took an internship working at Madame Butterfly's Bridal Boutiques. I was the personal assistant to the owner for three years. She paid me a lot of money. A wealthy guy walked in to the boutique. He was the father to a real bridezilla. Rosa saw him come in and she was mesmerized. She had me take lead so that she wouldn't fall all over herself. She fell in love with him. His daughter was such a bitch. We catered to everything she wanted. We had her dresses pinned and ready to send them out for the final steps and she canceled the dresses. It was a big account. Rosa's partner was hospitalized for three days from stress."

"Why"

"Why what?"

"Why would she need to be hospitalized?"

"We all worked very hard to pull this wedding together. There were so many aspects to it. Different venues. She wanted three dresses. No detail went ignored. Rosa made sure of it. We worked long hours." I laugh. "I got so wrapped up in my job, I failed three of my classes. I did all the work for them. The day I was supposed to turn them all in, I was in a coma of sorts. I slept through my finals. I slept three days straight."

"Oh my god. And you took over for her?"

"Not exactly."

"What?"

"The father of bridezilla came in and paid for everything. He took the dresses and he auctioned them off. One sold for twenty thousand dollars. That was the least amount that he got for them. He split the amount between all of us that were dealing with his bitch daughter and he married Rosa. I went back to school and tried to deal with my classes. My adviser never liked me much and was waiting for me to slip. He told me that there was nothing he could do for me.

"I took those same fucking classes the next semester and passed them. Rosa had found out what had happened and said that I was more than professional that I didn't take any of my problems with me to work. No one knew. She signed her company over to me."

"So how does Beth play out in this?"

"She is Rosa's niece. She wanted the company. She was jealous when Rosa put everything in my name. I didn't know it. I was offered a job as a commentator in Atlanta. I was on my way there when I was served with papers that I needed to meet with lawyers. I didn't know about the dresses being sold or any of it. Rosa's husband had opened up a bank account in my name. Beth tried to sue for the money. She had nothing to do with any of it but she wanted the benefits."

Cody takes out the last picture and holds it up. It's a picture of me with my dad. My college graduation picture. He looks at it. "Jack is your dad?"

"Jack is my dad."

"He is not Kyle's dad?"

"My dad adopted Kyle and Brandon after their father passed away. My sisters and I got along with them from the moment we all met. Joanne doesn't like my dad's children but she never kept him from adopting her sons." I take the picture from him. "She took this picture. She wouldn't be in it. It was the last time I saw my dad."

I go into my bedroom and close the door. Cody knocks on the door softly. He walks in my room. "Are you alright?"

I look at him. "Why did you kiss me?" I look out the window. "I recognized you on the flight. I am sure you just walked past me. So why would you kiss me?"

He runs his fingers through his hair. He has long fingers. Piano fingers. "If I tell you, you won't be my plus one."

"Tyler put you up to it?" I ask. "He wanted you to live up to your nickname?"

"He told me to kiss the prettiest girl I saw."

"I think you should go." I tell him.

"You don't believe me?"

I turn and face him. "I have to get showered and dressed for a rehearsal wedding party that I am crashing." I smile.

"Can I ask you a question?"

"Of course."

"Did Kyle ever talk about me being his roommate?"

"Never to me."

"Why are you holding my jersey in that picture?"

"Cody, why the hell not? You were so quick at bat. You threw the ball with such precision." I blush.

"Why are you blushing?"

"You are the reason that I won my scholarship."

"Come back to the resort with me and get all dolled up there. Let the professionals do your hair and makeup."

"Beth would have a heart attack." I say.

"She shit canned you. What do you care?"

I take my purse and my car keys. I put them on my lap.

"You won't need your purse or your car keys." Cody says.

"I am bringing my purse with me."

"Can I ask you a question?"

"I haven't stopped you yet." I smile at him.

"Where did you get that teddy bear from?"

"My dad gave it to me when I graduated college. He has traveled all over the US with me."

"He?"

I cover my face with my hands and laugh. He stands in front of me. He takes my wrists in his hands. He gently removes my hands from my face.

"He?"

"Don't make me say it." I say.

"Did you name the bear?"

"Oh my god!" I giggle.

"What is it?"

"LB Parker." I cover my face and scream.

Cody takes my wrists again and holds my arms over my head. He kisses me. "LB Parker?"

"Cody!"

He kisses me again. "We have to go."

I open the door and there on the door step is the most beautiful arrangement of flowers. There are balloons attached and a stuffed hippo. I burst into tears.

Cody picks up the flowers and carries them in. He puts them on the kitchen table. He reads the card.

Sweetheart,

I hope that you enjoy your new home. If you need anything changed or adapted to your needs, please feel free to let me know. I am so glad to have you back. Your hungry hippo couldn't wait to see you again. I love you.

Daddy

Cody looks at me. "We need to go." He says.

"I think I have cold feet." I say.

"Good thing you aren't the bride." He laughs.

Fifteen minutes later, we are in the lobby and Cody is off making plans for me at the spa. I look around the lobby. Lee walks over. "Can I chat with you a moment?"

"Not on a cold day in hell." I tell him.

"When I contacted her, I didn't know she was going to fire you."

"You have questions about how she operates, ask her."

A guy walks over and spins me around. "Always so strong." He says taking me into his arms.

"Kyle!" I cry. "What are you doing here?"

"My friend is getting married."

"Your name wasn't on the guest list."

"My name is on the guest list." He says.

"I printed out the guest list. Kyle Steele was not on the list."

"I know. I have had to hide my identity so that I could surprise you." Kyle says.

Cody walks over. He puts his hand on Kyle's shoulder. "Its good to see you."

Kyle smiles. "Its good to see you too."

"Kyle, where are you going to stay until next week when you are supposed to get back in town?" I ask him.

"With my favorite little sister." He says brightly.

"Kyle, we are all younger than you are."

"Not all of you are my favorite." He smiles brightly.

"Ash is popular." I say. Referring her to being with Brandon.

"Only if I want to throw up daily."

We laugh.

"That's not nice." I tell him.

"You still laughed when I said it."

"I will deny I ever did." I smile.

Cody takes my hand. "We have a spa treatment starting in five minutes."

"We do?" I ask.

"I wasn't going to turn you over to the wolves." He says.

Kyle looks at Cody. "What does that mean?"

"I have been fired from my job." I say. "And the bride thinks that Cody's kissing me was all my doing."

"I am sorry, what?"

"To which part?" I ask.

"Cody kissed you?"

"I did." Cody says. He takes my hand in his hand and holds it to his chest.

"You kissed my favorite sister?" Kyle asks.

Beth walks into the lobby. She walks over to me. "What are you doing here?"

"She is a guest." Cody says.

"I went looking for you darling." Beth says and stands on her toes to kiss him on the lips. He steps back. Beth stumbles.

"Don't call me darling. You and I are nothing. We have been nothing for over ten years. You have weaseled your way to take over the planning of this wedding but do not think for one second that you are anything to me." Cody says. He takes my hand and walks off with me. He turns and looks at Kyle. "Join us. I am sure they can squeeze in a surfboard."

I laugh at the reference. I know what he is talking about.

"You laugh at your brother?" He asks me.

"You know about surfboard?" Cody asks.

I laugh. "We always teased him about being a surfboard." I look at Kyle. "He took me body surfing once and held my hand through the waves."

"I wish I was there." Cody says.

"Then you wouldn't have hit two grand slam home runs." I say. I push my wheelchair ahead of them.

"Where are you going?" They both ask.

"To the bathroom." I say. I open the door to a private bathroom and go inside. When I come out, they are both waiting for me.

"Ready?" Cody asks.

"I am ready." I say.

Jillian walks over. She looks at Cody and Kyle and then down at me. She only lowers her eyes to acknowledge me. "We have a problem and you both are needed to help out with the situation."

"No." Cody says.

"You are best man."

"I am not the best man. I am the man of honor. Your side of the isle."

"Oh for Christ sake." She says. She looks at Kyle. "Will you help out?"

"No." He says.

"Is every guy I know an asshole?"

"Did you have my sister fired?" Kyle asks.

"Excuse me. Who is your sister?" Jillian asks.

Cody and Kyle both hold their hands out to me.

"Excuse me. What?"

"Jillian, I would like to introduce you to my sister, Crystal Steele." Kyle says.

"No. You have a brother named Brandon." She says.

"And three sisters."

"Does Tyler know this?"

"Tyler has met two out of three of them. He never met Crystal." Kyle says.

"Do you all mind to stop talking over my head." I say. If I had my car, I would get in it and go.

"I hired Madame Butterfly's Bridal Boutique to do the details of my wedding." Jillian says.

"That was my sister's company." Kyle says.

"No. She stole the company from my dear sweet aunt." Beth says.

I look at Beth. I square my shoulders and look at her. "You know that is far from the truth. I worked for your aunt. I never knew that she was going to turn it over to me. I didn't ask for it. I was leaving for a job in Atlanta when the lawyers told me that MBBB was mine."

Chapter Three

Jillian looks at Beth. "Beth, I have known you forever. You told me that your aunt gave you the company."

"She bought me out." I say. "The only problem is she doesn't know what the fuck she is doing. So she needs me. Only because of you and Lee she fired me." I look at Cody. "Thank you for everything. I have to go." I want to leave before anyone sees me cry.

"Is your car here?" Kyle asks.

"No. That doesn't mean I won't get home."

"Let me take you." Cody says.

"You are needed here." Jillian says.

Beth reaches out to put her hand on Cody's arm.

"Beth, if you touch me again, I will be the owner of a bridal company and I will have you arrested for harassment." Cody says.

"Darling, please." She says.

"We had this conversation already."

Tyler walks over. "What the hell is going on?" He looks at his soon-to-be-wife and the wedding planner. He looks at Cody. "The spa called. They are waiting for you and your plus one to get there for your appointments."

"I am sorry. He doesn't have a plus one." Jillian says.

"Yes I do." Cody says.

Beth steps in front of me. He steps back and takes my hand.

"Jillian, you better tell your wedding planner to cut the shit or you will have to replace me in the wedding party." Cody says. He takes my hand. "Come on, they are waiting for us."

"Gold digger." Beth says. That is the cat calling the kettle black.

I look at her like she is crazy. She is crazy.

"You think my sister is a gold digger?" Kyle asks.

My cheeks burn. I feel heat prickle on my forehead.

"How could she not be? Going after the number one bachelor on the planet?" Beth asks.

"Were you not throwing yourself at me just now and in the lobby? What does that say about you? You saw us on Facebook and couldn't wait to fire her." Cody says.

"It was the first time you ever saw her and you kissed her like that?" Jillian asks.

I try to push my wheelchair away from all of this. Cody and Kyle both take my hands. "Please. Just let me go." I say.

Cody squeezes my hand. I look up at him. "Actually, I had the pleasure of being her seat partner on a plane first from Indiana to Atlanta and then from Atlanta to Fort Lauderdale. The pilots had heard that she was flying solo. They asked me to be in charge of her safety."

"I slept on the plane from Indiana to Atlanta." I say.

"I know. I am surprised you don't have a bruise on your cheek from my bony shoulder."

"You slept with my sister?" Kyle asks jokingly.

"No. I watched a movie while she slept on the plane." Cody says and glares at Kyle. "Don't fuel the fire."

I look around and wonder if its possible to sink into the carpet underneath my chair.

The clerk who was so nice to me walks over. "Miss Steele?"

I look at him. "Yes."

"If you don't get to your spa appointment now, you will be late for your nail appointment. My staff are very patient, but if clients are late, they bitch about it to me. I wouldn't want someone who is as nice as you to lose out on people who genuinely want to lift your spirits. You lifted mine when I got that box of cookies today. Thank you so much. How did you know?"

I smile at him.

He looks at Cody. "You have made all my staff weak kneed."

"Because he so good looking." Beth says.

"Um no." The clerk says.

"Then why?" She asks.

"They all wish that they were the ones that got that kiss last night. That was the most romantic thing that has ever taken place in the lobby. I have worked here for years, and to date, I haven't seen anything so romantic in my life."

Cody smiles at him. That one smile that reaches his eyes.

We finally make it over to the spa. When we get there a beautiful, tall blonde is standing waiting for us. She looks at Kyle. She looks at me. "Please tell me that this is your beautiful sister." She says.

Kyle steps up to her and kisses her on the lips. "Thank you for saying that." He says quietly into her lips. He turns back to me. "Crystal, this is Lacey."

"Its nice to meet you." I say to her.

"It's a pleasure to meet you." She says. "I have heard so much about you from Kyle and Brandon."

"Brandon lies." We both say at the same time and laugh.

Kyle steps close to me and kisses me on the head. "I love you."

Lacey looks at Kyle. "We are in room two." She looks at Cody and me. "You are in room four."

"Thank you."

"We will see you when we are done."

Lacey hugs me. "I am getting my nails done next too. You and I are sticking together." She says. "I need dirt on this guy."

I smile at her.

Cody and I each lay on the massage tables on our stomachs. Two women walk in the room and put soft music on. One dims the lights and then they start the massages. Forty-five minutes later, I feel so relaxed. The one who massaged me shows us to the locker rooms. She tells us that we can get showered if we want to. I go in the locker room and quickly shower. I get dressed and wait for Cody in a private room.

A woman walks over pushing a cart. "Are you Crystal?" She asks.

"Yes."

"I am here to do your nails." She says.

She sets up her cart next to a desk. She sits on one side of it. I sit on the other. She turns the light on. She does my nails. When she finishes I have the best French manicure I have ever had. I open my purse and attempt to tip her.

"No. Everything has been paid for." She tells me. "Enjoy your stay."

"Thank you." I tell her.

"Your boyfriend is waiting for you by the deck."

"Thank you." I look around.

"Go out that door to the right and follow the path."

"Thank you again." I say. I wiggle my fingers and look at my nails. "Are you sure that I can't tip you?"

"Crystal, I am positive. It was a pleasure."

I leave the lobby and follow the path. I smile as I continue down the path. There are baseballs leading down the path. When I reach the last baseball, I don't know which way to go.

The clerk walks over. He points to the tiki hut. I smile at him. I push my wheelchair down the path to the tiki hut.

Cody stands there with his feet crossed. He looks so handsome standing there. He is in a fitted blue shirt that makes his eyes shine a warm green. He extends his hand to me.

"Thank you for the spa and my nails." I say.

"I did the spa. The nails was set up by Kyle. He is fuming mad right now. He is livid that Tyler would let Jillian be so out of control."

"I feel so relaxed. Thank you."

"I am so glad."

I look at him. "Why did you lie to everyone?"

"What have I lied about?"

"You said that I slept on your shoulder on the plane. Why did you say that?"

He takes his phone out of his pocket and scrolls a moment on it. He holds his hand out to me. I take his phone and look at it. There is a picture of me sleeping on his shoulder.

I look at him. "But you were sitting across the isle from me." I say.

"You were so nice to all the people around you. I heard you when you were helped on the plane. You said thank you to everyone who helped you. The pilots came down the isle and asked me if I would change seats with the lady who was supposed to sit next to you. They asked me if anything happened in case of an emergency would I be in charge of you. I said yes immediately."

"Thank you."

"Don't thank me. I wanted to do it. You were wrong when you said I walked past you and didn't notice you. I did."

"I didn't see you afterwards."

"Its me who lost sight of you. When we landed in Atlanta they told me that I had to get off the plane. You were the last one to disembark. I waited for you. I didn't see you in the airport at all. When I boarded the plane for Fort Lauderdale, I couldn't believe that you were on the plane. You were on the plane and you had your iPad on the little table top. You were going over something and smiling."

"My sisters were sending me messages that I was one step closer to being their neighbors."

"They live in the same development?"

"No. I am in the middle of the two of them. Ten minutes equally from both of them."

"You are close to them?"

"I am. My older sister is very protective. My younger sister goes out of her way to make sure that everyone is nice to me."

"What would they say if they knew that you got fired?"

I laugh. "Actually I am surprised my phone hasn't been ringing all day. I told my mother that I got fired. My dad too."

"Are your sisters in touch with your dad?"

"Secretly yes."

"Why have you been distant?"

"I don't want to do anything secretly."

He kisses me. He looks down at me and smiles. "My kissing you wasn't a secret."

"Far from it." I say. I smile brightly.

"Come lets go get changed."

"Cody, I don't have anything with me."

"Your dress is hanging in the room. Actually two of them. One for tonight and one for tomorrow."

"Cody, what did you do?"

"Lacey did it."

"Kyle has told me about her."

He takes my hand and we leave the tiki hut. He uses the key and opens the door. He then hands me the key.

"What is this?"

"It was your room first." He says.

When we enter the room there are two dresses set out on each bed. "Oh my god. Those are beautiful." I look at Cody. "Which one should I wear tonight?"

"Pick one."

I take one off the bed that I slept in last night and go into the bathroom. I put it on and come out.

He looks at me. "You will be the most beautiful girl in the room."

"If that's true your cousin may have me arrested." I say.

We both laugh.

"Should I try the other one?"

"No. I am glad you picked this one for tonight. The other matches my accessories." He looks around. "Make yourself at home. I will just be a minute."

"I can wait for you in the lobby."

"No way. We stick together. You are my date." He walks into the walk in closet.

"Cody?"

He turns and looks at me. "What?"

"Thank you."

He smiles and turns back into the closet. He gets dressed quickly. When I look up, its like I am looking at a GQ model. "Do I look good?"

"Cody, no one ever needs to tell you if you look good or not. If I was standing up my knees would be weak right now."

He steps in front of me and kisses me. When he breaks the kiss we are both gasping for breath. He takes my hand and we leave the room.

There are flashes of light. Someone took a picture of us. Cody takes my hand in his hand and walks next to me. We enter the lobby. The clerk is standing behind the counter. He looks up when we enter. He takes his personal phone and snaps a picture of us.

We find the banquet room that the rehearsal is taking place in. When we go in the room everyone looks at Cody and me.

"You draw attention." I say to him.

"Its all you." He kisses my lips softly. "Promise you won't leave without me."

"Yes." I tell him.

I stay in the back. I would if I was working the event. Beth is in the front of the room acting as if she is running the show. In reality the bride is running the show.

Jillian looks stunning. She is in a white fitted dress that hugs her curves perfectly. She stands in the back of the room with her father. He looks at me and then says something to Jillian. She turns her head slightly but doesn't look at me. She says something to him. He steps away from her and walks towards me.

"Are you Ms. Steele?"

"I am." I say.

"I wanted to take a moment to tell you how sorry I am for all that happened today."

"Sir, today and tomorrow its all about your daughter. I appreciate you saying something but really its not necessary. My boss just wanted to take point to make sure that your daughter gets exactly what she wants."

He looks at his daughter.

I look at the front. "They are going to be ready for you and your daughter in just a minute." I tell him.

"Thank you." He says. He walks over to Jillian. He takes her arm and they wait for Beth to give them their cue to come to the front.

I look up to the front of the room and Cody is watching me. I smile at him. There is a girl standing behind him. She flashes me a bright smile. He turns slightly to her and says something. She nods her head.

Kyle walks over and stands next to me. He leans against the wall. He puts his hand on my shoulder. "I spoke to dad."

I look up at him. "And?"

"He will be here tomorrow to have brunch with you."

"You all have to stop making plans for me." I say.

"I heard what you told Jillian's dad. That was very nice of you to not throw anyone under the bus."

"Its not about me. Its about the bride. No matter how good or evil they are. We do all of this to make sure that they get what they want."

"You got fired."

"I know. People like reminding me of it."

"So why not bad mouth Beth?"

"She is sue happy. If I say anything against her no matter if it's true or not she will sue me. She thinks that I stole her aunt's company."

"Brandon and I are legal." He tells me.

I laugh at him. "You all are. I am surprised I didn't hear from Kelsey and Ash."

"Brandon told them to give you the day."

"How nice of him."

"On a scale of one to a hundred, how happy are you that Cody kissed you last night?"

I look at him and smile. "A thousand." I beam.

"That good?"

"I have never been kissed like that in my whole life." I say.

When the rehearsal wedding ceremony is over, we are ushered into another room where there is a buffet set up. This is not what she wanted. I look around. Jillian's dad walks over.

"Why do you look like someone dropped the ball?" He asks.

"Beth is going to blame me for the mess up. This is not what I had set up for your daughter and Tyler." I look at Beth swooning over Cody and honestly I feel sick.

Jillian walks over. "I have all the plans that you did for my wedding. I have the original contract. I know this—" she looks at the buffet set up all around the room. "I know that this is not your doing."

I feel sick. "You look beautiful." I tell her.

She looks in the corner of the room. There is a tower of cupcakes that looks like a wedding cake. "I know that that is your doing. Thank you for listening to what we wanted. Tyler loves cupcakes."

Beth makes her way back to where I am. "What the hell is with the cupcakes? That will be removed immediately."

Tyler walks over and hugs me. "Cupcakes! Thank you so much for the cupcake tower."

"I am so happy for you both. You are going to be the best looking groom and you, Jillian are stunning tonight. Tomorrow I know you are going to be equally stunning."

She looks at Cody. "My cousin really likes you."

"I really like him too." I look at the two of them. "This is where you need to make your way around the room and thank your guests for coming tonight. There is a birdcage set up next to the cupcakes for your guest tonight to put their cards and gifts in."

Jillian looks at me. "Beth said that we couldn't have that."

"Its not something that she does. That's my touch."

I feel like someone is watching me. I turn and see Joanna, my step-mother, watching me. I look at Kyle.

"She is friends of the father."

"The universe just wants to slap me in the face." I say.

She walks over. She stands on her toes and kisses Kyle on the cheek. She kisses me on the cheek next. She notices the birdcage. "Can I ask you a question?"

I look at her.

"You were ten when your dad and I got married. How did you know about the birdcage?"

"I was fourteen when you and my dad got married. My grandma told us girls that when she and my grandpa got married all their guests put their gifts for the couple in a white birdcage. I always liked that detail. When I first got my job, there was a couple that wanted a box. They had this designer box for their cards. One of the guests took the box and threw it on the floor. I remembered grandma telling me about the birdcage. We were at a resort that had a Bahama style store. They had a birdcage. I went in and purchased it. I took all the cards that were all over the floor and I put them in the birdcage. On top, I added a card from Rosa and me that just read 'congratulations and best wishes to you always'. They were so happy. They called Rosa to find out how they could repay the money for the birdcage. She gave them the information. When the money came, Rosa gave it to me. I sent the money back to the couple."

Joanna looks at me. "We never knew where the birdcage came from. You know we still have it."

I smile.

"I saw you on Facebook. I am so happy for you." She says.

"Thank you." I say.

"Your dad and I want to take you out for dinner. We are so glad that you are back in our area." She looks at me. "Your dad is so excited that you are in one of his bungalows.

"Thank you for the flowers and the balloons." I tell her.

"I am so glad that you got them." She says.

"Thank you for my hippo."

"You left him at our house a long time ago."

Cody walks over with two plates of food. "Come sit with me." He hands the plates to me and pushes my wheelchair to the table that he is sitting at. I feel awkward. "Whats the matter?"

"Nothing." I say.

"Who was that lady that you were talking to?"

"Joanna, my step-mother."

"Did you know that she was going to be here?"

"No."

"Is she friends of the bride or groom?"

"She knows your uncle." I say. I look at him. "You were roommates with Kyle and you never met his mom?"

"Your dad would go to a lot of the school functions. I never met her." He looks at me.

"Eat something." He kisses my bare shoulder.

I look at him and smile. I put my hand on Cody's shoulder and he flinches but then pulls me against him and kisses me on the lips.

We walk hand in hand back to the room. We go in the room. The dress that was left on the bed is ripped to shreds. I look at the dress. Cody looks at me. I turn to the door and try to leave.

"Don't leave." He says. He takes his phone out of his pocket and calls for security. "I need someone to call the police."

On the dress is a green post-it note that reads, Your a Bitch.

"Do you know who did this?"

"The only one I could think of is Beth. She spelled you're wrong." I roll my eyes.

There is a knock on the door. Two police officers come in the room. They take statements from both of us. They take pictures of the shredded dress.

Kyle and Lacey knock on the door. Kyle hugs me.

Cody walks out of the room with the two officers. "I want to press charges. That is an expensive dress."

"Do you have any enemies?"

"The dress is my girlfriend's. She just got fired yesterday."

"Maybe she did it." The one officer says with a bite in his tone.

"She didn't do it."

"How do you know?"

"She is the girl in the wheelchair."

The one officer looks at Cody. "You are the couple that is on Facebook kissing."

"Yes."

"Is it true that you just met her yesterday?"

"No."

They all hear someone crying. Cody scans the courtyard. The police do the same. They see Beth standing off by the bushes. She's a hot mess. Her lipstick is smeared all over her face. Her eyeliner and mascara are smudged down her face. She is holding a pair of scissors in her hand.

Cody walks over to her with the officers behind him. "Why would you do that?"

"Why her?" Beth asks.

"Why not her?" Cody yells.

"You don't even know her."

"I do know her."

"You just met her last night."

"I kissed her last night. I met her on a flight." Cody says.

"Prove it." Beth says.

"Why did you do that? How did you get in my room?"

"Why are you two sharing a room?" Beth asks.

"There was a mixup in booking." Cody says.

"Sir, you don't have to answer her questions." The officer says. He looks at Beth. "You do have to answer our questions."

She blinks a few times.

"Have you been drinking?"

"I had a drink." She says.

"Did you take any drugs?"

"I don't do drugs."

"Do you know the victim?"

"She is my former employee."

"You fired her?"

"Yes."

"Why?"

"She was flirting with the clients. She knows better." She looks around. "She is sleeping with the client."

"I am not a client. I am the cousin of the client. We didn't sleep together. There are two beds. She was in one and I was in the other."

"Sir, again, you don't have to talk to her." The police officer says.

"Can I ask you a question?" Cody asks her. "What were you looking for in the room?"

The officer looks at Beth. "What were you looking for in the room? How did you get the key to the room?"

"I told them that I was his wife. I was looking for her stuff. None of her stuff is here. Why is none of her stuff here?"

"You fired her yesterday morning." Cody yells at her.

Beth looks at him. "Lover boy, come on. You know you want me."

Cody walks away.

The two officers repeat his nickname. One of them steps closer to Beth. "You need to put the scissors down."

She drops them on the ground. "Everyone likes her best. My aunt gave her the business. She steals my clients." She laughs. "Her last name is Steele." She throws her hands in the air. "She stole him."

Cody returns to the room. The dress is still on his bed. I am not there. He walks out of the room. He runs into the lobby. He looks at the new clerk that is at the front desk.

"Hi. Did you see a woman in a wheelchair come through here?"

"Yes."

"Did you see where she went?"

"She left with an older woman."

"Oh come on." Cody says and runs his fingers through his hair.

The clerk bends behind the counter and picks up a bag. He straightens and hands the bag to Cody. "She left this for you."

Cody looks inside the bag. Inside is the dress that I wore tonight.

Kyle walks over. "Cody, what's going on?"

"She left." Cody says.

"Crystal is sharing a room with Lacey. I am going to share the room with you."

"The clerk said that she left."

"She walked my mom out. Then she went on the outside path to Lacey's room."

Cody looks at the clerk. "Is there a gift shop that is open?"

"It closes in fifteen minutes. Its over there." He says and points his finger to the sign that reads gift shop.

Cody runs into the gift shop. Kyle joins him. "What are you doing?" Kyle asks him.

"I want to get her something."

"What?"

"What does she like?"

"I don't know."

"You claimed that she's your favorite sister and now you are telling me that you don't know what she likes." He walks around the gift shop and picks up a picture frame. He then walks over to where they have stuffed animals. He looks at Kyle. "What's the story about the hippo?"

"The hippo?"

"Kyle! Are you sure you know her?"

"The hippo is at my parents' house. How do you know about the hippo?"

"When we were leaving her she shed—"

Kyle laughs. "It's a bungalow."

"When we were leaving, there was the most beautiful flowers with balloons that read welcome home and a stuffed hippo was with it. She burst into tears when she saw the hippo. What's the story of the hippo?"

"Jack, our dad, bought each of his girls a different stuffed animal before he left their mom. Before her graduation from college she stayed at our dad's house. She left the hippo in her room. My mom was so mean to her and her dad took my mom's side of it. Brandon and I were on her side. Jack told all of us that when she returned to us, he would give it back to her." Kyle looks at Cody. "She burst into tears?"

"Yes." Cody picks up one stuffed animal and then puts it down. "What's her favorite color?"

"Red and blue."

"Why?"

"I have no idea." He says.

The lady behind the counter looks at them. She looks like she is exhausted. "We close in five minutes." She says. She walks around the counter and over to them. "Who are you buying a gift for?"

"My girlfriend."

Kyle's head jerks up.

Cody ignores him.

She looks at Cody. "I watched you grab her and kiss her. It was the most romantic thing I have ever witnessed." She walks to the cabinets. She opens it and takes out two teddybears that are joined together hugging one another. "This?" She suggests.

"Oh that's perfect." Cody says.

She takes them up to the counter and she rings him up. He pays and gives her extra money for staying open longer for them.

"Sir, this is too much money." The lady says.

"Its not." He says.
"Thank you."

Cody and Kyle leave. "What room is Lacey staying in?"
"She is in room three-fourteen."
"Is she eating pies in there?"
They both laugh.
Cody starts walking over that way.
"Give it to her tomorrow."
"I will." He says. They go back to his room. "I want to hold her and kiss her."

Kyle calls Lacey. "Hey."
"Hi." She says softly.
"How are things?"
"She's sleeping I think."
"Thanks for letting her stay with you." Kyle yawns.
"Oh don't mention it."
"Sleep well. I will see you in the morning."
"You too."
"Love you."
"Love you too."

When he puts his phone on the nightstand he looks around the room. Cody is sitting at the table with his computer in front of him checking emails. He looks at Kyle.
"How come she knows so much about me?"
"I brought her to school with me once and she wanted to see the baseball fields and the softball fields. You were practicing. She had a notebook with her and she kept jotting things down. I never questioned her until later. Then she showed me."
"What"
"It was all notes about you. She could tell the pitch that you were going to throw based on how you stood."
"What?"

"I took her notes to the coach and he watched you. I didn't tell him that my little sister did the observations in an hour."

"She watched me for an hour and knew how to make corrections?"

"I took her notes to the coach. I had to photo copy them a few times because she draws fucking hearts on everything."

Cody laughs. He opens his wallet and takes out the note that I left him. Kyle looks at it and laughs.

"Coach said that he wanted to meet the person that could watch one of his athletes in just an hour's time and had an eye to make corrections. He took those notes and he said he would use them." Kyle laughs. "She even had notes on how you hit the fucking ball. She noticed that when you wiggled your ass, you weren't into it. When you stomped your foot just before you took your stance in the box, you hit a home run."

Cody stands up. "You are joking?"

"I am not. When she applied for college, she saw that sports commentator was an option. Kelsey and I went with her for her orientation. She took her notebook out of her back pack and started reading. Every other person was animated when they were doing their audition. She wasn't. She went in with this attitude that if she got it she got it, if she didn't she would find something else. She was spot on. She did your play-by-play and then you hit that grand slam home run. If she could have, she would have jumped out of her wheelchair and ran a victory lap around the bases with you. She was so excited. The guy teaching the classes, wanted her. Not for anything else but her enthusiasm."

"Oh wow."

"Your cousin got my sister fired." Kyle says.

"I know."

"Why?"

"Why did she get her fired?"

"No. Why did you kiss her?"

"I had such a reputation in school of being a player. A woman recognized me on the plane and made a big deal about it. She was like 'oh my god! It's Lover Boy' I walked past her like I didn't hear it. I saw Crystal smile and then she shook her head. She said to no one at all 'that stupid bitch wouldn't recognize a nice person if she was sitting next to him.' She looked up at me and I know she knew who I am. She smiled. It was a smile that is one you reserve for a person you love. Her smile melted my heart. I was across the isle from her. She was reading something on her phone and she was upset about something. Then she threw her phone in her purse and closed her eyes.

"At first, I thought she was blowing off steam or something. Then I noticed that her head dropped forward. I stood up and asked the lady who was going to sit next to her if I could switch seats. She was grateful because they put her kids in the isle with me. I sat next to Crystal and she immediately put her hand on my arm and used my shoulder as a pillow. She was sleeping the whole time. The pilots came down the isle and asked me if I would take charge of her if there was an accident. I told them that it was a no brainer."

"How did you wind up in the same room as her?"

"I really have no idea."

"You didn't notice her wheelchair in the room?"

"The room was dark when I came in it. The bed closest to the door was available and I jumped in it. I fell asleep immediately. I woke up to her voice. I heard her laugh. She said that she would have to call her mom back. Then her phone rang and it was Beth yelling at her. She stood her ground. I told her to stop yelling and she turned so quickly I think she banged her elbow on the table. She looked at me and asked what the hell I was doing in her room. Then she was out of the room in the lobby trying to deal with the mixup. Then she got fired. She came back here and cleaned out all of her stuff and she was gone."

"How did you find her at the house?"

"Her She-Shed?"

"Her house." Kyle laughs.

"She left her earrings on the nightstand and her teddy bear was under the bed. It had her name on the tag and a post-it stapled to it with an address and the word new circled a lot. I went to the clerk who had helped her and asked if he could help me find this address. Four matches came up. But I saw her get into her red Mustang with a box on top. I was blown away watching her. She got fired and didn't shed a tear. She just got in her car. She gunned the engine and left the parking lot. The first little house I got to had her car in the driveway."

"She left her teddy bear?"

"I don't think she knew she left it."

"The teddy bear with the creepy belly button."

They both laugh.

Kyle walks around the room. "So why did you kiss her?"

"We did Tyler's bachelor party. Sort of. We all had drinks by the pool. They dared me to kiss the prettiest girl I saw and when I walked in the lobby, I wasn't drinking. I can't drink."

"I know."

"Anyway, I saw her and I couldn't resist. I had to kiss her."

"How did it wind up on Facebook?"

"I have no idea." Cody says. He looks at Kyle. "I was lost in that kiss. I couldn't get enough of her. I didn't want it to end. Then stupid Tyler kept saying Lover Boy that's enough. He told me that I proved my point. I kissed her again."

Kyle takes out his phone and he opens his Facebook app. He watches Cody kissing me. He gives the phone to Cody. He watches it.

Cody looks at Kyle. "We need to get her a dress for tomorrow."

"Lacey will give her something." Kyle says.

They turn the lights off and go to sleep. Cody just lays in bed looking up at the ceiling.

Chapter Four

I sit at a table in the beautiful atrium. There are flowers all around and butterflies flutter about. I sit sipping an iced coffee. I look around and think that this is the most beautiful place I have ever been in. This would be a perfect spot for a wedding.

I hear male voices. "She has to be around here somewhere."

I look around. I see Kyle and Cody walking around.

"Lacey said that she asked about the atrium. We are in the atrium." Cody says. He looks down from where they are standing on the upper level. "There she is." He says. He sprints down the stairs and runs over to me. "Hi. You are the hardest person to find." He looks at me and smiles.

"Then I did something right." I say.

"You were trying to hide?" Cody asks.

"No. I don't hide."

He takes my coffee and takes a sip. "This is so great."

I laugh. "What is with you eating my food and drinking my drinks?"

"I like what you like." He says.

Kyle sits down. "We need to get you a dress." He too takes my coffee cup and finishes the coffee in it.

"I have a dress."

"Where did you get a dress from?"

"I went home and got something from my closet."

"How did you get home?" Kyle asks.

"Dad."

"You called him?"

"I did."

"How did it go?" He sits with the back of the chair against his chest. He puts his arms on the top of it.

"It went well. He went to get Joanna and then they will be back for brunch."

Cody looks at me. "I am going to find my cousin and see what the plan is."

"There is no plan." I tell him. "She is getting a spray tan. When she is done with that, she is getting her nails done. Then she gets her hair and makeup done. She will get into her wedding dress and at five tonight you will stand on the alter with her while she exchanges her vows."

"You know the whole itinerary?"

"I do know it. You will actually be needed at three to do pictures with the bride and the bridesmaids. Then there will be a quick snack so that no one passes out on her lucky day."

"What will you do?" Cody asks.

"Well it seems that I have to oversee this wedding because Beth was arrested last night." I want to gloat but I don't. Either way, I am not taking over the business again. If it flops, I am all for it.

Lee walks over. "Crystal."

I look up at him. "Did you want something?"

"You have a phone call."

"No one is calling me."

"There seems to be a problem with the flowers."

"Lee, there is no problem with the flowers."

"Will you please just take the phone?"

I take the phone from him. "Hello."

"Causing trouble everywhere you go." Rosa says lightheartedly.

I laugh. "Hi Rosa."

"I heard what happened. How are you?"

"I will see this through until the end. This is the last one I will do."

"Oh please don't say that. We have seven waiting brides."

"I don't. She fired me. She couldn't wait to get rid of me. I won't press charges so she can get everything she wants. I am here in Fort Lauderdale and I will find another job. Trust me, I have money saved up. I will be good for a while."

"We will talk soon." She says.

"Sure."

I give Lee his phone back. I look at him for a moment. He is bridezilla's brother.

"You know who I am?" Lee asks.

"You are Lee Caster."

"My dad is so mad at me." Lee says.

"I hope that you and Beth are happy. How is Becky?"

"She is livid." Lee says.

"Oh sure. I did my job again and she's disappointed."

"Not at you. She is livid with me."

"Why?"

"She is pissed off that I got you fired." He looks at Cody and Kyle. "You are both guests of the wedding party."

"We are." Kyle says.

"Jillian wants to have everyone for brunch. It will be served in a half hour." He stands taller. He looks like a light post. He is so skinny. A walking coat wrack.

"Where will that be?"

"In the banquet room we were in yesterday." He says.

I look at all of them. "There has been a change of plans. Brunch will be in the atrium in forty-five minutes per the bride. Because its not raining, she has decided to do it here." I look around again as a staff of people start setting up tables. They set up the table for the couple. "Lee, you just have to watch that they put no live candles out. Tyler's son will be here."

"Where are you going?" Cody asks warmly.

"I don't work for the company any more. My job here is done." I say. I take my empty coffee cup and leave.

Lee chases after me. "The photographers won't work with me."

"That's not my problem."

"Can you just tell them that I am who they need to talk to?"

I leave the atrium and slowly make my way back to the lobby. I see my team of photographers. They work with us a lot. They walk over to me and hug me.

"What the fuck is going on?" Oscar asks. He is my head photographer.

"Beth fired me." I say.

"Are you fucking kidding?" Marcus asks. He is the second photographer.

"Nope."

"Well where is she?" Marcus asks.

"She got arrested." I say. I look across the courtyard. "That tall guy is Lee."

"We know who Lee is. Why is he here?"

"He is taking lead."

"When did that happen?"

"Oh for Christ sake, I have no idea what Beth and him are up to. But when I got here I didn't recognize him yesterday when he was being a pain in my ass. He calls it a seminar. He is taking lead. You have to work with him." I look at both of them. "Please give your best. The bride is worth your hard work."

"Are you saying we would sabotage our work?" Oscar asks.

I look at him. "Was it you who captured the kiss and plastered it all over Facebook?"

He looks around.

I look at Marcus.

"Don't be mad." Oscar says.

"I am not mad."

"We got a call from Becky. She is livid." Marcus says.

"Just say that you will do what you do best."

"We will do the job." Oscar says. "I was hired to do a side job. I need you and Cody for these shots."

"Oscar, I already lost my job. I won't let you get fired."

"Who's going to fire me? As I hear it, Beth lost her shit and cut an innocent dress to death."

"How do you know that?"

Marcus looks up and then all around.

"What are you two not telling me?"

"She was arrested because there is footage of her sneaking into a room that is not hers and going on a rampage."

"Did you two have anything to do with the mixup?"

The clerk walks over. "Ms. Steele, could you come with me please?"

I follow him into a small banquet hall. There is a big box on the table with a big red bow and blue ribbons. On the top of the box are two bears hugging each other.

"Is this a gift for the bride? This isn't her room?" I say.

"No. This is a gift for you." The clerk says. "My name is Kent. My boss heard what happened and he wants to offer you a job. We have three locations. This is the biggest of the three. We have a smaller golf resort and another location closer to the ocean. He will be back here on Monday. He wants me to host you."

"Is this from your boss?" I ask.

Kent shakes his head. "This is from a guest in our resort."

"Who is it for?"

"You."

"Me?"

"Yes." Kent says. He puts it on a chair and opens the lid of the box and holds it on his lap. Inside the box is the most beautiful dress that I have ever seen. Kent stands and takes the dress out of the box.

I gasp. "Oh my god. That dress would cost me all my savings." It's a beaded black dress that is cocktail length. It is spaghetti strapped with a sparkly short sleeved bolero.

"It's a gift. This dress was purchased for you." He looks up as a woman steps into the room. "Pam, thank you for coming."

She looks at him and smiles brightly. "Glad I can offer my service." She looks at me. "Come with me, I will help you get dressed."

"Who bought this dress?" I ask.

There is a note pinned to the dress. "Stop asking questions and just come on already."

I smile.

Pam says, "Come with me."

We leave the room and she carries the box and the teddy bears. She goes into the spa and into a dressing room. I take my shirt and pants off. I fold them up nicely. I put the dress on over my head and then stand up while holding on to the wall railing. The dress slides down my body and Pam steps on the side of me and zips the dress.

I sit back in my wheelchair.

"Do you have shoes?"

"I can't ware heals." I am wearing ballet flats. They stay on my feet with elastic bands that are thin and cris-cross on the top of my feet.

"You don't need heals. You look beautiful." She says. "I will be right back." She leaves the room. She comes back moments later with Oscar and Marcus.

Oscar walks over. He takes my hair and pulls some of it forward on my shoulder. He steps back and starts taking pictures of me.

"This feels wrong." I say.

"Why do you say that?"

"Its about our bride."

"No. We have an assignment first before the bride. Besides Kammy is here to work with the bride." Oscar says.

"I didn't realize that Kammy was assigned this job too."

"She wasn't." Marcus says. "When she heard what was going on, she wouldn't let us leave without her." Marcus walks over and stands in front of me. "Angle your body in your chair." He says.

I do.

He snaps what seems like a hundred shots. "Now put your hands on your knee. Cross your wrists." We do this pose with a lot of our brides. It does two things, makes cleavage and looks glamorous. Marcus steps back again. He gets the teddy bears and hands it to me. "Hold this."

I put the bears on my lap and hold them. Oscar steps closer and he takes over taking pictures. Pam walks over. "The atrium is ready."

"The atrium is ready for what?" I ask.

"Just go there. We will be right behind you."

I leave the room and push my wheelchair to the atrium. Cody walks over and takes my hand. He is already dressed for the wedding. He looks so handsome. I hear the cameras clicking behind us.

Kammy stands in front of us. She takes pictures of the two of us. We continue on to the atrium. A gazebo that I didn't noice before is in front of us. Cody steps behind my wheelchair and tips me back to go up the one step that is about seven inches high. Once we are back on solid ground, Cody holds my hand. He sits on the bench seat and spreads his legs. He pulls me to him and kisses me. He then stands and kisses me like he did two nights before.

A couple walks by. "Oh my god." The woman says. "Look how beautiful that looks. We should tell my dad that we want to get married here."

"We told your dad that we were just looking." The guy says.

She looks at me. "She is beautiful."

"She is beautiful." The guy agrees.

Then she looks at Cody and recognizes him at the same time that her fiancé does. They both look at each other and than back at the two of us. "Do you know who that is?" They both say together.

Cody deepens the kiss. Oscar steps in front of the couple and takes pictures. Marcus does as well from a different angle. Kammy sits on the floor and angles up.

"Ok, we have one more spot that we need you to go to." Oscar says.

I look at him. "Where would that be?"

"Up there." He says. He points to the dome. "There is an elevator on the left."

We sit at a table in a separate atrium. This one is smaller but even more beautiful than the bigger one. My dad and Kyle sit at the table with us. Joanne sits between my dad and her eldest son. Cody sits next to me.

"You look so elegant." Dad says.

"Oh thank you." I say.

The food on our plates is half eaten. It is so delicious.

Lacey sits next to Kyle. They look like they totally belong together. She looks at me. "So what is your plan now that you are back here?"

"I am back here." I say.

"Have you seen your sisters?" Joanna asks.

"I have not seen them yet. We are planning to get together at the end of the week. Brandon is putting it all together." I say,

"Have you seen your mom?"

"I just got here two days ago." It seems like I have been back for a year and yet not at all at the same time.

Lacey looks at Cody. "How did you two meet?"

"Hello!" I hear Kelsey's voice. She looks at me. I pull away from the table and my older sister sits on my lap. She hugs me.

"Hi." I say.

"Hello!" She stands and hugs Kyle. She hugs Lacey next. She makes her way around the table hugging everyone. She looks at Cody.

I look at Kyle and then I say. "Kelsey, this is Cody Parker."

"Thee Cody Parker?" She asks.

"Lover Boy." Lacey says.

He stiffens a bit next to me. I put my hand on his hand. "This is my boyfriend."

"Since when?" Dad asks.

"Dad, did you see the kiss seen around the world?" Kyle asks.

"Excuse me, I have to go. My cousin is getting married and I am in the wedding party." Cody says.

"The best man?" Joanne asks.

"Something like that." He says. He stands and puts his napkin over his plate. He looks at me. "We have to go." He says.

"Are you leaving?" Kelsey asks. "I just got here."

"I know, but I have obligations."

"How does a person who has been fired have obligations?" Joanna asks.

Cody takes my hand and we leave.

As we walk away, I hear Kyle's voice. "You haven't spoken to her in years and you were so nice to her last night. Why all the fucking questions?"

"How long has she known your former roommate?" Kelsey asks.

"Its theirs to tell. Not mine."

"He is a player." Lacey says.

"He was a player."

"A leopard doesn't lose its spots."

"Its not for us to judge." Kyle says.

We finally get out of the atrium. I push my wheelchair in front of Cody and I stop and look at him. "I apologize for my family. The way they see things is not how I see them."

"You don't ever need to apologize for your family." Cody says.

Jillian walks over. "Cody, grandma is here and she is waiting to be escorted by you."

"I am coming." He says.

I look at him. "Go. I don't want to keep you from your wedding duties." I look at Jillian. "Wow, you are stunning. You are the most beautiful bride I have ever seen."

Jillian spins around a few times. I see when she turns the second time that a few of her buttons are not fastened. "Do you really thinks so?"

"I do. Some of your buttons in the back are not fastened. Let me get Kammy, she can help you." I say.

"Oh thank you."

Cody steps behind her, he takes the fabric in his fingers and fastens them. "I am the man of honor." He says and kisses his cousin on the cheek.

"Cody, if people talk shit about you, promise me that you will let it go in one ear and out the other. Your dad will be here."

"Jillian, I will be alright."

"Not everyone believes the rumors." She says.

I reach my hand up and take Cody's hand.

"Jillian looks at me. "What do you think of my cousin?"

"He's my hero."

"How so?"

"Cody, had not one but two grand slam home runs in the last game that he played. When he hit the second of the two out of the park, I was in a class and failing my test miserably. When I heard in my ear that Cody Parker scored a second grand slam home run. I was writing his statistics in my notebook and my teacher walked by. He was getting ready to accuse me of cheating and when he looked down and saw it, he gave me an automatic A."

Cody looks down at me and smiles. He looks at Jillian, "Can you have Kyle show grandma to her seat. She loves him more than any of us." He looks at me. "I need a minute."

"Cody, I release you from your man of honor duties, you have proven yourself more than worthy." She says. She looks at me. "I apologize for all my wrong doings."

"Its more than ok." I tell her.

"I will be on the alter with you." Cody says. He takes my hand. "Come lets go find you a great seat."

I start to laugh.

"What is it?" They both ask.

"I bring my own seat." I smile brightly.

Cody kisses me. "Lets find a good placed to put it."

Jillian laughs. She steps into Cody. "Put her in front of you on the isle."

He looks at her.

"I am serious." She says. "You are the last to come down. You don't have a lady to walk with down the isle. She will be your partner."

"Why?"

"My wedding, my rules." She says. She steps back and then leans in to kiss him on the cheek. She kisses me on the cheek. "Thank you for making sure I am perfect."

"You look like you just walked off the pages of a bridal magazine. You will be the star bride of Madame Butterfly's Bridal Boutique. Trust me, every bride will want to look as elegant as you." I say it and mean it. We showcase all of our brides. Jillian is the most beautiful girl that we have had.

Two beautiful women walk over. "Jillian, you need to get out of the sun. You will melt in this heat."

One of them looks at Cody. "Come on. You are needed in the bridal suite."

"Cody, please. You have been a disappointment." The other one says.

"Why would you say that to him?" I ask defensively.

They both look at me. "Who are you?"

"I am his girlfriend." I say. I look at him. "Sweetheart, don't let anyone tell you that you are a disappointment. You are far from it." I pull him to me and hug him. I kiss him on the lips and hold him close to me for a moment longer. "I will wait for you by grandma." I tell him. "We have a special place for her so that she doesn't miss a sight." I push my wheelchair away from them.

I find the grandmother. "Hi, ma'am. My name is Crystal. I am the wedding planner and I have come to show you to your seat."

"I will follow you, dear." She says.

"Right this way." I tell her.

Kyle walks over. "Please let me escort you to your seat." He says. "Its nice to see you again grandma. This is my sister Crystal."

"The wedding planner is your sister?"

"The one overseeing the details of this wedding." I say. "This is my last one."

"It wouldn't have anything to do you with you getting kissed by my grandson?"

"No." I say. "I am moving on from this line of work." I talk as we approach the seats. "You are the third seat on the left." I smile at her. "Enjoy."

As I am leaving, I hear grandma say, "I think Cody finally found himself a winner."

Kyle hugs her. "If you need anything, let me know."

The first of the bridesmaids line up in the back of the atrium. The groomsmen line up on the other side of the sidewalk. They each walk three feet on their own before they join hands and walk down the isle.

Tyler is the last one to line up. He walks down the isle by himself. He walks half way down and then turns back and takes his son's hand. The most adorable three year old walks with him.

The wedding march starts and the back door of the atrium opens. Jillian and her dad walk through. He walks her down the isle. When they get to the front of the canopy, her dad stops just before handing his daughter's hands over to Tyler and takes her hands and kisses them.

"I love you. You will be great entering your new journey." Her dad says.

The ceremony starts. When the priest says that Tyler can now kiss his bride the whole atrium erupts in cheers.

Cody steps forward and squats to gather her train for her. She starts down the stairs and Cody lays the material ever so carefully behind her. Tyler takes Jillian's hand and they walk back up the isle. Tyler carries his son too.

I am waiting for them when they leave the atrium. Oscar is with me to get shots of them as they leave. They stop walking when they reach where I am.

I look at her. "Your second dress is hanging in the bridal suite."

"Thank you." Jillian says.

"My assistant Kammy is in there waiting for you. She will help you get changed. Then she will bring your dress that you are wearing to your room."

"Thank you again."

"You don't have to thank us." I say.

Jillian leans close to me. "Is there a photographer that is going to take pictures of me in my wedding lingerie?"

"Yes. Kammy." I tell her.

She smiles brightly.

The rest of the bridal party comes out. They are ushered into the reception hall. An open bar is set up in one corner and servers greet them with plates of finger foods. When Jillian's grandma walks in the door, violins start to play her favorite tune. She is ushered to a table where she makes herself comfortable. A server walks over and places a plate of variety foods in front of her.

"She got every detail down to the cucumber finger sandwiches." Grandma says.

"That was a special order from the wedding planner." The young woman server says.

"That wasn't included in our package?"

"You would have to talk to the wedding planner."

"Do you know whom that would be?"

She turns around a few times to look for me. When she sees me she turns back to grandma and says. "The pretty one in the wheelchair."

"You don't know her name?"

"She just came to this location like three days ago. She is the best wedding planner that we have worked with. She doesn't leave any detail out. Her notes for all of us were so thorough. There was no guessing where to put things."

Another server walks over with the stuffed mushrooms that grandma likes. He puts them down in front of her. They are piping hot just how she requested. "These are just for you." He says. He gives her a few napkins. "Is there anything else we can get for you?"

"No. Thank you."

A third server walks over with two drinks for her. One is a martini and the other is an iced tea. "Here you are." She says.

Grandma sips the martini. She closes her eyes.

"Is everything alright?" The three servers ask together.

She smiles brightly. Her smile matches her grandson's smile and reaches her eyes. "Minty." She says.

"That was what you wanted?" The server that brought it over asks.

"Its perfect. Its exactly what I wanted." Grandma says. She smiles again. "Tell me, was this a special order?"

"This was on a different ticket than our original order." The third server says. She comes with us from Madame Butterfly's Bridal Boutique. "This went in as a special order. Our wedding planner goes over all the details and you are an honored guest." She says.

"Beth did this?" Grandma reads the third server's name tag. "Kat? Did Beth do this?"

"Beth didn't take lead on any detail for this wedding. She usually takes no interest at all in the weddings that we coordinate. She only took an interest when she saw Facebook."

"What does that mean?" Grandma asks.

"Nothing." Kat says.

Sam also works with us. He brought over the mushrooms. He looks at Kat.

"We were dealing with Beth." Grandma says.

"I can tell you for sure that you never spoke to Beth." Kat says. "All these details are perfect." She walks away.

"Where is Beth? I heard that she flew here to make this event special." Grandma says.

"She had an emergency and had to return to Orlando." Sam says. "If you need anything please let us know. We are here to serve you."

"Was Crystal the one who organized this event?"

"Every detail was overseen by her. Then Beth wanted to make her look bad and sent her to Indiana on a wild goose chase. Once she landed in Indianapolis, Beth called her frantic and said that she needed Crystal to fly to Orlando. She did. No questions asked. Then when she touched down in Orlando, Beth told Crystal that she had made a mistake again and she needed to meet with a bride in Ohio." Sam laughs. "Crystal did have a temper about that, but never the less, she did in fact get on a plane and flew to Ohio. Beth sent over twenty-five text messages to Crystal. When she got them, she then flew to Atlanta where she got stuck for three hours. Then she finally flew to Fort Lauderdale. She came here with a big smile on her face that she was finally here."

"So when did she kiss my grandson?"

Cody walks over and hugs her, "Are you causing trouble?"

"Just digging some dirt."

"She didn't kiss me. I kissed her. She didn't know I was going to do it." He looks at his grandmother and takes one of her mushrooms. He looks at Sam. "Who made these?"

"They were made by Crystal."

He leaves them to find me.

I am outside looking out at the most beautiful sunset I have seen in a long time. This day has been a long one. I should have been at home getting my house all set up the way that I want it. But instead, I worked for an unpaid event. I am not going to get paid for it. I got fired.

I look out at the sun setting. I take my phone out of my purse and take a picture of it. I snap the picture and then put my phone back in my purse. I stay outside listening to the music playing. The DJ rocks it. I sway back and forth in my wheelchair.

"Can I dance with you?" Cody asks softly.

"Of course you can." I say and turn around.

"How do we do this?"

"Just like everyone else." I say.

He stands in front of me.

"Stand next to me. Put your hand on my shoulder and hold my other hand. Just sway to the music. Just like everyone else." I tell him.

He does. We dance to one song. The song changes and he keeps dancing with me. Oscar takes pictures of us.

"I have a favor to ask of you." Cody says.

"What would that be?"

"Can I stay with you for a few days in your she shed?"

I laugh. "Don't let my dad hear you say that."

"Can I?"

"Why would you want to?"

"I have to stay in the area for a week."

"You can stay with me. That would be fine."

"Tomorrow there is a breakfast and a lunch with the newlyweds." Cody says.

"I know. I planned it. Its for the family only."

"I want you to be there with me." He kisses me. He puts his hand behind my head and puts his other arm around me. He holds me close. "You are going to be my family." He says and kisses me again.

"I will be going home tonight."

"You are a guest."

"I am not. I was the wedding planner. I lost my job. I am tired. My shoes are killing my feet." I laugh.

"You are my invited guest."

"I will be going home. Kyle is going to take me."

"I will take you."

"Cody, you know where I live. You are welcome to stay with me as long as you want. I have to go. I need to go find a big sandbox." I need a sand box to go bury myself in.

"What?" He asks.

"Nothing." I say. I pull away from him and try to leave.

"Crystal? How did you know about my grandma's favorite mushrooms? And the chocolate mint martini?"

I look at him. "It was my job to cover every detail."

"Jillian is the most selfish person on the planet. She wouldn't know my grandmother's favorite things if her life depended on it." He holds my hands. "How did you know about them?"

"She called and tried to add them to the menu. Beth told her it was too late. Your grandma seemed so nice and Beth was a bitch. I was taking lead on this one, so I had the say. I made the mushrooms myself so that it wouldn't cost an additional fee. The chocolate Martini was just my treat to her. When she came to pay the additional, I took the money and then mailed it back to her saying that we were overpaid."

"Where did the money come from to pay for that martini mix?"

"Stop it. I wouldn't ask you where you got money from."

Jillian walks outside. "Cody, we are doing the last dance of the night."

"Congratulations on your wedding. You are the most beautiful bride we have ever had." I tell her.

"You will come for breakfast tomorrow?" She asks.

"No. My job is done. Lee is lead on the rest of this. Beth should be back tomorrow."

"It was very nice of you to add my grandma's favorite things. The little petti fours. How did you know?"

I look at her. "It's my job to make sure that the honored guests get exactly what they want. Your grandma wanted to pay extra for these things."

"The petti fours? How did you get them from her favorite bakery?"

"Jillian, go be with your guests. And enjoy your wedding. The last dance is coming up. Enjoy it. Tyler is a lucky guy."

"Thank you." She says.

I look at Cody. "Go. Dance with your grandma."

"I want to drive you home."

"We'll see." I say.

They both leave. He walks her back inside. I watch them go in.

Oscar sits with me. "I am only going over the pictures that we took with you."

"Oscar, please. Beth will be back tomorrow. She fired my ass. I am going home. Reality will hit me."

"Don't do that. You are the best fucking person I know."

"That's because I get you all the chocolate candy kisses you want."

"I am serious."

"So am I. I will go home and wake up from this dream."

"What dream is that?"

"Cody Parker. It has to be a dream."

"We have pictures to prove that its not." Oscar says.

"We have to oversee the clean up." I say. "I do."

"That's not your job anymore."

I smile. "It has to be for now."

"Lee wanted lead. Give it to him."

"I did nothing to these people. They think I am after their father's fortune. I was Rosa's assistant. She taught me what she wanted me to know. Beth wanted nothing to do with the fucking business." I blink a few times. "I have an interview with the manager here next week."

"I will leave. I want to work with you."

"Oscar, I don't even have the job. I don't know that I will get it. But you have your young family and I live here now."

"I will only work with you. My wife and the twins will move here."

"Lets see what happens." I say.

"Cody really likes you."

"Oscar, please stop. I am going to get all silly."

"Get silly."

"I want to jump up and down. In my heart, I am jumping up and down. Cody Parker kissed me. Oscar, I have never been kissed like that. No one will ever kiss me like that again."

"Does he know that you dreamed of him?"

I laugh. "Every girl dreamed of him." I look at him. "What happens next?"

"Will you say goodnight?"

"No." I say. "It's not about me. Jillian and Tyler, its about them." I hug him. "I have to find someone to give me a ride home. I have to stand up for a while. I have been sitting too long. I have to stretch my neck. I have to exercise. I have to take this dress off. Can you find out who needs this back?"

"Yes." Oscar says. "Are you going to change before you go home?"

"Yes. This dress feels like it cost more than I have saved up."

"You don't think you deserve to be in a beautiful dress?"

"I am being silly. I am tired. I really need to stand up."

"So stand up."

"I need to find something to hold on to."

"Come with me." Oscar says.

He takes me back to the gazebo. I release the feet hangers and I stand up. I stand in the corner of the gazebo so that I could just lightly hold on and stand up.

Cody walks over. He looks at me. "You can stand?"

"I walk with a walker. I mostly use my wheelchair. I need to hold on to something."

"Can you hold on to me?"

"Yes." I say. "But don't let me go." My heart screams DON'T LET ME GO! I LOVE YOU!

"I won't." He says.

The two violinists walk over and they both start playing softly.

Cody wraps his arms around my waist. I put my hands on his shoulders. He sways to the music.

My knees buckle because I have been standing too long. He lifts me and dances with me. My feet are off the ground.

"I know why they call you lover boy." I say.

He looks at me.

"You meant it for the love of baseball."

"How is it that you know so much about me?"

"Google."

He walks over to the wicker loveseat and sits down. "Is this alright?"

"If we sit here too long, I am going to fall asleep."

"If you do, what would be the worst thing?"

"When I wake up, this will all be a dream."

"You don't think this is real?"

"Have you seen some of the comments on Facebook?"

"Does it matter?"

"Its not you they are saying mean things about."

Chapter Five

My phone ringing wakes me up. I sit up and look around. I am in the resort bedroom. The one that Cody and I shared the first night. I look at the other bed and Cody is sleeping above the sheets all sprawled out. I look for my phone. I look at my wheelchair and the phone is on the cushion.

"Hello." I say.

"Hi sweetheart."

"Hi mom."

"Have you seen the pictures that are on Facebook?"

"The kiss?"

"No. There are pictures of you dancing in a gazebo."

"What?" I squeak.

"There are pictures of you dancing in a guy's arms." She takes and audible breath. "You should pull it up."

"I will."

"Where are you?"

"Finishing up at work." I tell her.

"What work? You got fired." She laughs.

"Thank you. Thank you for reminding me. Are you laughing?"

"Not at the fact that you got fired. I am laughing at the fact that Beth is going to lose—"

"Don't gloat."

"I will because you won't."

"I have to go."

"When will I see you?"

"Mommy, I will drive up to Delray and we will have lunch at my favorite Italian restaurant. On me." My favorite Italian restaurant is on Atlantic Avenue.

"Absolutely not on you. You just lost your job."

I laugh. "I love you. I will be in touch in a few days."

"Are your sisters going to help you move into your house?"

"Um I am not sure."

"Kelsey told me about lunch with daddy."

"Mom, it creeps me out when you call him daddy."

She laughs.

"We will talk soon. Love you." I put my phone back on my wheelchair. I lay back against the pillows.

Cody opens his eyes. He looks over at me and watches me. He doesn't say anything at all, but he never stops watching me.

I take my phone off my wheelchair again and look at Facebook. I look over at Cody. He is flat on his back with his arm over his eyes. I look back at my phone.

Image after image are of Cody and me dancing in the gazebo. He is holding me around the waist in a few. In a few other's Cody holds me as my knees buckled. Then he is holding me completely off my legs. The last ones are of me on Cody's lap, in his arms, sleeping.

I get in my wheelchair and take a shower. When I come out, I get dressed in pants and a dressy shirt. I put my makeup on. When I finish I look at the other bed and Cody is still sleeping.

Cody's phone rings. He answers it. "Hello."

"Mr. Parker, you are needed in the lobby of the resort." A male's voice says loudly on the other end.

"I will be there shortly." He says.

"The sooner the better."

"Sure." He says. He looks around the room. Everything is neat. His clothes that were in a heap on the floor are now folded on a chair. He gets out of bed and notices that one teddy bear is on top of his clothes. "Crystal?" He picks up the teddy bear. It has a key to my house. He reads the note. "Just let yourself in when you get to the house. I had to deal with something. Thank you for everything."

He calls Kyle. "I need Crystal's phone number?"

"What's going on?" Kyle asks.

"She keeps leaving."

"She had to take care of something."

"What?"

"Something at her house." Kyle sounds distracted.

"What?"

"I don't know. I dropped her off at her request and came back for the brunch."

"She left the teddy bear." Cody says.

"She took half of the set with her."

"Kyle, you got to cover for me."

"You are supposed to make a speech."

"You do it."

"Wing it?" Kyle asks.

"I will text it to you."

"Did they call you to come to the lobby?"

"They did."

"Are you coming?"

"I want to find your sister." Cody says. He runs his fingers through his hair and then takes the teddy bear and throws it on the bed.

I am pulling pots out of a box when the front door opens. I have music playing loudly so I don't hear anyone. Cody walks over to the counter and takes my phone. He shuts off the music. I drop the pot on the floor.

"I didn't mean to scare you." He says bending down to pick the pot up.

"You are supposed to be giving your speech for your cousin and Tyler." I take it from him and put it on the counter.

"Why did you leave?" He asks. He stands leaning against the counter next to me.

"I broke out in a rash. That hasn't happened in a long time. I was covered."

"Why didn't you wake me?"

"I couldn't stop itching." I tell him.

He looks at me and laughs. "Why didn't you wake me up?"

"I just had to go. I was going to have a melt down on top of a rash."

Cody hugs me. "I heard you on the phone with your mom."

"I thought you did."

"Do you know who put the pictures on Facebook?" He asks me.

"I have an idea. I know that he will deny it."

"Are they good?"

"You didn't look?"

"Lets look together." He says.

There is a knock on the front door. I go over and open it. My mom stands there with a big arrangement of flowers. She hugs me tight. "Hi." She says excitedly.

"Hi."

"There are two cars in your driveway. Are one of the boys here?"

"No. Kyle is out of town and Brandon is off with Ash." I say it and want to cringe.

"That's a thing?"

"Its been a thing for a long time. He loves her. She loves him. They are moving in together."

"So who's car is in the driveway?"

"Why don't you come in?" I look at the flowers. "You and daddy must have got them from the same florist."

"He was here already?" She is disappointed.

"No."

"How did he get you flowers?"

"Mom, he built these houses."

"It's small." Mom says.

"For a large family, its small. I am one person. Its fine. There are three bedrooms. So I have the master which is beautiful. I have two guest rooms and an office. The office makes me the happiest. That was the selling factor."

"Who owns the car in the driveway?"

"Cody Parker."

"Cody Parker? He is here?"

"Come meet him." I say.

I show her around the house. The master bedroom is very large. There is nothing but the bed in the room and a nightstand.

"You are staying here?" Mom says.

"I haven't stayed here at all. I stayed at the resort."

"Where will you stay tonight?"

"I have a bed right here."

"You can't stay here without your stuff." She walks around. "Leave it to your father."

"What are you talking about?" I ask her.

"Nothing."

"Mom."

"He let you move in without your stuff."

"He let me?"

"Let, that might be the wrong word."

I leave the room.

Mom walks after me. She walks into the kitchen. "Where is he?"

I look at the couch where I had the television box on and notice that my television that was delivered, now sits on the stand and is plugged in. The television is on softly. I look at the couch again and see that Cody is on it sleeping.

Mom walks over to the pictures that are now hanging on the wall. "You hung these?"

"Cody must have hung them." I say.

She looks at them. "I don't remember this one." She says about the one of me holding Cody's jersey. "Why would Cody hang your pictures?"

"You weren't there. And he was snooping and took them out of the box."

"I am glad that you are back, but why here? Why this house? Why not closer to me?"

"Daddy didn't know that I was moving back. He didn't know that Ashley and Brandon brought me to this little home. I fell in love with it the second that I saw it. I didn't know that it was daddy's developing. I fell in love with it. It was like it was designed just for me."

She looks at Cody sleeping on the couch. "Its so strange that you brought home a guy that you just met in a hotel who was a guest at a wedding that you were planning."

I look at her. "Mom, you have dated men and knew them for a shorter time that I have known Cody and you brought them home to meet us girls. We never judged you."

"I am not judging you."

"Aren't you?" I ask. "Ashley is dating her step-brother and you don't have a problem with that."

"She knows him."

"I know Cody."

"You are a fan of his?" She asks this with annoyance in her tone. She looks over at Cody.

"I am a fan." I look at him and I have a feeling that he is not sleeping anymore. "I know him. I know a lot about him."

"What does he know about you?" She snaps at me.

I look back at Cody and I hope that if he is not sleeping, that he just stays out of this conversation.

"You are right." I start saying to her. "You are right, he doesn't know anything about me."

"Then why would he kiss you? What did you do to get him to notice you?"

I look at him. I love my mother but right now, I want to kick her out of my house.

"I am waiting." Mom says.

"I am an adult. I don't have to explain anything to you."

"Obviously you planned this."

"What are you trying to make me feel guilty about? Should I be guilty that I moved into the cutest development that I didn't know that Jack Steele designed? Should I feel guilty that a handsome guy picked me out of all the women that were in a lobby of a resort and kissed me? What? Should I feel guilty that I have pictures hanging on my walls that you don't know about? That picture was taken on the day of my college orientation. I asked you to go with me. You told me to grow up and do it on my own; I was an adult after all." I say. The words come out just louder than a whisper. I look at Cody. I know he heard what I said. "Its because of Cody Parker that I was accepted into the program I wanted to be in."

"You are getting emotional. I think I am going to go." She looks at her watch. "I have to meet up with Stew."

Tell that judge mental man I send my love. I think to myself. I say to her, "Oh, how is Stew doing? How are his children?"

"Stew is great. He doesn't talk to his children."

What's with dads not talking to their children? I think. "I am sorry to hear that."

"Do you still keep in touch with his kids?"

"I haven't seen them since they came to stay with me in Orlando. I still didn't get a chance to visit with them. They were going to the theme parks and I was working two weddings."

"So you had them as house guests and ignored them?"

"Is that what you heard? I know that's not what I said." I smile at her. I know that this bothers her and it makes me feel better. I look at her and for some unknown reason to myself, I invite her to stay for a bit.

"I should go." She says.

"Thank you for the lovely flowers."

"Do you want me to do anything for you?"

"No." I say. I walk her to the door.

I close the door and take a deep breath. I feel the urge to break something. I love my mother and we have a great relationship. I don't know why she couldn't just come to my new house and say how cute it was or that she wished me luck in my new home. Instead she found flaws.

I look at the couch and Cody isn't there any longer. I look around and don't see him. "If you have decided to leave, I don't blame you." I say to the air around me.

Cody walks over to me. "I was trying to give you space."

"Are you calling my house small? Again?" I laugh.

"This is a she shed."

"It is not a she shed." I laugh.

"Wow, your mom."

"She's not normally like that." That is the truth. She is normally very kind and very supportive. Well most of the time she is supportive. She is always nice to have phone conversations with.

"I was going to say something but then I thought it was best if I stayed out of it."

"Thank you."

"She doesn't know that you are a fan of mine?"

"My sisters are involved with other things. I like sports and weddings. They like fancy things and weddings. My mother sees their accomplishments and gloats about them. The things that I do seems to be expected. My grandmas make big deals about what I do with my life. They don't do the same for my sisters. They do the same for my step-brothers who are technically not related to them at all. A few of mom's boyfriends knew that I am a baseball fan. They would encourage me."

"So your mom disapproves of you being with me?"

I turn away from him. I look at the wall clock. "You have a speech to give."

"Come with me." He steps close behind me and puts his arms around me.

"I want to."

"Then come."

"Come back when you are done."

"You can't stay here, there is no furniture." Cody says.

I turn back to look at him. "I don't need furniture really. I always bring my own chair."

He embraces me and kisses me. "I won't have any fun without you there."

"Cody, you have known all these people long before you ever knew me. You will have fun with them regardless if I am there or not."

He kisses me again. He kisses me deeply. "Are you sure that you won't come?"

"I can't go." I tell him. "I broke out in a rash and just thinking of going back makes me itch."

"I will be back." Cody says.

"Have fun. Dance. Give a great toast." I look at him. "Did you ever find out what they wanted from you this morning?"

"How do you know that they wanted me this morning?"

"There was a woman demanding to know why you were kissing a perfect slut stranger." I say.

"Who are you talking about?" He asks.

"A woman named Nicole."

He takes his phone out of his pocket and angrily punches the numbers. He puts the phone to his ear and walks outside. He walks back in the house and kisses me on the lips. "I will be right back." He says.

I sit at the table. My phone rings. I look at it and decide whether or not to answer it. Rosa is calling me. I do answer the phone.

"Hello." I say.

"Where are you?"

"Excuse me." I say.

"There is a wedding happening and you are not there."

"Rosa, of course, I am not there. I was fired. Beth took over. She fired me. Why would I be needed there?"

"I gave you my company."

"That's the problem. I was happy being your assistant. You should have given the company to Beth. She got it anyway."

"I am going to lose everything." Rosa says. "My reputation is done."

"That has nothing to do with me."

"It does too."

"Rosa, call Beth and talk to her about it. I am done. Thank you for calling me."

"Did Cody ever meet up with his girlfriend, Nicole?"

"What?"

"Nicole, his girlfriend, did he ever meet up with her? He was going to ask her to marry him."

"How do you know that?"

"You were going to host that."

"I was? This is the first that I am hearing of it. Who was going to set it up?"

"Cody Parks."

"Cody parks?"

"Yes."

"So Nicole is going to be proposed to by Cody Parks?"

"Yes." Rosa says.

"And what does Cody Parks do?"

"He is a musician."

"Beth is planning Cody Parks engagement and wedding?"

"No you are."

"No I am not." I say.

"Come on, don't be such a brat."

"I am not being a brat. I got fired. Please talk to Lee."

"I don't want to talk to Lee."

"I have to go." I say. I don't wait for her to say another word.

Cody comes back in the house. "Do you have something to wear that is a bit fancy?"

I look at him. "Why? Am I going to clean my house wearing fancy clothes?"

"No. You are going to come meet one of my friends."

"Where?"

"They are at the resort. I promise you that they are excited to meet you."

"Cody, you have a speech to give."

"I will only give the speech if you come."

"Cody, I can't."

"I want you to."

"You go ahead, I will come in a little while."

"Are you sure?"

Yes. I am totally sure that I am not going. I look at him and smile. "Either way, I will see you later."

"Either way?" He says. He walks in my room and looks in my nearly empty closet. He takes a dress out and comes back into the dining room. He takes my hand and he pulls me outside.

"What are you doing?"

"You are going."

"Cody, please. You will have a good time with your friends and your family. Your girlfriend is waiting for you."

"I don't have a girlfriend. You know that. You defended me on a plane when you didn't even know me personally."

"I know that you are nice."

"Why do you say that?"

"You have a speech."

"I want to know how you know I am nice."

"Should I drive?" I ask him.

"Why are you trying to get rid of me?"

"I want to keep you." I say without thinking.

"What?"

"Nothing."

"How do I do it?"

"You don't know how to do it? And you want me to tell you?" I laugh.

He looks at me and laughs. "I meant." He laughs again. "I meant how do I fold your wheelchair?"

"Oh, I will show you." I say.

We enter the lobby that has become both my favorite place and a place that I equally hate. Kent sees us coming and he smiles. He floats over and hugs me.

"Hi." He says.

"Hi." I say back.

"You look beautiful." He looks me up and down from head to toe.

"Thank you." I smile at him.

A guy walks into the lobby from a side back door. He sees Cody and walks over. They both hug each other.

"Lover Boy!" The other guy says.

"Music Man." Cody says.

I look at both men and I smile. I see a woman watching them just like I am. When Cody looks at her, she beams with love. Then she looks at the other guy and she nearly falls all over herself.

Oscar walks over to me. "So you are back?"

"I am not. I am a guest."

"A paying one?"

I look at him. "I always pay my own way."

"I see that Nicole has found Cody." Oscar says.

I look at Oscar. "I thought that you were the one who was encouraging me to give myself to Cody."

He looks at me. "You are leaving us."

"I got fired." I say. I snap my head up. "Right, I got fired. I don't belong here." I leave the area. I sit in a spot that no one can see me but I can see all that is going on.

Nicole is all over both guys. I watch Jill walk over and hug all of them. They are all enjoying themselves.

Tyler walks over and looks around. "Cody, what's going on?" He smiles. "You didn't come to the lobby this morning. Where have you been?"

I watch Cody scan the lobby looking for me. He looks at all of them and turns and walks away. He walks over to Kent and talks to him and the lady next to Kent. They point outside at the same time.

Lee walks over. "Hi can I talk to you?"

I look at him. "No."

"Obviously you are here because you can't get enough."

"I am staying here at the resort as my house is not yet ready to live in."

"You are staying with one of the guests?" He looks at me. "My stepmother always trusted you. Maybe you were always sneaking off with the guests."

I look at him. "Are you calling me a slut?"

Becky walks over. She looks at her brother. "What did you say to her?"

I feel my skin prickle. The rash takes over my skin all over my face.

Becky looks at me. "Are you alright?"

I look at her. I lift my chin and round my shoulders. "I think that I am allergic to this place. Excuse me." I say.

I hear Becky ask Lee again "What did you say to her?"

"I told her that Rosa trusted her and maybe that was a mistake because she was probably sneaking off with the guests."

Kyle stands on the balcony watching the whole thing. He follows with his eyes where I go. Then he looks back at Becky and Lee. He watches Beth walk over to them.

Cody walks over to Kyle. "Where is your sister now?"

"I am not sure." Kyle says. "Maybe she watched you with your friend and your girlfriend."

"Kyle, I don't have a girlfriend. I do have a mad crush on your sister. She keeps disappearing."

"Did you expect her to sit on the sidelines and watch you? She has done that before and she was your biggest fan. It's a different stadium this time and I think she thought she was a contender."

"What are you talking about?"

"Did you or did you not get a call that you were needed in the lobby this morning?"

"I did. I never went to find out why. Your sister left and I needed to find her."

"Where did you find her?"

"At her she shed."

Kyle laughs. "My dad will be so offended if he hears you say that."

"Her mom showed up. It wasn't a nice visit."

Kyle looks around to see if he can still see me. He can't. "No fucking way."

"I thought that her mom sounded so supportive up until she showed up with flowers that are beautiful." Cody looks at Kyle. "Your dad sent the same big bunch of flowers. Where is she?" Cody asks.

"I don't know."

"She gave me the spare key to her house."

"You are going to stay with her?"

"I want to."

"Did you see the pictures of the two of you on Facebook?"

"Not all of them." Cody says.

"You should see them."

Cody takes his phone out and looks at the pictures. The last one that he sees is the one of us in the lobby from the first night. He stares at it.

Chapter Six

I sit on the balcony at Brandon's apartment. His balcony faces the ocean and I let my hair blow wild from the wind. Brandon and Ashley give me space. I have been here for a week.

Ashely walks outside the sliding door. She looks at me. "Your phone is ringing."

"Let it ring." I say.

"How long are you going to ignore all your calls?"

"Fine." I say. I reach for my phone and take it from her. I throw it over the balcony.

"Why would you do that?" She yells at me.

The phone lays in the sand unharmed because of the case that it's in. A guy picks it up and looks up. Ashley looks at him. "I dropped it." She says.

"I will bring it up." Brandon says.

"Thanks." Ashley says. She looks at me. "Its been a week."

"Do you want me to go? Am I invading your space?"

"No. Not at all." She says. "We are worried about you. All of us are worried about you. Mom says you won't talk to her. Dad said that you won't talk to him. He wants to know why you have someone staying in your house other than you."

"He needed a place to stay for a couple of weeks. I told him he could stay with me."

"Stay with you." She repeats my words back to me.

"I feel like a fool." I look at my younger sister. "I never felt so much passion in a single kiss. Only I feel that same feeling every time he kisses me." I look out over the ocean. "I know better not to get caught up with clients' guests."

"You shouldn't feel like a fool."

"Yeah well I do. I broke out in fucking hives. I haven't had hives since I was twelve."

"The doctor told you that stress caused it." Brandon says. He hands me the phone. "Don't throw it over again."

"Don't tell me what to do, I am older than you are." I say laughing.

He smiles and hugs me. "Just a year. A year almost to the day."

I look at him. "My birthday is in August. Your birthday is in September that is more than a day."

Brandon looks at me. "Kyle wants to get together for lunch. Kelsey wants to come too."

"You don't need me to go to lunch with the two of them."

"We want you to come with us." Ashley says.

"No."

Brandon and Ashley exchange looks. "How is your work search going?"

I look at him. "Why?"

"I was just wondering."

"I have money. I will pay for whatever you want me to."

"Stop. It's not about money." He says. Brandon sits on the railing of the balcony and looks at me. "Kyle wants to go to lunch with all of us. Will you go?"

"I will go." I tell him. "I just don't want my mom, dad or anyone else I don't know to be there to go. I don't want to be ambushed."

"I won't let you be ambushed."

"When are we going?" I ask. I look out at the ocean.

"When do you want to go?" Brandon asks.

I look at him. "Just tell me when and where and I will show up." I turn my wheelchair and go back in the house. I go into the guest room that I am staying in and close the door. I look around the room and the teddy bear that I left in the hotel room with Cody is sitting on the bed.

I turn and leave the room. "Brandon!" I yell.

He walks over.

"Where did that teddy bear come from?" I ask him.

"I brought it." Cody says.

I look at him and then back at Brandon. "You said I wouldn't be ambushed."

"No one is ambushing you." Brandon says.

I look at Cody. "What are you doing here?"

"I have been calling you for days."

"I know."

"Why are you ignoring my calls?"

"Is your girlfriend staying in my house with you?"

"I don't have a girlfriend. You know that." He looks at Brandon and Ashley who both seem to be hanging on every word. "Will you go somewhere and talk to me?"

"Yes." I say. "Just give me a few minutes."

"Ok." He says.

"Have you met my sister and brother?" I ask Cody.

Kyle hugs me. "I will introduce them." He hugs me. "Where are you going?"

"To change my clothes." I tell him.

"Hear him out."

I look at Kyle. Then I go back in the room that I am using. I look at the clothes that I have with me and the only thing that I think is appropriate is a pair of pants and a black shirt. It dips low so I put a tank top on underneath it. I do my hair and my makeup quickly.

Cody and I sit on the pier. He sits on a bench that is at the very end of the pier. He looks out at the horizon. It is beautiful. There are people around us. I notice that some of the men fishing recognize Cody.

A woman walks past us. She looks at Cody and smiles. He nods his head letting her know that he is acknowledging her. The woman comes back and sits next to him. He moves away from her. She moves closer. She never saw me. Or if she did she never gave me a second thought.

I approach Cody. "Sweetheart, we should go meet up with the others." I reach my hand out to him. Kiss me. Please kiss me. The little voice in my head screams out to him.

He stands up and then gets on his knees on the side of my wheelchair and kisses me. The woman gasps. The men around us hoot. I wrap my arms around him and he deepens the kiss.

Cody breaks the kiss and stands. He takes my hand and we leave the pier. We still haven't spoken to each other. When we reach the Cove which is a diner, he pushes the button for the elevator. Once we are inside, he kisses me again.

He looks at me. "We need to talk." He says.

"That's why I am here." I tell him. "Cody, my life is difficult right now. You don't need my drama."

"Your drama started with me. Your drama happened because I kissed you. I want to kiss you everyday of my life." He says.

"You don't know anything about me." I say.

"That's not true. You told me about yourself."

"I told you tidbits so that if my family and your family questioned you about what you knew about me, you could tell them things that are true."

"Where have you been?" He asks.

I feel the hives starting to emerge on my skin. They are prickling.

Cody looks at me. "Is this something that always happens to you?"

"I haven't had a breakout of hives since I was twelve."

"Lets get you some water." He says. "Maybe you are allergic to my kisses."

"I am not allergic to your kisses. I am allergic to stress." I say and roll my eyes.

"Let's get you out of the sun and in the AC." He takes my hand and we enter the diner.

The host walks over smiling. "Pick a table anywhere you want." She says. She looks at me. "Can I ask you a question?"

"Yes." I say expecting her to say something about Facebook and the famous kiss. She surprises me completely.

"How do you like your home in Gulfport?"

"I love it." I tell her.

"I moved into Gulfport about a year ago, I am on the committee. If you need anything please let me know. You and your husband." She says.

I jerk my head up and look at Cody. "Thank you. I will do just that. I am Crystal. This is Cody. And you are?"

"Dotty."

"Its nice to meet you, Dotty." I say.

"Like I said, just pick a table anywhere you want to sit."

"Thank you." I say.

"Can we get two waters right away, my wife needs a drink." Cody says the word wife and my heart flutters in my chest.

"Let me get that for you right away." Dotty says.

When she walks away I look at Cody. "What? Your wife? I am sorry, did I sleep through the wedding of my dreams? Am I in the twilight zone? Is Alice and the white rabbit going to run past looking for Tweddle Dee and that other idiot?"

Cody looks at me. "Someone came with the police asking why I was staying in your house. The only thing that came to mind is that I was your husband. That seemed to satisfy the police officer."

"Cody." I laugh. "For Christ sake, we are strangers."

"Well lets stop being strangers and become friends."

He looks at the server who walks over with the waters. The young guy puts the glasses on the table. He hands us menus and then walks away quickly. Cody takes the glass and sticks a straw in it. He pushes it in front of me.

The server walks back. "Excuse me. Can I ask you a question?" He asks Cody.

"Yes."

"Are you by any chance coaching baseball?" He turns and walks away quickly.

I can't help but giggle. I try to stop laughing but I laugh harder.

"Are you laughing because I coach?"

"Of course not. I think its wonderful of you to want to teach the youths how to be as great as you are."

"I am not great anymore."

"Cody. Please." I say.

"You will be saying that in a different setting." He says.

"Oh my god, you are sure of yourself." I laugh.

"I am just telling you what to expect." He says smiling.

I look at him. "What about your security job?"

He looks at me. "How the hell do you know of that?"

"Do people not know anything about you past your baseball career?" I take a sip of water and gag on it.

He jumps up. "Are you alright?"

"It tastes like soap."

Dotty runs over. "What's the matter?"

"The water tastes like soap." I say.

"I am sorry. Let me get you another one." Dotty says. She looks at the young server. "Did my son bother you?"

Cody looks at her and then at him. He looks back at Dotty. "He was asking about my coaching."

"Oh, that's right." She looks at me. "You have married a sport hero." She looks over at her son. "He is a big fan. He wants to follow in your footsteps."

Cody looks sad for a moment. I reach out and take his hand. I hold it.

"Those are some big shoes to fill. Not everyone hits three grand slam home runs in one game." I say.

Cody's head jerks up and he looks at me. He is still standing next to me and he drops down in the chair next to me and takes me in his arms. I feel his heart beating against my own.

"Cody, sweetheart, I think we have to go."

He looks at me. He holds me closer to him.

"Please stay and have lunch on us." Dotty says.

"We can't stay." I say. "We thought that we had more time, but we don't."

"I will see you both in the neighborhood." Dotty says. She looks at Cody. "I am sorry about my son."

"No. No need at all. My wife caught me off guard. We will come back." Cody says. He takes my hand and we leave. He looks around when we are outside.

"Cody, what are you looking for?"

"A private spot."

"Why?" I ask.

The young server walks over. "Mr. Parker, I am so sorry. I didn't mean—"

"Its fine." Cody says.

"What's up there?" I ask pointing to an observation area.

"That's the observation deck. Its private. The only things up there are pigeons."

"How do we get up there? Can we go up there?" I ask.

"Yes. Take the elevator up to T-level."

"Thank you."

"I hope that I didn't upset both of you. I am sorry about the water. I was just told to bring it over to you."

"What's your name?" I ask.

"Brad." He says.

"Brad, thank you. You have nothing to worry about. We will be back. We need a little while."

"Take your time. Mom doesn't close the observation level until midnight." He leaves us.

Cody and I get in the elevator. We get out on the observation deck. It's a pier looking structure that is covered. It is private. There is no one else up there but the two of us.

I reach my hand out to Cody. He laces our fingers together and I can feel my heart beating in my fingertips. I feel his heart beating as well. "Cody, what's going on?"

"You surprised me. You literally caught me off guard." He says. He looks around.

"Cody, talk to me."

"I want to know about you. You know a lot about me."

"What do you want to know?"

"What makes you happy?"

"What makes me happy? Well my job used to make me happy. Seeing people happy makes me happy. My sisters generally make me happy. Watching you play baseball made me happy."

"You said that you dreamt of marrying me."

"Cody, I think every girl who knows you exist dream of marrying you."

"But you did?"

"Yes."

"Why?"

"I don't know if you would believe me."

"Tell me."

"When I saw on the news that you were mugged and that you were injured as a result, I found out what hospital you were in and I sent you a teddy bear. It was wearing a shirt that said I wish you well." I turn my wheelchair and push down the covered pier.

"Wait! That was from you?"

"I was so emotional when I watched it on the news. I wanted to make sure that you knew that you were loved. I sent you a note too."

"I have it. I have the bear and the note. I keep them in my room." He says. "Come talk to me.

"Cody, my neighbor thinks that we are married. This is going to get back to my family. They know so much about me. I am surprised my phone isn't ringing already." I no sooner say it when my phone blows up with text messages.

Kyle: CALL ME NOW!

Kelsey: Tell me you are fucking joking

Brandon: What's going on? Call me. Ky is calling me and wants to know what the hell is going on. Call me.

Ashley: wait….. what? You are married?

Mom: I am not amused.

Dad: Dotty sent me a text message that you are married. You are married?"

Oscar: what's going on? When did you get married? Are you married? You just met him. What did you do?

Kyle: Crystal! CALL ME! Where are you?

Brandon: Crystal, call me.

Mom: Young lady! What are you thinking?

My phone rings. I look at it. Kyle's face fills the screen on my phone. "Hello." I whisper into it.

"Have you lost your fucking mind?" He yells.

"What are you talking about?"

"There are wedding pictures of you and Cody online."

"What?" When did I get married?"

"Don't play games with me."

"Ky, I am confused."

"Why am I looking at wedding pictures of you?"

"I have no idea. I never even tried on a wedding dress." I stay away from the beautiful white dresses. I don't think that I am ever going to get married. I want to. I want that more than anything. I want to marry Cody Parker.

"Did someone photoshop you in a wedding dress?"

"I have to go." I tell him.

"Don't hang up." Kyle yells as I toss my phone into my purse.

Cody looks at me. "It seems that I have added to your drama."

"Dotty called my dad." I push my wheelchair to the end of the observation deck. I push my wheelchair as fast as I can.

Cody runs after me. "What does that mean? You are an adult."

"My dad hasn't spoken to me in years. Now they want to all yell at me." I say.

Cody's phone rings. He answers it. Its Kyle. "Hey brother what's going on?"

"Cody, what are you doing?" Kyle asks.

"What do you mean?"

"This is how the trouble started the last time. It took you years to get out of it. That girl had you attacked. You were the one who was hurt. This time it will be my sister that will be broken."

"I am not going to allow that to happen."

"Cody, its happening. My sister lost her job. My sister won't call her family."

"Her losing her job had nothing to do with me. It had everything to do with a jealous woman. And her not calling her family, well you all sent her text messages at the same time. Are you all going to listen calmly to her side. You are the one who told me where I could find her. Did you set this up?"

"No."

"Neither did I." He says. He looks around and I am gone. "I have to go, she is gone."

"What do you mean gone?"

"Ky, she is gone."

"That's her thing. Always running from her problems."

"Ky, that is so not true. When she got fired she stood her ground. She showed up even after the fact that she was fired so that my cousin could have the wedding of her dreams after my cousin aided in having her fired. Do you even know her?"

"I grew up with her."

"That doesn't mean that you know a person." Cody looks around. "Do you know that she is the most supportive person I have met in my life. I want to know details of her life, and she tells me what she knows about my life. You know that bear that came in the shirt, I finally found out who sent it."

"Who sent it?"

"Your sister." Cody says.

"My sister sent you the bear?"

"The bear and the note." Cody runs his fingers through his hair. "She told me that she dreamed of marrying me."

"Cody, I am sure that every woman who knows you exist wants to marry you."

I come up behind him and take his hand in my hand and squeeze it. He turns and looks at me.

"I have to go." Cody says.

"Don't hurt her."

"I don't plan on it."

"Cody, I will hurt you if you hurt her." Kyle says.

"Ky, don't think the worst of me. Everyone does. You never have before, please don't do it now."

"I don't." I say.

He looks at me.

"I don't think the worst of you. I would never think the worst of you." I tell him sincerely.

He puts his phone back in his pocket. He gets down on his knees and kisses me. I pull back. "What's the matter?"

"Nothing." I say.

"Are you sure?"

"Of course I am. Nothing is wrong."

"Tell me."

"You don't have to get on your knees to kiss me. When you kissed me in the resort, you made me feel so desirable."

"I don't want to make you feel uncomfortable."

"I don't want to make you feel uncomfortable either." I say to him.

He stands up and steps to the side of my wheelchair, he puts his hands on the back of my head. He kisses me. My body reacts to this kiss. It has reacted to all the others as well but now I feel all my nerve endings buzzing. I feel like I was struck by lightning.

"Cody, please." I say against his lips.

"Please what?"

"Oh, Cody." I cry against his lips.

"What?"

"I need more." I nearly beg.

"More what?"

"Of. You." I say. When I hear the words come out of my mouth, I am almost embarrassed.

"Where do we go?"

I look at him and smile against his lips. "I have a house just a few blocks away."

He laughs against my lips and they vibrate. I feel the vibration all the way in the pit of my stomach and a bit lower. "Do you want me to drive?"

"We." I pant for a breath. "We can take my car." I say.

"Will you be able to drive?" He laughs again.

"Kiss me." I tell him.

He does. He kisses me and I feel my body again react to him. He smells so good. He kisses me and I feel like if the whole world fell apart, I wouldn't notice it at all. I am so wrapped up in Cody Parker.

I pull my car into my driveway. I feel silly that I stayed away from my own home. I don't know what to do. Before I can think about anything else and how ridiculous I am being, Cody pulls into the driveway behind me in his own car.

"I thought you would wait for me." He says.

"I am waiting for you." I say.

"I stopped to get something for lunch for us. We were going to have lunch and then never had lunch. Your family seems to make you a little crazy."

"Which room are you using?" I ask him.

"The one furthest away from the master bedroom." Cody says.

"That's the smallest room and my unofficial office."

I take the key out of my purse and unlock the door. When I enter the house, its like I have entered the model home. The furniture is all set up. My family supplied me with living breathing plants. I look around and it looks like it did when I was just thinking of buying the house.

"Cody, did you do all of this?" I ask.

"No. Joanne showed up and insisted on setting up the place."

"I wonder if she has hung my clothes color coordinated like she did when I was visiting her and my dad." I have to admit it looks beautiful and its just how I have set up the last three places I have lived. Its almost like I never moved at all. All my stuff is in the same places. I take my cell phone out of my pocket and send Joanne a quick text message.

Me: Joanne, thank you so much for setting up my home. It's beautiful.

Joanne: I have wanted to do it so badly. I was hoping your furniture would have arrived before you did. I wanted to do this for you.

Me: thank you again

Joanne: Are you with Cody Parker? Are you married?

Me: I am with Cody. We are not married

Joanne: Good I was getting worried that you are... well you know

"She just can't wait to be mean to me." I say.

"What?" Cody asks.

"My step-mother only thinks that you would be with me because I am pregnant." I say. "I need a minute." I go into my bedroom and close the door. I go into the walk-in closet and cover my face with my hands.

"Crystal?" Cody calls out.

I wipe my tears out of my eyes.

"Crystal? Your phone is ringing."

I open the door that joins the bathroom to the closet. I wash my face. When I leave my room, I look for Cody. I hear my voice fill the silence. I squint my eyes for a moment and listen to what I am hearing. Its one of the many videos on my phone and me talking to a bride to be.

I hear her say, "I can't believe its finally here and I feel like a princess."

"You are absolutely stunning." I tell her.

"I am so lucky."

"You both are lucky." I tell her.

"And you promise that he's going to show up?" She asks me.

"He is already waiting for you at the alter. He looks so handsome and he can't wait for you to join your hands, your hearts, and your lives. Lets get you down that isle." I tell her. "You are stunning and he is waiting with baited breath."

"What if I am not the one for him?"

"What if you are? What if his world would end if you weren't apart of it?"

"He is very handsome." The bride says.

"You will have the most beautiful children."

The bride turns quickly looking at me. "Who told you that I am pregnant?"

"No one. I was saying that you are a beautiful couple and you will have beautiful children." I say.

The father of the bride opens the door and as Cody watches the video of me doing my job, he sees me take a deep breath that I was holding. Cody looks around the room and sees that I am watching him watch me.

"Are you ok?" He asks standing and walking over to me.

"I want to go throw myself in a volcano." I know it sounds dramatic but I think it would be the right thing to do.

"Why would you say that?" Cody asks.

"Cody, I don't want you to feel bad, but my life has changed because you picked me."

"I am sorry I ruined your life."

"Cody, please I have fantasized of you doing exactly what you did to me."

"Tell me something about you."

"I dreamed of being a a ballerina when I was little. I wanted to be a gymnast. I dreamed of being a cheerleader on the top of the pyramid." I stop talking. "I have a great life. I am smart. I graduated the top of my class. My parents spoiled me and my sisters. They were always competing in wanting to make us happy. Kelsey was ready for them to divorce and move on to having separate lives. She loved that my mom had boyfriends and that my dad went from my mom's bed right to Joanne's bed."

"How did you feel about it?"

"Cody tell me something about you."

"How did you feel about it?"

"My parents fought all the time. It was about me. It was about the money that they needed for my physical therapy and the operations that I had."

"How many?" He asks.

"I had six in one day. Three on each leg."

He gets down on his knees and takes one of my legs in his hands. He looks at my heel and rubs his fingers over the scar that runs about three inches up my leg. He then looks and runs his hand up my leg behind my knee. This raised scar runs about two and a half inches behind my knee on each leg. He rubs the scar there too. He looks at me. "Where is the other one?"

"My hip flexors." I say.

"I will have to examine them later."

I laugh. "I might enjoy that examination."

He still holds my leg in his hands. "Did you feel guilty for them not working out?"

"No." I look into his green eyes and feel like I can get lost in the forest that leads to his soul. "Can I kiss you?" He leans close and lets me kiss him. He allows me to have control of the kiss. I put my hands around his neck and he deepens the kiss. I could get lost in his forest green eyes and his kisses. I want to kiss him for the rest of my life. I don't want anyone else. I want him. I have dreamt of him kissing me, but my dreams don't even come close to this reality.

Cody looks at me. "What made you like baseball?"

"My dad took to Kyle and Brandon. I thought I was being replaced. Brandon loves baseball but he is no good at it. I sat with him and nagged him for weeks to teach me about baseball. I wanted to know the dynamics of the game. I wanted to know the differences between a strike and a fair ball. He did. He encouraged me to go with him and my dad to a professional baseball game and oh my god, I nearly died of excitement." I giggle.

"What game was it?"

I look at him. "The LA Dodgers were here playing the Marlins. They were showcasing amateur athletes. I watched you pitch. Every single pitch you threw was a strike. Every single pitch you threw made my heart stop. The best one that I watched was when you narrowed your eyes and looked up in the stadium. I am not sure if you were looking at anyone in particular, but Brandon told me to cheer loudly. I did and threw my arms up in the air. You threw that ball with so much speed the catcher cursed you and the batter threw his bat on the ground and had a tantrum. You looked up in the stands and it was like you saw me. You smiled and took your hat off and waved."

"I wish I would have seen you. The truth is, I was looking for my dad and my mom. They were supposed to be in the stands. I never found them."

"They must be so proud of you."

"To be honest, the happiest day of my mom's life is when she was told that I would never play again."

"Cody, that can't be true."

"My mom never got it. My dad was my coach up until I was in high school and he was thrown out of a game because he attacked me."

I hug him. "I am sorry to hear this." I say. I kiss him. "I am sorry that they don't see what I see."

"Crystal, a lot of people don't see what you see. Most people I know don't see what you see in me. I took a job as a security guard and my dad laughed at me. One night he went to dinner with my mother at a place that they had gone to a hundred of times. When they came out, there was a group of guys waiting to hurt both of them. They knew that they are my parents and they wanted to get revenge because they had lost money betting against my team. I was across the street when I heard the commotion, I ran across the street and I took charge of the situation. I told my parents to get in the car and drive away. The next day, I had to go to a luncheon. My grandma was there. She knew how my dad was with me. She couldn't stop talking about me using my muscles for good." He kisses me. "It would have been nice to know that I had a fan out there for me."

"Cody, every young and old woman at that game was there cheering you on."

He hugs me tight.

"Do you have siblings?"

"I have one brother and one sister."

"Are you close to them?"

His phone rings. He looks at it and smiles. "My sister is calling me." He says.

"Get it." I say.

Chapter Seven

"What are their names?" I ask him.

"Gianna is my sister and Landon is my brother."

"Landon Parker is your brother?"

"You know my brother?"

"Cody, answer your phone."

He smiles. "Hi Gianna." He beams when he says her name.

"Hi!" She shrieks. "Cody, you are all over the internet. You got married?"

He looks at me. "I meant to say my fiancée. I slipped when I said wife. I want to marry her."

"Where did you meet her?" Gianna asks.

"We met on a flight. Then I kissed—"

"The kiss seen around the world." Gianna gushes. "Is she nice? Jillian told mom what happened and mom lost her shit."

"Gianna!" He laughs.

"Mom did. She was yelling at Jillian and Tyler for the way that Beth treated the wedding planner."

I busy myself while he is on the phone. All I want to do is make myself comfortable with a bowl of popcorn and watch him on the phone with her, but I don't do that. I go into my office and I am surprised to see that it is all set up for me.

I sit at the desk and open the drawer. I take out a notebook and start writing in it. Cody knocks on the door.

"Hi." He says.

"Hi."

"You didn't have to leave the room."

"You needed your privacy."

"They want to meet you."

"What?"

"My family wants to meet you."

"When?" I ask.

"Tonight for dinner." Cody says.

"Tonight?"

"Yes."

"Where?"

"My mom wants you to come to their house."

"Where do they live?"

"Highland Beach." Cody says.

"You should go."

"Crystal, I am not going without you. My family wants to meet you." He walks around the desk and squats down next to me. "You recognized my brother's name? How?"

"He and I took a statistics class together." I look at Cody. "He played volleyball right?"

"Yes." He says.

"And Gianna, is she an athlete too?"

"Gianna is a dancer. She teaches dance to children and old people."

I laugh at him. "What do your parents do?"

"My parents are retired." He looks at me. "I never talk this much about my family."

"You did refer to me as your fiancée."

"We have to make a stop."

"What?" I ask.

"My mom will know I am lying if you are not wearing a ring."

"Cody, I have rings in my jewelry box. Go pick one out of there. I don't need you to buy me a ring until its real."

Cody looks at me.

"Squatting can't be good for your lower back." I say.

He stands and then sits on the edge of the desk. "How do you know about my back injury?"

"I took a class with your brother."

"What did he tell you about it?" He looks at me. "Do you want to meet my family?"

"Yes."

"You know, I never met your mom the other day. Or whenever that was."

"I know." I tell him. "What should I wear?"

He looks at me. "What you are wearing is good."

"Cody, you said that your family lives in Highland Beach, I am sure that what I am wearing right now isn't appropriate."

"You always look beautiful. Please they are just people."

"They are not just people, Cody. They are your family."

"Crystal, they are just people."

"Did you meet my dad?"

"I did. I met him through Kyle."

"Did you ever meet Kyle's dad?"

"Yes."

"Kyle and Brandon's dad died." I say.

"I know, I went to the funeral with Kyle. I held him up." Cody says. "Did you go to the funeral?"

"My dad told me he didn't want me there. My sisters went. I met up with the two of them afterwards and stayed with them for almost two weeks. Their dad was always nice to me."

"Kyle was a mess for a long time."

"Did you meet my mom?"

"Never." He says.

An hour and a half later, Cody and I look like we just stepped off a runway red carpet. My hair hangs around my shoulders and I am wearing a basic black dress. He picked a ring for me out of the jewelry box and it looks like an engagement ring. He holds my hand as we drive up to the gated house.

"What if they don't like me. Cody, my mother and step mother think that I have acted slutty. What if your parents think the same thing?"

"Stop it." He says. "You are making me nervous."

"Are you nervous?"

"There is always a bit of nerves when I come home."

"Cody." I squeeze his fingers. "No one can take away all the good things that you have done with your life. Does your family know that you opened a school for kids with learning disabilities? Do they know that you established a scholarship fund for athletes that can't afford to go to school?"

He blinks a few times. "How do you know that?"

"How does anyone not know it?"

"Crystal, where have you been my whole life?"

"Waiting for you to find me." I say and smile.

He pulls the car on the driveway. Sawyer Parker stands outside waiting for us. Cody gets out of the car and gets my wheelchair for me. His dad walks over and opens it. He sticks the cushion on it. I open the door and use my arms to put my legs out of the car.

"Do we lift you?" Sawyer asks.

I look at him and smile. "No, thank you." I hold on to the door and the body of the car and stand. I then reach for my wheelchair and sit in it. I adjust myself and then get my purse. I put it in my seatbelt and then close the door. I take the box of cookies that I made Cody stop for out of the car and hand them to Sawyer.

"It's important to always be safe." Sawyer says. He smiles. I smile back at him. "I am Sawyer Parker."

"Its nice to meet a celebrity." I say to him. "I am Crystal Steele."

"Its nice to meet a celebrity." He says back to me. "Come out of the heat." He looks at Cody and smiles. He embraces his son. He looks at the cookies in the box. "These are my favorite cookies. Thank you." He looks at Cody. "Hide them, I am not sharing them with anyone." He looks at me. "If anyone asks, you didn't bring anything with you."

I laugh. "I hope you enjoy them." I smile.

When we go to enter the house, there are two platform steps in front of the house. Cody looks at me. He looks around to see if there is any other way to get into the house. There is not. Something that they think nothing of is an obstacle for me. The one thing that I notice is that they are wide step so my whole wheelchair will fit up them as we go.

"How can I help?"

"Just tip the wheelchair backwards and go up the steps one at a time." I tell him.

When we get into the house, Landon hugs me. "Its nice to see you again."

"You too." I tell him. I look around and the house is amazing. It looks like a model home. Nothing is out of place.

"Come meet my mom and my sister." Cody says.

A beautiful woman takes Cody in her arms. "Cody!" She says hugging him.

"Hi mom." He says. "Crystal, this is my mom, Catalina."

I look at her and smile. "The model? Wow, you are even more beautiful in person."

"Thank you for saying that." She says warmly. She hugs me. "Its nice to meet you."

"You as well." I say. Now it makes sense a bit why she would want Cody to stop playing baseball, he is really good looking. With his brownish hair and those popping green eyes, he looks like a model himself. I look at him and my heart speeds up. Butterflies flutter in my stomach. I think to myself, HE PICKED ME. HE KISSED ME!

Gianna stands next to Sawyer and just watches for a moment. She looks at my finger. She is the first to do it. The ring that I am wearing is not a big diamond. The design is two hearts side-by-side that are diamonds. It is an actual engagement ring. I needed it for one of my jobs that I did. The designer of the ring was trying to sell her rings to the couple that came into Madame Butterflies Bridal Boutique. She did well enough that she moved in next door to the boutique. We would refer business to her and she would do the same for us. She gave me the ring. She wanted me to have it so that when anyone would ask, I could say where it came from. I only wore it a few times and then stuck it in a jewelry box. No one ever saw me wearing it.

"Where did you get that beautiful ring?" Gianna asks Cody.

"My friend Monica designs them." I say.

"Oh that's beautiful." Gianna says. She looks at Cody. "You picked a beautiful ring for her."

He smiles and kisses me.

Catalina ushers us to the table. It is set with the most beautiful place settings I have ever seen. Joanne, my step-mother, is a designer and her tables were never set as lovely as this table is. Cody removes a chair for me to join the table. He stands behind me and pushes my wheelchair into the table. He kisses me on my forehead after he tilts my head back.

Catalina looks at me. "You are familiar to me." She says. "Where do I know you from?"

I have met her before. "Did you come to Orlando with Jillian?"

"I didn't." She says. "We missed her wedding completely. Sawyer, Landon, Gianna and I just got back from Argentina. There was a runway event down there."

I smile at her. "I saw some of the pictures of you on the catwalk event. You are stunning."

She smiles at me.

"I saw Sawyer was your escort."

She looks at Sawyer. They smile at each other and then at me. "My escort fell sick at last minute. Sawyer was there and I wouldn't have wanted anyone else there. He saved me from a big spill."

"When I was watching, it never appeared that anything was wrong. You are a beautiful couple."

"Thank you for saying that." Sawyer says.

"I can't help but think that I met you somewhere before." Catalina says. She looks at Cody. "Tell us how you met?"

Cody looks at me. He is sitting next to me and is bouncing his leg under the table. I put my hand on his leg. He looks at me.

"We met on a flight." I say.

"I hope it was a good experience." Landon says jokingly.

I look at him. "Why wouldn't it be a good experience?" Landon is always the jokester but right now, I am annoyed that he would say something shitty about his brother.

Gianna hits Landon. "This is why he doesn't come home."

Cody bounces his leg again.

"Stop this!" Sawyer says. "Cody, stop bouncing your leg." He says calmly. "Tell us about that beautiful picture we saw on social media of the two of you."

He looks at me. "Excuse us one moment." He says and pushes away from the table. He takes my hand and takes me with him. He walks outside to the backyard. Its all level so he doesn't need to help me. He holds my hand. He raises it to his chest and I feel his heart beating both in his hand and against the back of my hand.

"Cody, you are not doing this alone. Just tell them how we met. Make it as big as you want it. I will go along with whatever you tell them." I say softly.

"We should go." He says.

"Cody, your parents have made me feel more at home in the short time that we have been here than my parents have ever made me feel. Its going to be ok." I tell him.

"The thing is, I don't want them to chase you away."

"Somehow I think you would find me." I tell him and smile brightly at him.

After everyone has enjoyed a delicious meal, Catalina tells everyone to go outside. They all do. I stay back a moment and use the bathroom. When I come out, I go into the kitchen and clean up. I stack all the clean dried dishes on the counter. I put the forks and knives that we used on a cloth napkin.

I then leave the kitchen and join everyone outside. They are all chatting nicely. I don't want to interrupt their conversation so I turn around and go back in the house. I watch them from the kitchen. I can see them. They can not see me.

Cody walks in the house. "Crystal?" He calls out. He walks in the kitchen. He looks around. "Did you clean up?"

"You all were so involved with conversation, I didn't want to interrupt."

"Come outside." He says.

"What were you all talking about."

"My mom is wracking her memory to where she knows you from."

"Cody, I have no idea." I say.

"Come outside. Be with us." He says.

We sit outside and the warm Florida temperature seems to be melting me in my black dress. I am sweating hot. I can feel my hives prickling. I feel like I am going to be sick. All I want to do is scratch the hell out of my skin. I look at all them. "I have to go inside." I say.

"Of course." Catalina says. "Are you alright?"

"I break out in hives. I am afraid I am breaking out right now."

"Can I get you anything for it?"

"No, thank you." I say. I feel the urge to scratch my whole body.

"When did the hives start? Maybe you are allergic to Cody." Landon says.

I look at him. "Landon, do you have a problem with me being with Cody?"

"No." He says honestly.

"So then why the banter?" I look at Sawyer and Catalina. "Landon cost me a big grade when we were in a statistics class together."

"What does that mean?" Gianna asks.

Landon's face turns the same color as my hives that are now crawling up my neck. Landon looks at me. "I didn't know that she was going to fail you. I did own up to what I did." He says.

I feel like I want to rip my clothes off and scratch my whole body until I pass out. "I am sorry, I do need to get out of the sun." I say.

Cody takes control of my wheelchair and pushes me in the house. He pushes me into a hallway and he pulls my dress away from my skin. "Holy shit, why didn't you say anything?"

"I didn't want to be rude."

"I think you should go to the hospital and let them test you."

"I just need a glass of water and cold air."

"I think you need medical attention."

"Just kiss me." I say.

Cody takes me in his arms and kisses me deeply.

Sawyer walks over to us. He clears his throat. He hands Cody a tube of Calamine lotion. "Take her in the bathroom or somewhere private and rub this on her hives." He looks at me. "It should help."

"Thank you." I say.

He hands me a pair of shorts and a shirt. "This is Gianna's. I think you will be more comfortable."

"I am comfortable." I lie.

"Crystal, we are just hanging around the house. You look like you are ready to go plan a wedding party."

"Your wife is one of the most glamorous women, I think that she would be offended."

"She's the one who told Gianna to get you something comfortable." He looks at Cody. "Does she share your fondness for carrot cake?"

I look at Cody. I smile at him. "You are the one who took my piece of cake on the flight."

He looks at me with a wicked smile. "They didn't say it belonged to anyone."

"Oh my god, they did too. They asked who was the attendee at a wedding." I say.

"I love carrot cake. It was delicious."

"Its my favorite of all cakes. I asked the bride to send me a piece for the flight."

"It was so good." Cody says again.

Sawyer looks at the two of us. "Calamine lotion and water. Then carrot cake and a movie." He says. "I might share my cookies after all." He puts his hand on my shoulder and then squeezes Cody's arm as he leaves us.

"Thank you." I say.

We go into a room and Cody closes the doors behind us. He lifts me out of my wheelchair and walks over to the bed with me. He supports me until I am secure on my feet. He then unzips my dress and lets it fall to the floor around my ankles. He lifts me and sits me on the bed. The hives are all over my chest and my neck. They are on my back as well.

He kisses me on the lips and puts his arms around me as he lays me back on the bed. He opens the tube of lotion, he applies it to my skin and then starts rubbing it in. He rubs gently at my chest and up my neck.

"Cody, don't enjoy this too much." I say.

He laughs against my ear. He rubs it all over my chest above my lacy bra. He does keep his hands off my breasts even when they perk at his nearness. He laughs. "Behave yourself, my whole family is lurking in this house."

I laugh. Once I start, I can't contain my giggles. He tickles me and I giggle more. "Cody! Stop."

"Let me do your back." He says. He helps me sit up when I reach my hand out to him. He sits behind me and rubs the lotion on my back. "Pull your hair off your neck. I will do the back of your neck." He says.

"I didn't bring anything with me." I say.

"You don't have protection?" He asks.

"Cody!" I laugh.

"Get dressed. I will get you a hair thingy from my sister."

"Thank you." I say to him. He leaves the room and I get dressed. When he comes back in the room, I am back in my wheelchair and dressed in the most comfortable outfit I have worn in a long time.

Cody walks back in the room. He hands me a black scrunchie. I take it and pull my hair back. He steps behind me and rubs the lotion all over my neck. "They are waiting for us to watch a movie."

"What are we watching?"

"The Wedding Planner." He says.

"Cody, please be joking." I smile.

"You don't want to watch that movie?"

"No. My line of work that I was just fired from isn't something I want to watch right now."

"Jillian found out that you are here with me. She wants to come over."

"Cody, this is your parents' house. They can have anyone over that they want."

"Would it bother you?"

"Your cousin thinks that I orchestrated the whole thing with you. Your cousin told Lee and Beth that I set it up. The truth is, you weren't a guest on the guest list."

"I know."

"I didn't know that you were going to be there. Cody, I didn't know that when we were on the same flight that it would change my life forever." I look at him. "I don't remember you sitting next to me."

"You really did fall asleep. The pilots wanted to make sure that you were cared for in case of an emergency." He sits on the bed and holds my hand. "I sat next to you and you made yourself comfortable against me."

"We should get out there with your family. They might think that we are—"

"Do you care?"

"I do care. I want them to like me."

"They like you." Cody says.

We sit on the couch watching a movie. Cody sits next to me with our hands laced together. When the movie is over, Cody stands up. He looks at me. "Are you ready to go?"

"As soon as you are." I say.

"We didn't have cake." Gianna says.

"Save it for us." Cody says.

"Thank you for inviting me." I say. I look at Gianna. "I will get the clothes back to you."

"No worries." She says. "Whenever you do its fine."

Sawyer walks us out to Cody's car. "Can I ask you both a question?" We both look at him.

"When can we have an engagement party for you?" He looks at me. "And when do we get to meet your family?"

"You already know my brother."

"Your brother?"

"Kyle."

"You are Kyle's sister?"

"One of three of them."

"Is Kyle your only brother?"

"No. I have a younger brother too. Brandon." I say.

"You really want to throw an engagement party for us?" Cody asks.

"Cody, I haven't seen you this happy and relaxed in years." Sawyer looks at me. "Cody was telling us that you are a fan of his since he played baseball."

"Its true." I say. "Cody hitting three grand slam home runs in one game got me a spot in the program I took in college."

Sawyer looks at Cody. "You scored three in one game?"

Cody looks down at me and then back up at his father.

"Oh my god, you didn't watch it?" I ask. "It was beautiful. He got up in the second inning and he cracked the first ball pitched to him. The commentator was so rude when he talked about Cody." I don't wait for them to ask what he said, I just continue on. "The commentator commented that Parker is a pitcher and you don't expect much from him." I look at Cody and take his hand in my own. "Then he swung at the first pitch and that ball sailed into the grandstands. The commentator literally choked on his words. Then Cody was up in the fifth inning and Cody got two strikes and then he cracked the ball and it sailed in the same spot. I was so excited. I was sad that I missed being at the game. I had tickets to go with my brothers but I had my interview for school. Then Cody got up in the ninth inning and bases were loaded again. He had a full count. Three balls, two strikes and then he hit the home run. The stadium was on their feet." I look at Cody. "In my own way, I was jumping for joy."

"I didn't know that happened." Sawyer says.

"They played it on the sports highlight reel over and over. When I was able to watch it, I did over and over and cried tears of joy."

"We should go." Cody says.

"Was that the only three grand slams that you hit?"

I look at Sawyer and if I had the ability, I would jump on him and choke him. "Cody's the record holder for having the most grand slam home runs in his short career."

"We have to go." Cody says.

Sawyer hugs Cody. He looks at me. "It was a pleasure meeting you."

"You too." I say. "Thank you for making me feel at home. You really made me feel welcome here." I get in the car.

Cody puts my wheelchair in the car. He gets in and drives slowly on the long driveway. When we get to the street, he speeds up a bit.

"Cody, can you make a stop?" I ask.

"I need to get you home."

"Cody, please." I say.

"Where do you want to go?"

"Can we stop at the jetty?"

He looks at me. "Why?"

"I don't want anyone to interrupt us." I say.

He drives to the jetty. He parks the car and gets my wheelchair. I get in it. "Why are we here?"

"I want to talk and I don't want anyone to interrupt us."

"Are you going to push me into the water?"

"No." I tell him. I push my self as he walks next to me.

There are benches set up on the jetty. We walk down further to where the water could be felt in mists as it sprays in the air.

Cody looks at me. "You embarrassed my dad."

"I didn't mean to."

"To be honest I am glad you got so into the details of my play-by-plays."

"Cody, why don't they know more about how wonderful you were. Do they know that every time you hit a home run you paid for someone's hospital bill."

He looks at me. "No one knew that. How do you know that?"

I turn and look out on the horizon.

"How do you know that?" He asks. He stands and walks over to me. He stands in front of me an takes my hands in his own. "How do you know that?"

"You paid my hospital bill."

"What?"

"I was in the hospital. I was involved in a car accident. I was stopped at a red light. A car coming in the opposite direction ran the red light and hit a car in the intersection. She spun out of control and hit my car three times. They had to take me out of the car with the jaws of life. My car was destroyed."

"I didn't know that I paid your hospital bill. The truth is, I was watching the news with Kyle and they played the accident over and over. I found out what hospital and called. I just said that I wanted to pay the bill for the victim of the accident."

"Thank you." I say.

"Were you hurt badly?"

"My car took the brunt of it. My car crumbled from the impact. If I controlled the car like you do with my feet, my leg would have been pinned. They couldn't figure out why my leg wasn't pinned. Then the firefighter saw the hand controls and they treated me so gently. I was injured, but I healed nicely. Kyle didn't tell you it was me ?"

"Actually now that you are saying that it was you in the accident, his tears make sense." He kisses me. "Where were you hurt?"

"I broke my tailbone."

"What did they do for it?"

"Cody, I just want to know if your parents know that you did that. Do your parents and your family know how great you are?"

"They love me."

"I don't doubt that. But do they know how great you are?"

"I don't think so." He looks at me. "I want to know as much about you as you do about me."

"I am boring." I tell him. "I plan weddings for women and couples who are in love with each other but they are so rude to people around them."

"Boring? I think not. I watched that video of you encouraging a bride."

"I did do that a few times."

"Is that how Rosa taught you to do it?"

"No. Rosa was a great boss and I am glad that I was her assistant, but in reality she had no patients for the brides and the families. She made the weddings elegant and everything the brides wanted but her heart wasn't in it." I look out to the horizon again. "I was leaving. I was all packed, and ready to fly to Atlanta. I was hired over the phone. I was heading to Georgia to be a sports commentator when Rosa told me that she was giving me the boutique. Lawyers met me at the gate at the airport, I mean that's how ready I was to leave. They told me that I had to come with them. They made it seem like I had done something bad. I felt like I was tricked into taking over for Rosa. Beth thought that she was cheated. I think so too in a way. Beth became my assistant. She was good but she was very resentful. She bought me out. She did it behind my back. A lawyer showed up and demanded that I sign it over immediately and then I was the assistant again."

"Wow, that's awful." He says.

"She had me on five planes. She wanted me to be so tired that I made mistakes during your cousin's wedding. I was exhausted but then you kissed me." I look at him. "Why did you pick me?"

"When we were on the plane and that couple was rude to me, I heard you say to no one in particular but you said that I was a nice person. When I walked past where you were sitting, you smiled at me. I thought for a split second that you were going to be rude to me, but then the flight attendant walked over to you and addressed you about obnoxious athletes and you looked right at him and said that you didn't see any obnoxious athletes but extremely rude people who only believe what they read in gossip magazines. He said something else to you and you brushed him off. What did he say?"

I shake my head. "I don't remember." I say.

"I think you lie."

"No."

"What did he say?"

"I don't remember."

"Maybe one day you will tell me."

"Its over and he was fired."

"Fired over what?"

I look at him. "Let it go." I say.

"Was it something about you?"

"No."

"What was it?"

I try to push past him.

"Tell me."

"Cody, stop it."

"I want to know." He looks at me. "Crystal tell me."

"He said you are a piece of shit. He said that it was right that you were mugged and beaten up."

"So you had him fired?"

"Cody."

"Crystal."

"He said other stuff. He wanted to know if I thought if Cody Parker was better off dead."

"What did you say?"

"I flagged over another attendant and told her that the guy threatened your life. Then I googled the mugging and saw that he was there."

"What?" He looks at me. "Crystal, that's very serious."

"Cody I know that."

"Show me."

"I am sure you have seen it."

"No."

A wave crashes on the rocks of the jetty and sprays us. He takes my hand and we leave. We get in the car. He looks at me.

"Please show me." He says.

I give him my phone and show him. He watches. He looks so sad.

"What are you thinking?" I ask softly.

He drives in silence. When he pulls into my driveway he looks at me. When I get in my wheelchair he hugs me. "I have to go, but I will be back." He says.

"Cody, what are you thinking?"

"Why do you think I am so worthy?"

"How do you not think that you are?"

"Crystal, my dad doesn't even know my fucking career best. I am what people say I am."

"No." I say. "Please come inside with me. Let's talk. Please."

Dotty drives by and stops the car in the street in front of my driveway. "Hi, is everything alright?"

"We are fine." I tell her.

"Do you need help?"

"Why?" I look at Cody, "Let's go inside."

We go in the house together.

My cell phone rings. I look at it. "Hi dad."

"Hi. I got a call from Dotty saying that I needed to check on you."

"Tell her to mind her business." I snap at him. "I don't need a fucking babysitter."

"She told me that you haven't been home in a week."

"Dad, I am dealing with something more important. I just met Dotty outside of my neighborhood. I don't want people to report to you and mom. That's not fair."

"Is everything ok?"

"Call Brandon, he will tell you."

"I am asking you."

"Go call your sons. They seem to know a lot about my life."

"Don't be like that." He scolds me.

"I have to go."

Cody and I sit on the couch together. His phone rings and he ignores it. I watch him. His phone rings again.

"Cody answer the phone." I tell him.

"I don't want to talk to them. They are just going to tell me how disappointed they are. Its always the same shit."

"I don't think that's whats going to happen." I say tenderly to him.

"Why do you believe in me?"

"Because when I watched you on the mound at one game, there was a kid in the stands who was crying that he missed out on getting a signature from his favorite player. You ran over and signed the kid's baseball and he was so elated."

"Crystal, my parents were at that game. Do you know what they would say about it? They would tell me that I didn't play my best."

"In that game, not only did you make a kid's dream come true, but you hit two home runs. So you didn't pitch well."

"My dad told me I was a let down."

"Stop it." I say. "Your dad should see that great person that you are."

"I don't know that they ever saw that."

"Well then they are blind."

His phone rings again. He looks at it. He attempts to put his phone in his pocket but I take it from him. He nods his head allowing me to answer his phone.

"Hello."

"Hi Crystal, its Sawyer."

"Hi." I say.

"I would like to speak to Cody."

"He is sleeping." I say.

Cody relaxes a bit.

"Crystal, I wanted to thank you."

"Why?"

"You bring out something remarkable in my son."

"Your son is remarkable all on his own."

"I agree. It was so nice of you to be so excited about his baseball career."

"Its more than that. He is such a nice person. He is caring for no other reason than he really cares."

"What does that mean?"

"Every time he hit a home run, he would donate money to a charity. When he hit the grand slams he would pay random people's hospital bills."

"Is that true?"

"Absolutely."

"Did you really meet him on a flight? Jillian is telling us that he met you at the resort after he kissed you."

"We really were on a few flights together." I say honestly.

"How did you meet?"

"He gave up his seat to a woman who couldn't get a seat by her children."

Cody looks at me.

"Can I ask you a question and then I will let you go?" Sawyer asks.

"Yes." I say.

"Does my son know as much about you as you know about him?"

"I don't know."

"When he wakes up, will you hug him for me?"

"I will."

"You really make him happy."

"Your son has made me feel so loved just by kissing me. I feel in my heart that he is the best person I have ever met."

Cody and I snuggle on the couch together watching television. We watch For The Love of The Game. I fall asleep before the end of the movie. Cody lifts me in his arms and carries me into my room. He lays me in my bed and lays with me. It's the first time that we have been in the same bed together.

Cody holds me throughout the night in his arms. "Why do you think I am so great? How is that you see such greatness in me when no one else ever has. You make me feel very special." He pulls me closer to him. "I want to know about you and your life. I am going to search for the answers I need. I love you. I will come back for you. I will come back to you. I will love you always for the way that you love me."

When I wake up in the morning, I get in my wheelchair and I am overcome by sadness. I don't want to leave my room because I know that he is gone. My heart is braking.

I go into the kitchen and see that there are flowers all over. There are floral arrangements on the kitchen table, there are two on the dining room table. There are flowers everywhere.

I push my wheelchair over to the table. There is an envelope in the middle of the table. I reach for it and open it.

Sweetheart,

I love you. I want you to know that I will be back. I have to go take care of something important. You make me want to be the best version of myself because you see the best version of me. Thank you for pointing out that you think I am a great person. Don't be sad, I am coming back for you.

As I watched you sleep last night, I am so glad that you got the job working as the wedding planner. I know its not the job that you wanted, but it brought us together. I am not sure that our worlds would have merged otherwise. I will be in touch.

Love you, Cody

I put my head down on the table and cry. It's the first time that I have allowed myself to cry. I am not crying over all the things that have gone completely to shit since I moved back. I cry that I may never see Cody again. I cry because I have never been treated so nicely. I cry that his family doesn't see what I see. I cry for not telling him more about my life.

Chapter Eight

Kyle and Kelsey stand outside of my house watching the front door. They look in the side glass panels to see if they can see me. I see them through the glass and let them in. They both hug me equally as tight. Kyle kisses me on the top of my head like he has done thousands of times before in such a big brother fashion. They stand on the welcoming soft carpet. Kelsey slips out of her shoes and enjoys the softness under her feet. She loves her bare feet on carpet.

"Come in." I say. I try to hide my sadness from them. I think I fail miserably.

Kyle doesn't waste any time. He stands in front of me. "Where is Cody?" He blurts out. "You are engaged now? God! What are you thinking?"

I blink the tears away. "I don't know I haven't seen him in a week. We are engaged. I was thinking that I have loved him for so long so why not."

"What happened?" Kelsey asks. She is more tender about it.

"He brought me to meet his family."

Kyle softens then. He becomes overprotective in the matter of seconds. "Were they nice to you?"

"They made me feel very welcome." I say honestly.

"What happened?" Kelsey asks again.

I tell them what happened. I tell them all of it from the time that I left Brandon's apartment. I tell them about meeting his family. I tell them about Landon and how he thought he was only joking but in reality he was being hurtful to both Cody and me.

"So wait, when did he propose to you?" Kelsey asks.

I look at her. She is right to ask. He never did. I don't answer her. We have lunch together. I refuse to have any regrets. Even if I never see Cody Parker again, I will always remember how cherished he made me feel. His kisses will stay on my lips forever and in my heart even longer.

They leave shortly after lunch. I busy myself with things that I am working on. I go into my room and get changed for an interview that I am having for a job I really don't want. I take the ring that is supposed to be my engagement ring out of my jewelry box and I put it back on my finger. Then I take it off. My sister was right. Cody and I are not really anything. He isn't even my boyfriend. I feel a stab of sadness in my heart.

I lock up my house and turn to get in my car. Cody is leaning against my car. I look at him.

"Hi." I say.

"Are you mad?"

"Cody, I am not mad. I am going to be late."

"Can you change it?"

"Why would I?"

"I want to spend the day with you."

"You want to spend the day with me? Why?"

"I feel like I owe you an explanation."

"You owe me nothing."

"I do." He says. "I owe you everything."

"Cody, I have to go. I have an interview for a job. I don't even want this job, but I have to go. They are going to call my mom if I don't show up."

"Don't show up."

"Cody, I have expenses. I have taken care of myself financially since I was in college."

"Please give me an hour."

I look at him and see bruises on his face. "Were you in a fight?"

Dotty drives by. She waves at us. "Hi you two." She says cheerfully.

"Hi Dotty." I say. I fight the urge to roll my eyes.

She looks at Cody. "I wanted to thank you for taking time to work with Brad. He feels really bad about you getting hurt."

"Its ok." Cody says.

"He wants you to know that he didn't hit you with the ball to hurt you."

"I never thought that he did."

"He's not going to practice today."

"Dotty, he has to show up."

"I will bring him there myself." She says. She looks at me. "How are you doing?" She asks me. "You look lovely."

"I am fine. Thank you." I tell her. Fine. I am far from fine. I want my life to be less complicated. I mean having Cerebral Palsy makes my life on a daily basis complicated at times and when I get stressed out my muscles get agitated. Since I have been back in south Florida I break out in hives on nearly a daily basis.

Cody takes my hand. "We need to talk."

"Fine." I say.

Dotty smiles and drives away. "Have a nice day you two!" She calls out the window.

My phone rings. I look at it. It is the guy who is supposed to interview me. I answer the call. "Hello."

"Is this Crystal Steele?" A male voice carries through the phone.

"Yes."

"Ms. Steele, I am sorry to tell you that the job has been filled."

"Thank you for letting me know."

"I will keep your resume on file."

"Thank you."

Cody and I go in the house. I bring my purse in my room and get changed. Cody stands in the door frame watching me.

"I am sorry." He says. He doesn't wait for me to talk to him. "I had to deal with things. You brought it to my attention that there was another guy when I was attacked. I always said that there was more than two. My dad went with me. He watched all the sports highlights that he could find. He was so nice to me for the first time in a long time. It's because of you. I told him that we are not engaged. He told me that is a mistake. He told me that I found someone who loves me for all of me. My dad talked to Landon and wanted to know why he kept making remarks when we were there that made me look bad."

"Cody, I don't allow people's opinion of others to make up my mind of how I feel about people. I know Landon. He has more faults than you do. Trust me, he is not a nice guy."

"Why do you say that?"

"I failed my statistics class because of him. I had to take it again. I had to take it at another campus because the teacher that we had told everyone that I was the cheater. Luckily for me, her husband didn't believe her. I passed the class because I did all the work. I know that Landon didn't mean for me to fail, but when he looked over my shoulder and made it obvious what he was doing, she confiscated both tests. I worked my ass off in that class. I hated it. I only passed it because I had a crush on you and I plugged all of your stats into the problems and then I gave a shit. The teacher that I had at the other campus asked whose stats I was using and when I told him it was you, he told me I was getting an automatic A. He told me that I still needed to do the work but he was a fan of yours. He was grateful for something that you had done for his brother who is disabled."

"Every time I hear you talk about me, I know what you are saying is true of the things that I have done, but it seems that you are only seeing the good."

"I know you are not a saint. I wouldn't make you out to be one, but why is it ok with you for people to only know the bad stuff? Cody, your baseball skills caught my attention but what draws me to you is the fact that you are a nice person. I feel its easier for people to only see the bad and overlook the good. I want the opposite. I want to see the good. I don't ignore that there is bad too, but you are great."

"My dad wants to have lunch with the two of us. Would you want to go?"

"Yes." I say. "Tell me about where you have been."

"While I was spending time with my dad, I was doing some research."

"What were you looking into?"

"Finding out about you."

"What do you want to know?"

"You don't talk much about you." He crosses the room and kisses me on the lips. I moan against his lips. "Crystal, I have never had anyone ever react to my kisses the way you do."

"Cody I have dreamed of you kissing me for a long time. Only I never dreamed it would be this good."

"You really know how to make a man feel good about himself."

I touch his bruises on his face. "You promise you weren't in a fight."

"I wasn't in a fight. Brad found me and asked if I would help him train. I said I would. I was giving him directions and he threw the ball. I have a —"

"He threw it in your blind spot?" I ask.

He hugs me. He tickles me. "You know all my secrets."

"I don't." I laugh.

"It seems that you do."

I laugh harder when he tickles me harder. "Cody!" I laugh.

"How have your hives been?" He asked.

"They pop up whenever they want." I say.

"How many boyfriends have you had?"

"How many have I had? Four. Two of them were serious."

"Did they treat you well?"

"They did." I say.

He still has me in his arms. He is still standing in front of me holding me in his arms. "Did you?"

"You want to know if I am a virgin. I am not."

"When was your first?"

"Are you sure you want to know this stuff?"

"I wouldn't be asking if I didn't." He grins.

"I haven't had a boyfriend in almost two years. I took my last breakup hard. We were together for almost two years. He did ask me to marry him."

"Was he the one who—"

"No. I had sex for the first time when I was a junior in high school. I dated an athlete. He played football and all sports really. He was so nice to me. We were together all of ninth, tenth and junior year. I lost my virginity on Homecoming night."

"Were you ready?" He takes a strand of my hair and twirls it in his fingers.

"More than ready." I tell him. I laugh.

"What happened to him?"

"We out grew each other. We were together through the year and then I went to prom with him. We were back at the hotel afterwards and something didn't feel right for both of us. We stayed friends."

"Really?"

"Its Oscar."

"The camera guy?"

"Yeah." I say and laugh. "Then I dated two guys and nothing ever serious happened with them. I mean they were nice and romanticish—"

"Romanticish?" He asks laughing.

"Is this hurting your back?" I ask him.

"No. I want to hold you so you can't get away." He tells me. He kisses me stealing my breath. My body reacts to his passionate kiss. When he breaks the kiss, we both pant. "Ok so romanticish?"

I laugh against his chin. "One gave me a stuffed monkey because he thought that it reminded him of me."

He looks around the room. He had seen a stuffed monkey when he was helping Kyle put my apartment together.

"What are you looking for?" I ask him.

"The monkey. I know I saw a stuffed monkey when I was helping Kyle unpack your stuff."

"I put it in the guest bedroom." I say.

"Why do you still have it?"

"I thought it was cute. Its not my favorite but I thought it was cute."

"Are you still friends with him?"

"No. But through him came boyfriend number three. I think he took notes from number two and was just not all that into it but he tried to always make me feel like he was in it. It felt forced. We only dated for a month. Then I took a break because I was in college. My grades slipped one semester and my parents were livid. They told me that I had to get my head out of my ass and buckle down. My mom's boyfriend at the time told me that the only thing I had going for me was my brains. He meant at as a compliment. I called Kelsey and she called my mom. The boyfriend was gone. Then my mom met Stew and he introduced me to boyfriend number four. When four and I broke up, I was concerned that he was going to leave my mom. They are still together."

"Did you ever date my brother?"

"No."

"Did you ever think about it?"

"No."

"Really?"

"Cody, I knew his last name was Parker, I didn't know he was your brother until you said you have a brother named Landon. We took a few classes together. He hung out with girls on the dance teams. He was always nice to me, but he wasn't anyone that I wanted to be with. I met my last boyfriend when I went for a broadcasting commentator seminar. He heard my voice and the excitement in my tone while I was on the radio."

"So you were on the radio?"

"Yes. I got the job in Atlanta to do the sports center for baseball and hockey."

"Did you love him?"

"Cody, you got me talking, I promise I will continue talking. I think you are hurting your back."

He sits on the floor in my room on the carpet and spreads his legs. I stand holding on to my bed and when my knees bend, I lower myself carefully on the floor and sit across from him. I spread my legs. We sit with our shoes touching each other.

"Did you love him?"

"I almost married Quinn Daniels."

"You were with Quinn Daniels?"

"Yes."

"He is married now to Michelle."

"You know her?"

"She is a sports agent. She was never mine. I didn't trust her."

"Yeah. She and Quinn had dated a long time before he met me. Then they broke up and he asked me out. I think he asked me out to make her jealous. I don't think he knew he was going to fall in love with me. She was dating a tennis star and when they broke up, she came looking for Quinn. To be honest, I was ready to move on anyway. I mean I was sad that it ended and I was broken-hearted over it, but in the long run if I would have married him, I think I would have had the marriage annulled."

"Why do you say that?"

"I just found something about him that I wish he wasn't involved in. He wasn't really but he stood by and watched something happening and didn't do anything to stop it or prevent it from getting worse."

"What was it?"

"I signed legal papers saying that I wouldn't talk about it."

"Did he know that I was attacked?"

I don't say anything.

"Is that it?"

"Cody, I can't tell you."

He moves on to his knees in front of me. "Did he witness them attacking me?" He asks softly.

"If I tell you, and it comes out that I was the one who said anything he will sue me."

"What did he see?"

"Quinn saw the model pay out the money to three guys. The next thing he saw was you drive up to meet her. You were getting the car so that she didn't have to cross the street in her ten thousand dollar shoes."

He laughs. "Her shoes looked like they were expensive and the ones she wore on the catwalks and runways were, but she had fabulous fakes." He kisses me on the lips. "What else did he see?"

"He saw the guy standing in the shadows with the bat. Someone went and made it looked like they were attacking her. The guy held her around the waist so that she couldn't stop what was happening to you. Then the one guy came out and started attacking you. The second guy came out of the shadows and attacked you. Quinn stood across the street and he did tell the detectives afterwards but he didn't do anything to stop it from happening to you. When I found out that he knew first hand what had happened, my feelings for him changed almost immediately. He accused me of loving you more than him. He told me that he was leaving me and going back to Michelle. He said that Michelle told him that she was ready to have his children and he was ready for that move. He wasn't ready to make the commitment to me." I say quickly.

"His loss is my gain." Cody says and kisses me. He puts his arms around me and lowers me backwards on the carpet. He runs his hands up and down my body.

"Cody, please." I say gasping.

He kisses me and I can feel his heat. I feel his hardness. I feel his heart beating against my own chest. He deepens the kiss and cups my center. He moves his palm back and forth. The friction gives me tingles throughout my whole body. My toes curl in my shoes. He reaches under my right leg and bends my knee. "Am I hurting you?"

"No." I say breathlessly.

"No, you want me to stop?"

"No, you aren't hurting— me." I pant. "Oh god, Cody. Please." I beg.

He kisses me again and takes my panties off. He caresses the inside of my thigh and inches closer and closer to my sex. He thrusts his tongue in my mouth and his finger inside my folds.

I whimper against his mouth.

He pulls his finger back and pushes deeper. He does this a few times and my body responds immediately. My nerve endings are humming with joy. I have wanted this to happen for so long with this magnificent man. He pulls his finger back again and then pushes deeper again. My vision goes black then I see white fireworks and my body erupts with a mind blowing orgasm.

I cry out. "Please, don't stop."

Cody lifts my leg a little and pushes in again. He kisses me again. "We have to go meet my dad."

"Can we cancel?"

He laughs against my lips. "We can not cancel. He is going to meet us here first."

I put my hands on his shoulders. "I have to sit up." I say.

He looks at me.

"If I am flat on my back, I struggle to sit up." I say.

"Oh, you should have told me."

"I am telling you now." I smile. "What should I wear?"

"Something comfortable." He says. He puts his arm around me and the other under my knees and he picks me up. "Is this ok?"

"Yes." I say. He sits me in my wheelchair. I go into my closet and pick leggings and a dressy shirt. I get dressed. I leave my room and look for Cody.

He is sitting at the kitchen counter with his phone in front of him. When I put my hand on his shoulder, he jumps.

"Oh I am sorry. Did I come up on your blind spot?"

"No. I didn't hear you."

"Are you ok?"

"Yes."

"What are you doing?"

"I am looking into something."

"How do I look?" I ask him.

He looks me over from head to toe and then back up. His eyes dart to my breasts. He smiles.

"Are you wearing a baseball bra?"

"No." I say.

"The design looks like baseballs."

I lift my shirt up to prove that its not baseballs. He smiles. "Why did you think that I was wearing a baseball bra?"

"I saw one in your room."

"Its part of a Halloween costume." I tell him.

"Later you will have to put it on so I can see it."

I laugh. "Um no."

"Come on. Be a sport."

I laugh at him. "When you lifted me up did you get hurt?"

"Crystal, I am fine. You didn't hurt me. I didn't get hurt."

"What time is your dad coming here?"

"He should be here any time now." Cody says. "Crystal, don't be nervous." He takes my hand in his hand. "You should wear that ring."

"Why? Your dad knows that we aren't really a couple."

"We are a couple." He reaches for my hand. "I am going to marry you. How could I not want to? You make me feel like I have never felt before."

"What's that?"

"Loved." He says.

I reach my arms up and hug him. "You are so lovable."

"Women have only been with me because I was an athlete."

"You were dating gold diggers. I am not after you because of what you did for a career. I wanted to be with you since I first saw you play. But the reason wasn't because you are Oh My God, Cody Parker, but because you were so nice to everyone who wanted your autograph or wanted to take a picture with you."

"Did you take a picture with me?

"Kyle has it."

"Why does Kyle have it?"

"He took the picture of us. I only saw it once. He wanted to prevent me from dreaming about you. He has the picture, I have the memory and no one can take that away from me."

Cody picks up his phone and dials a number. "Ky, its me. Good. I have a question, do you have a picture of me and Crystal from when I played? Can you send it to me? Thanks. I promise to always love her."

I look at him when he puts the phone back on the counter. His phone buzzes with a text message. He picks the phone up again and looks at it. An image of him in his baseball glory looking so handsome in his uniform with stains running the length of his leg from him sliding into home plate. The smile on my face seems to fill my little house. The look on my face is pure joy. He is squatting next to me with his arm around my shoulder. I am holding a small teddy bear in my hands that has his jersey.

"That was my first professional game." He says.

"I know." I smile at him.

"I asked my team to get me a bear. I never got one."

I leave him for a moment and go into my office. I open a box and take out a teddy bear. I close the box and slide it back into the closet and close the door. I return to the kitchen and hand him the bear.

"I can't take this from you."

"I have a few of them." I say. I put the breaks on my wheelchair and take my feet off the hangers. I push the buttons one at a time to release them. I stand up pulling myself up at the counter. I put my arms around Cody and hug him.

"Do you know if Ky has more pictures like this?"

"I don't know." I say.

"Are you alright?" He asks. He puts his arm around me.

"I am ok."

"Where is your walker? I only saw it one time."

"Its in my bathroom."

"Do you use workout equipment?"

"I have a stander that I use."

"Where is that?"

"My dad said he had it sent to his house."

"Why?"

"I don't know."

"Have you spoken to any of them in two weeks?" Cody asks.

"I usually go a while without talking to my family. I keep in touch with my sisters and brothers. They usually tell my dad what's going on with me."

"Maybe he should hear it from you."

"Cody, don't push." I tell him.

He lifts me off my feet and sits me on the barstool next to him. He puts his legs on either side of my legs. He squeezes his legs together causing my legs to squeeze together as well. "Does this hurt you?"

"No."

"Are you still doing physical therapy?"

"No. I work out in a gym."

"Can I watch?"

"Yes." I tell him.

"When are you going to work out?"

"I have to find the right gym."

"We can find one together."

"Women will be staring at you." I say.

"I know how to go incognito to a gym." He says kissing me.

"Cody."

"What?"

"We have to find a way that I can initiate some of the kisses. I know that Quinn told me time and time again that he always thought that he was chasing me."

"Let me clear something up with you right now, we will work on a way for you to initiate some of the kisses, but I would chase you to the end of the world and still that wouldn't be far enough."

"Cody, I want to jump into your arms."

"I will catch you. I won't let you fall." He says. He puts his arms out and I throw myself at him. He takes me in his arms and I laugh uncontrollably. He does too.

Sawyer stands on the other side of the front door listening to us laugh. He smiles to himself. He raises his hand to knock once and then lowers his hand. He stands listening to my screech of laughter. He smiles. He hears Cody laugh as well.

Sawyer knocks on the door. Cody opens the door holding me in his arms. Our faces are flushed from us laughing.

"Please come in." I say. I kiss Cody on the cheek. "You need to put me down."

"I need to keep you forever."

Sawyer doesn't say anything. He smiles as he follows Cody in the house.

"I am yours forever and longer than that." I tell Cody.

Sawyer takes his phone out and takes a picture of us. "Cody, put her down." He says kindly.

Cody sits me in my wheelchair ever so carefully. Sawyer never stops taking pictures of us. He sits on the couch.

"What time are we going out?" Cody asks.

"Whenever you are ready." Sawyer says.

"We are ready whenever." I say.

He looks at me. "You both need to fix your hair."

I flip my head and my hair falls perfectly around my shoulders. I take my hands and fluff my hair. I laugh. "I am ready."

Cody grabs my sides and tickles me again. He laughs wickedly.

I burst into a fit of laughter. "Cody! Stop."

Sawyer sits on the arm of the couch watching us. "Cody." Sawyer says gently. "Stop it." He looks at the two of us. "Crystal, I can honestly tell you, you will be a welcomed member to our family."

I look at Sawyer. "I do love your son."

"I saw that the moment I watched you drive up to my house. I saw my son in a different light. He seemed so relaxed about coming home. I know that hasn't always been the experiences of the past."

I turn to Cody. "When Cody kissed me ever so passionately on the lips, at the resort, he changed my life forever."

"Gianna showed us the pictures on Facebook."

"I didn't know that my friend was going to put them all on Facebook. Actually he is a coworker and if I was still employed, I would have him fired." I say about Oscar.

"Why do you say that? The pictures are stunning."

"He didn't have any approval to share any of them." I say.

"Do you follow everything by the book?"

"In my line of work, it is the most important thing to do. When there is even the slightest bend in the rules, that welcomes trouble." I look at both of them. "I am sorry."

"No. Please always feel free to speak your mind." Cody says.

"Cody told me about the flight that you were on. He told me that when he heard you come to his defense, his heart melted." Sawyer says.

"I think that people should keep their opinions to themselves if they don't know the person at all."

Sawyer turns to Cody. "Some of our family members are going to meet their match with her."

Cody laughs.

We leave for the restaurant. The second that we enter the lobby of the restaurant, I see that my dad is sitting at a table. He is by himself. I look at the profile of him. I haven't seen him since the resort. I look at Cody. He holds my hand.

"Cody, one thing I hate most of all is being ambushed." I say to him.

"No one is ambushing you."

"Did you know that he was going to be here?"

"No." Cody says.

"Did your dad know?"

"I don't think so.

We stand waiting for the host to seat us. As we wait for someone from the restaurant to come over, I see Kelsey and Ashley sit with him. Joanne joins them. I feel like I want to run in the opposite direction.

Joanne sees me. She smiles and stands up. "Sweetheart, come join us."

"Hi Joanne." I say. "Joanne, this is Sawyer Parker and you remember Cody."

"Its nice to meet you, Sawyer. Cody, its nice to see you again."

"You too." Cody says.

Sawyer doesn't say anything right away. He watches the interaction. When he does speak its very calm. "You know, I was taking my son and your step-daughter to lunch and it occurs to me that we came in the wrong restaurant. We have a reservation in the other restaurant." He looks at the two of us. "If you want to say hello to your family, we will wait for you."

I look at Sawyer and I feel like I have missed out on having a great dad. I know that Cody has had a tumultuous relationship, but he seems like a great dad.

"Come meet my sisters and my dad." I say to both Cody and Sawyer.

Joanne turns quickly. She walks over to the table and informs dad that I am here. He stands and looks around the restaurant.

Cody takes my hand and Sawyer walks behind us. Sawyer puts his hand on my shoulder. I feel his support. Dad looks at Cody and hugs him. Cody embraces dad.

"It's good to see you." Cody says.

"How are you doing?" Dad asks him.

"Good. Thank you."

I look at Ashley and Kelsey. "Cody and Sawyer, these two are my sisters. This is Kelsey and Ashley."

A woman sitting at the booth next to where my family sits looks over. "Cody Parker as I live and breathe." She says.

He glances at her but doesn't give her a second look.

"Are you just going to ignore me?" She asks.

Sawyer clears his throat. He looks at the woman. "Do you want something with my son."

"You are not his dad." She says.

"I am not?" He looks at Cody. "Do you have another father somewhere?" He smirks.

"I met Cody Parker's dad and you are not him." She says.

I look at Cody and I can't control myself, I pull him to me and I kiss him. He puts his hand behind my head like he did when he first kissed me and he deepens the kiss. He kisses me like we are the only two in the restaurant.

Joanne clears her throat. "Young lady." She says.

Sawyer looks at Joanne. "Are you disciplining her?" He asks in a tone that is just louder than a whisper.

Joanne looks at him. "You don't know her."

"I think the one who doesn't know her is you." He says.

Dad puts his hand on Joanne's arm. "Stop this. I have missed out on my daughters' lives long enough. Stop this. My ex-wife has taken to your sons like she is their own mother. It makes me sad that we can't say the same about you."

Brandon walks over. "She barely likes us." He kisses me on the cheek.

"Brandon!" Ashley says.

He steps closer to her and kisses her on the lips. He knows that Joanne doesn't condone public displays of affection. He hugs his mother. He hugs me and Cody. He shakes hands with Sawyer.

Sawyer looks around at everyone by just moving his eyes. "It was nice meeting all of you. We are at the wrong restaurant and need to get to our reservation." He reaches over me and shakes dad's hand.

"Before you go, what do you think of our children being together?" Dad asks.

I feel the hives start their raising process. My neck itches almost immediately.

Sawyer is still standing behind me in a protective way. He looks down at me and then at Cody. He looks at dad with narrowed yellowish-green cat eyes. His eyes are so much different than Cody's warm welcoming green eyes. "I think they are the perfect couple. I think that they both bring out the best in each other and I can't wait for them to get married and have this beautiful creature in my family. She has stolen the hearts of not only my son, but of my wife and our family."

"You haven't known her long at all, how do you know that she is going to be a good addition to your family?" Joanne asks.

My dad chokes on his water. "Jo? Why would you say that?"

"In the short time that I have known her, I can honestly say she has changed lives." He looks at Joanne with narrowed eyes. "What a pity that you don't know how spectacular she is." He takes control of my wheelchair and pulls me backwards. He walks to the door and we leave.

I feel the heat of hives climbing up my chest and neck. I look at Sawyer. "Thank you for saying all of that to my family."

"Sweetheart, I meant what I said." He says. "Come we should go." He looks at the two of us. "We need to go quickly, my knuckles are itching to hit someone in the eye."

Cody looks at his dad. "We shouldn't tell mom, she wouldn't settle for not hitting someone."

I get in the car in the back seat. Cody takes my wheelchair and folds it. He puts it in the trunk of the car. They each get in the front seat. I cry quietly. The tears fall down my cheeks and I wipe them away. Sawyer is driving and he looks in the mirror and watches me.

He pulls the car into the parking lot. He parks the car. Cody and him get out of the car and walk to the back of it. Sawyer looks at Cody. "She has been crying this whole time. If you think we should reschedule, that would be fine."

"No."

"I don't know what Jack sees in that woman." Sawyer says.

"He loves her sons."

"Time has past. It's a long time and he should pick the side of his daughter and not that bitch." Sawyer looks at me. I haven't moved to get out of the car.

"Dad, I have to tell you, I love her. I love her even more now. I think every day with her, I love her more. When I was with you dealing with all that shit, I couldn't get her out of my mind. I wanted to run to her."

"Run to her now. I listened to the two of you laughing. I feel sad that I took you away from that."

"She threw herself at me." Cody says smiling. "She was sitting on a barstool at the counter in her kitchen and she said that she wanted to throw herself at me. I told her to do it that I would catch her. She just fell into my arms and I swear my heart melted. I love her."

I open the door. "Cody?"

He walks over with my wheelchair. I get in it. I look at Sawyer. "I am sorry." I say. "I know that you had reservations there. I know that its one of your favorite spots."

"I will get a new favorite spot." Sawyer says. He walks over to the door of the restaurant and holds the door.

Cody pushes my wheelchair in the restaurant. We are greeted by the most lovely woman. She smiles at all of us. "Welcome. Do you want a table inside or out? We have tables in the atrium."

I smile when she mentions an atrium. Sawyer and Cody see my smile. Sawyer looks at me. "Please let my daughter-in-law pick."

I look at him and beam. "The atrium, please." I follow the host. They follow behind me. When we get to the table, Cody moves the chair for me. The host takes the chair and moves it to the side of the room. "Thank you." I tell her.

"Enjoy." The host says. She puts the menus on the table in front of us and then leaves us.

I look at both of them. "Sawyer, thank you so much. This is the most beautiful place I have ever been." I smile. I feel giddy. The hives that threatened to take over my body, have decided that they are at rest. I am excited.

Sawyer and Cody both take their seats. Sawyer looks at me. "Have whatever you want." He says to both of us. He looks at me. "Is it weird that your brother and sister are in a relationship?"

I laugh. "They have always been close. It would be weird if they weren't together. Brandon only kissed her on the lips to piss his mom off. I think he read the room as he approached. Kyle and Brandon do a lot to piss Joanne off because she is rude to me. They can sense when Joanne isn't being nice to me. She isn't nice to my sisters either but they show up to see my dad secretly. I won't do anything secretly."

The server brings over shrimp cocktails. There are Dungeness crab legs on plates. He also brings over stuffed mushrooms. He walks away.

We have lunch. The food is delicious. When the dessert comes I am so excited that its carrot cake.

"Can we walk around?" I ask the server when he brings the bill.

He looks at me. "You can go where ever you want."

"Thank you."

We walk around the atrium. Sawyer starts off walking with us. He then takes his phone out. He steps in front of us. "You both stay as long as you want. Enjoy each other. I have to return this call."

"If you need to go, we can come back." I say.

"No. I just need to return this call. The sooner the better." Sawyer says. He hugs Cody. He then hugs me.

We walk around. It's a large atrium and covered by a glass roof. I look up and notice that it's a heavy rain. Cody takes my hand in his hand.

"How are you?" He asks.

"I am embarrassed."

"Why?"

"I hate that Joanne did that. She thinks that I am not good enough for you."

"I am not good enough for you." He says.

"Oh my god, Cody. Please don't say that. You are perfect for me."

"You are perfect for me." He says.

"Do you know that woman who recognized you?"

"Yes. I didn't date her or anything. I went to school with her. She would follow me around like a puppy. I am friends with her brother."

"Does he play baseball?"

"No." He says. He looks at me. "Why doesn't she like you?"

"Does Joanne need a reason not to like anyone? There is no one specific reason why she doesn't like me."

My cell phone rings the same time that Cody's rings. He fishes his out of his pocket. I just let mine ring. He looks at his phone. He takes my hand in his hand and holds it firmly. He sits on a butterfly shaped bench and holds my hand. He puts his legs around the frame of my wheelchair.

"Hello." Cody says.

I hear the person's voice come across loud and Cody doesn't have it on speaker. "Cody, I go out of town for a week and have been away from social media. Cody, who is she?"

I try to pull my hand away from him. His grip tightens but he doesn't hurt me.

"Her name is Crystal Steele."

"Kyle's sister?"

"What?" He chokes.

"I am pretty sure that's Kyle's sister."

"Adam, how do you know that?"

"Dude, he had her pictures hanging up in our apartment."

"I never noticed."

"He brought her to baseball games."

"I never knew."

"She won a scholarship because of your scoring. Two grand slam home runs and one single home run. When she announced you on the radio she gave me goosebumps. How is she? How old is she now? Twenty-five?"

"Adam, how do you know all this about her?"

"She was in a massive car accident. I don't think she was hurt but I know that she had to be rescued from the twisted metal."

My phone rings again. I still don't get it.

"Adam, let me call you back."

"You look like a great couple. Don't do anything to fuck it up." He says.

Cody puts the phone back in his pocket.

"It seems that my friend Adam knows a lot about you." Cody says.

"I heard." I say.

"Its rude to ease drop."

"He spoke loudly." I say.

"I want to hear you announcing me."

I blush a bit.

"Adam makes it sound like it was the best thing that you ever saw."

"Are you kidding? It was fucking amazing." I say. "He thinks that I am twenty-five. I am twenty-eight."

"I know that."

My phone rings again.

"Crystal, answer the phone."

"No. I am on a fabulous date and I don't want anything to spoil it. Joanne already tried to ruin the day. I won't let anyone else ruin the day."

Someone screams out and we both look around. Beth is standing with Lee on the other side of the atrium. When we look at her, she is stamping her feet like she is a child who just had her ice cream stolen.

"How did they find us?" I ask.

"I don't know but we don't have to talk to them."

"I am not going to talk to them."

Beth walks over. "Hi." She says.

"What the hell do you want?" I ask.

"I need to talk to you."

I look at her. "No."

"There are brides that won't book with us unless you come back."

"I am not coming back."

"Rosa won't talk to me."

"That's not my problem."

"Beth, I told you not to say anything to her." Lee says.

I look at him. "Please don't think that you are going to get me to come back by using reverse psychology. You don't understand, I was the owner of the boutique and Beth here wanted it. She did some weddings on the sly to get enough money to buy me out. She did. Then she couldn't do the job because she doesn't even like the business. Much like Rosa. Rosa didn't like the business either. I don't know why she didn't sell it when she had the opportunity. I know that she got a really good offer. Then she put in a clause that I couldn't sell the business for two years. Beth made me an offer after the two and a half year mark and why not. Then I was the assistant who was really running the business." I look at Beth. "There is a buyer who wants to buy the building and the company. Sell it if you want out."

"I don't want out. I want the business. We are losing out because you are gone."

"You should have thought about it."

"The thing is, you don't even know Cody." Beth says.

"How do you know that I don't know Cody? Did I ever say to you that I didn't know him? I love Cody."

"You only know who he is because I have his pictures all over the place at work."

"Um no."

Sawyer watches us. He watches what is going on. He sits at the table that we were at earlier during lunch and he watches. I look over and see him. He smiles at me. I smile back.

Cody walks over to his dad. He sits down with Sawyer. "Its so bad, I should interfere with this but I like to watch her lose her shit."

"She is radiating anger."

"Is that a thing?" Cody asks. He has my purse because when they walked over, I left it on the bench with Cody. My phone rings. He opens my purse and looks at my phone. Kyle's face fills the screen. "Hi." Cody says.

"Is something wrong? I am calling my sister."

"She's having a confrontation."

"Not with our family." Kyle says.

"No. She's telling Beth off."

"Watch out for her. When she argues with people she breaks out in hives." Kyle says.

"She's had hives since I met her." Cody says.

"Cody, just watch out for her. She loves you."

"I love her."

"Cody."

"Ky, she has to do this. She has to stand her ground. She has to stand up to these people."

Beth screams on the top of her lungs. "Are you fucking kidding me?" She stomps her feet.

Lee looks at her. "What's going on?"

"I just got a notification that someone bought out the building."

Chapter Nine

Cody and Sawyer walk over. Beth is crumpled on the carpeted floor crying her eyes out. They watch her. There is a crowd of people that gathers to watch.

Lee reaches down and wraps his hand around her arm. "Get up." He snaps at her.

She looks at me. "You did this." Beth glares at me.

"I did what?" I ask her not knowing what she is talking about.

"You told them that we were selling."

"I haven't spoken to anyone. I live here now. I don't want anything to do with weddings ever again."

"Do you think that Cody is going to marry you?" Beth asks. "He probably feels sorry for you."

I turn quickly. With my hands on the rims of the wheels, I push myself as fast as I can out of there. I leave the restaurant. I don't even know where I am, but I take off down a sidewalk. Hot tears burn my face.

Cody runs after me. He takes me in his arms. "Stop." He pants.

"I had nothing to do with the building being sold."

"My dad did it. He bought the building."

I feel the muscles burning in my arms. My lungs are burning. My heart is pounding in my chest. "Do you?"

"Do I what?"

"Do you feel sorry for me?" I ask.

"Why would I feel sorry for you?"

"Is Beth right?"

"Beth is a bitch. I hate Beth. She said that to make me angry."

"What is your dad going to do with a bridal shop?"

"My mom and sister always wanted to have one." He says.

"No they don't."

"I don't know what he is going to do with a bridal shop. That was the phone call he had to make."

"Your dad must think the—"

"I think the best of you. I am sorry that today happened. I am not sorry that you are going to be in our family." Sawyer says. He looks at Cody. "She traveled ten miles quickly."

"Ten miles?" I ask.

"That's the distance I drove to reach you." He smiles at his exaggeration.

I look at Cody. "You ran after me. Are you alright? Did you hurt your back or your knee?"

Sawyer looks at me. "You are the one who has had a horrible day and you are worried about Cody?"

I look at Sawyer. "What are you going to do with a bridal shop?"

"Its yours to decide."

"Mine?"

"I bought it for you."

I look at Cody and then at Sawyer. "I need a drink." I say. I feel my weight shift in my chair and realize that I have a flat tire. "Oh no, I have a flat tire." I say sadly.

"How do we fix it?"

"We go to a bicycle store. Its just a bicycle tire." I say.

Cody lifts me out of my wheelchair and carries me to Sawyer's car. He sits me in the front seat. He kisses me on the lips.

Sawyer puts my wheelchair in the trunk like it is something he has done a thousand times. He hands Cody the keys to his car. He gets in the backseat. I turn and look at him.

"Do you want me to sit in the backseat?"

"No." Sawyer says.

Cody looks at me. "What bicycle shop?"

"I just moved back, I don't have one that I go to yet."

Sawyer looks on his phone where the nearest bicycle shop is. "Three miles south of us." He says. "Really just make a U-turn and go back in the direction that we just came from." Sawyer says.

Cody drives the three miles and pulls into the parking lot. He jumps out of the car and gets my wheelchair. "Just the one or should it be both?" He squeezes the tire that is not flat and it pops. "That answers that question." He smiles brightly. "I will be right back."

"When you go in, tell them that you can't leave it and come back for it." I say.

"Of course." He says.

When he walks away I look at Sawyer. "He acts like he has done this a time or two."

"He went to school with a young lady who is disabled in a wheelchair. She too has Cerebral Palsy. She uses a wheelchair. They weren't close but she was a fan of his too."

"Do I look like her?" I ask without thinking.

"No." Sawyer says laughing. "Cody only knew of her. He didn't really know her. He would recognize her if they were in the same room, but he doesn't know her."

"He doesn't know me either." I say quietly.

"He knows you." Sawyer says.

"What does he know about me?"

"Ask him."

Cody walks out of the store. He puts the wheelchair in the trunk. He gets in the driver's seat. He kisses me on the lips. "Benny is delighted to do your wheels for you."

"Thank you." I say. "How much do I owe you?"

"Stop it." He looks at me and then looks at his dad. "You both look like you were deep in conversation."

I don't hold back. "Cody, why did you pick me? Why did you kiss me? What do you know about me?" My heart is breaking and I don't want it to. I have never felt more loved in all my life. I haven't ever been kissed the way that Cody kisses me. I wouldn't want that to stop. I wouldn't want anyone else.

"What do I know about you? Well let's see." He looks at his dad and takes my hand into his own hand. He laces our fingers together. "You have the best giggle in the whole world. You trust me with your life, or at least trust me to catch you. I know that you love me unconditionally and I am honored. I know that when you were given the bridal shop that you donated dresses to girls who couldn't afford dresses for homecomings and proms. You also donated tuxedos for boys."

I look at him. "No one knows that."

"My dad and I do. We also know that Rosa and Beth never shared your good deeds. We know that you rent out a ball room twice a year for young people with disabilities to have a dance."

I feel my heart pounding in my chest. My family doesn't even know that I have done things like this. Cody looks at me because he feels my heart beating in my finger tips. "Please don't tell Kyle." I say softly.

"Does your family not know that you have done these great things?" Sawyer asks.

"No."

"Can I ask you a question?" Sawyer asks.

"Yes."

"Are you ashamed of what you have done to bring happiness to others?"

"No."

"Then why not let your family know?"

"Do you know all the wonderful things that Cody has done?" I ask. "Do you know that your daughter gives free dance lessons to children with disabilities?" I can't say anything nice about Landon because I don't know about him.

"What?" They both ask.

"She hosts a runway event for them on the night of their big recital."

"How do you know that?" Cody asks.

"We crossed paths a few times." I say. "I didn't know she was your sister. Parker is a popular last name. She doesn't look like you at all."

"You don't have to justify yourself." Sawyer says. "Now that I just said that, I am going to ask you a question. You don't have to answer it if you don't want. Why did you do it? How did it start?"

"Why did I do it? A girl and her mom came into my shop when it was mine and she is a bit on the larger side so she couldn't find a dress that she liked in her size. When she walked into my shop the first dress she saw she wanted. It was very expensive." I laugh. "Actually it was one of my most expensive dresses in the store that wasn't a wedding gown. Her mom never looked at the price tag she told the daughter to try it on.

"I was dealing with a bitchy bride-to-be and when I saw this girl and her mother I sent someone else to deal with the bride. I turned my attention to the girl and her mother. The mother was so encouraging. The dress was the exact color that the girl wanted to wear to her dance. She was excited because a boy had asked her to go with him. She was so excited. She was all giggles. It was like the dress was made just for her. She put that dress on and she looked like a princess.

"I still have her pictures hanging in the shop. When her mom helped her take the dress off, she noticed the price and her heart sank. I watched it happen. The mom was going to go broke to make her daughter happy. When she went to ring up the dress, I had told my sale's clerk to tell them that upon looking over the dress, they found imperfections and the dress was one-third of what it cost. The mom knew I did something to alter the price. She told her colleagues about the shop. They all came to me to plan their weddings. Some of them came back and gave back the bridal party dresses. I can't resell them so I donated them."

"Why doesn't your family know about it?" Cody asks.

"Why doesn't your family know how great you are?" I ask him. "How did you even find out about this?"

"Actually the girl that you were just telling us about recognized Cody when we were in Orlando and she told us about it. She also told us that you were always so nice to people no matter how mean and rude they were to you. She said that you have a folder that you bring with you with Cody's number on it. She told us that she was with her boyfriend at a baseball game and when people in the stands had mentioned Cody in a derogatory manner that you shut them up."

I put my hands over my face.

"What are you doing?" Cody asks. "Did you do that?" Cody takes my hands in his.

"One time at a game I did. You had been injured from the mugging. I think you were just released from the hospital. The guy was there with his cute girlfriend and she had said something about how cute you are. The guy turned to her and started talking shit. I was going to stay out of it, but I often watch that show What Would You Do and I knew I had to say something."

"Wow. Thank you."

"The young lady told us that the guy threw stuff at you."

"He did. A half eaten hotdog loaded in mustard. He threw pretzels at me. Then he got a drink and he opened it up and threw it at me."

"I am sorry that happened to you." Cody says.

I smile. "I got free stuff. That's the reason I have so many of your stuffed teddy bears."

"What teddy bears?" Sawyer asks.

"They had teddy bears wearing my jersey number."

"I want one." Sawyer says.

"I have a few at my house." I say. "I will give you a few of them."

Cody looks at his dad. "Where do you want to go now?"

"Am I keeping you both from anything?" Sawyer asks.

"No." We say together.

"Cody, I would like to go home. I want you both to come."

Cody pulls the car onto the driveway of his parents house. Catalina is standing outside waiting for us. When we are all out of the car, she hugs each one of us. The second that she embraces me, I can't help the tears that come. I can't stop them.

"Come inside." She says.

Cody pushes me right to the front door. I put my hands on my wheels to stop us from going any further. "What's the matter?" He asks.

I turn around and look around.

"What are you looking for?"

I look at Cody and burst into tears. "There's no steps."

Cody hugs me. "There are steps. We added ramps so that you feel welcome here anytime."

"Oh my god, thank you so much." I cry.

Catalina stands watching us and she cries. She wipes her eyes.

"Don't cry." Cody says. "I love you."

"I love you too. So much. Thank you."

"Come inside." Catalina says and kisses me on the cheek.

We all go in the house. Sawyer leads us into the den. Its all bright in there. I look around and see a picture of Cody and I kissing. It was the night that he kissed me. It is blown up in a poster size. It hangs in a black shiny frame.

I look at it and gasp. "Oh my god." I say and reach out for Cody. "How do you have that?"

"Landon did it." Sawyer says.

I look at myself being kissed by Cody Parker and I can't believe what I am looking at. I was there and I feel like the moment that we are sharing was captured completely. "I will have to thank him." I say. I look at Catalina and Sawyer. "Why do you have it hanging in here?"

"This is where we have family photos." Catalina says. "I have to tell you that I am excited that Cody has met such a wonderful person. Cody has never been this happy."

"Its true." He says. "I have never been this happy with any woman that I have dated."

Sawyer looks at Catalina. "I wanted to tell you that we have acquired a wedding shop."

She looks at him. "Why?"

"It seems that a wedding planner was wrongfully fired from her job because of a random incident. I don't like when people are mistreated. I found out some information that we will share with you and I think that you will agree that owning a bridal shop is the best thing."

She looks at her husband the way I look at Cody with so much love. "Sawyer, if you think owning a bridal shop is the right thing, then I am with you a hundred percent." She looks at me. "Are you sure that its what Crystal wanted?"

"We didn't talk about it. She just found out about it as well." Sawyer says.

I look at the three of them. "Is it alright if I use the bathroom?"

"You don't have to ask. Of course you can," Catalina says.

I leave the three of them and push my wheelchair down the hallway. I go into the bathroom and close the door.

I find all of them outside sitting around the patio table. When they see me, Cody and Sawyer stand up. Cody walks over and kisses me on the lips. This is not a passionate kiss but it still makes my lips vibrate.

"Can I hug you?" I ask him.

"Of course you can." He says. He stands almost over me and I hug him tight.

"Crystal, do you want the bridal shop?" Sawyer asks.

I look at him and Catalina. "I just moved here. I love my bridal shop in Orlando and I am so grateful that you would do this for me."

"Before you say that you are done with it completely, let me just share with you that the bridal shop can be moved here. I bought the building, I can always sell it. A lot of people are interested in that space." Sawyer says.

"I know." I smile. "I should have sold it to someone else but Beth presented to me that she was the only one interested in it and she would sue me if I didn't let her buy me out."

Landon walks outside and looks at all of us. "What's going on?" He asks.

"We are the owners of a bridal shop." Sawyer tells his younger son.

"What?" He asks laughing.

"It was the right thing to do." Cody says.

Landon looks at me. "I would agree. Crystal has done a lot of good not only to the women who have purchased dresses and wedding packages from her."

I look at Landon. "What do you know about what I do?"

"I have followed up with you a bit over the years. I know we are not friends, but I know that you have done some remarkable things."

Catalina looks at me. "Your parents must be so proud."

"They don't know." I say.

"Why not?" Cody asks.

"Cody, did your family know how magnificent you were at your job?"

"No."

"We are grateful that you brought it to our attention what we sadly missed out on. You must think we are awful."

"No, I think you are wonderful. You all have made me feel more welcome here than my own family does. My brothers are great."

"Your sisters don't treat you right?" Landon asks.

"They are over protective but at the same time they don't want to be bothered to know what I do on a day-to-day business."

"You never told them what you were doing?"

"I told them I was working, they never asked for details about the jobs."

"Do they know that you paid for six families who couldn't afford a real wedding, you gave them the wedding of their dreams and you bought their honeymoons too." Landon says.

"How do you know that?" I ask him.

"I was a guest at one of those weddings." He looks around at Cody, Sawyer and Catalina. "My friend had been hit with a big medical expense. The place that they had booked the wedding at canceled on them at last minute saying that they had double booked. They wouldn't give back the money that he and his now wife had paid out. He was devastated. She was beyond devastated."

Sawyer looks at Landon and then at me. "How did you find out about this?"

"The bride came to return her dress." I say.

"Aren't all sales final?"

"There are exceptions." I say.

Cody's phone rings. He reaches in his pocket and answers it. He doesn't even look at it. "Talk to me." Cody says.

"Where are you guys? I need to see my sister." Kyle says.

"She's with me and my family."

"I am coming." He says. "I am pulling in right now."

"I will meet you at the front door." Cody says. He stands up and walks in the house. He opens the front door and Kyle hugs him.

"Where is she? How is she?"

"She's outside with my—" Cody turns and follows Kyle out of the house.

Kyle runs over to me and takes me in his arms. The second that I am in his arms I cry softly. "Don't let her ruin you." Kyle says. "Kelsey, Ashley and Brandon are looking for you. They told me that they were calling you."

"I couldn't talk to them." I say. I wipe my eyes. I look around at everyone. "I am sorry."

"Don't be sorry." Catalina says. "Come in the house. You are getting splotches. Are you feeling ok?"

"I am feeling ok." I say to her.

"I think you need a drink."

We go in the house and my phone rings in my purse nonstop. Kyle takes my phone out of my purse and answers it. "Hi Kelsey." He says.

"How is she? Where is she? Where are you and why are you answering her phone?"

"She is sad."

"Your mom was so mean to her. I am really sick of it. I told her off."

"Brandon told me."

"Ky, I am sorry."

"You and I will talk later. I can't be mad. We are with Cody. I will call you when I am home."

"I called her."

"She can't talk."

"Can't or won't."

"Both. Either. She will call you when she is ready."

"Ky, the last time something upset her she went four months without talking to us."

"I know."

"Why is she talking to you?"

"Kels, don't be mean. I am friends with Cody."

"Whatever." She says and hangs up.

My phone rings again. Kyle goes to answer it and I grab it from him. "My phone." I say. "I am not a kid anymore. I am not going to be told what to do by any of them or you. I love you all, but no more. My mom who is always supportive of me made a comment that I was being slutty.

Your mom said almost the same thing. It makes me wonder if they have become friends over the years."

"They have coffee together twice a week." Kyle says.

My phone rings again and I see that its Stew. He has always been supportive of me. My parents and my siblings don't know a lot about me, but Stew does. I look at Cody. "Can I go somewhere private?"

"Of course." He takes my hand and leads me to a side office. "Go in here. You can close the door or not."

"Thank you." I say. I call him back.

His voice fills the office so I close the door. "Sweetheart how are you?"

The second I hear his voice, I start to cry.

"Tell me."

I join them all at the table. I look at Cody. "Can you take me home?" I ask him.

"Of course." He says.

"I am sorry to be rude to you." I say to Sawyer and Catalina.

"No." Catalina says. "You don't need to worry about anything."

"Thank you for making me feel so welcome." I say to them.

Kyle looks at me. "I can take you home."

I look at Cody. "Kyle can take me home." I say.

"No." Cody says. "I will take you."

I look at Cody. "Your car is at my house."

Kyle looks at both of us. "I will drive both of you."

Ten minutes later we are in Kyle's car. The two of them are in the front seat. I sit in the backseat. They talk softly among themselves. I say nothing. I look at my phone at all the text messages that I have received.

Dad: I am sorry that lunch was ruined. Call me.

Brandon: the shit really hit the fan! Call me.

Ashley: I feel so bad that things happened the way they did. Please don't think it was an ambush. That was never our intention. Brandon and

I want to know if you are coming back to the apartment or what you are doing? Don't stay away like you do.

Dad: Sweetheart, I am concerned, I have called and left messages. Where are you? Call me. I want you to know that I am on your side.

Mom: I am sorry that I lost my temper with you. Please call me. I love you. ♥

Stew: Hi darling girl. When you get a chance can you call one of us to let us know that you are ok. Oh wait… you are calling back.

Kelsey: Hi Crystal, I told off Joanne. I stood up for you. Dad is mad at me. ♥ I don't think he is going to talk to me.

Brandon: I just found out some information and before I tell everyone what I found out, can you call me? Did you really donate dresses? Did you really pay for weddings for your clients? Why didn't any of us know this? I asked Ash and she burst into tears that you don't tell her anything. I just have one question? Why didn't you tell me? We always shared secrets.

"Earth to Crystal." Kyle says.
I look up from my phone at him. "What?"
"Where do you want to go?"
"My house."
"We will be there in a few minutes."
"Thanks." I say.
Kyle looks at Cody. "Do you want to stay with me?"
"I am going to stay with Crystal." Cody says.
Kyle pulls into my driveway. He gets out of the car and gets my wheelchair. He stands behind my wheelchair and waits for me to get in it. I do and then go into my house.
Kyle follows Cody in the house. When they come in the house, they don't see me. They both look through the house for me. The house is not large by any means, but neither of them find me.
They both sit on the couch.

"Where do you think she is?" Cody asks.

"Maybe she went to the bathroom." Kyle says.

"Kyle, we have checked the whole house. Its not that large. She is not here."

"Well she didn't leave, she has to be somewhere."

I am using a rowing machine. My wheelchair is behind the seat and I pull back on the rowing machine. The tension is tight. The sweat pours off my body.

A timer goes off. A woman trainer walks over to me. "Time is up."

"Thank you." I say to her.

She takes the cables from me so that I don't just release them.

"Do you need me to help you with anything else?" She asks.

"No."

"If you need anything, let me know." She says.

I push my wheelchair over to equipment that looks like a monkey bars for adults. I reach my arms up and do pull-ups. I lift myself out of my wheelchair and lower myself back into the seat. I do fifty pull-ups.

Cody walks in the gym. He looks around and sees me working out. He stands against a mirror watching me. Women walk past him and try to get his attention. He sees no one. He never takes his eyes off of me.

A woman looks around to see what he is looking at. She sees me. She looks at Cody and than back at me. "What does she have that I don't?" She asks out loud.

"My heart." Cody says. He never looks at her. He shifts his weight and walks over to me. He waits until I am done. He sees that my body is covered in sweat. He takes a towel out of his bag and hands it to me. "Hi."

I look at him. "Hi."

"I have been looking for you all over." He looks around the gym. "How did you find my gym?"

"Your gym?" I ask.

"This is my gym." Cody says.

"I have a membership to this gym in Orlando. They told me that it works here too."

"You have been working out in my Orlando gym?"

"For a long time."

"I never saw you in the gym."

"They told me that the owner doesn't go there regularly. I didn't know they were talking about you."

"Are you done?" Cody asks me.

The trainer walks over. "She should be done. She's been here for two hours."

Cody looks at me. "You worked out for two hours?"

I laugh. "No. I explored a bit."

"Did you like what you saw?"

"Yes." I look at him. "Its beautiful."

"What do you like the best?"

"The batting cages." I say.

Cody looks at me. "The batting cages impress you the most?"

"Oh yes." I say.

"Why?"

I look at him and smile. "I can picture you in there getting situated to hit a home run."

"What?"

I throw my hands in the air.

A woman walks over. She looks at me and Cody. She looks back at me. "I have never seen anyone workout harder." She looks at me. "You are amazing."

"Thank you." I say. My ponytail is dripping wet like I just came out of the shower or a swimming pool.

"Are you training for an event?"

"No."

"Do you always workout like that?" She asks.

"Just when I need to blow off steam." I say. I smile.

She smiles. She looks at Cody. She looks back at me. "I recognize you from somewhere." She says.

"I recently moved here." I say.

"From?"

"Central Florida."

"You look familiar. Did you live here before?" She asks.

"I was born in the area."

"Are you Kelsey's sister?" She asks.

I want to roll my eyes. I want to hit someone. I want to throw something. "I am Kelsey's sister."

"How is she?"

"She's good."

"Does she know that you are back in town?"

I look at her. "She does know that I am back."

"Does she know that you workout here?"

"No. This is the first time that I have worked out—" she interrupts me.

"The first time you have ever worked out?"

"No." I laugh. "It's the first time that I have worked out at this location."

"I am going to call Kelsey."

Lucky me. I think to myself. "Tell her I said hi." I say.

Cody looks at the woman. "Who are you?"

She looks at Cody. "Are you her trainer?"

"I am her boyfriend." Cody says.

She checks Cody out right in front of me. "I am Samantha."

"Samantha, please excuse us. We have to go." Cody says. He takes my hand and walks off with me. "It was nice chatting with you." He says over his shoulder to her.

I sit at the kitchen table with a bowl of salad in front of me. Cody is in the kitchen getting the rest of the meal ready. Kyle sits at the table with me. He looks at me.

"What?" I ask him.

"I just don't understand how you got out of here and left the house as fast as you did." He says. "Why didn't you say you were going to the gym?"

"I didn't want a lecture. I didn't want to feel like I was being treated like a child. I didn't want anyone to find me." I look at Cody. "How did you find me?"

"I got an alert." He says.

"What does that mean?"

"It means that I got an alert."

"What was the alert?" I ask.

"That someone was working out in my facility that didn't have a membership." Cody says.

I push away from the table.

"Where are you going?" They both ask me.

I go in my room, I come back into the dining room. I put my gym membership card on Cody's placemat.

Kyle reaches over and takes it in his hand. He looks at it.

"Ky, ask her what she liked the best about my gym?"

"Did she like that everything is accessible?" Kyle asks.

"Ask her."

Kyle looks at me. "What did you like the best?"

I smile and giggle.

"What's going on?" Kyle asks. "What did you like best?"

"The batting cages." I say.

Kyle looks at me and then at Cody. He smiles. He looks back at my gym membership card. "Does the Orlando gym have a batting cage?"

"No." Cody and I say together.

"There is a baseball field." I say.

"Did you go there?" Kyle asks.

I shake my head.

Cody carries over three plates. He puts one in front of each of us. He reaches over Kyle and takes my membership card. He looks at it. "You showed this to the trainers?"

"I did. I showed it to three of them." I say. I take my fork and play with my food.

"What aren't you saying?" Kyle asks. He watches me. "Crystal?"

I look up at him. I don't say anything because I don't want to cause any trouble for Cody's employees. I can easily go find another gym. He isn't likely to open up a new gym location because his employees weren't nice to me. The female trainer was extremely nice and showed me all around. She stood by allowing me to show my excitement over the batting cages.

Cody looks at me. "Are you not saying something?"

"What do you want to hear?" I ask them both. "I went to the gym and had a fabulous workout." I take a bite of the food even though I am not hungry at all. "This is so delicious."

Kyle laughs. "You don't have to tell him that. He knows his food is crap."

"Kyle, that is so mean." I say.

We finish dinner and the two of them clean up. I go in my room and close the door. I get in my bed and lay back against the pillows. I close my eyes and drift off to sleep.

Cody and Kyle sit on the couch. Cody pulls out his laptop and accesses the gym's security cameras. He watches me go in the gym. He watches my excitement when I enter the facility. He watches me approach the counter where there are two male trainers standing shooting the shit between the two of them. At first they ignore me. Cody turns the dial for the volume and he listens through his earbuds to the conversation taking place between his two workers.

"Yeah, I heard that he was back in town. I heard that he has a girlfriend. There is talk that he is going to marry some chick that he met at a hotel and kissed." The one says.

The other looks at his coworker. "Yeah, I heard that this chick is trouble. I heard that she set it all up that he would sleep in her room with her. I heard her boss flew here and fired her."

"No—" the first one says.

I look at both of them like they are not talking about me. Clearly they are. "Excuse me." I say.

They both ignore me like I have said nothing.

"Um, excuse me."

They finally look at me. They don't realized that they were just talking about me. The second one looks at me. "How can we help you?"

A man walks over and hands his membership card to them over my head. They take it and scan it.

"I am sorry, did you not see that they are helping me?" I ask nicely.

"I need to get my workout started." The client says.

"Here you are, sir." The first one says.

"I have a membership card." I tell them.

"I have never seen you here before." The first one says to me.

I open my purse and take out the membership card. I hand it to them.

"What do you want us to do with this?" The first one asks.

"Scan it." I say.

"This is not for this branch." The second one says.

"I have a valued membership card. I can workout in any of the locations nationwide."

"Name some of the other locations." The first one says.

"There are facilities in Atlanta, Indianapolis, Jacksonville, Orlando and here." I say.

The female walks over. She takes my card from the two of them. She scans it. "Let me show you around." She says with a welcoming voice.

"Thank you." I say.

The two guys look at each other. They return to their conversation like I was never there.

Cody closes his laptop. He walks Kyle to the door. Kyle stops just before he leaves. "Can you make sure that she shows up for lunch with her mom tomorrow?"

"If she wants to go." Cody says.

"We haven't had a lot of time with her." Kyle says.

Cody leans back against the wall and crosses his arms over his chest. "Ky, with the exception of you, Ashley and Brandon has anyone been nice to her? Her mom sounded all encouraging when she was on the phone with her. I heard them talking. Then when she came here and saw her daughter for the first time in her new she shed." He laughs at the reference to my house. "She made her sound like Crystal is a slut. Then your mom. Well you know what happened there. Beth has had it out for Crystal since I kissed her."

"I know all of that. But her family wants to spend time with her."

"If she wants to come, I will not keep her from coming. With that said, I won't let her go alone. The guard in me wants to protect her."

"I know all of that." Kyle says. "What were you watching on your computer?"

"My staff needs to be trained or fired." He says.

Kyle reaches for the doorknob and opens the door. "She went to the gym and now you are going to fire your employees?"

"Ky, mind your business." Cody says. He closes the door behind Kyle and locks up the house.

He walks into my room and sits on the bed with me. I feel the bed dip but I don't open my eyes. He slips his shoes off and stands unbuttoning his jeans. He steps out of them and then sits back on the bed. It dips again. He stands a second time and walks over to the side of the bed. He pulls the sheet back and then slides into bed with me.

I lay with my arm over the pillow. Cody slides his arms around me and curls into me. He closes his eyes. He reaches his arm over me and laces our fingers together.

"Cody?" I say softly.

He opens his eyes and looks at me. "Yes." He says.

I say nothing more.

"Crystal?"

"Hmm."

"Were they mean to you at the gym?"

"Hmm."

"Is that a yes or a no?"

I don't respond to any thing else. He snuggles closer to me.

I wake up in the morning and I am laying half on top of Cody. I move immediately knowing that his right arm is where he sustained his injuries. When I settle myself back on the mattress, Cody pulls me back on top of him.

"No." I say.

He opens his eyes. "What's wrong?"

"I don't want to hurt you."

"Crystal, I am all healed. You will not hurt me."

"Are you sure?"

"I am." He looks at me. "Were you treated well at the gym?"

"It was fine." I say.

"Are you sure?" He asks. He kisses the top of my head.

"Cody, I lost my job because of a misunderstanding. I don't want anyone to lose their jobs because of me."

"I am going to make sure that they get a sensitivity training."

I giggle into his chest. "They were talking about you when I approached them. I don't think that they knew who I was until that lovely girl came over. They held my membership card between the two of them. They might have recognized my name."

"Did they tell you that you couldn't work out in the gym?"

"They didn't say anything like that. They weren't welcoming either, but they didn't tell me that I couldn't workout there."

"Your family wants to have lunch with you." Cody says.

"No."

"Kyle wants you to know that your family wants to have lunch with you."

"Um, I am still saying no."

"What do you want to do today?"

"I was thinking of getting on the train and seeing how long it takes to get to Orlando and back." I tell him.

"Are you going to do this alone?"

"I was going to ask you to go with me if you want to."

"I will go with you." He looks at me. "I could drive you."

"Well I know by car it takes a little more than three hours. I wanted to see how long it takes by the train. Its supposed to be faster." I say.

"When do we leave?"

"As soon as we are ready." I say smiling.

He pulls me further up on his body and kisses me. He wraps his arms around me. "Cody?"

"What?"

"Make love to me." I say kissing him.

He kisses me and lays me back on the mattress. He runs his hands up and down my body. He kisses his way up and down my body. He takes my nipple in his lips. He sucks it in his mouth and I gasp. He kisses a trail down my flat belly. He goes lower.

"Cody!" I cry out.

Cody pushes a finger into my center and then another. I gasp and cry out. He kisses my lips.

"So wet." He says.

"Cody." I cry out again.

He opens a condom wrapper. He covers himself and then he enters me with one quick push. He pulls back and then pushes back into me. I cry out. I arch my back and he wraps his arm around me to help me get closer to him.

In a quick move he rolls over and now I am on top. He lets me take control. I cry out. "Cody, please." I say.

"Please what?"

"Roll back over." I cry out. "I need you deeper. Please go deeper."

He rolls again and pulls back. He pushes deep inside me in one quick movement. My body convulses with my orgasm. When he erupts in me, my body reacts again and I feel my insides clutch him. I want to stay like this forever. Connected to him. We are one and I am the happiest that I have ever been. Cody rolls out of me and I feel completely naked without him.

Chapter Ten

We sit together in side by side seats on the train. The train stops in Palm Beach before it cuts through the state and speeds through to Orlando. Less than two hours later, the train pulls into the station and we wait to get off.

My friend Emma waits for me inside the station. When she sees me she embraces me warmly. She looks at Cody. She smiles at him.

"Cody, this is Emma. Emma this is Cody." I say.

"I know who he is." She tells us. "Remember, you and I roomed together since the womb."

I laugh at her. "You are ridiculous."

"Its nice to meet you." Cody says. "So you lived with Crystal?"

"She and I lived together all through college and then she got me a job working at the bridal shop."

"Do you still work there?" Cody asks.

Emma looks at me. "Someone bought us out."

"I know." I tell her.

"Why didn't you tell me?"

"Beth fired me."

Emma looks at me. "Why didn't you tell me?"

"Shock." I say.

"Are you hungry?" Emma asks.

"We are hungry." Cody says.

Emma looks at my hand. "Oh my god, you are engaged?"

"I am engaged." I say smiling at her.

Emma looks at Cody. "Congratulations." She knows that I have loved Cody Parker forever. When he got injured, she heard me sobbing. She knew I was concerned. She knew that I never trusted the model that he was dating.

"Thank you."

Emma looks at me. "That is why that bitch fired you."

I don't say anything. Cody takes my hand and we follow Emma to her car. When we get to the car, she opens the passenger door for me. She stands behind my wheelchair as I get in the car and then she folds my wheelchair because she has truly done this lots of times before. She opens the trunk of the car and puts my wheelchair in the trunk.

Cody stands next to Emma. "I could have done that."

"I am so used to doing it. Thank you." Emma gets in the car. She looks at me and smiles. "What did your family think of you being engaged?"

"Joanne called me a slut. My mom told me that I was acting slutty and well my dad never speaks against Joanne. Stew is happy for me." I say.

"Stew?" Cody asks from the backseat.

"Stew is my mom's on-again off-again boyfriend. Over the years I have stayed in touch with him. When I graduated from college, they all came. Stew was up front. No one knew that he was going to be there. When I came off the stage he grabbed me in such a hug and told me that he was so proud of me. He was excited about the job in Atlanta. He had called his friend to tell him that I was coming and to have the basement apartment that was accessible ready for me. I was so sad that I disappointed him. He assured me that everything was fine. My mom left him shortly after. Then they got back together. Stew was always telling me that I could do whatever I wanted to do. He is the only one who knows about the donations that I do."

Emma pulls the car into a parking lot. Beth is standing there with her hands on her hips. I look at Emma. "What the hell is she doing here?" Emma asks.

I look at her. "Did you set this up?"

"No." Emma says. "The last I heard, Beth was down in Miami sucking—"

"Em-ma!" I say.

Cody laughs from the backseat.

"Emma, lets go somewhere else."

"This is my dad's place. He is waiting to see you." Emma says. She gets out of the car. "I will see what Beth wants."

Cody looks at me. "Is your friend trustworthy?"

"She's the best." I tell him and honestly mean it.

Ten minutes later we enter the restaurant and an older guy with salty black hair is hugging me tight. I feel like I am being hugged by a loving dad. He is not mine, but he has always made me feel loved.

"Crystal!" He says hugging me again. He looks at Cody. "Oh my goodness, did he walk out of one of your photographs?"

"Hi Angelo." I say.

Cody smiles. "She has photographs of me?"

"That's how that bitch Beth got pictures of you." Angelo says.

"That's not true." I say. "Beth has pictures of Cody with her at an event that they both attended."

"An event that she stole from you." Angelo says.

"That part is true. But it happened so I can't do anything about it."

Cody looks at me. "The event where I met Beth, you were supposed to be there?"

"It was Crystal's event. She planned the whole thing. She planned every detail of it. She planned the guests." Emma says.

I look at both father and daughter. "Ok, we know how awful Beth is. The fact is that she was the owner of the Madame Butterflies Boutiques. I did all the work for a lot of events."

"All of them." Angelo says.

I smile at him. "You don't have to keep promoting me, Cody and I are going to get married." I say to him.

"Oh my goodness, I am so excited for you." Angelo says. He looks at Cody. "Do you prefer eggplant parmigiana or chicken parmigiana?"

"I like both of them equally." Cody says.

"Do you like salad with your lunch or soup?" Angelo stands next to Cody beaming like a proud dad.

"What kind of soup?"

"Broccoli cheese is our famous soup. But we have chicken noodle, we have minestrone, we have an Italian meatball soup too."

Cody looks at me. "What's your favorite?"

Angelo looks at me. "Sweet girl, anyone you want, I know you like them cold."

"Cold?" Cody asks. "Why cold?" He asks me.

I look at him. "I don't like eating hot soup. It makes me hot from the inside out." I look at Angelo. "I like them warm."

Cody looks at me and smiles. "If you like cold soup, I think that's fine. Its how you like it."

"She also doesn't eat cereal with milk." Angelo says.

Emma looks at Angelo and glares. "Ok. That's enough."

"Well if Cody is going to marry her, he should know that she only drinks cold coffee. She only eats scrambled eggs or hard boiled ones."

I look at them. "Excuse me." I say. I want to leave the room quickly, I don't. I make my way to the bathroom and just sit in the large lounge area. I sit at the counter and just stare at my reflection.

There is a knock on the door. Cody walks in the bathroom lounge area and looks around. "Are you ok?" He asks.

"I am ok."

"Why cold stuff?"

"Its just what I like."

Cody kisses me on the lips. "Come back and have lunch with everyone."

"I just don't want anyone to ruin anything."

"No one is going to ruin anything." He looks at me. "Did you ever get to the event where I met Beth?"

"No." I say.

"You didn't get to see it all finished what you planned?"

"I was there the next day to oversee the cleanup."

"You missed out on the fancy part of it."

"Yes."

"Why?"

"Beth demanded that she needed to be there and make sure that everything went well. Beth knew that you were the guest of honor and she wasn't going to give up a chance to be with you. She didn't know that I knew who you were. She threw it up in my face that you would never be in love with someone like me. She told me that if you and I were in the same room, you wouldn't give me the time of day."

Cody looks at me and kisses me again. "Well she was right, I didn't give you the time of day, I kissed you senseless."

I laugh and wrap my arms around him and hug him tight.

We sit at a table in the middle of the restaurant. Angelo put the food on platters in the middle of the table so that everyone could take what he or she wants. He has both eggplant parmigiana and chicken parmigiana on the table. There are soups and salads as well.

By the time everyone is done eating there is no food left on the platters. Emma's mom has joined us as well. Cass walks in. When she sees me she runs over and hugs me. "Crystal, its so good to see you. I thought that you moved."

"Its good to see you too, Cass. I did move. I am only here visiting."

"Someone bought the bridal shop." She shares with the room like none of us know. Emma works there and I did too.

"I know." I tell her.

"Someone is interested in buying the whole building." Cass says again like no one knows about it.

"I know." I tell her again.

"Why are you letting it go?" Cass asks.

"Beth fired me." I say. "She did me a favor." I mean it.

"How long are you here for?" Angelo asks.

"We leave to go back tonight." Cody says.

Angelo looks at Cody. "Can you tell me what made you pick Crystal?"

"Why wouldn't I pick her?" Cody asks.

"What made you kiss her?"

"We met on a flight." Cody says. He kisses me quickly on the lips. "Someone was being rude on the flight that we were on. Crystal defended me. She then closed her eyes and fell asleep on me. I lost sight of her in the airport and then we were on yet another plane. She defended me again. The pilot asked if anything went wrong on the flight, if I would make sure she got off the plane. I agreed to watch out for her. We got safely to Fort Lauderdale and by the time I got my luggage, I lost sight of her again. When I was in the lobby of the resort that my cousin's wedding was at, I saw her and couldn't help myself. I had to kiss her." He looks at me. Then he looks at everyone else. "I couldn't get enough of her. I didn't want that kiss to end."

"Me either." I say.

Emma looks at us. "What are you going to do while you are here?"

"I just came to get somethings that I left behind."

"Me." Emma says.

She catches me off guard by saying that. We have been friends a long time.

"Tell us about your house." Cass says.

"My house is cute." I say.

"She bought a she shed." Cody says.

I laugh. "Its not a she shed. My dad built it."

"You are living in one of your dad's homes?"

"I didn't know it was his development." I say.

"They must be so glad to have you back." Angelo says.

"So glad." I say sarcastically.

"Why do you say that?" Angelo asks.

"The truth is, I have been there for a month and I haven't seen a lot of them. Don't get me wrong, they text me every day. My dad gets wrapped in Joanne and how she thinks and feels. It seems that my mother, who has always hated Joanne, is now besties. They both said pretty much the same thing to me. My mom and Joanne said I was being slutty."

Cass jumps up from the table and hugs me. "This surprises me about your mom."

"Me too." I say.

A short time later, I am standing in the middle of the bridal shop. Cody looks around. "Wow."

"What?"

"Look at all these dresses." He says.

I laugh. I look at him and laugh more. "What did you expect?"

"Like one dress in a style." He looks around. To his left, there is a section that is for men. Suits and cummerbunds in a ray of colors. I have Tuxedos, I have ties and other accessories. Cody looks at me. "You have a section for men?"

"Have you ever been in a bridal shop?" I ask.

"Yes. I have never seen a section for men in bridal shops."

"Well it's the only bridal shop around in a fifteen mile radius."

"Do a lot of men come into the store?"

"I would say that one-third of my sales yearly are from men buying tuxedos and cummerbunds for homecomings and proms and weddings too. I try to get in the latest styles. Or I did."

"So which one of you was in charge of getting the styles of dresses and other stuff?" Cody asks.

"Me. Rosa had me do it when I was her personal assistant. She hated talking to the dress makers. She hated a lot of the things that go along with being a wedding planner. She did it well but she hated all the ins and outs."

"What do you want to do with all of it?"

"Well I just moved across the state."

"Do you want to sell the building?"

"A long time ago." I say.

"So you wouldn't mind if my dad sold the building?"

"No. He owns it." I say.

"What would you do with all the dresses?"

"Send them back to the designers."

"Will you lose money?"

"There will be a loss of commission."

"If you could pick one, which one would it be?"

I look at him. "The dress that I wanted to wear for my perfect day, was sold last year." I look at the dresses all hanging around the room. "It was here for years. It went unseen or overlooked by bride after bride. I wanted it since I saw it. It was just the perfect dress. A bride came in was looking for an affordable dress. Beth knew how much I loved the dress. She dropped the price because she was looking to clear out some of the dresses. She made it so affordable it sold in literally ten minutes after we opened the store for the day. I was crushed when I came in later that day and my dress was gone." I look at Cody. "I dreamed of the perfect dress that I would wear and I would dream of getting married, but every time I saw myself walking down the isle I never saw who the groom was waiting for me at the front of the church."

"What did the dress look like? Maybe you can tell my mom about it and she can help find the dress. What made it so special?"

"It was just the right one." I say smiling. I look around. "I will be right back." I say. I turn and leave him. I go into the back room. I go into the office and get my belongings that I had left in the office. I didn't know that I was going to be fired.

Cody walks into the office. He looks around. He sees the pictures of him and Beth from the charity event that I planned. "I dated Beth a long time ago. She hated that I played baseball. The night of the charity event she made a big deal that we could finally be together because I no longer played stupid baseball."

"Oh my god, I hate her." I say.

"I hate her too." Cody says. He looks around the room and sees the Barbie doll and Ken doll in the shadow box. Ken is dressed in a baseball uniform.

I look at Cody. "I can explain why Ken over there is wearing the wrong number on the jersey."

He looks at me.

"I couldn't tell her. I didn't want her to know. I didn't want her to steal my favorite number from me. It had seemed that she had taken everything else."

"What's your favorite number?" He asks.

I smile at him. "Sixteen." I say.

"That wasn't always my jersey number." Cody says.

"I know that. You also wore thirty-two."

He kisses me on the lips. We get lost in that kiss for a while. When my cell phone rings Cody pulls away from me. He sees a book on a shelf that catches his attention. He walks over to the bookshelf and picks the book up.

"Hi Emma." I say.

"Hi." She says. "I am calling to invite you and Cody to join Bruce and me for dinner."

"Let me see what Cody wants to do. We didn't bring a change of clothes with us." I say.

"Well, if we don't do it tonight, would you be willing to come back and plan a dinner with us?"

"Well, yes. I will have to come back." I tell her.

"Bruce has a job in Fort Lauderdale next week. He has invited me to come with him."

"Come with him." I tell her.

"Are you sure?"

"I am sure."

"I am sorry about my parents. They were excited for you. They are excited that you are with Cody. They are extremely upset with your parents. My dad called your dad and your mom."

"Oh boy. The last time he did that was our graduation." I say. Angelo did call my dad and had a heart to heart with him that he had some nerve not taking my side. Angelo yelled at dad for always sticking by his trouble making wife.

"Whats going to happen to the shop?"

"I am not sure." I tell her. "I think the new owner is interested in selling."

"What are we going to do with all the dresses?"

"We will have a meeting about it in a couple of weeks. Nothing is set yet."

"Do you need me to drive you back to the train station?"

"Actually yes." I say.

"What time are you going back?"

"We are scheduled on the seven-thirty train back." I say.

"What time are you going to get there?"

"We are required to be there an hour before we leave." I say.

"You have your tickets for the return trip?"

"Yes."

"Want to grab something to eat before you go?"

I look at Cody. He shakes his head. "No." I say. "We are still full from lunch. Your dad's eggplant is my favorite thing in the world."

"I will tell him. Kiss ass." She teases me.

"Be here in a half hour." I tell her.

"I will." She says and hangs up.

Cody looks at me. "What are you going to do to pass the time?"

"Spend time with you." I tell him.

"You don't have anything that you need to do?"

"Technically we are trespassing."

"No." He says.

"Yes." I say back. "I got fired. I don't work here any more."

"My dad is not going to report you for trespassing." I go into Beth's office. I take one of the appointment books off her desk and open it. "Oh crap." I say.

"What's wrong?"

"She has a wedding booked for next week. I don't know if anything has been finalized. I am sure that Beth has no clue."

"Will Emma know?"

"Emma does fittings only." I say. "She doesn't work on bookings."

I take my cell phone out. I call Rosa. I don't want to talk to her really but, what choice do I have. She answers on the fourth ring. "Hi Rosa."

"Hi." She says and I can hear the sob in her voice.

"Is everything alright?"

"Between you and my bitch niece, my shop has been sold."

"Not because of me." I say.

"Yes. Because of you!" She yells. "Why couldn't you let her win Cody Parker?"

I know that Cody hears her yelling at me.

Cody looks at me and walks the distance that separates us. He takes me in his arms and kisses me on the lips. He moans against my mouth causing me to moan as well.

"Are you having sex?" Rosa yells at me.

Cody pulls away and then kisses me again.

"Hello!" Rosa yells.

"Rosa, stop yelling." I say to her.

"You called me while you are in the middle of having sex with my niece's boyfriend."

"They never dated."

"They did date. He is a player that Lover Boy."

"Rosa, everyone has a past."

"Well does he know about your past?" She asks like she has some great knowledge of my sexual behaviors."

"What should he know about my past?" I ask her.

"Oh—" she draws out the word. "So he doesn't know that you are a virgin slut?"

"How is that even possible?" I ask her. "And who ever told you that I was a virgin? I met you when I was in college. I have had past boyfriends and we were intimate."

Cody looks at me. He writes down on a sheet of paper. Tell her why you are calling her and hang up!!

"Rosa, I am calling because it looks like Beth and Lee have booked a wedding for next week. Has everything been taken care of and finalized for the wedding?"

She tries to act all innocent. "Well how should I know?"

"Because I am looking at the book and I see that you have co-signed on all of the bookings."

"What? How do you know that?"

"The owner of the shop has given me the approval to check that all appointments and bookings have been kept."

"A Sawyer something or another bought the shop."

"Rosa, I don't know why you are getting all bent out of shape about it. You gave the business to me and you never once signed off on any of my bookings and appointments, so I guess what I am asking, why are you co-signing on bookings with Beth?"

"Bitch!" She snaps.

"Should I call the bride and make sure that everything has been taken care of?"

"Let me ask Lee." She says.

"Just so you know, I will not be working with any of them."

"Bitch!" She snaps again. I hear her talking to Tony. "I am talking to Crystal." She says. I hear a bit of a commotion. "Give me back my phone." I hear her say.

"Crystal?" Tony Caster asks.

"Hi Tony." I say.

"What's going on?" He asks.

"Well I came to Orlando for the day. I am leaving in a few minutes to head back to Fort Lauderdale. I was looking in the appointment book and I see that there is a wedding scheduled for next week and out of habit, I am just making sure that everything is set for them. I will not be working with Beth and Lee at all."

"I hear you. Let me check out the information for you and I will get back to you." He says. "How will I get back in touch with you?"

"Rosa has my contact information."

"What's going to happen to Rosa's shop?" Tony asks.

"Tony, you and her are married five years. This shop has not been Rosa's in all that time."

"She's an investor."

"When did that happen?"

"When Beth bought you out."

"I should have left all those years back." I say. "I know I am not smart."

"Don't!" Cody and Tony both say at the same time.

I look at Cody. "Don't say that again." He says to me.

"Listen, Crystal. I will get the information that you are asking about and get back to you. If things are needed—"

"Just let me know, I will drive back and take care of everything that needs to be done."

"Her stupid photographer friends are not working with us." Rosa says in the background.

"What did she expect?" I ask.

Emma walks in the store. She finds us in the office. I look at her. She looks at me and looks guilty of something.

"Emma, what's going on?" I ask her.

"That's my first booking." She says.

"Emma, you do fittings. You don't do bookings. You are not authorized to do bookings."

"Well someone had to do them. You got fired. Beth was arrested. What was I supposed to do?"

"Close the store. That's our policy."

"We have a policy that if your boss is thrown in jail and your coworker is fired that we are supposed to close?"

"I need your keys." I tell her.

"No."

"Why?"

"Because Bruce and I are running the shop."

"Bruce is a contractor. What does he know about wedding planning?"

"Bruce's mom is a wedding planner." Emma says.

"I am aware of that. She is the competition."

"She's been helping out." Emma says.

"Emma, that goes against our policy and you know it."

"Are you bringing up the policy to me again?"

Cody looks at me. "Hun, we have to go." He says. He takes my hand and the appointment books. He walks outside still holding my hand. Emma walks out with us.

Landon stands outside the bridal shop. He hugs Cody and me. He closes the door and padlocks it.

"What are you doing?" Emma asks.

I look at Landon. "How did you know?"

"I will drive you both home." Landon says.

Emma looks at Landon. "Why are you being so nice? We know what a jerk you really are."

I don't agree with her. Landon wronged me in college. He didn't do anything to Emma but turn her down.

Landon looks at me. "I hope that with time, you will see that I made a mistake back then and I am sorry that you were the one who took the blame for it." He looks at Emma. "Emma, I said no to you. I didn't want to date you. Bruce was my friend. You had him beat me up because you told him that I came on to you."

Bruce stands on the sidewalk behind Landon. "Is that true?"

Emma whips around. "He did come on to me." She says.

"Emma, tell your parents thanks for a lovely lunch. I will talk to you soon." I look at Cody and Landon. "Can we go?"

"You have all that you need?" Landon asks.

Then I remembered why I came back in the first place. "Can you open the doors for a quick minute? I remember why I came back here." I say. "I just have one thing that I need to get."

Landon unlocks the door and holds it open for me.

I rush back in and go back into my office. I open all the drawers of the desk. "Where is it?" I ask to no one. I close the drawers and open them again like some how I think what I am looking for is magically going to appear. "Where is it?" I ask again.

Cody stands in the doorway. "What are you looking for?"

"Something I have had for years." I say.

"What is it?"

"A signed autographed picture."

"Who signed a picture?" Cody asks.

"You did. I had it in my desk for a long time. Its gone." I open the drawers again and look through everything. I slam the drawer and catch my finger. "Ouch!" I scream.

"I will sign another one for you." He says. He stands in front of me and takes my hand in his hand. My finger is throbbing and he can feel it. "How did you get a signed picture of me?"

"I bought it at a silent auction."

He looks at me. "The person who paid for that picture paid a lot of money."

Landon walks in the room. "Everything ok?" He asks.

"I can't find something that I know I left here." I say.

"What is it?"

"An autographed picture."

Landon looks at me. "My dad has it."

We both turn our heads and look at him. Cody looks at Landon. "Why?"

"He didn't know if Crystal." Landon looks at me. "He didn't know if you would come back here." He looks back at Cody. "Crystal has it in a frame that must have cost a bundle."

They both look at me.

"Why?" Cody asks.

"Why what?"

"Why do you have it?"

"Because no matter how many awful things I heard people say about you, in my heart I knew that couldn't be true." I look at Cody. "You paid my hospital bills."

Landon looks at me. "When were you in the hospital?"

"I was in an accident. My car crumbled around me. They had to take me out with the jaws of life."

"When?"

"A few years back." I say. I look at Cody. "I need that picture."

"Why?" They both ask.

"It has the contract in the frame."

"What contract?" They both ask again.

"The one that I had drawn up by a lawyer that guarantees that I own this place no matter what. It guarantees that I can't get fired and can't be undermined." I look at Landon. "I need that picture." I say.

"Why didn't you tell my dad? Why didn't you say anything?" Cody asks.

"To be honest, I forgot all about it. Not the picture. But the contract. The lawyer sent me an email when he drove by and saw that the shop was sold. He told me that no one can buy it from Beth because when I allowed her to buy me out, I didn't allow her to buy me out of the building."

Landon looks at me. "What lawyer would do that?"

"Jake Jackson."

Both brothers look at each other.

"We should go." Landon says. He looks at me. "How much did you pay for that picture of Cody?"

"It was a silent auction. The price I paid for it is confidential."

"Did Jackson tell you that?" Landon asks.

"It was an anonymous purchase." Cody says.

Landon looks at Cody. "Well now we know who bought it. Its no longer anonymous."

"Landon!" I snap. "Let it go!" I push past the two of them and go into the bathroom. I use the bathroom and then leave the store.

A half hour later, Landon pulls off at a rest area because I have to go to the bathroom. Cody gets my wheelchair out of the trunk. I get in it and take my purse. I rush into the building and find the lady's room. I come out of it immediately. Cody and Landon are standing waiting for me.

"Did you go?" Cody asks.

"No its out of order." I say.

Landon runs to the men's room. He runs back. "We will stand guard." He says.

"She can't go in there." Cody says.

"I have to." I say. "The companion bathroom is out of order too."

Landon takes my hand. He jogs across the building to the bathroom and he stands outside the door while I go in. Cody stands next to him. He looks at Cody. "How much to the picture go for?"

"Four." Cody says.

"Four?"

"Yes."

"She paid four thousand dollars for a signed picture of you?"

"Apparently."

Landon looks at Cody. "You know, when I was in school with her and people would talk baseball her hearing was perked. She would sit reading a book or working on a paper and she would listen to what was being said. When anyone ever mentioned you — they did because they knew it pissed me off when they talked shit— when they mentioned you, she would pack up her stuff and leave the area. I thought that it was because she didn't like me. She left a paper on the table that she was sitting at and I took it. I read it over and over. She wrote on it. That everyone who was talking didn't know a thing about you and didn't know or understand the good you bring to the world. I didn't know what she was referring to."

"I was watching television with Kyle. We were in our apartment and I watched on the news an accident that they were covering. The accident was bad. Her car rolled over, they showed it over and over again."

"Did you know it was her?"

"No."

"Why did you pay for her hospital bills?"

"That's kind of my thing." Cody says. He looks at the door. "She's been in there a long time." Cody says. He opens the door and comes in. "Crystal?"

"Cody! The door won't open."

He pushes on it. "Which way does it go? In or out?"

"I don't know." I say honestly.

"Was it inside with you or did you pull it closed?"

"Neither." I say.

"Well then how did the door shut?"

"It just slammed." I say. "Cody!"

"Wait, let me get Landon."

"Cody!" I yell.

"What?"

"I am stuck."

"I know."

"No! I am stuck. When the door slammed, I started falling. I am stuck. I can't hold on much more." I say.

He calls for Landon. "Landon!" He yells.

Landon runs in the bathroom. "What's going on?"

"She's stuck." Cody says.

"I am falling!" I say with a shaky voice.

Cody slides under the door. In one quick move, he grabs me. I really can't fall because I am caught on the toilet dispenser and my wheelchair. "Landon, it seems that we need you in here too." Cody says.

"Cody!" I say. "I am going to fall."

"You are caught up so good, you can't fall." He says.

Landon lifts the door on the hinges and the door pops open. He looks at me. He puts his hands on my waist and lifts me up. Cody supports me from underneath. I wrap my arms around Cody.

"You are ok." They both say together.

A guy walks in the bathroom who works in the facility. "What the hell is going on in here?"

"The disabled stalls are out of order." Landon says.

"They are."

"Its against the law for all of them to be out of order." Landon says.

"This door gets stuck and the toilet paper dispenser drops out." The guy who works there says.

"It seems like that's how my wife got caught." Cody says.

Landon moves my wheelchair. My purse strap breaks and my purse dumps out all over the floor. The contents goes all over the place.

Cody is still holding me in his arms. "Lets get the hell out of here." He says.

"My stuff is all over the floor." I say.

"Take her, I will get her purse and all her stuff." Landon says.

We sit at a table in the service area. I am in my wheelchair. Cody sits next to me. Landon is on line getting us something to eat. He is at the chicken fast food restaurant line. When he has the food, he walks over. I watch women walk by and look at Landon. They turn and look at him a second time. Landon doesn't notice.

"How are you doing?" Landon asks.

"I am sad about my purse."

"Women are always so attached to their bags."

"I bought that purse with my first paycheck. I only have three purses."

"Three?" They both ask together.

"My mom has like three thousand. My sister has a couple hundred purses. Why do you only have three?" Cody asks.

"I donate them when I am done with them." I say. "I think that I am fortunate enough that I can buy an expensive purse. I love my purses, but when I am done using it, I am not going to use it again." I look around us and then look at the two of them. "I know how that sounds, but—"

"Stop." Cody says. "You don't have to explain yourself. My mom and sister should take a page out of your book and follow your lead."

"Your mom and sister give back in their own ways." I say.

"What do you know of their giving?" Cody asks.

"I am sure that you both know the good that your mom, dad and sister do."

Cody looks at Landon. "I can honestly say no." He laughs.

"We should get going soon." I say.

Before we go to the car, Cody checks out the bathrooms to see if they have been fixed. And the only one that I can still use is the men's room. I go into the bathroom and use it quickly and come out fast. Cody waits for me.

We get back in the car. Landon and Cody sit in the front seat. I sit in the backseat. Cody puts his head back on the headrest and falls asleep within a few minutes of us being back on the road.

Landon keeps his eyes on the road ahead of us and watches me in the mirror at the same time. I look up and see that he is watching me.

"What are you thinking?" I ask him.

"Nothing." He says.

"Make something up. We are still two hours from Fort Lauderdale." I say.

"How come you stuck up for him?" Landon asks me.

"It was the right thing to do. The woman looked at him and was all flirty and I wouldn't have said anything at all, but then she just turned into the biggest bitch. She was saying how rude he is and calling him names. I just said something quietly. I didn't think anyone heard me. Apparently Cody did." I look at Landon. "I really wish I could have stood up and threw myself at him and kissed him on the lips yelling Oh My God, its Cody Parker."

Landon laughs. "No girl has wanted to yell Oh my God, its Landon Parker."

"You rub people wrong." I say.

"Ouch! Don't hold back." He says.

"Landon, I don't mean anything bad by it. You just seem like you throw yourself in people's faces. Its like you try too hard for people to see you."

"I always feel like I go unseen."

"Trust me, you catch people's eyes. Women notice you. We should have had this conversation at the service station. I would have pointed out all the women who were watching you."

"They were looking at Cody."

"Not everyone notices him. You both look so different. Both of you are very attractive. Extremely attractive. Cody—" I start to giggle.

"What about him?" Landon asks. He looks over to see that Cody is still sleeping. He looks completely relaxed.

"I always noticed that he was nice. When I went to games, he was always taking time to thank the fans for coming and showing their support. Then when he stepped up to the plate and hit grand slam home runs. Oh my god, he made baseball fun to watch. It wasn't like he was a one hit wonder. He could do it every time he was up to bat. But he knew the pitchers that were trying to strike him out. He knew their games better than they knew his. If they struggled, he didn't take advantage of it. He would hit a base hit. If the pitcher was an asshole he would crack it."

"How do you know this?" Landon asks.

Chapter Eleven

Landon pulls the car into my driveway. Its late. Its almost midnight. Cody gets my wheelchair out of the trunk. I get in it. I take my broken purse and get my keys out. I unlock the door and look back at both of them.

"Landon, did you want to stay the night?" I ask.

"I should go home." He says.

"Stay the night." Cody insists. "You have been driving all day."

We go into the house. Landon looks around once he steps inside. "Its bigger than it looks."

I laugh. "I know right."

"Wow, this place is cute."

"Make yourself at home. I am going to change my clothes." I tell them. I go into my room and close the door.

Cody and Landon sit on the couch. Landon looks at Cody. "She knows a lot about you."

"She does know a lot about me."

"Do you know much about her?"

"Everything I learn makes me love her even more."

"Cody, she knows things about you that no one else does."

"Landon, I know she knows a lot about me."

"She thinks that I am a jerk. She told me that every woman in the rest stop noticed me. I haven't had a girl friend in almost a year."

"She called you a jerk?"

"Not right out." Landon looks around. He stands and walks over to look at the pictures that are hanging on the wall. He looks at the one that I am holding up Cody's jersey. Landon looks at Cody. "We were at this game." He sees a picture of him and me smiling. He smiles. Crystal has a picture of me. He thinks and smiles again.

"I didn't know." Cody says.

"Did you know her then?"

"No. I met her on a flight. I went to school with Kyle. Kyle stayed in touch and he was always so great because he never asked me for tickets or anything free." He looks at the picture of me holding his jersey and the smile on my face. "If I would have known that Crystal is his sister, I would have put them in my section. It would have been nice to have someone cheering me on."

Landon looks at Cody. "Do you think she is ok?"

Cody walks over to my bedroom door and opens it. He walks into my room and sees that I am sprawled out on my bed wearing a tank top with his number on it and underwear. He walks over and kisses me on the lips. "Sleep well." He says.

He returns to the other room and looks at Landon. "She's sleeping."

"I sent dad a text message about the picture that he has."

Cody looks around the room. He sees photo albums that he didn't see before. He sits on the couch and looks through one.

I am little in the first picture. I am sitting in a high chair smiling brightly. I have both my arms raised above my head. Landon looks at the picture. Cody looks at Landon. "Tell me about her at school.

"We weren't friends." Landon says.

"You took classes with her. Tell me about her. What did you observe about her? You are a really good judge of character."

"You think so?" Landon says.

Cody turns the page. I am wearing a tutu while standing on my walker. I have one arm raised above my head. "We should show this to Gianna."

"Awe, she is so cute." Landon says. He looks at the picture. "She was always just so nice. If anyone asked her questions, she would always take the time to talk to them. When people talked baseball around her, she would listen intently. When someone would misspeak, she wouldn't argue, she would pack up her stuff and leave the area. She would mumble under her breath, assholes."

Cody looks at his brother and laughs. "She didn't argue?"

"Nope."

"Why?" He asks.

"I don't know." He says. The teddy bears that are wearing Cody's jersey sits on the shelf. Landon picks them up. "What the hell is this?"

"She apparently bought all of them." Cody says. "When I got mugged, they released the bears at the next game. I asked the staff at the stadium if I could get one. A few days later, I was told that there were none left."

"Well you had a lot of fans." Landon says trying to be nice.

"No. That's just it. I know that I didn't have a lot of fans. There were guys that I played with who had more fans and the stuffed animals were always left. We were told that they weren't good sellers. Mine were all gone."

"Maybe people wanted to show support when you were hurt." Landon says.

Cody looks at the stuffed animal. "Did mom and dad care?" He asks quietly.

"Yes. Of course they did. Mom flew back from Spain and dad was at the hospital."

"He was never at the hospital."

Landon lays on the couch and watches television. He falls asleep. Cody sits with my photo album on his lap. He flips through it. One picture catches his attention. He takes it out of the album and looks at it. I am standing on my walker with my braces on my legs. My knees hyperextend or roll back. My toes are elevated because I am standing on my heels. Cody looks at the picture. He really studies it.

I get up to use the bathroom. When I finish, I hear the television. I leave my room and watch Cody studying a picture in his hand. "Hi." I say.

He looks at me. "Hi."

"What are you doing?"

"Looking at your pictures."

I look at Landon. "I have an extra room. Landon might be more comfortable in the guest room."

"He's fine." Cody says. Cody looks at the picture. He sees again that I am standing with the aid of my walker. I am again wearing braces on my legs and my knees are hyperextended. I am standing on my heels. He looks around.

"What are you looking for?" I ask him.

"Do you still use your walker?"

"Yes." I say.

"I have never seen it." He looks at the picture. "Where is it?"

"In my room." I say.

"Show me." He says. He gets up and takes my hand. We go back in my room. He looks around my room.

"Cody, what are you looking for?"

"Your walker." He says.

I maneuver my wheelchair to the side of the bed where my walker stands folded next to the wall. I open it up. I push it to the end of the bed so that I have room to stand up. I take my feet off the hangers. I stand up and walk to Cody. I stand holding on to the walker. "What is it that you want to see?" I ask him. "What were you studying in the pictures that you were looking at?"

"Just stand there." He says. He steps closer to me. "I have done research on cerebral palsy." He tells me.

I don't say anything. I just stand with the aid of my walker. I shift my weight from one leg to the other.

"What's wrong?" He gets on his knees next to me and runs both hands up my legs from my ankle to my knee. He rubs his hands back down to my calf.

"I don't usually stand in one place on my walker. I usually use it to walk with."

"Can you just stand for a little while longer?" He asks. He looks me up and down.

"What are you trying to see?"

"In the pictures I noticed that you were standing more on your heels then flat on your feet. But now you are standing flat on your feet."

I sit back in my wheelchair. "I can explain that to you." I say.

He moves my walker and gets on his knees in front of me. He takes my barefoot in his hand. He flexes my foot.

"Cody, what are you doing?"

He lifts my leg so that its extended straight in front of me. "Does this hurt?"

"No."

"I went to school for sport's medicine." He looks at me. "You think that's stupid?"

"Cody!" I say loudly.

Landon jumps off the couch and bursts into my room. "Everything ok?"

I laugh. "Everything is fine."

"Cody? Why are you holding her leg up? Is this part of something kinky that is going to happen?"

I laugh. Cody glares at him.

"Are you doing something that is sports med related?" Landon asks.

"Cody, can I have my leg back?" I ask him.

"Can you lay on the floor?" Cody asks me. He looks at Landon. "Get out."

"Its four in the morning." Landon says.

"Out of the room." Cody says. "Get out of the room."

"Show me what you do." Landon says. He sits on the floor next to him.

Cody looks at me. "Can I help you get on the carpet?"

"Can I put clothes on?" I ask. I am in my underwear and a tank top. I take the brakes off my wheelchair and push my wheelchair over to the dresser. I take out leggings and another shirt.

"You don't have to change." Cody says.

"I am putting clothes on." I take the pants and put one leg at a time and then I stand up holding on to the dresser. Both Cody and Landon see the dresser pulling away from the wall. They both run to hold it in place while I quickly pull my pants up. I sit in my wheelchair quickly.

Landon moves the dresser to see if there is anything on the back of it that can be used to secure it to the wall.

Cody is hugging me. "Oh my god, I saw the dresser falling on top of you."

"I didn't think about it. I usually test to see if surfaces are secured. In my last place that I lived it was. I should have checked it." I say.

Landon looks at me. "Do you have tools?"

"What?" I ask.

"Do you have tools?"

"No." I laugh when I think of myself using tools.

"I will secure your furniture to the walls for you." Landon says.

"I can tell my brothers to do it or my dad for that matter." I say. "I am sure that my dad would love to come over and tell me how silly I was for not testing the—"

Cody kisses me on the lips. "No!" He says. "You didn't know. It didn't happen." He says. "I want you on the floor."

I laugh. "You have had me on the floor." I say.

This catches both brothers off guard. Landon looks at each of us and laughs. Cody kisses me passionately on the lips. Landon takes his phone out of his pocket and takes a picture of us. We are lost in each other. Landon captures the intimacy just like Oscar did.

Landon clears his throat. "Cody, how about you do your evaluation of Steele in the morning." He called me Steele. I look at him. "Cody, its in the middle of the night. I want to watch how you are going to evaluate her, but I am exhausted." He looks at both of us. "You both look exhausted too."

"Tomorrow it is." Cody says.

Landon leaves the room. He walks back in and walks across to where I am and takes me in his arms. He hugs me tight against him and kisses the top of my head. "Good night." He says. He hugs Cody and then leaves the room again.

I am laying on the floor on my back. Cody is sitting on the floor holding my leg up. He supports my leg with his shoulder. He runs his hands down the back of my leg. My knee does hyperextend. Landon watches Cody. Cody lowers my leg and flexes my foot. After his evaluation both brothers tickle me. Cody lifts me in his arms and sits me in my wheelchair. Landon hugs me. I leave my room and order something for lunch for the three of us.

Cody leans against the dresser that almost toppled over on me. He looks at me. I look at him. "Talk to me." He says.

"What do you want to know?"

"Everything."

"In the pictures that you were looking at, I was standing on my heels. Its because I hyperextend my knees. With the braces that I used to wear all the time when I was young, they added support that was much needed, but they brought my toes up. So if I was tired or didn't think about what I was doing, I did walk on my heels more than I didn't. If I don't wear the braces, which I don't do as much now, I still hyperextend my knees but I don't walk on my heels."

"Does it hurt?" He asks sitting on the floor again taking my leg in his hands.

"It doesn't hurt." I tell him. "You said that you went to school for sports medicine. Why would you think that I would be surprised to know that?" I reach my hand out and touch his shoulder.

"Because everyone who learns that I have done sports med tends to think that I am too stupid to know what I am doing."

"Cody. You are anything but stupid. I am not surprised that you went into sports medicine. I am surprised that you say it like that and not that you graduated with a degree in physical therapy."

He raises up on his knees and gently puts my leg down. Then he takes me in his arms and crushes me in a hug. "Where the fuck have you been my whole life?" He asks. He kisses me tenderly. "Every time you open your mouth you speak so highly of me. You know more details of my life than my own fucking family does. And you make me feel like I am standing on a fucking mountain." He kisses me again. "People know Cody Parker."

"No." I tell him. "No, they think they know you. They think that you are just Cody Parker the injured baseball player." I say. I look at him seriously. "Why didn't you go back?"

"My arm hurt. Every time I tried to throw the ball I could feel all the muscles contract. They would tighten up. I would get a pain in my neck. It was worse when I tried to bat. I worked with trainers and physical therapists. I knew what I needed to do to get myself back on the field. But when I stood in the batter's box and I took my stance, everything froze up. My body tensed. I could hit a home run without even thinking about it. After my injuries, I couldn't hit a bunt if my life depended on it." He says.

"Do you think you will play again?"

"No. I think everyone is happier that I can't play."

"Not everyone." I tell him. "What made you become a security guard?" I ask.

He hugs me and talks against my ear. "I went to school with a girl who is disabled. She uses a wheelchair. She was stalked by an asshole teacher. I mean this fucker showed up everywhere she was. She fought back and got away from him on her own, but when my career fell apart, I thought about her a lot. She endured a lot of shit and there were guys who tried to protect her. They did a shitty job of it. When I was working as a guard, I didn't feel the pain in my ribs, my arm, and my neck. Everything that I went through, I thought of her. I thought to myself what she went through was so much worse than what I was going through."

"Cody, I love you." I tell him.

"Why?" He asks quietly against my ear.

"Why not?" I ask him.

"I am not all you think that I am." He says.

"You are so much more." I say it and mean it. "Cody, you should get off your knees. You might hurt yourself."

In one quick movement, he is on his feet and I am in his arms. "Tell me about you. Don't change the subject and talk about me. Tell me about you." He says and gets in my bed with me.

"Tell you about me." I say. "Um— its hard for me to talk about myself. There's nothing exciting about me. The most thrilling thing that has ever happened to me in my whole life was you kissing me."

"That can't be true."

"Cody, I am not blowing smoke up your ass. I am telling you the truth. I fear that I will never meet another person that will make me feel so enveloped in love."

"Is that something true."

I sit up in my bed and throw myself at him. I get on my hands and knees on the mattress and crawl up on the bed and then put my left arm across his body to the other side of the mattress and lay on top of him. I kiss his neck. I kiss his chin. I kiss his lower lip. I kiss his upper lip and then I push my tongue in his mouth.

He moans against my mouth. The moan vibrates against my lips. I push up on the mattress on either side of him and pull my body closer to him. "Let me help you." He says. Then he laughs. "Are you trying to seduce me?" I laugh against his neck. He moans again.

I lower my head and kiss his nipple. I put my hand flat on his belly. I run my hand up and down his chest.

"Crystal." He gasps.

I kiss his nipple again and again. It perks up to meet my lips. I suck his nipple in my mouth.

"Crystal, you are killing me." He says breathy. He pulls me up his body and uses his legs to spread mine. He slides his hand between our bodies. He touches the waistband of my leggings. He stops and sits up. He takes me in his arms and lays me back against the pillows. He gets on his knees next to me and pulls my pants and undies off of me. He pushes the tank top up on my chest and pulls it in one jerk over my head. He looks at my naked body and I squirm under his touch.

"Cody. Please!" I cry out.

He kisses my bottom lip. He then lowers his head to my nipple. He takes it in between his lips and sucks it in his mouth.

"Cody! Oh my god, Cody please!" I say.

He slips his hand down my body and palms my core. He then sticks his fingers inside me. My body convulses with an earth shattering orgasm. Cody kisses my lips. He captures my scream from my orgasm . He pushes his fingers deeper and pulls them back then pushes them in again. "I am going to enter you." He says against my lips.

"Please. Please. Please." I say.

He pulls away from me for a moment and pushes into me with a force that no one has ever attempted. He pulls back quickly and then pushes back into me. I feel like a virgin being ripped for the first time. I want to cry out but then he moves inside me and I feel him swell. My muscles grab him. He pulses a few times. He goes stiff with his own orgasm.

"Cody, please." I say. I grab the sheets in my fist. I pull the sheet up and feel my own orgasm coming from my toes. I feel energy surging up my legs. I feel it growing in my belly and then— "Cody!" I cry out.

He pulls out of me and gets off the bed in a flash. He goes into the bathroom. He comes back with a cloth. He gets back on the bed and he rubs the cloth over my body which is so sensitive. He rubs the sweat off of my chest. He runs the cloth down my flat belly and then between my legs.

I roll to my side and put my face in the pillow. I scream with the orgasm he forces from me. I breathe deeply. "I have to pee." I tell him. I get out of the bed and go into the bathroom. I get right in the shower.

Cody lays on the bed with his naked body covered by the sheet to his waist. He lays against my pillows and drapes his arm over his eyes.

I come back in the room and I get dressed. I close the lights in the room and get back in my bed. I move as little as possible to not wake Cody up. When I get settled in my bed, Cody rolls into me and puts his arm around me. "Sleep well." I whisper.

Landon enters my room with the tools that he needs to secure my furniture to the walls. Cody helps him in the room. Cody holds the furniture.

Landon secures the dresser and stands in front of it trying to pull it forward. It goes no where.

"Tell me about Crystal." Cody says to his brother.

Landon looks at him. "Why this again?"

"She finds it hard to talk about herself." Cody says. "She can open her mouth and tell me all about me. She can tell me all the good and the bad things about me."

"At least she's not delusional." Landon laughs.

Cody's phone rings. He reaches back on the night stand and answers it. "Hello."

"Mr. Parker, my name is Justine. I work at your gym." She says.

"Yes."

"I wanted to tell you that there is a woman here trying to workout and a few of the trainers won't allow her to continue."

"I will be right there." Cody says. He pushes his phone in his pocket. He looks at Landon. "We have to go to the gym."

Landon drives to the gym. They both jump out of the car and run into the gym. Cody walks over to find Justine. He knows her well because he hired her. Landon looks at Justine and smiles.

Cody looks around and sees me sitting on the leg press machine. The two trainers are standing there over me. They look pissed off. Cody stands there watching me.

I push my legs and move the machine just a little bit.

Landon walks over.

One of the trainers looks at me. "You are going to hurt yourself."

Cody and Landon each walk over closer and they each squat down on the side of the machine. Cody reaches underneath and changes the tension making it lighter. "One. Two. Three. Push. Push hard." Cody says.

"If my knees lock out—"

"We will release them. This is all you. Stand up." Cody says.

Landon looks at me. "Do it. You used to do this in the gym at school."

Cody looks at Landon. Cody feels my muscles shake. "Ready. Only when you are ready. Breathe. Push. One. Two. Three. Go!" Cody coaches me.

I push and my knees do lock so that I am laying down, but my legs are straight.

Landon slips his hands behind my knee as Cody directs him.

Cody looks at me. "One more." He says. "Want to do one more?"

"Yes." I say.

"Ok. When you are ready." He says.

I push half way and my legs shake. Cody and Landon both at the same time slip their hands under my legs and help me. When my knees lock out, they both hug me. They both release my knees. I reach my hand out to Cody and he helps me sit up. Landon picks me up and sits me in my wheelchair.

Cody looks at both of us. "Take her away from here."

I look at Cody. "Before I go, can I hug you?" I ask.

He steps in front of me and spreads his legs a bit. He hugs me tight.

"Thank you." I say to him.

"Don't thank me." He says kissing my lips.

I look at Landon. "Spar with me."

"You got it." He says. We both walk off to the boxing room.

Cody stands looking at his two trainers. He looks at Justine who has walked over to join them. He looks at her. "I need you to pull all of the staff together. We need to have a meeting in fifteen minutes.

He looks around. He looks at the two trainers that were giving me a hard time. He looks around again and his anger grows. He sees that I am doing the rowing machine. He never takes his eyes off me when he speaks to them. "I want to know why you both had a problem with Ms. Steele working out here."

They both look at Cody. One of them steps back. "I am sorry, who are you? And why do you care?"

Justine looks at the trainer like he has lost his mind. "This is Cody Parker. The owner of this gym. The one who pays your salary."

The second trainer looks at Cody. "I am sorry. I didn't know that you were here."

"I want everyone who walks in these doors to be treated the same as everyone else. Not everyone who walks in this building will be an athlete but that doesn't mean that they shouldn't be treated like one." Cody says.

Justine looks at Cody. "The staff will be ready in five minutes."

Cody finally breaks his stare and looks at Justine. "Thank you. Make sure that the music is loud because I may yell."

The second trainer looks at Cody. "I didn't have a problem with her working out. She has been here working out for a long time. The thing is she slipped getting on the equipment."

Cody walks quickly over to where I am. He takes the gloves away from me. I look at him. "Did you slip getting on the equipment?"

"I did, but I am ok." I say.

He gets on his knees in front of me and touches my legs, my arms, and my hands. "Did you hurt yourself?"

"Cody, I am fine. I broke a nail." I say. My finger has a band-aid on it. He can see that it was bleeding.

"Did you bleed a lot?" He asks.

"Cody, I am fine."

He takes my hand in his hand and takes the band-aid off my finger. He looks at my finger. My nails are my own but I get them done with acrylic to make them strong. The acrylic tip covering my nail broke breaking my nail with it. Cody squeezes my finger and it still bleeds. "Do you need stitches?"

I open my bag that is sitting next to my wheelchair and take out another band-aid. I open it and attempt to put it on my finger. "No stitches needed. I have broken a nail before. It will be ok."

Cody takes the band-aid from me. He opens the wrapper. He puts the band-aid back in the wrapper packaging and sticks it in his pocket. He stands and leans over me releasing the brakes from the wheels. He pulls my wheelchair back away from the equipment and pushes me into a private office. He pushes me up to the sink. He turns the water on and pumps soap into his hand. He takes my hand between his hands and washes my hand. He holds my bloody finger under the water. The water turns red running down the drain. "I think its going to need a stitch."

"Cody, it just needs a band-aid. It will be fine." I say to him.

He takes paper towels and dries my hand. He adds pressure to my finger. He feels it pulsing in his hand. "I think you need medical attention."

I laugh. "Just put the band-aid on it. It will be fine." I look at him.

"How did you slip?"

I shake my head. "I didn't plan it right." I say. That's not true. When I was getting on the leg press machine, the one trainer grabbed my arm. I don't know if he was trying to help or trying to prevent me from getting on the machine. I started falling so I put my hand on the machine and my nail caught.

"Don't cover up for my staff. I will fire all of them."

"No." I say.

"Crystal, I will look at the cameras and see what happened." Cody tells me.

My finger really hurts me. In reality it probably does need a stitch or two. It pulled my nail away from the nail bed. I have had nails break, but nothing like this. If I had the ability to jump up and down, I would. Its really that painful.

Cody takes the band-aid out of the wrapper again and wraps it around my finger. Cody looks at me and kisses me on the lips. "Come with me to this meeting that was just scheduled."

"Cody, I don't know." I say.

Landon comes into the private office with Justine. Landon walks over to me and sits on the table. "Wow, Steele. I saw you on the cameras working out, you are incredible."

"Thanks Landon." I say.

"How's your hand?" Landon asks. He takes my right hand in his hand. I wince. Cody takes my hand from Landon and runs his fingers over it. I again wince. Landon puts his hand on Cody's chest. "I can take her for x-rays."

"They can do it here." Justine says.

"I am fine." I say. The top of my hand is hurting me.

"Stop it." Cody says. "If you are in pain, say you are in pain."

"I am in pain." I admit.

"So your nail breaking is the least of it?"

"Oh no. Equally, I am in pain." I say. My hip hurts as well because I hit my hip trying to save myself from the fall. I can tell that I am bruised.

Landon looks at me. "Does anything else hurt?"

"Landon! For Christ sake, shut up." I say.

He lifts me out of my wheelchair. He holds me in his arms so that my right hip is away from him. "Check her hip." He says.

"Cody, I am ok." He pulls my pants away from my skin and sees my bruises.

Justine looks at all of us. "You can take her to the PT room and we can do the x-rays. I will tell the staff to plan for a staff meeting tomorrow."

"Thank you." Cody says. He takes me from Landon.

"Cody, put me in my wheelchair. I can find the PT room. You are going to strain yourself holding me."

"I can hold you." He tells me.

All I want to do is cry. If I was in a gym and I didn't know anyone, I would have found a private place. I would have found somewhere where no one could see me and I would cry. My finger on my left hand is hurting. The top of my right hand is hurting. My hip feels like its on fire.

Cody brings me in the room and puts me on the mat. Cody lays me flat on my back. He runs his hands up and down my body evaluating me for injuries. He puts his hand on the outside of my legs. He puts his hands under my leg and pushes a bit of pressure. He watches my reactions. "Am I hurting you?"

"No." I say honestly. "I just need to take a warm bath."

"Can you take a bath?"

"A shower." I say.

"Come, I will take you home and you can take a bath. I will get you out of it."

"Cody, am I keeping you from your life?" I ask.

"No. This is my life." He says. "Tell me what happened and how you got hurt." He gets on his knees and works his way around me. He slides his hands under my right hip and I cry out. He stands up and walks around me. He gets back on his knees and rolls me to him. He slides my pants down a bit and looks at the bruises on my hip. "How did that happen?"

"I kind of fell onto the machine when the trainer went to help me on the equipment."

"Help you on or keep you off of it?" He reaches up on a counter that looks like its floating on the wall. He gets an ointment in a tube and rubs it on my hip. "The ointment is going to get cold and then heat up." He rubs it hard. "I am going to push a bit harder. Its going to be painful but it will feel better. It doesn't feel like anything is broken."

"It hurts so much." I say.

"I know." He says tenderly. "I am going to push a bit harder." He says. He adjusts my pants so that he is not touching my skin any more. He takes his phone out of his pocket. "Landon, can you come to the PT room?" He puts his phone back in his pocket.

"Cody, can I just go home?" I ask.

"Yes. We are going to go home." He says.

Landon walks in. "What?"

"Just support her from behind." He says.

Landon gets on his knees behind me. His knees are at my side.

"I am going to just shift her back." Cody says.

"I got it." Landon says.

Cody kisses me on the lips. He leans me into Landon's knees. Then he presses his palm into my hip. I feel a jolt of pain and then its gone. He looks at me "You ok, sweetheart?"

"It feels better." I say honestly. "My hand still hurts like hell."

Cody lifts me into his arms. Landon walks over with my wheelchair.

Landon takes my hand in his hand again. He feels the top of my hand with his fingers. "Make a fist."

I do.

"Wiggle your fingers."

I do.

"Make a fist and rotate your wrist up and down and sideways." Landon says.

I make a fist and rotate my wrist. When I move it in a circle, a sharp pain shoots up my arm.

Landon takes my hand back in his hand and feels up my wrist. He rubs his fingers on either side of my wrist.

I look at Landon. "I thought you went to law school."

He looks at me with a smirk on his face. "Um no. Law school? No."

"I know you are a lawyer."

"I am now, but I have experience with sports medicine too. Actually you inspired me when we were in school together."

I look at him. "I inspired you?"

"You have no idea." He says. "Make a fist." When I do he takes my arm in both of his hands and assists me when I rotate my arm. "Its not broken. I think you bruised it good." Landon says. He looks at Cody. "You should wrap her hand and her wrist. She needs to be immobilized for a few days."

"Are you nuts? I need to be able to push my wheelchair. I have to be able to hold on to my wheelchair. I am not that hurt."

"You are too. Crystal." They both say together.

"It would just be a few days. You can let someone take care of you." Cody says.

I put my hand on my wheels and push myself out of the room. I gather my stuff which hurts my hand when I pick it up, but I do it anyway. I push my wheelchair as fast as I can to the door and try to leave.

They both block me. "Why won't you let anyone take care of you?" Cody asks.

I see Kyle and Brandon walking to the doors with Ashley. I turn quickly and look at both of them. "You called my family?"

"No." They both say.

Justine walks over. "They are members of the gym."

"Shit!" I say.

Cody takes me in his arms. "Let me take care of you."

"They are going to yell at me. They think they all know what's best for me. Please don't tell them that I got hurt." I say. "I should have stayed in Orlando. My family never knew what I was doing. They never gave a sh—"

The door opens and Kyle takes me in his arms. "Hi."

Brandon looks at me. "You ok?"

"She had a hard workout." Landon says.

Ashley looks at him. "What kind of workout?" She gets a grin on her face.

"Oh yes because that's what I do, I go to a public place to have sex." I say.

Brandon looks at Ashley. "What is wrong with you?"

Landon looks at my siblings. He looks at Cody. He looks at me. "If I can say one thing that I know is true about Crystal Steele, she always has class in everything that she does."

I look at Landon. I look around at my family. I look at Cody and Landon. "I will catch up with you later."

"Don't walk away!" Ashley says.

A member of the gym is walking in the doors and I push through the doors and to my car. I put my bag in the car. I get in my car as carefully as I can. I close the door and leave moments later.

Cody looks at my siblings. He looks at Ashley. "It was rude of you to insinuate that Crystal had sex in the gym."

She turns into Brandon. "I was only teasing her. I didn't mean anything by it."

Kyle looks at Ashley. "You have to understand, my mom, your mom, and now you have made her sound like a slut. I am telling you right now, it stops."

"Kyle, I didn't mean anything by it." She looks at Cody. "Why are you rushing into a relationship with her?" She looks at Kyle and Brandon. "Why are you allowing her to rush into a relationship?"

Brandon looks at Ashley. "Why do you think that we have any say in how she runs her life? She has been on her own since she was in college. She was on her own since she graduated high school. Kelsey, Kyle and I have no say in how she lives her life. Dad is a wimp and doesn't stand up to my mom. Your mom is always so supportive of Tally and now she is singing a different tune."

Ashley looks at Cody. "Why are you rushing into a relationship with my sister?"

"Love at first sight." Landon says.

Brandon looks at Landon. "You know my sister?"

"I went to college with her." He says.

Cody finally answers. "When anyone meets someone like your sister, in my case, when I met your sister my heart nearly leapt out of my chest. I know that I have found the love of my life." He looks at everyone "Excuse me.

Landon leaves with Cody. They get in the car and leave the parking lot.

Justine looks at my family. "I can't believe for one second that anyone would think anything bad about her. She is the kindest person in the world."

Kyle looks at her. "Thank you for saying that."

"I am not just saying that." Justine turns and walks away.

Kyle runs after her. "Justine, whats going on?"

"You don't even know her and she's your sister. You don't even try to see how wonderful she is. You didn't even notice that she got injured."

"I do know her." Kyle says.

"What do you know about her?"

"I know my sister."

Brandon walks over. "What do you mean she is injured?"

"She hurt her hip and her hand."

"We will check on her." Ashley says. "I am going to workout." Ashley flips her hair and turns to the treadmill.

Chapter Twelve

Mom and Stew sit at their table having a late breakfast. Kelsey and Ashley sit at the table with them. Stew looks at the three women around him. He loves them deeply. He watches them. He looks at mom after a long moment.

"What are you not asking?" Kelsey asks him.

"Have you spoken to your sister?" He looks at mom. "Have you spoken to your daughter?"

"She has been busy ignoring us." Ashley says.

"Its because you all have made her out to be slutty. My girl is anything but that. Have you been to her house?"

"I went." Mom says.

"Were you nice about it?" He looks at Kelsey and Ashley, "have you been to her house? Have you had her over at your homes?"

"Yes." Ashley says.

He looks at Kelsey. "You?"

She looks down at her plate and then pushes the food around on the plate. "I live on the third floor and there is not an elevator.."

"Have you asked if you could go to her house and spend time with her?" Stew asks.

"She is never alone anymore. She lives with Cody Parker."

"Didn't you like Cody Parker?" Mom asks.

"No." Kelsey and Ashley say together.

Mom looks at both of them. "Tell me what inspired her to want to know about baseball?"

"She wanted to connect with dad." Kelsey says. "Dad took the boys to baseball. Dad replaced us with Kyle and Brandon."

"Is that what you think?"

"All of us." Ashley says.

"So why baseball?" Mom asks.

"She was looking to connect with him. She sat with Brandon and had him teach her all the ins and outs of baseball. And he did. Kyle was really good. He was a great player. Brandon loves baseball, but he wasn't any good at it. He can break down all the parts of baseball. He taught it to Tally and she made a career out of it. Or she went to school to make a career out of it." Ashley says.

"No. She always wanted to be a wedding planner." Mom says.

"She never wanted to be a wedding planner. She took a job as Rosa's assistant. She was good at it. She has an eye for what works. She is great with the people. She is great with the staff. She is good at listening to details and then making it above and beyond what the wedding parties want." Kelsey says. "She does a lot to give back."

"What does that mean?" Mom asks.

"Do you know anything about her?" Stew asks.

"That's not fair." Mom says.

"Isn't it? You encourage her over the phone to go for her dreams and follow her heart. Then when she does you call her slutty." Stew says.

"She pulls away from me." Mom says.

"She pulls away from all of us." Ashley says.

"Do you reach out to her?" Stew asks. He looks at all of them.

Kelsey looks at all of them. "If she wants to get in touch with me, she knows where I am."

"If you want to get in touch with her, you know where she lives." Ashley snaps at Kelsey. "We were the ones that planned for her to see dad's houses."

"She is in Gulfport?" Stew asks.

"Yes." Ashley says.

Stew's phone rings. He looks at it and sees my face smiling at him. He excuses himself from the table and walks into his office. He closes the doors and sits at his desk. "Hello my sweet girl." He says.

"Stew, why couldn't you have been my dad?" I ask. "You always make me feel loved."

"What's going on?" He asks.

"I need some advice and I don't know who to turn to."

"What's going on?" He asks.

I tell him about the contract I have for the building. Its legally binding that it can't be sold without my approval. I tell him that Sawyer Parker bought the building and now that's were the problem stems. I don't want to create any problems for the family that I want so desperately to be apart of.

"Do you have the contract?" He asks me.

"I do."

"Do you want me to come to you?"

"Yes."

"Have you seen your family?"

"Not lately." I say.

"Why?"

"They seem to judge me. I think that I made a mistake."

"What's that?"

"Moving back here."

"Sweet girl, don't say that. If you didn't you wouldn't have met the love of your life." He says.

"Oh my god! Stew, I love him."

"I know you do." He says sweetly.

"Stew, I have never been with someone that makes me feel so loved in all my life. And his family is so nice and welcoming. Cody makes me believe in Disney fairytales. He makes me feel like I am the only woman on the earth." I get all giddy.

"When do I get to meet him?"

"You can come over." I tell him.

"I will be there in a half hour." He tells me.

"Stew."

"What?"

"I love you."

"I love you too." He says.

Cody and I sit on the couch. He sits with my legs over his legs. He rubs my hand that is still in a bandage. Its been a week since I got hurt in the gym. Cody rubs it gently.

Cody looks at me. "Have you seen anyone in your family?"

"Not lately." I say.

"Why do you pull away from them?"

"Because they don't always make me feel like they want to be with me. Or that they don't want me around." I look at Cody. "I don't ever get the feeling that my family misses me." I try to keep the sadness out of my tone.

The doorbell rings. Cody watches me get in my wheelchair before he jumps up to beat me to the door. He opens the door. Stew stands looking at Cody.

"Can I help you?" Cody asks.

Stew looks at him again. "I am looking for Crystal." Stew says smoothly.

I come up behind Cody. "Cody, stand down." I say with a bright smile. "This is Stew. Stew this is my Cody."

Cody steps aside and Stew takes me in his arms. He takes me in his arms the way I wish my dad would do, but never does. He used to hold me in his arms when I was little and I would feel like the world could shatter and I wouldn't notice. That's the way that I feel as Stew holds me in his arms. That's the way I feel when Cody holds me in his arms.

Stew kisses the top of my head. "My beautiful girl."

"How are you doing?" I ask.

He hugs me again. When he stands straight, he looks at Cody. "Mr. Parker, its good to see you again." Stew says.

Cody extends his hand and when Stew takes Cody's hand they embrace. "Doc! Its good to see you."

"You know each other?" I ask. I know that they know each other.

Cody looks at Stew and then at me. "Stew is the one who did my surgery for my shoulder."

Stew puts his hands on Cody's shoulder and pushes his fingers into his flesh. "Any tenderness?"

"Not anymore." Cody says.

"Have you been practicing?"

"No. Those days are over." Cody admits.

"I know that you were cleared to play." Stew says.

"Its been too long." Cody says.

Stew looks at me. "Maybe you can convince him to go back to his first love."

I smile at Stew. "I would love to be in his family box seating screaming as loud as I did when I was just a fan." I say.

Cody looks at me. "You say that and mean it, don't you?"

Stew doesn't let me answer. He speaks for me. "Even if it was just one game and you struck out every time you were at bat, she would scream loud cheering you on with every ounce of her heart."

Cody looks at Stew. "Doc, I mean no disrespect to you, but I am going to kiss her."

"Please, son. Kiss my girl. The Whole world has seen the way you kiss her." He looks at me. "If it makes you feel better, I will put your favorite cookies in the oven for you."

"You made my favorite cookies?" I ask and get excited.

"Yes. Always." He says. He walks into the kitchen and opens the oven. He looks around the kitchen and it is large. He puts the oven on and puts the cookies on the counter waiting for the oven to heat up. He walks around the house.

Stew looks at all the pictures hanging on the walls. There are pictures of Stew and me. He turns around and looks at the two of us. Cody is still kissing me. "Leave her some oxygen."

We laugh.

"You have pictures of me?"

"Stew, you are my dad." I say.

"Don't say that in front of your dad." He says putting his hands on his chest and closes his eyes briefly like he knows something that no one else does.

"I will say that in front of the whole fucking family. My dad would pick Kyle and Brandon over his girls everyday. He would pick his wife over me every chance he gets."

"Your dad loves you."

"Stew, he knows where I live. I am in one of his houses. He sent me flowers. He never came here once. I have been here almost two months."

The oven beeps indicating that its at the set temperature. Stew puts the cookies in the oven. He comes back in the room with us and looks at us. "Did you ask him to come over? Did you invite your mom and your sisters? Did you invite Jo—?" He makes a gagging noise.

We laugh.

"Stew, when Kels moved into her apartment on the third floor mom threw her a housewarming party. When Ash moved in with Brandon she threw them a housewarming party. When I moved here, I got matching flowers from mom and dad and then they called me a slut." I look at Cody. "Did I leave anything out?" I look back at Stew. "Did she tell you that I was back?"

"Sweetheart, Ashley and Brandon told me that you moved here. I was at the resort when you first arrived. I am the one who took the picture of you and Cody. I sent it to my sister and she put it on Facebook." Stew says.

The two of us look at him. Cody looks at me. "I thought that your photographer friend took the pictures of us."

"Oscar did take a few of the pictures. The initial photo of Lover Boy kissing the beautiful stranger was my doing." Stew says.

"Why didn't you let me know that you were there?" I ask. "I could have used a father's love."

"Sweetheart, I saw you were in good hands."

"Want to see my house?" I ask him.

"It's a she shed." Cody says.

Stew throws his head back laughing. "Oh my god, Parker, that's rich!" He looks around. "Cody, how is your family doing?"

"They are great. Thanks for asking." Cody says.

We sit on the couch and visit for a long time. Stew watches us interact with one another. He takes mental notes that we never stop touching one another. He notices that when one of us talks the other listens intently to the other.

The smell of the cookies burning causes Stew and Cody to jump off the couch. The kitchen fills with smoke. Stew opens the oven and takes the cookies out of the oven and puts the cookie sheet right in the garbage.

Cody looks at Stew. "You come for one visit and you try to burn down her she shed."

The two of them laugh in the kitchen. He stays a while longer. He takes pictures of the inside of the house to show mom. He doesn't leave until I have fallen asleep on the couch with my head resting on Cody's leg.

"Don't get up." Stew says. "I will let myself out. Cody, take care of my girl."

"Let's get together and have lunch." Cody says.

"I will be in touch, son." He says.

"Stew, can I ask you a question?" Cody looks at me and continues rubbing my shoulder with his fingertips. "Why hasn't Kelsey reached out to her? Why hasn't her mom come to see her? Do you know what my family did for her?"

"She told me. She cried tears of joy that your parents put a ramp in the entrance of their house so that she could come and go freely. She was elated. She was so surprised."

Cody looks at me again and runs his fingers through my hair. "Stew, you should hear her. She talks so highly of me. She makes me feel like I am on cloud nine. The way she talks about me. The way she builds me up, how do I even come close to doing that for her?"

"Just love her."

"Stew, I have never had anyone be that supportive of me. My parents didn't even know all the things that I have done both on the field and off of it."

"Cody, its something that you and my sweet girl have in common. You do all these remarkable things and you don't tell anyone that you do it, how do you expect them to know?"

"She knows. She knows more than anyone ever once tried to find out about me."

"Tell me something." Stew says looking at me. He looks at Cody.

"Anything"

"Why did you kiss her?"

"I couldn't let her get away." Cody says and rubs my shoulder again.

"What does that mean?" Stew sits back down on the couch across from Cody.

"We were on a flight together. There was a woman who looked up when she saw me coming down the isle to my seat. She was flirty at first. The guy sitting next to her called her out on it. She had recognized who I was and then she started talking shit." He looks down at me again. He looks back at Stew. "Crystal said in a low voice that they shouldn't talk shit about people that they don't know."

"You heard her?"

"I thought I made it up. But then the couple kept talking shit and Crystal got mad and called them stupid people. We were on a second flight together and she was doing work on her iPad. I watched her close it in anger and shove it in her bag. Then she closed her eyes and she fell asleep. I sat next to her. I traded my seat with a woman who couldn't get a seat with her children. She was grateful. I was grateful that I had a chance to sit next to an angel. She slept the whole flight so I didn't get a chance to talk to her. Then I lost sight of her when we were in the airport. When she came into the lobby of the resort, the only thing that I wanted to do was kiss her. I couldn't get enough of her. I didn't want to stop kissing her.

"Then the next morning I woke up and I thought I was dreaming. I heard her laugh. I heard her yell. When she saw me laying in the other bed, she didn't seem scared. She seemed like she was stuck in a dream herself." He looks up at Stew. "I had to battle with myself not to jump out of bed and kiss her. All I wanted to do was kiss her. Then my fucking cousin helped get her fired and I wanted to take Crystal in my arms and leave." He looks down at me. "She is so strong."

"She has worked very hard to be as strong as she is. She is just this close." He holds his fingers close together. "She is this close from falling apart." Stew says.

"I will try to keep her from doing that."

"Are you serious that you want to marry her?"

"I have never wanted anything more in my life. I love her. I want to know as much about her as she knows about me. She knows my whole life. She knows things that I never told anyone."

"Try to get her to have her family come and see her house." Stew says. He stands and walks over to the couch and kisses me on the head. He kisses Cody on the top of his head. "Keep in touch."

"Thank you."

I wake up in my bed and sensations fill me. I reach my hand down between my legs and Cody stops me. He pushes deeper in me and I cry out. "Cody, plea-se. Oh god, Cody. More. Please. More."

"Like this?" He asks and he pulls back.

"No. Deeper."

"Like this?" He asks and pushes in.

The orgasm grips me and steals my breath. My inner muscles pulse. I tighten around Cody and then there are fireworks erupting. "Cody, kiss me." I say.

He does and pulls back before he pushes deeper again. "Crystal, you have to relax." He tells me.

"Cody!" I cry out. My body stiffens uncontrollably.

"Crystal, you have to relax."

For a moment, I see stars. Its like I left earth and I am in the Milky Way. I pant for breath. My body flails under Cody. He pushes deeper again and then his body goes stiff. He puts his hand under my head and puts his mouth on mine. There is hunger in his kiss.

"Crystal." He says quietly.

I open my eyes.

"I am going to pull out." He says. In one quick movement he is out of me and leaves me feeling empty and incomplete. He gets out of my bed and enters the bathroom. He comes back moments later.

I hold my arms out to him. He comes back and lays next to me. We lay with our naked bodies together. I run my fingers in his hair. He pushes his fingers inside me.

"Don't be upset." He says.

"Why would I be upset?"

"I invited Stew over with your mom and sisters. Kyle is going to come too. He may bring your dad."

"Come where?" I ask him smiling.

"Not funny."

"Did you invite your family too?"

"You want my family to come?"

I roll into him. I look him in the eyes. "Cody, your family— even Landon has made me feel more love from a family than my family has my whole life. I want them to be here. I know they are busy, but—" I close my eyes as he pushes his fingers in deeper. He toys with my sex.

"Stop. I will invite them." He says and kisses me.

"Cody."

He smiles at me. "Crystal."

"My family isn't always nice."

"Its going to be fine." He says. He notices my insecurity when it comes to my family. "I am going to be here. Stew and my dad will be here. Your family will be fine. Maybe they wanted you to invite them over."

"The thing is, I don't need anything from them. I have been on my own since I was in college. I mean I had Kyle, Kelsey and Brandon. But my parents kind of stayed away and I guess that was my doing because each of them thought that they other one was there for me."

"Why?"

"Because my mom always competes with Joanna and my dad thinks that he doesn't measure up to Stew."

"Does he?"

"My mom and Stew have an on-again off-again relationship, but he was always there for me. I don't know if he was there for Kelsey and Ash, but he was for me. I don't know how he did it but he would show up to things that I had at school that I never mentioned to my parents. Kyle would come. Kelsey would come. Stew was always there. When I graduated from high school and college my mom was on one side of the auditorium. My dad was on the other side. Stew was right in the middle." I look at him. "Your mom was at my college graduation."

"My mom? How is that?"

"She was the speaker. She gave a very inspirational speech."

"My mom?"

"Yes."

"What did she say?"

"You can watch it."

"I would like that."

"She gave the commencement speech and I wondered if she ever told you the same thing."

"I don't know what she said."

"When we get out of bed, I will show it to you."

"I bet you graduated top of your class."

"Um no. I was in the top twenty."

"Your parents must have been so proud of you."

"They never said."

"Maybe you can invite some of your friends over." Cody says. He again toys with my sex and my inner muscles grip his fingers. He kisses my lips as the orgasm over powers me.

"I was thinking the same of you." I smile against his lips.

My house is not big by any means. Cody teases me about it and refers to it as a she shed. To be honest, its not much bigger than that. It is spacious and feels homey to me. With three full sized bedrooms and an office off the kitchen, it does offer room. There is no formal dining room but I I have two tables. The kitchen is spacious. When I was buying the house, I had actually looked at the larger model and thought that was what I purchased.

My family is coming and it seems that I can't get my house clean enough. I have dusted the furniture and vacuumed the floors over and over again. I mop the floors two times. I see streaks on the floors.

Cody has gone to the grocery store to pick things for lunch. When he gets back he walks in the house. He looks around. He sees me in my office. He walks in. "What's the matter?"

"Its not clean enough." I say.

"Crystal, Stew could perform surgery in this house." He says. He again sees my insecurity. "Crystal, they are going to be happy to see you. I am sure that they are going to be happy that you invited them." He kisses me and I melt against him. "Crystal be confident." He tells me.

"Cody, your dad is going to be so mad."

"What? Why do you say that?"

"When the papers were drawn up for me taking ownership of the bridal shop, there was a clause in it stating that the building couldn't be sold without my knowledge. I know what your dad did was for me, but now he is going to be sued for interfering."

"Crystal, my dad has good attorneys."

"I just don't want him to not like me."

"That's not possible." Sawyer says from behind us startling both of us. "Today is a day to celebrate. We will talk about the bridal shop tomorrow or in a few days. Your lawyers have contacted me on behalf of the building and I want you to know that I did what I did to put a freeze on it so that Beth and Lee couldn't do anything to screw you out of money." He says. He looks at the two of us. "You should lock the doors. I walked right in." He says smiling.

"Is mom here with you?"

"She is coming with Gianna and her boyfriend."

"Catalina has a boyfriend?" I ask and laugh."

Cody and Sawyer laugh along with me. "Very funny." Sawyer says.

My mom is the first of my family to arrive. I open the door and let her in. She has been here before when I had first moved in. She hasn't been back since that first time. When she walks in the front door of my house, she is in awe.

I have changed a few pictures. I have added more pictures of my family. Me with my mom, me with my dad, me with my siblings and me with Stew. There are also pictures with me and Cody. I have little two-by-two photo images of Joanna. There is a large ten-by-twelve of Stew, Cody and me. It is not a real photo. The three of us had never been photographed together.

When he came to spend the day with us, we found it hanging on the wall and I laughed so hard because right next to the largest picture on display was the smallest picture of Joanna. Stew did it and I left it.

One of the pictures of my mom and me is one of my favorites. We were both wearing basic black dresses. It was for an event for Kelsey. Oscar had taken it to surprise me. It was a really nice moment caught because we were actually both happy to be with each other. Those moments didn't happen often enough.

The picture of me with my dad was at the brunch at the resort. Oscar had taken that picture too. From the angle of it, it appears that I am sitting on my dad's lap.

Mom looks at all the pictures. Kelsey follows mom and looks at them too. She sees the one of Joanne and laughs. She looks at me. There are pictures of me with Cody and his family. Mom looks at those pictures for a while.

"Dad is going to be mad." She says.

"What are you talking about?" I ask.

"Could the picture be any smaller?" Kelsey asks.

"I didn't do that." I say.

"Who did?"

Before I can say anything, Stew stands behind me. He puts a supportive hand on my shoulder. "I did."

Mom looks at the picture of Stew, Cody and me. It looks like a real image. It looks like we are at his favorite place in Fort Lauderdale. "This is lovely." Mom says.

"Oscar took it." He says about my former boyfriend who turned out to be my friend. When I look at the picture, I know that Oscar did in fact take separate pictures of me, Cody and Stew.

Mom looks at the picture. She looks at Stew. "That was from our anniversary." She says.

"I am aware of what the image was first of." Stew says.

"Why not have Oscar take a real picture of the three of you?"

"He will."

"I will what?" Oscar asks. At the sound of his voice I turn and he takes me in his arms. "Hi girlfriend." He says.

"Hi Oscar." I say.

"Thanks for inviting me to your house."

I look at him and smile. "Could you have made her any smaller?"

He looks at all of us because Joanne and my dad aren't at my house yet. "I tried making it a postage stamp size but we thought that it would go overlooked."

I clearly didn't know he was going to say that. I laugh. I throw my head back and laugh. "Oscar!" I say.

He kisses me on the cheek very close to my lips. Cody steps closer to me. I turn my wheelchair towards Cody and he kisses me like we are the only two in my house. I feel everyone watching me. I hear the gasps when he doesn't stop kissing me. I hear the clicking of Oscar's camera.

"Oscar, why do you encourage her?" Kelsey asks him.

Oscar knows my family well. We were friends and lovers once. He knows how my family treats me. "I love her." Oscar says.

I feel Cody tense. I wrap my arms around him and hold him closer to me. I want to tell him that Oscar doesn't mean anything to me. He is my friend. He is my employee. Cody is my choice. Cody is the one person that I have dreamed of and have wanted for years. Cody makes me believe that love is worth waiting for. I wanted Cody before I ever knew who he was. I wanted to be his.

Dad walks in the house with Joanna. She has been in my house with out me being here with her when she decorated the house for me. I am really grateful. I did change a few things but overall I have left her design style. She watches Cody kissing me and she smiles. Oscar actually captures her smile. He is taking random pictures of everyone in my house.

She looks at dad. "Take notes." She says.

That stops everyone in the room. He looks at her. "What?"

Its like she is another person. It almost seems like Joanna has a twin sister that showed up in her place. "I want you to kiss me like that. I want someone to take a picture of you kissing me and capture that you love only me."

Kyle looks at the room. "Mom, don't ever think that dad doesn't love only you. Sometimes you are the only one at all that he loves."

She looks at Kyle. "Are you saying that I don't allow him to love anyone else?"

"Stop this." Sawyer says. "Your daughter has invited you to come celebrate her house. There will be no harshness today. There will be no hard feelings." Sawyer puts his hand on my shoulder. "Show us your house."

Dad looks at Sawyer. "I am Jack."

Sawyer takes dad's extended hand and shakes it. "I know who you are." He looks at me. "Your daughter speaks so highly of you."

Gianna and Catalina walk in the front door and its like time stands still. Mom looks at Cody's mom and she seems to shrink behind Stew. Gianna looks just as stunning as Catalina. With everyone in my house, it seems like the air has evaporated completely. My little house feels just like a little house.

Brandon breaks the tension that has taken over my house. "I heard that someone referred to these houses as she sheds."

I look at him with wide eyes. I am grateful that he didn't come right out and say that Cody said that about my house.

Dad looks at the five of us that call him dad and he laughs. "The she sheds and man caves are in the other development." The room fills with laughter and it seems that from that point on everything goes smoothly.

Chapter Thirteen

Cody did go to the grocery store and picked up finger foods that we can all enjoy. He also planned for food to be brought in for a beautiful sit-down formal dinner. When the doorbell rings, Cody answers it and lets the catering company in. He ushers us out to the backyard.

Catalina has worked with the catering company before so she takes over and tells Cody to join the rest of us. Before he steps outside she touches his arm and draws his attention back to her. "Cody, do they know that you are living with her?"

"I don't know."

"Do you think that she is keeping it secret?"

"If she is, its only to keep people from ruining me." He says honestly. "She doesn't keep secrets."

"Not saying something, like you not telling us about things that were and are important to you is the same as keeping secrets."

He kisses the top of her head.

"Do you have your own room?"

"We share her bed."

"Cody." She says.

"You were trying to remember where you know her from."

"You know?" Catalina asks.

"You gave the commencement speech at her college graduation. She showed me the video of her graduation."

"She let you watch it?"

"Technically, yes."

"What does that mean?"

"She didn't let me hear it. She said I will hear it later. She wanted me to see how beautiful you are."

Catalina looks at the catering company workers. "Let me do what I do best." She says.

"You do everything best." Cody says.

"Cody, she has pictures of us hanging in her house." Catalina says with a smile that reaches her eyes.

"She loves that you and dad love her."

"Anyone who doesn't love her is an idiot." Landon says.

The two brothers embrace.

I sit outside. My backyard is big. There is a lot of grass and bushes that fill the backyard making the yard look really pretty to look at. There is a nice patio area which is why I really liked the house. Everything was easily accessible in the house and the outside patio sold me. I purchased the outdoor furniture with the house. They charged me more than I would have paid if I would have purchased the furniture on my own at one of the fancy patio places. I didn't care, I had to have it because it was exactly what I wanted.

My sisters and brothers sit next to me. My dad looks at the five of us sitting together. He notices that Kelsey seems to be on the edge of the seat that she sits on like she is ready to bolt at any time.

I engage her in conversation. "Kelsey what have you been up to lately? How is your boyfriend?"

She looks at me like I have just outed something she was keeping to herself. Which is ridiculous because we all know about her boyfriend. He has been around for a long time. "We have taken a bit of a break."

"I am sorry to hear that." I say. I really am sorry to hear that because I know that she feels for him the way that I feel for Cody.

"We aren't seeing other people, we are just taking a break."

"If you wanted to invite him to join us, please do." I say.

Kelsey looks at me. Kelsey is two years older than I am but she looks at me like I am the older sister at the moment. "I will send him a text message." She says. She looks at dad and then looks back at us. "Dad is mad at Trevor."

"Who cares. Its not work hours." Brandon says.

"Dad doesn't get in your business." Kelsey says to Brandon.

There is truth in that statement. Brandon loves sports but he is not good at any and dad bonded with Kyle. Dad is turned away a bit from Brandon for dating Ashely. The two of them don't care. Kelsey wants dad's attention. She wants his approval. She wants the same as I do. She wants him to acknowledge that she is important to him.

Kelsey takes her phone off the table and texts Trevor. Her phone rings almost immediately. "Hello." She says and finally settles into the chair she is occupying. She leans back and slips her ballet slipper flats off her feet and puts her feet on my lap. We smile at each other. "I am over at Crystal's and she has extended an invitation to you." She listens to whatever he saying. "I want to see you." She listens again. "No, the whole family is here. Cody and his family are here too." She listens and smiles. "The address is 248 Gulfport Street." We all year Trevor hoot with excitement. He says something to her and she smiles again. "She did. She bought your house."

Cody walks over to us finally and smiles. He looks at Kelsey. "Someone else built the she shed that she bought?"

Kelsey laughs. "Her boyfriend thinks your house is a she shed." She laughs again. "Fighting words." She bends forward in half laughing. "Ok. I will see you soon." She says smiling. My older sister is beautiful. When she smiles she makes Catalina seem ordinary. Kelsey arches her foot so that her toes are on my leg. She makes them do a happy dance and we both smile at one another.

"Kyle, where is your girlfriend?" Ashley asks. She knows that Kyle is in a new relationship and the rest of us don't know anything about it.

"This is why I stay away." He says.

I look at Kyle. "You can invite her if you want."

"I don't want her to come. This is a family day." Kyle says.

"I just wanted to extend the invitation if you wanted to bring someone."

"Thank you." He says.

Catalina comes outside and tells everyone that the meal is ready. Everyone makes their way back in the house. Just as everyone is seated around the table, there is a knock on the door. Kelsey gets up from where she just sat down and opens the door. Trevor stands on the welcome mat with a big smile on his face.

Trevor goes around the table and hugs everyone. He hugs me last. "So you bought my house." He looks at Kelsey. "How did she even find out about it?"

"Brandon and I brought her to the development." Ashley says. "We wanted her to look at my dad's development."

I look at Trevor. "The house is wonderful."

Kelsey looks at Brandon and Ashley. "I thought that you brought her to see the bigger house."

I look at Kelsey. I never said anything to anyone. I did look at the bigger version of this house. Then when I got the keys they said bungalow and I thought that's what they were calling it. I didn't realize that it was because it was the smaller house.

Kelsey looks at me.

"The address is the same." I tell her. "I looked at the house on Gulfport Street."

Trevor looks at everyone. "This isn't Gulfport Street."

"What?" Everyone asks.

"When I put the address into the GPS this is where it brought me." Sawyer says.

"Well it doesn't matter now, I have moved in here and all my stuff is here." I say.

Trevor gets up from the table. He walks over to where I am sitting and he pulls my wheelchair away from the table. He looks at everyone. "We will be right back."

Cody stands up and goes with us. Trevor walks to the back door. He walks across the lawn pushing my wheelchair. Cody follows behind us. When we have reached the door of the house behind my house, Trevor takes my key and opens the door.

"Why does the key open this house too?" I ask.

"Because this is your house. And that house that you are living in is the guest house." Trevor says.

I look around the house and I know that this is the house that I looked at. I look at Trevor. "Wow, I feel stupid." I say.

"No, please don't." Trevor says. "I will have some of my guys take your stuff out of the guest house and set up your house for no charge."

"Thank you." I say. "The guest house is beautiful. I love it." I look around the house and go from room to room. I start in the kitchen. I take mental notes of what needs to be fixed.

"What's going on?" Trevor asks.

"I am just noticing that somethings are not going to work for me."

"Don't hold back. We can change stuff out for you because it's a naked house." He says.

"What made you fall in love with it?" Cody asks. His voice echoes a bit and seems to bounce off the walls and the tiled floor.

Being in the house now, I don't know what made me want to look at no other house. I look around. I push my self into the master bedroom and into the master bathroom. It's a no entrance shower. There is no step or any barricades. There is a built in vanity. The linen closet doesn't go from floor to ceiling but is more like a built in cabinet that is perfect for me because everything is at my level. It seems to wrap around the bathroom.

I make my way back into the bedroom and open the closet doors and then I remember why the house caught my attention. Everything was on my level.

Trevor walks in the room. "Crystal, make a list of things that work and things that don't."

"Did you really not know that the house came with a guest house?" Cody asks.

"I really didn't know." I say.

"Are you ok?" Trevor asks.

"It just seems different."

"How so?" Cody and Trevor ask together.

"I don't know."

I leave the room and go into the next room. It's a big room. Almost as big as the master without the bathroom attached.

Cody walks in the room. "You ok?" He asks.

"I guess it was staged so I could see what it would look like. This is just an empty room." I look at Cody. "I feel stupid." I say.

He walks over and hugs me.

Trevor walks over. "Let me ask you a question."

I look at him.

"Did your dad know that you were buying a house here?"

I shake my head and say. "No."

"I am going to work on something. I know that we have to make adjustments in the kitchen and I think in the laundry room."

I leave the room and go into the laundry room and its perfect. I can reach everything. "Trevor!"

He and Cody come running.

"Don't touch anything." I say.

He laughs. "Just the kitchen then. I will work on that this week. I will do it personally. If you need anything else, please don't hesitate to ask for it. As long as you are in the guest house, you can just come right over and see the changes."

"Thank you." I say.

"Has Kels seen you a lot since you have been here?"

"Not really."

"She is going through a lot."

"She keeps her life from me." I say without thinking about it. What I said is true but I shouldn't have said anything.

"Has Joanne been nice to you?"

"No."

We go back to the house. It is loud. My dad's voice is the loudest. "That's not true." He is saying.

"You never defend me." Joanne says equally as loud.

Kelsey, Kyle and Brandon all say at the same time. "What are you talking about?"

Kelsey continues. "He only takes your side. He has stopped paying attention to his daughters since the day after he met you." She says. She looks at me. "If you want me to leave just let me know." She says it like I am the one yelling at her.

"I don't want you to go." I tell her.

"What's going on? What did we miss?" Cody asks.

Joanne walks over to the three of us and bends slightly at the waist so that we are eye to eye. "Is that how much you think of me? A two-by-two picture frame of me?"

"We told you, she didn't do it." Brandon says.

She stands straight as a board and looks at him. "I want to hear it from her."

"Can I ask you a question?" I ask her.

She whirls around and looks back at me. "What?"

"How many times have you asked me over for a visit?" I look at my mom. "How many times have you asked me over for a visit?" I look over at my dad. "I received the most beautiful flowers from you. Thank you." I look back at Joanne. "You came here and you decorated. Were you laughing about how dumb I am for being in the guest house and not in the main house?"

She looks at dad. "I didn't do that."

"What brought this up?" Trevor asks.

"There are pictures of her with Cody's family and none. Not one is with her own family." Joanne says.

"We don't have any family photos." Ashley says. "We do his and her family pictures." She looks at Joanne. "You don't even like us. Why would she have pictures occupying her walls of people who don't like her? She endured a lot of that when she was working with Beth."

Sawyer looks at me. "Is that true?"

Landon looks at everyone. "This is a house warming party."

Gianna looks at me. She is holding the teddy bear that is wearing Cody's jersey. "You are the one who sent Cody the teddy bear wearing a shirt that says, 'I wish you well.' How do you have his teddy bears?"

Everyone looks at her.

"I bought them. I bought the box of them." I say.

"Why?" Landon asks.

"He did something kind for me."

"What was that?" Brandon asks.

Kyle looks at everyone. "Stop." He says. "Everyone just stop." He looks at his mother. "I know your feelings are hurt, I don't blame you, but you have to know that what we all say is true. You came into Jack's life and you made sure that he only saw you. He sees Kelsey and Ashely secretly. Crystal doesn't want to meet secretly."

They all continue talking. I slip away and no one realizes that I am missing. I listen to them all talking about me like its not my house and they are not my guests. I just listen. I refuse to cry. Not because I don't want to. I do. I really want to cry my eyes out. I don't cry because if I start, I may not stop for weeks.

Stew walks into the office. He sits down on the chair in the office and takes me in his arms. "I am sorry I stirred up so much trouble. I really didn't think it was going to get this bad."

"I am sorry I missed it." I say with a big smile.

"You doing ok?"

"This is why I decided to stay away as long as I did. No one seems to get a long when they all have to be together."

"Kelsey seems to know about what you do to give back. She was telling everyone in a bragging way really."

"Kelsey does? Are you sure it wasn't Gianna talking?"

"Kelsey has hurt feelings because Gianna was at one of your events and you didn't tell her about it."

"I didn't tell Gianna about it. I rented the venue and paid for the event, she was there as a chaperone."

"Why do you keep that from everyone?"

I smile at him. "I tell you."

"Why don't you tell them?"

"I don't want them to take away the feelings I get when I do what I do. They have never been supportive of what I do. I have for each of my sisters. I have Kyle and Brandon. It was never reciprocated. Kelsey always had something more important to do and Ashley always wanted to do her gymnastics. You grow up with that, when you are an adult you know to keep it to yourself."

"Can I ask you a question?"

"Of course." I say.

"Do you know your sisters and brothers as well as you know Cody Parker?"

"Do they know me?"

"Don't be ten." He says.

"I know that Ashley can put Joanne out of business if she wanted to. Her interior designs are beautiful. I know that she started dating Brandon just to piss Joanne off but then they really fell in love with one another. I know that Kelsey loves Trevor and wants to start a life with him but with dad being mad at him, she has pulled back from Trevor so that dad doesn't get mad at her. I know that Kelsey owns ten dance studios and that Gianna is one of her instructors. I know that although Kelsey was supportive of me liking baseball and getting into college on a full ride, she is bothered that I never got over my love for the game and my love for Cody Parker."

"Why do you have all his teddy bears?"

"I bought the box of them."

"Why?"

"The store owner said that if they didn't sell one of them, he was going to take the box of them and burn it. He was going to tell the Parker family that the merchandise came defected. He kicked the box. Then he stated that Cody was a has been. I asked how much he wanted for the box of them and he gave me a price. I paid it and he walked me to my car carrying the box."

"You said he did something nice for you. What did he do?"

"When I was in the car accident, he paid the bill."

"What?" Stew asks and sits up straight in the chair.

"When I left the hospital, they told me that I had to pay before I left. I took my credit card out of my purse and went to pay. They told me that it was taken care of. When I left the hospital, there was a car waiting to take me anywhere I wanted to go."

"Where did you go?"

"I went back to my apartment. I was stiff for weeks."

"How do you know he did it?"

"He sent with the payment an envelope for me. It read open when I was alone. The driver gave me an envelope too."

"What was in the envelopes?"

"Autographed pictures of Cody."

"Where are they now?"

"I think his dad has them."

"How is that?"

"His dad bought my bridal shop."

Kyle knocks on the door. He doesn't wait for me to say anything he walks into the office and takes me in his arms. He hugs me in one of his best big brother embraces that always made me feel completely safe and loved. Not that I had any reason not to feel safe, but the warmth I feel in his arms, is something that is totally him.

"Kyle, I didn't mean to cause any problems." I say.

"You didn't cause any problems. Everything that was said needed to be said years ago. My mom thinks that dad takes everyone else's sides. We wanted her to see that its not true. Especially when it comes to you. Sadly its more when it comes to you."

I hug him.

Kyle looks at Stew. "You tried getting a postage stamp picture of her?" He laughs.

Stew just smiles. "You know, you can tell your sisters that they are wrong about her. What they don't know about her, she does know about them." He stands. "Don't hide out. We have a wedding to plan." He walks out of the office.

"Kyle?" I say and pull away from him. "Are you mad at me?"

"What?" He steps back two steps. "Why would I be mad at you?"

"Cody is your friend."

"Tally, listen to me. I am happy that you are with him. You love him."

I put my hand on my chest. "I do love him. I love him very much. I love him more than I have ever loved anyone in my life."

Kyle knows that I was in love with Quinn. He doesn't say anything. "Tally, we feel the love you have for Cody. It fills this whole house."

I laugh. He looks at me. "Cody. Calls. It. My. She. Shed." I say between fits of laughter.

"Well now we know that you are in the wrong house."

I get serious. I stop laughing and tears sting my eyes.

"You haven't explored your neighborhood?"

"Of course I have."

"You didn't notice that the house around the block has the same address?"

"Kyle, I know this sounds stupid, but it seems like its reversed. It seems like I got the wrong house. Everything here fits me and is accessible but this is not the house that I saw. It is the same house address but it's a different house. I love it. I could sell the big house."

"We will work it all out." Kyle says.

I turn from him. "I am really sorry that your mom has hurt feelings."

"We will work it all out." He says again.

"Is your girlfriend—"

"We will talk about her soon. But not today." He says. He steps behind my wheelchair and pushes me out of the office.

Brandon hugs me.

When I look around I only see my siblings, Cody and his siblings. "Where did everyone go?" I ask.

"They went to see the clubhouse." Kelsey says.

Behind the table is a hutch. I go over to the hutch and take out three boxes. I then go back over to where my siblings are sitting. I hand Kyle, Kelsey and Ashley a box. I then go back over to the hutch and take out three more boxes. I go back over and hand a box to Brandon, Landon and Gianna.

"What is this?" Gianna asks. "We should have brought you a present."

"I don't need anything." I say. "Open them when you are ready." I go back over to the hutch and take out one more box. I go back over and hand one to Oscar.

"You have one for me?" Oscar says.

"I love you. We didn't work out as a couple, but you have become my family." I say. I look at Trevor. "I don't have one for you."

"You didn't know me until today."

I look at my family. "Open them."

Brandon opens his first. He takes out a family picture of us. It was from his college graduation. He looks at all five of us standing together. I am standing in the picture because I am holding on to Kelsey on one side and Kyle on the other. "This is the best." Brandon says. He stands and hugs me.

Ashley opens hers next. She takes the picture out of the box. Its another family picture of just the five of us. In this one we are all dressed for Halloween. I am sitting in my wheelchair in her picture. She is lying across my lap. Brandon is holding her feet up. Kelsey is holding her head. Kyle is standing behind me. We are back to back and he has his head bent back on top of my head. Ashley holds the picture up. "I have looked all over for this picture." She hugs me. "Thank you." She says. "Mom thought that I made it up."

"Nope." Oscar says. "I won a first place prize for your silliness." Oscar opens his next. It's a picture of the two of us. We are in the gazebo that I danced with Cody in. But in this picture, Oscar is standing next me. Again in this picture I am standing. We are looking at each other smiling. "Marcus told me about this shot." He says.

Landon opens his box next. He looks at the picture and smiles. He closes the box. "Thank you." He says.

"Show us." Cody says.

Landon opens the box again and takes the photo out of the box. He holds it up. It's a picture of the two of us sitting next to each other at a baseball stadium. We are holding a sign between the two of us. The sign reads 'Cody Parker Fan Club'. We are both smiling. Landon looks at me. "Thank you again for this."

Gianna opens her box next. It's a picture of the two of us dressed up. It was at a charity event that I pulled together. She is kneeling next to me. We each have an arm around each other. We are holding a sign. This one says. 'Let love lift your heart'. Gianna looks at me. "I forgot about this event. This is where my mom recognized you from."

"What was the event for?" Kelsey asks.

"It was just an event that I did." I say.

Cody looks at me. "I need to talk to you. Privately." He takes my hand and we go into our bedroom. "You have pictures with my siblings supporting my charity and me."

"I didn't know they were your siblings until you invited me to your parents' house." I say. "Are you mad?"

"Mad? How can I be mad? It just shows me how fantastic you are." He looks at me. "How did you know about my charity?"

"I looked it up when you paid for my hospital bill." I say. "I wanted to pay you back."

"You didn't have to do that." He kisses me on the lips. He leaves my room and returns minutes later with the picture that Gianna opened. "You raised ten thousand dollars?" He asks me.

"No. That was the goal. That night brought in thirty thousand."

He looks at me. "The anonymous check." He looks at the picture again. He sees Catalina is standing behind Gianna and me. "Why did you do it?" He asks.

"I wanted to give to your charity." I say.

He sits on the bed. I push my wheelchair right up to the bed and kiss him. "I didn't know that Catalina was your mom. I think I suffer from tunnel vision when it comes to you." I say.

He laughs loudly. He falls back on the bed. He holds his stomach and laughs hardily. He stands up quickly and takes me in his arms. He hugs me tight and kisses me like he did the night we first kissed.

We leave the room and join everyone again. He hands the picture back to his sister. She smiles at him.

Kelsey looks at us. "We heard a big laugh." She says.

"She said the cutest thing. I couldn't help but laugh." Cody says.

"What did she say?" Kyle asks.

"She told me she has tunnel vision when it comes to me."

The room erupts in laughter. I smile along.

Kelsey opens her box next. It's the five of us all dressed up in black and she is dressed in her white ballerina outfit. Marcus took the picture of us. She is standing on point with her one arm up in the air. In this picture, Kyle is standing behind me and I am standing. He is supporting me. She gets off the couch and hugs me. "I knew someone captured that moment. Thank you." She says. She kisses me on the cheek loudly.

Kyle opens the box and gasps audibly. He leaves the box open on the couch and jumps up. He runs and takes me in his arms. "I will treasure it always. Thank you. Thank you. Thank you." He says.

Brandon takes the box and looks at the picture. It was at Kyle's college graduation. We are all gathered together. He is in the graduation gown, he is holding me in his arms and I am wearing his cap. We are all smiling.

There is a second picture attached of him and me at my graduation from college. He was the only one there.

Kelsey looks at it. She joins in the hug. Brandon and Ashley do too. Oscar takes a picture of us. Cody hugs us. Landon and Gianna join in the hug. Oscar keeps snapping. Trevor takes pictures too.

All the parents return. We have the leftovers from lunch for dinner. When all the food is gone, we all sit together watching a movie. One by one, someone leaves. Catalina and Gianna leave first. Shortly after, Sawyer leaves. Landon stays a bit longer. My dad and Joanne leave. Mom and Stew leave together in separate cars. He follows her out. My siblings leave one at a time. Kelsey is the last one to leave.

"Before I go, I just wanted to thank you for having me." She says. "Listen, I am sorry that I have stayed away. I thought that's what you wanted."

"I wish that you were here when I saw the house with Brandon and Ashley. Kyle was in China so he couldn't have been here, but I wanted you to come. I swear, this is not the same house. The address is the same but the house is not."

"I will talk to Trevor about it."

"He said that he is going to fix the kitchen in the house. There are others things too, but I don't want to say anything."

"Say something. That's what he does. That's why dad got into a big argument with Trevor. He knows about ADA codes and what works and makes sense. Dad wanted to do something with one of the houses and Trevor flipped the design. Really the way dad was doing it was wrong."

"Thank Trevor for me for paying attention to details."

"I will." She says. "He likes you."

"I think he is perfect for you. Lets double date soon."

"I agree." She says. She hugs me. "I love you."

"I love you too."

"I know just the spot that I am going to hang that picture of us."

"You really like it?" I ask her.

"Oh my god, yes." She says. "Trevor and I are moving in a few weeks. We can't wait to have you and Cody come over."

"I can't wait." I tell her.

Trevor walks over. "Hun, we have to go." He says.

She hugs me one more time and laughs. "Was Stew really looking to make her picture postage stamp size?" She laughs into my shoulder. She tries to pull herself together. She does for a moment. "That's wrong of us." She says. Then she bursts out in laughter again. "I love you."

"I love you too." I tell her. I hold my hand up like I am handing her a postage stamp. The two of us put our heads together and laugh again.

She hugs me one more time before Trevor hugs me and they leave. They blow the horn when they get to the end of the street and both stick their hands out the windows and wave. I wave back at them.

Chapter Fourteen

Cody and I are in my bed. He is sleeping flat on his back. I sit up and scoot myself closer to him. I put my hand on his chest. I rub my hand over his chest. I take one of his nipples and rub my fingertips over it. I look up at his face and his eyes are closed but I am not sure that he is still sleeping. I move my hand lower to the hairline at his waistband. He puts his hand on my hand.

"What are you doing?" He asks.

"Exploring." I say with a big grin.

"Don't start something that you can't finish." He says.

"Let go of my hand so I can play."

"I am going to—" He gasps.

"Can I touch—" I never finish my sentence. He flips me on my back and slips a condom on before he slips into me. "Cody! Oh my god, please." I say.

Cody pulls out and lays next to me. He then gets out of bed and takes care of the condom. He gets back in bed.

"You don't play fair." I tell him.

"Are you accusing me of being a cheater?"

"No. I am just saying that you don't play fair." I don't give him a chance to move closer or away because I take him in my hand and feel the smoothness of his skin. I pump my hand once and then again.

He closes his eyes. "Cryst—tal." He says my name in broken syllables. I just touch my lips to the tip and he twitches from the light touch. He groans as I slide my hand from the tip to the root. "Cry—stal." He says.

He is completely erect under my touch. I pump my hand around him and he erupts. He squeezes his eyes as he groans and his pelvis rises off the bed.

I put my hand on his stomach and he just lays back and lets me touch him. I touch the scar that is on his side. When I touch the scar he winces. "Does that hurt?" I ask him.

"No." He says.

"Does this bother you?" I ask him in a timid voice.

"No."

I touch it again and again he winces. "Cody are you sure?"

"I never let anyone touch it before." He says.

"Is this from the attack?"

His breathing is labored.

"Cody if it bothers you, I will stop."

"No."

"No what?" I whisper.

"I want you to touch it. I want you to touch every part of me. I want you to feel comfortable touching me. I feel comfortable touching you." He says.

"I don't want to hurt you." I say.

"Crystal, you are not hurting me." He puts his hand on top of my hand and pushes my fingertips into the scar. He winces under the pressure of our combined touch.

I try to pull my hand free. "Cody, tell me about it." I say.

He opens his eyes and reaches his arms out taking me in his embrace and pulling me over his body. He then rolls on top of me and puts his head down on my chest after he settles me in the plush pillows that smell of his shampoo and him. "You know what happened?"

"I know what I read." I tell him. "I know what Quinn, that asshole, told people about it. You tell me." I run my fingers through his hair and over his shoulders.

"Like you know, I went to get the car for her. When I got back to where she was waiting, I noticed that she was standing with two guys. At first it looked like she was just talking to people she knew. I got out of the car and walked over to her. I felt pain the second that I was on the sidewalk. I guess the guy I didn't see was waiting for me. He hit me in the arm. One of them had a knife. He was threatening her with it and when the guy struck me, I fell forward. The knife cut me."

I pull his hand up to my lips and kiss it.

"Not everyone thinks that I am a good guy. People think that I am a player."

"Cody, I don't make judgement on people based on what others think. The flight wasn't the first time that we encountered each other."

He pulls back and looks at me.

"I was in a Target store in Indiana and I couldn't reach what I wanted. I asked people to help me and no one did. You were wearing a baseball cap so that people wouldn't recognize you. When you walked down the isle that I was in, you looked at me. You smiled at me. I asked you to reach what I wanted and you got it down for me. You put it in my grocery cart. You looked at all the items that were in there for a brief moment. You asked me if I was done shopping. I said that I was and you walked away. When I was online to pay, I was looking at a sports magazine and you came up behind me and told me not to believe everything I read. You looked over my shoulder at the article I was reading and you touched the magazine page and told me that the writer of that article knew her shit."

He sits up and looks at me. "What? That girl in Target had pink hair."

I laugh. "I know. I look different with pink hair."

"Why was it pink?" He reaches for a strand of my hair and pulls it through his fingers.

"My friend fucked up when she was coloring it." I laugh. "You paid for everything in my cart. The article that you pointed to was the one that I wrote."

"No. Bella Steele wrote that."

"I am Bella Steele. My full name is Crystal Bella Steele."

He looks at me. "Why didn't you tell me?"

"When I saw you on the plane and that woman was so rude to you, you looked at me. I thought you recognized me."

"I thought for a second that I had seen you before." He says.

"Cody."

He kisses my shoulder.

"Cody, do you remember?" I cover my face with the sheet.

"Remember what?" He asks pulling the sheet back.

"Do you remember when you were coaching those little kids at the park in Indiana?"

"I often coached kids." He says.

"The day it started to rain out of nowhere."

"What about it?"

"I was struggling to get my stuff together. You walked over with that big umbrella and handed it to me. You gathered all of my stuff for me and then handed it to me. You pushed my wheelchair across the lot to that building for shelter."

"Crystal, I am sorry."

"Why?"

"I thought that I had made those events up. And the one at the car lot?"

"No, you didn't make them up. You were nice to me. So when I heard that lady on the plane make those comments I had to say something. I wanted you to hear me say them."

He smiles. "I heard you."

"I heard you giving a speech to kids. You were supposed to talk to the little boys. You addressed everyone. There was a girl who caught my attention because she was standing in the children's museum at the commenter's booth and she was reading my words loudly that I had said about you."

"I didn't see you there. I would have noticed and adult in a room full of kids."

"There was a big life size poster of you, I was behind it."

"Why?" He asks.

"I wanted to listen to your voice. I couldn't get enough. I wanted to listen to you talk all day. There was a lady there with you. She said that you were doing a speaking engagement somewhere else. I jotted it down. I showed up and heard you talk and I felt that if I wasn't in my wheelchair I would have been in a heap on the floor. You made my knees weak." I say. Heat rises from my shoulders to my hair.

"God." He puts his forehead to my forehead. "I wish I would have known you then."

"You looked at me, I felt a jolt of electricity."

"You say that and I have to tell you, I felt a jolt of electricity too. You looked at me and you smiled. I remember you looking right at me." He kisses my lips. "You know, they tell us when we give speeches to find someone in the crowd, for whatever reason I looked and looked around the room for a while and I spotted you smiling at me. You made my knees weak too. That smile. Your smile gave me confidence."

"Cody, I wished on every star that I could be yours."

"Your wishing paid off." He says. He kisses me. He looks at me. "We are having lunch with my mom and dad. Then we leave for Indiana."

"I know." I kiss him.

"I am going to pack up my stuff. I am going to sell my house."

I hug him. "Where ever will you put all of your stuff?"

He tickles me. "You have an empty house that is just wanting to get filled." He says.

"Are you using me for my house?" I ask him laughing.

"Is your house where your body is? That's where I want to be my whole life."

I burst into tears. He takes me in his arms and just holds me.

"Why are you crying?"

"I feel like the luckiest girl on the planet."

"I am the luckiest man on the planet. I have never met anyone like you. You make me so happy."

"I love you." I tell him.

"I love you too."

I drive my car to the resort where Cody kissed me in the lobby. I park my car in the lot. We walk into the lobby hand in hand. When the doors of the lobby open for us, everyone stops and looks at us.

A woman stands at the front desk where I was that first night and she looks at Cody. "Lover Boy." She gushes.

Kent is standing behind the counter with Pam. They both look at us. Pam looks at the woman standing in front of her. "That's uncalled for." She says. Pam looks at the two of us. "Welcome back." She looks at the woman in front of her, "Excuse me, if you go to the next counter, they will help you get checked in." Pam walks over. She smiles at the two of us. "Follow me." She says.

Cody takes my hand. We follow Pam to the atrium's diner. Catalina, Sawyer, Landon and Gianna are there. Cody and I join them. We have lunch together.

Sawyer looks at Cody. "What time is your flight?"

"We leave at four." Cody says.

Catalina looks at Cody. "Who is going?"

"The two of us." Cody says to her.

"Crystal, do you want to go?"

"Oh yes." I say.

"Have you gone on any dates?" Gianna asks.

Cody looks at me. "We have been a bit busy."

"Its romantic to go on dates." Gianna says.

"Well, actually we are going to double date with my sister and her boyfriend when we get back. We would love to plan something with each of you." I say. I can feel Cody's leg bouncing under the table. I put my hand on his leg. "We have been busy." I say.

Landon looks at us. "I am flying out to Indiana too." He looks at Cody. "I want to offer to help you pack up your stuff."

"Are you going to drive it back?" Gianna asks.

Cody looks at Gianna. "No."

"I was just asking." She says.

I look around feeling my hives that have been dormant start to prickle my skin. I get itchy almost immediately. I feel the itchiest on my throat. Cody looks at me. "You need to drink some water." He says.

Catalina looks at me. "Sweetheart, do you want us to move our meal indoors?"

"No." I say. "This is fine."

Cody looks at me. "You haven't had hives in weeks."

"I am ok." I say. I want to rip my skin off. I am so itchy.

"Maybe its something here." Landon says. "When did you first get hives?"

"When I was here." I say.

"Maybe its something in the air here, or something that you are allergic to." Catalina says.

Cody takes me by the hand and we go inside. He walks into the gift shop and buys a bottle of water. He comes out with it and holds it out to me. "Drink this." He says.

I look at him.

"Crystal, drink some water."

I take the bottle from him and drink almost the whole thing.

He looks at me. "Did you get hives the first night that you were here?"

"No."

"I wonder what it is about this place that gives you hives?"

Confrontations. I think but don't say it.

He looks at me. "What are you thinking?"

"Nothing." I tell him. "I am excited to go with you to Indiana." Nervous too. His life was there. His friends are there. Will he want to go back and not come back with me? All of this plays in my head.

"Are you feeling better?"

"I wasn't ever not feeling well." I say. I felt like I was being put on a barbecue.

"Are you sure you want to go with me?"

"Yes." I say to him. "I want to spend time with you. I want to be with you. I want to see your life."

He puts his forehead against mine. "You know about my life. You know more about my life than anyone I ever met in my life."

Gianna walks over. A guy walks behind her. He has his hand on her waist. They look like a beautiful couple. As they walk over to us, he sizes Cody up. He looks at me. When they finally get to where we are, Gianna looks at me. "How are the hives?" She asks.

"They are ok." I say. "Thank you."

"Cody, Crystal, this is Jason." She turns into him. "Jason, this is my brother Cody and his fiancé Crystal.'

Jason looks at both of us. "Congratulations."

"Thank you." Cody says.

I look at Jason. I recognize him. He too was a baseball player. When he looks at me he knows that I know who he is. "Jason, its good to see you again." I say.

Gianna looks at him first and then me. "You know him?"

"She interviewed me when I was just getting started." He says. He looks at Cody. "You are a lucky guy. She finds out every detail and then spins it so that you seem like you are a fucking superhero. When I heard her talk about me, I was dumbstruck for a moment and had to think, was she talking about me." He says.

"That's not true." I say.

Landon walks over. "Its nice that she liked you. When she knows all the details that she digs for, she tells it the way it is."

Jason looks at Landon. "I know what you did on that test day. I know that you meant it as a joke, but she was the one that had to take the class over on another campus."

I never said anything to anyone about what Landon did. "That's not true." I say.

"She never said anything. Other people talked about what you did. Some people laughed about it. Some people were pissed off about it."

Gianna looks at me. Her smile is as wide as her face. "So you can dish dirt on my boyfriend."

"I can tell you his baseball stats." I say. And that he is not the right guy for you.

She hugs him. "When you get back, you will have to come over for dinner."

"We will." Cody says.

"Where are you going?" Jason asks.

"Indiana." He says.

We sit side by side on the airplane. Landon sits in the row behind us. He sits at the edge of his seat and pokes Cody in the arm. Cody looks at him. "There are steps leading up to your house." He says.

"I am aware of that." Cody says.

"Is she going to stay with you?"

"Yes." Cody says. He looks at me. I am again sleeping on his shoulder.

"I didn't mean to upset her."

"Just drop it."

"Are you mad at me?" Landon asks.

"No." Cody says. He kisses the top of my head.

"Can you tell me something?"

"What?"

"What drew you to her?"

"I just felt it was meant to be. I love her. I want to spend the rest of my life with her."

"Whats going to happen with the bridal shop?"

"I don't know."

"You know, I remember years ago when we were in school with each other. She had just taken the job at the Butterfly place. She had picked out a wedding dress. She told her friend about the perfect dress. Then time passed and I remember her crying. She was so sad. I watched her and I made my way to where she was so I could hear her talking. She was crying over a wedding dress. Then she told her friend that she didn't know why she was crying. She said that Joanne was probably right and no one would love her. But she cried. I mean big crying like Gianna has done when some asshole guy breaks up with her."

"Awe." Cody says.

"She looked at her friend. I swear to god, she said to her friend. It was the perfect dress for when she married Cody Parker."

He kisses my head again. "She didn't know you and I are brothers."

"Cody, I always heard her talking so highly of you and your stats. She would glow when she would get into conversations about baseball and you. She talked about every topic." Landon looks at me. "She could relate to everyone." Landon looks at me again and then back at Cody. "I know that Beth knew about that dress that was so special to Crystal. I know that Beth sold it for next to nothing."

"She told me about the dress."

"The designer is CP Designs." Landon says.

"How do you know that?"

I startle in my sleep and open my eyes. Cody and Landon both look at me. I look at the two of them and then out the window. I start to giggle. I put my head against the seat.

"You ok?" Cody asks.

"I was dreaming I was falling." I say. I look at the two of them. "Are you two ok? Landon, I didn't mean to upset you earlier."

"I am not upset." He says.

"How much longer?" I ask.

"You ok?" Cody asks.

"I just feel like I have to stand up."

He and Landon both stand. Landon stands in the row behind us. He reaches over the seat and helps me stand. Cody stands on my side. But he holds me too. I put my hands on my seat and the seat in front of me.

"Is this good." Cody asks.

"Can you bend my left knee? I have a Charlie-horse."

Cody looks at Landon. "You got her?"

"Yes." He says.

Cody goes down on his knees which is not easy because there is not a lot of room. He rubs my calf muscle. He lifts my foot up to flex my foot. He feels a surge run up my leg. Cody looks at me. "You ok?"

I smile at him. "It's better." I say. Then I get a sharp pain in my leg. He feels my muscles tighten.

"Landon, hold her." Cody says.

"I got her." He says. He has climbed over the seat and is now sitting in my seat. He looks at me. "Remember the gym?" He asks.

I look at him. I have tears in my eyes. From sitting too long, my muscles are rebelling.

"What happened in the gym?" Cody asks.

"Landon was doing a leg press. His leg went completely stiff. I was working out next to him and I went over and flexed his foot."

"Oh my god, it hurt like hell." Landon says.

I feel my knees buckle. Landon and Cody both support me.

A flight attendant makes her way down the isle. She stops where we are. "Everything alright here?" She asks sweetly.

"I was getting a Charlie-horse. I just needed to stand up for a minute." I say.

She looks at Cody. "Are you ok, sir?"

"My wife needed to stand, she is disabled so my brother and I are just helping her."

"Do you need some water?" The flight attendant asks.

"No, thank you." I say.

She looks at Landon. "Sir, you can't stay there."

Landon looks at her. "I will return to my seat." Landon rubs his hand over my knee. "Right now, I need to help out."

"Sure." She says. She looks at Cody again and checks him out. She looks at Landon again and winks at him.

I look at Cody. "I have to sit." I tell him.

Landon picks me up in his arms and sits me in the seat. He walks around Cody and to the isle behind us.

Cody sits down next to me. I take his hand in mine. "Cody, I can't wait to marry you." I say quietly to him.

We leave the airport and there are two guys waiting outside the airport for us. They are holding paper signs that read, Cody Parker We Love You!!

He greets both of them with hugs. They shake hands with Landon. They both seem to overlook me for a brief moment. Then they look at me and both at the same time hug me.

Cody takes my hand. "Crystal Steele these two are my friends. This is Todd Banks and Logan Davidson."

"Its nice to officially meet you both. I know who you are." I say.

"Crystal Steele? You were the voice on the radio." Todd says.

I smile at him.

"You did the best play-by-plays. My wife would record you talking about our games. She loved the excitement in your voice." Logan says.

"I met your wife." I tell him. "She came into my bridal shop and bought her dress and all the dresses for the bridal party. I remember she wanted everything to be formal black and white. She wanted black accents on her dress. She wanted to make you feel comfortable and not have anything pink." I say to Logan.

He laughs. "She told me that she had to find you. Then she told me all about you giving back."

"To be honest, I saw the pictures of the wedding because we supplied the photographer. Everything was so beautiful. It looked like a fairytale. Then three weeks later after the wedding, she came back into my shop and wanted to donate the dresses."

"Did those dresses get a second life?"

"They all did." I say.

We get into the mini van. Logan drives around the city and points out Indianapolis. I don't say that I spent a whole year living here. I just let him point out things to me like it's the first time that I am seeing it. I am still in awe of the city. I love Indianapolis just as much as I love Florida.

My family and friends didn't know that I lived in Indiana for a year. I wanted to be completely independent. I almost lasted the full year. The winter was harsh. I was lonely. I was trying to follow a dream, but it turned into a nightmare of shattered glass and brokenness. I returned to Orlando and never looked back.

Logan drives to one of the most beautiful houses I have ever seen in my life. He drives up the driveway and stops the car. I look at the steps leading up to the house. My heart sinks for a moment.

We all get out of the car. I get in my wheelchair. I look at the house and it really is stunning. I look around. "Can I go look around?"

"Of course." Cody says.

I want to leave them before my tears come.

Todd looks at Cody. "She's on the verge of tears."

Landon gets our stuff out of the trunk. He takes my walker out and carries it up the steps. He leans it against the front door.

"I would never do anything to hurt her." Cody says.

"Cody, look at all those steps." Logan says. "We think nothing of it. She sees an obstacle that she cant conquer on her own."

"I am going to help her." Cody says.

"Go get her."

Cody walks around looking for me. I am near a fence looking at two deers. He walks over quietly so not to startle the deer. He puts his arms around me. "Are you ok?" He asks.

"I am ok." I say.

"What's wrong?"

"I am excited to be here with you." I tell him.

"You don't seem happy."

"Cody, I am overwhelmed."

"What does that mean?" He asks.

"Are you kidding? Logan Davidson and Todd Banks? Oh my god!"

He takes me in his arms and hugs me. "You like them better?"

"Not a chance in hell, but oh my God !"

"It has nothing to do with the steps?"

I look at him. "I knew there were steps."

"Stalker?" He teases.

"No. I was here once. It was part of a tour I took. I lived here for a year and wanted to know if I should have packed up my stuff and moved back sooner."

He laughs. "You decided you were safe when you saw my home?" He asks.

I laugh.

A car pulls into the driveway and two stunning women step out of the car. They each approach Cody making the deer scamper. Brittany looks at me. She smiles and hugs me tight.

"Its good to see you again." She says with such warmth in her voice.

"You too." I say and smile.

Lynn looks at me. "Its good to see you again. I wanted to thank you for all that you have done for my charity."

Todd looks at Lynn. "What are you talking about?"

Cody looks at me. "What don't you do?" He kisses me. One of those earth shattering kisses.

Brittany and Lynn hoot and howl. Todd turns his back on us. Landon and Logan walk up the steps of the house. Logan walks over to the side of the house that one can only access by climbing the steps. Logan and Landon get the ramps that are hidden on the side of the house.

Todd looks at me. "Come with me for a moment." He walks behind me and takes control of my wheelchair. "Push the pink button."

I do. A portable elevator opens and I am completely overwhelmed. Cody runs over and hugs Landon first and then Todd. He hugs Logan last.

I get in the elevator and go up and down a few times. When I go up, I scream with happiness. When I come back down I get out and burst into tears. Happy tears run down my cheeks.

Lynn and Brittany stand next to me wiping their eyes. Brittany looks at Cody, "This is a very special girl you have here."

""We will have to talk Brit. She doesn't like to talk about herself." Cody says.

Landon sits on the steps and looks so sad. I go over and put my hand on his shoulder. "Are you ok?"

"I just feel like I am a third wheel. I am the only one without a girlfriend or wife."

I look at him. "I thought that you are dating Paige Walker." I say.

He looks at me. "Who told you that?"

"She did." I say.

"You keep in touch with Paige Walker?"

"Yes. She is one of my sorority sisters."

Brittany looks at me. "You pledged?" She asks.

"I did."

"Which one?" Brittany asks.

"There was only two that I was interested in. Bronte and Aglaea. I wound up going with Aglaea."

"Charity and grace." Landon says. "It suits you."

Cody looks at his brother. "You know that?"

"Paige was the one who got me to pledge." I say.

"Why didn't you pick Bronte?" Lynn asks. "That's my chapter."

"They were a bunch of weirdos at my school." I say.

Landon looks at me. "That's not true. They didn't want you." He says.

"Why didn't they want her?" Cody asks.

"She wasn't a cheerleader." Brittany says.

"What?" Cody, Logan and Todd yell together.

"Its not a big deal." I say. "I was friends with some girls that were in Bronte. We all hung out together and we all got along." I start to itch my arm. Hives start to pucker on my skin.

Brittany looks at me. "You still get hives?"

I smile at her. "Not all the time, but yes."

"We should get you out of the fresh air." Cody says. He scoops me in his arms and walks up the steps with me. He enters the house.

I gasp. "Oh my god!" I say.

Cody and his friends sit on the couches watching television. They have packed up Cody's bedrooms. They watch a baseball game that is on. They are so involved with the game that they don't notice that Brittany, Lynn and I are gone. Landon is gone too.

Todd stands up to get a drink. He looks around. "Where is everyone?"

Cody jumps up. "Crystal!" He yells. He runs through the house looking for me. He sees my walker standing folded by his bed. "Crystal!" He yells again.

"None of them are here." Logan says.

"When did they leave?" Todd asks.

"How did they leave?" Cody asks.

"Um through the front door. She used the elevator." Todd says.

"Why didn't they say they were leaving? Did they take Landon with them?" Logan asks. "She went to school with Landon, right?"

"Yes." Cody says.

"You think that they were dating back then?" Logan asks.

"I can tell you that she never gave me the time of day." Landon says. "She didn't know that I was Cody's brother until he injured his knee and I was talking about him in class."

"You didn't tell her that you are Cody's brother?"

"We had classes together. We weren't friends. She was nice to me but overall she didn't like me." Landon says.

"Romeo, who wouldn't like you?" Todd asks teasing Landon.

Landon puts the food that he went out to get on the table and walks out of the room. Cody looks at Todd. "Why would you say that?"

"Hey they still call you Lover Boy." Todd says.

They are best friends so Cody doesn't argue the point. He is mad at Todd for being dickish to Landon. Cody is very close to his brother. He walks off to find Landon. "Hey."

"Your friends just love to rub in my face that I don't measure up to you." Landon says.

"Landon, you are better than I am."

Landon looks at him. "Better than you? Are you fucking nuts? You have women lining up to be with you."

"Landon, that's just it, I don't want women lining up for me. I never did. Some bitch got her friends to say that I went from her bed to their beds and Lover Boy came about. The truth is I turned her down and she was pissed off. She said that she would ruin me. Little did she know that she sparked a match for women to be interested in me. The only woman I want to be interested in me is Crystal Steele. I am so blessed that she loves me."

"She baffles me." Landon says. "She knows details. She listens when you think she isn't listening. I am blown away that she knows about Paige."

"How did you meet her?"

Landon looks at Cody. "How did I meet Crystal?"

"Yeah." He says.

"I heard her voice on the radio. She was talking about you. She was so serious until you hit the grand slam home run and then there was this loud scream on the radio and she was animated. She reported every play by play. When I listened to her call the games I was inspired by you. But when you cracked that grand slam, I think she sensed that you were going to do it. Its funny because it sounded like there was a loud crash where she was. When I saw her after the game, she had a black eye."

"What?" Cody asks.

"She apparently threw her hands up in the air and she knocked over a shelf."

"Oh my god, really?"

"Yeah. They called in a few guys to raise the shelf up on the wall."

They hear the door open and the three of us getting back. Todd takes Lynn in his arms and hugs her. "Where have you been?"

"We went site seeing." She says.

"Everything ok?" He asks her.

"No." Brittany says.

"Everything is fine." I say.

Cody walks over and hugs me. He pulls back from me. "Do you have a black eye?"

"No." I say.

Brittany walks over to Logan and hugs him. He holds her closer. "What happened?" He asks in her ear.

Brittany kisses him on the cheek. "A woman punched her in the face."

"What?" Cody yells

Chapter Fifteen

Landon walks over and takes my face in his hand. He holds my face up and they all look at me.

"Landon!" I yell. "Why are you always so rough?" I say and put my hand on his wrist. I push his hand away.

"Let me see it." He says. He holds my chin in his hand and with his other hand, he pushes on my cheek bone.

"Are you crazy?" I yell at him.

"Stop being a fucking baby and let me see it."

"Landon!" I grit my teeth. "Don't push hard."

"Crystal, I am not even applying pressure yet." Landon says.

"Who punched you?" Cody asks.

Lynn takes her phone out of her purse and shows them. "We were having coffee at Baseball's Café. We were laughing and we were involved in conversation. We were taking selfies and this woman walked over to us and punched Crystal in the eye. She yelled at her saying that Crystal —" she turns and looks at Cody. "You only kissed Crystal because you felt sorry for her. The woman went— just watch the video." She says.

I look at all of them. "Cody, can I take a shower?"

"Of course you can. I put the chair in there for you." He says.

"Thank you." I say. I look at Brittany and Lynn. I also look at Logan and Todd. "If you are all gone when I get back, it was nice to finally meet the two of you." I say to Logan and Todd. I look at Brittany and Lynn. "Thank you for today. I loved seeing the sites. I loved touring the city."

They all hug me. Brittany and Lynn hug me like my sisters do. It's a warm embrace. When Logan hugs me, I wince.

Cody looks at me. "Are you alright?"

"I am ok." I say.

I go into Cody's room and into the joining bathroom. I take a shower and then get dressed in pajama shorts and a shirt. I go over to Cody's bed and get in it. I lay in the middle of the bed and fall asleep.

The six of them have dinner together. Cody watches the video again and again. Landon looks at Cody. "She's been in there a long time."

Cody gets up from the table and walks to his room. He opens the door and sees that I am in the middle of his bed. He walks over to the bed and sits on it. My black eye is facing up so he can see it. He touches my cheek. He leans closer to me and kisses my cheek. "I will be with you soon." He runs his fingers through my hair.

Cody walks back into the kitchen to join his friends and Landon. Lynn looks at Cody. "She is so strong. She didn't back down. She didn't expect the punch in the eye, but she didn't back down. She took the scone that she had just taken a bite of and she threw it at the woman. It hit the woman right in the mouth." Lynn and Brittany laugh.

"She literally had no choice but to eat the half eaten scone." Brittany says. She looks at her watch, "Hun, we should go."

Cody walks them out. Lynn looks at Cody before she gets into her car with Todd. "She is so much fun. She knows a wealth of information about just about everything. She communicates well with children that we encountered. She chatted with an elderly lady who saw that kiss. The lady told Crystal that she was prettier in the picture."

"We will have to get together and chat. I need to learn more about her." Cody says.

"Talk to her." Todd says.

"When we talk, she can tell me details about my life that I don't remember. When it comes to her, she is like a clam."

"I am so glad that you two found each other." Lynn says. "Good night."

"Good night." Cody says. He looks at his friends. "Thanks for everything."

"We will be back tomorrow around noon." Todd says.

"Drive safe. See you tomorrow."

Cody walks back into the house and expects he will have to clean up everything. Everything is clean. Landon is no where to be found. Cody looks for him. He walks outside and sees Landon sitting on the porch.

"You ok?" Cody asks Landon.

"Who the fuck punches a woman in a fucking wheelchair?" Landon asks. He drinks his beer. "I can't understand how anyone does this. We have to find that bitch and have her charged."

"I think its up to her." Cody says.

"Aren't you mad about this?"

"I am really upset about it. All I want to do is go hold her."

"Go." Landon says.

"She is sleeping. I don't want to wake her up."

"Maybe you should wake her up. She might have a concussion." When he says it they both run into the house.

I am at the kitchen table eating a sandwich. "Hi."

"Hi." Cody says.

"Hi." Landon says.

"I am sorry I was rude." I say.

"No." Cody says. He walks over and hugs me. I wince when he hugs me. "What's wrong?" He pulls the neck of my shirt. He sees I am wearing a bra. He takes my shirt off of me. He sees that there is a cut in my skin that travels down my side. "Crystal, what happened?"

"Its so stupid." I say.

"What happened?" Landon asks.

"When she punched me in the face, I hit my side on the table."

Cody gets on his knees next to me. "Put your arm up." He looks at Landon. "Stand behind her. Just hold her arm so she doesn't jerk." Cody's phone rings. He takes it off the table. He looks at it. "Hi Kyle." He says.

"Why am I watching my sister get punched in the face and slammed into a table on Facebook?"

Cody looks at me. "You were slammed into a table?"

I close my eyes.

"What the fuck happened?" Kyle yells.

"Ky, let me call you back." Cody says.

"Don't hang up." Kyle says.

Cody puts his phone back on the table. He looks up at Landon. Landon nods his head. Cody puts his hands on my side. His hands are cold against my skin. His touch is light at first. Cody pushes a bit on my ribs and I wince. "That hurts?" He asks.

"Yes." I say as calmly as I can.

"Does this hurt?" He touches underneath the abrasion.

"No."

"Does this hurt?" He touches the bruised spot again.

"Yes." I say through my teeth.

"Does this hurt?" Cody asks touching above the bruised spot.

"A bit."

He slides his hand to my back. "You got slammed against the table?" He asks.

"She shoved me first. Then when I righted myself, she punched me in the eye. I literally never saw it coming."

Cody pushes his fingers into my skin. "Does this hurt?"

"No." I say.

Landon lets go of my arm. He gets on his knees next to me as well. He puts his hand on my ribs and feels around.

"For fuck's sake, Landon." I say. "Why do you have to be so rough?"

Cody looks at Landon. He looks at me. "He is touching you lighter than I did." He looks at me. "Does it hurt that bad?"

I try not to cry.

"You have to tell me." Cody says.

I do start to cry. "Is there merit in what she said? Did you kiss me because you feel sorry for me?" When the tears run down my cheek my eye stings and my cheek stings.

"What she said holds no truth." Cody says. He puts his hands on my sides. He nods to Landon.

Landon touches my cheek. Pain radiates in me.

"Ouch!" I cry out.

Cody stands and pulls my shirt back over my head. "Grab my keys." He says.

Landon gets the keys off the peg that they hang from. He also takes my purse. He locks the door to Cody's house. Cody is pushing me down the ramp that they have secured on the front steps. We get in the car.

"The woman that punched me said that she was doing it for Beth." I say.

"Doing it for Beth?" They both ask together.

"She said that you are a player but that you were being tamed by Beth. She called me by name before she shoved me into the table and then she waited a moment before she hit me in the face." I say.

"What happened afterwards?" Cody asks.

"This guy who I thought was with her grabbed her. He held her there until the police came. That's what took so long, she was arrested. They told us to come down and file official complaints. We did. There was a police officer who kept watching me as I was writing what happened. He took pictures of my eye getting a shade darker by the moment."

Cody drives to a building that looks like a training center. Landon smiles in the back seat. He parks the car in the lot and gets my wheelchair out of the trunk. I carefully get in it. When we go inside there is workout equipment everywhere. A guy walks over to us.

"Becker Brewer?" I ask. I have surprise in my tone.

He used to play baseball with Cody. Becker had ended his career on a high. He too hit two grand slam home runs in a game. What was thrilling about it was it followed Cody's grand slams. Bases were loaded and Cody was up to bat. He cracked the ball on the first hit and it went into the grandstands. The pitcher then walked the next three batters. Bases were loaded again and Becker Brewer was at bat. He had a full count. Two strikes, three balls and then he cracked the ball and it went in the grandstands.

He looks at me. He smiles. He looks at Cody and Landon. "It's the Parker brothers." He says

"This is Crystal Steele." Cody says.

"The voice on the radio?" He asks.

"Yes."

He looks at me. "You know, your excitement was heard around the world."

"I didn't know my radio station was syndicated around the world." I say.

He looks at my face. "What's going on with her eye? As we are talking to each other, her eye is getting darker and darker."

"She was out with Brittany and Lynn and she got punched in the face." Cody says.

"Wow, if my wife was there, she would have pummeled the woman." I laugh. "Your wife is a WWE fighter." I say.

Landon looks at me. "How do you know all the shit that you know?"

Paige walks over and wraps herself around Landon. "Hi babe." She says. She kisses him.

He looks at her. "How did you know we were here?"

She smiles. "I tracked you." She says.

"What?" He asks.

She laughs. "I got to the house just as you were leaving. I followed you guys here."

"How did you know that we were here?"

Paige looks at me. "We are friends. She told me that you were coming to Indiana. I was supposed to be here earlier today but I got held up."

Becker looks at Cody. "Bring her back. Let me do some x-rays and see what's going on."

We follow him back to the interior corridors of the facility. Becker looks at Cody. "How is the packing coming?"

"We got a lot done." Cody says.

"Just the two of you wise guys?" Becker asks.

"No. Logan and Todd were with us. That's why Crystal was out with Britany and Lynn."

Becker looks at me. "Has anything changed since you lived here?"

I look at him. "It seems a bit cleaned up."

"Are you calling my facility a dump?" Cody asks.

I smile. "Not at all. When I was here last, this place looked like a warehouse unit."

Landon looks at me. "Did you train here?"

"I trained her for a month." Becker says. He looks at Cody. "All she did for weeks was talk about you."

I feel hives taking over my skin.

Becker looks at me. "Do you get hives a lot?"

"Recently." I say.

He lifts me and puts me on the table. He lays me back and puts the cage over my face to do MRI images of my face. I close my eyes as he slides the machine into place.

"Ok, let me go start the images." Becker says.

"Can someone stay with me?" I ask.

"I will stay." Cody says.

I can't see him because I am in the machine. I reach my hand out and he takes it. "Cody?" I ask.

Becker's voice fills the room. "Crystal just relax. Don't talk." He says.

Twenty-five minutes later Becker is sliding the table out of the cavity. He looks at me. "Ok, we are going to do your ribs now."

"Can I get a drink?" I ask.

"Lets do this first." He says. "The time is going to be longer.

"I have to go to the bathroom." I say.

Cody walks over to lift me up. I stop him. I stand and get in my wheelchair. I leave the room and go to the bathroom.

As I am pushing back to the room, a beautiful woman stands in the hallway. She looks at me. She walks over and takes my chin in her fingertips. She tips my head up gently. "Wow, that looks nasty." She says.

"The woman who did it called me by name as she shoved me into the table that we were at. Then she waited for me to right myself in my wheelchair and then she balled her fist up. She punched me right in the eye." I say.

She puts her fingers on my cheek and lightly touches it. "If I had to guess, I would say its just bruised." She looks at me and smiles brightly. "Want me to sock you in the other eye so you match?"

I laugh. "Thank you, but no. Your hands are lethal."

"You think my hands are lethal?" She asks.

"You are Stephanie Marz-Brewer."

She looks at me. "Wow, its nice to hear my full name spoken by someone other than myself."

I smile at her.

Landon walks out of the room that he is in. He walks over to me and picks me up in his arms. He carries me back in the room and puts me back on the table. He covers me with a weighted black blanket and he turns the machine on to slide me back for more images.

Cody takes my hand.

"Cody, talk to her. She can talk through this one." Becker says.

Cody talks to me. "Sorry that Landon came to get you before I could. He wants you to like him."

"I do like him."

"You don't have to." Cody says.

"Cody, I love him like a brother. At times he was there for me more than Kyle and Brandon. I guess because he was there at school with me." I can move my arms up so I move my free hand and wipe the tears out of my eyes.

"Why are you crying?" He asks.

"I feel trapped." I say.

Becker's voice fills the room. "Crystal, you are doing great. Its just a few more minutes." He holds his hands up to Cody. He holds up both hands indicating ten more minutes. "Take a deep breath in and hold it." I do. "Ok breathe normal." He says. The machine makes different noises. "Ok, one more time. Hold your breath in three, two, one." He says.

Landon comes back in the room. He slides me out and picks me up off the table. I wrap my arms around him and cry. He holds me like Kyle has done. He kisses the top of my head when he puts me in my wheelchair. "You are all done." He says.

Cody is sitting in the chair next to my wheelchair. I go to him and put my head on his shoulder. I cry. "You are all done." Cody says. He looks at Landon. "We have to talk later."

Landon nods his head. "I am going to stay with Paige in a hotel."

"Landon, I have a house full of bedrooms. You can stay with me."

"When does the real estate agent come?" Landon asks.

My hold on Cody slacks and he looks at me. "Lets get her home." He looks at Landon. "Support her for a moment." He says. Landon puts his arms around me and pulls me away from Cody. Cody stands and then scoops me up in his arms. Cody holds me as he follows Becker around the facility.

Landon walks out to the parking lot and puts my wheelchair into the trunk. Paige walks out with him. "What did she mean that she loves you like a brother?"

He looks at Paige. "I honestly don't know why she said that."

Paige looks at him. "You must have some idea."

He looks at Paige. "It really is news to me. I didn't give her a reason to like me when we were in school with each other. I cockblocked a few guys from dating her. I don't know what she even knew about it. I took a few classes with her. One of them I made it look like I was cheating off her. I wanted to make her laugh. She failed the class and got kicked out of the program."

Paige looks at him. She laughs. "You jerk."

"I know. I didn't realize all that she had to do to take that class again."

"What does that mean?"

"She had to go to another campus."

"That's how I met her. We didn't have classes together but she allowed me to sit at her table with her to study. She would always tell me that I could only sit with her if I promised to be loud." She laughs. "She told me about you."

"Oh god. I bet it was awful."

"No. The opposite. She talked about you like she was talking about one of her brothers that she wanted to pawn off. She said that there was a guy who would always berate her. One day when she was rushing into her class and rushing to get out of the rain, he ran out and helped her. She stayed in the rain for a minute longer. She couldn't believe that he was nice to her because he never was before. He finally went behind her and took control of her wheelchair and pushed her into the building. He went into the bathroom and got handfuls of paper towels. He took her feet off the hangers and dried the metal plates. She told me that she thought you had something to do with it. She told me that every time she went to talk to you, you would turn away and walk the other way."

"I did." He says.

"Why?"

"I didn't want her to know that I was attracted to her. I knew that she was in love with my brother. I wanted her to have that. I wanted to introduce them and then he got attacked." Landon says.

Cody walks out of the facility carrying me. Landon opens the door. Cody puts me in the car. "Come home so she doesn't think that she did something to upset you." He says to Landon. He looks at Paige. "You are welcome to stay with us."

"We will follow you." Paige says. "Can we stop for anything?"

"No." Cody says. He gets in the car and drives back to his house.

When he pulls into the driveway, he parks the car as close to the front as he can get. He gets my wheelchair out of the car and brings it up the steps. He puts it in the house. He then turns and walks down the steps. He opens the door and takes me in his arms.

Landon pulls Paige's car in the driveway. She gets out of the car. "You need me to get her wheelchair?"

"No. I put it in the house already. Can you just lock my car up?"

"Of course." She says.

Cody carries me in the house. He walks right into his bedroom and kicks the door closed behind him. He puts me in bed. He walks over to his closet and looks through a box. He takes out the bandage wraps and comes back over to the bed. He wakes me up. "Crystal, hun, I need you to sit up." He says sweetly.

I don't wake up. I snuggle more deeply into the pillows.

He gets off the bed. He walks out of the room and looks for Landon. Landon and Paige are lying on the couch. He looks at both of them. "I am sorry to interrupt. Landon, can you help me with something?"

"Sure." He says. He gets off the couch and follows Cody into his room. "What do you want me to do?"

"Support her for a moment. I am going to wrap her ribs." Cody says.

Landon sits on the bed and takes me in his arms. My head drops back. Landon puts his hand on my back above my sport bra. He supports my head with his other hand. Cody takes the bandage and starts wrapping my ribs. When he finishes he takes me in his arms.

"Thank you."

"If you need me for anything else, let me know. I will bring her wheelchair in here." Landon leaves the room and brings my wheelchair in the room. "Angle it so its easy for her to get in it." He smiles at Cody.

"Hey can you do me a favor?"

"Whats that?"

"Can you help me draw up legal papers against Beth?"

"Of course. We will work on it tomorrow." Landon hugs Cody.

♥

Cody and I sit having breakfast. My ribs are sore. My eye is swollen shut and more blackened than it was yesterday. I reach my hand across the table and take Cody's hand. Cody puts his hand on my hand. I finish eating my breakfast.

"I am going to call Becker and see if the results are in for your MRI."

"I am sorry I passed out last night. I have issues laying on my back for a long time. I think that Landon knew that and thought that I would sleep while I was in the MRI."

"How would Landon know that you pass out if you are on your back too long?"

I start to laugh. "He didn't tell you?"

"He didn't tell me."

I laugh again. "When we were in school, I was in a gym class. I went into a batting cage because they make me happy. I was getting ready to hit the ball and it came out of the machine at ninety miles an hour. It hit me in the chest. Landon was somewhere in the gym and he heard the hit and my whimper for help. It knocked the breath out of me. He came in the cage and got me. He brought me to the hospital to see if anything was broken. Nothing was. I had to have an MRI, he paid for it. Anyway, I was telling the technician that I couldn't lay on my back for a long time. He just ignored me. When it was all over, I got in my wheelchair, I found Landon waiting for me in the waiting room. I hugged him and passed out. He took me back to school."

"Why didn't you say anything?"

"I didn't know you were taking me to get an MRI."

"What did you think of the facility?"

"From what I saw of it, the MRI machine and the bathroom, it was lovely."

"Would you want to go workout?"

"Can I workout with broken ribs?"

Landon and Paige walk in. He kisses the top of my head like Kyle always does. Paige kisses my cheek. She puts her finger on my cheek. I don't wince under her touch. She looks at me. "I don't understand why its so black and blue."

"I don't know." I say.

"Do you always bruise so easily?"

"I haven't been punched in the face since I was a kid." I say.

Landon looks at my face. He pushes on my cheek. I don't yell at him. He observes that my eye is swollen shut. "It looks worst then yesterday and is swollen shut, yet we can touch it without you screaming at me." He says.

"Maybe she broke my eye socket." I say.

"We should call Becker to find out what the results are." Cody says.

Someone rings the bell. Then there is pounding on the door. Cody looks at his phone and sees who is outside. He gets up from the table and walks to the door. He opens the door.

"Where the fuck is my sister?"

"Where do you think she is?"

"Why is it that she is on Facebook yet again, only this time, she is being punched in the face?" Kyle asks.

"Come on in. She is at the table. We are having breakfast." Cody says. "How the hell did you get here?"

"I drove."

"You drove?" Cody looks at him incredulously.

Kyle follows Cody into the kitchen. Paige and Landon are sitting there eating breakfast. Kyle takes bacon off of the main plate and pops it in his mouth. He looks around the house that he stayed in with Cody years before. He looks at Cody. "Are you selling?"

"Yes. I am not going to live here. I am going to live in Florida."

"Who the hell hit my sister?"

"Someone who knows Beth."

"Where is my sister?"

"She went to change." Paige says.

"Change or hide?" Kyle asks.

"I don't hide from anything." I say. I look at him. "What are you doing here?"

"I came to bring you home." Kyle says like I knew exactly why he came.

"I am sorry, did I not get the memo that I am ten?" I look at him. "You came, you saw that I am ok, now get back in your car and go home. Report to your mom, my mom and dad that I got beat up."

"That's not what I would ever do."

"Kyle, I am here with Cody. I want to be here."

He looks at my face. He tries not to smile but he doesn't hide it well. "Its like when you were young." He walks closer to me and puts his hand under my chin. He tips my head up. "Is it the same eye that Kelsey socked you in?"

"Yes." I say.

Kyle looks at Cody. "You need to take her to have images."

"We did that." Cody says.

"What did they say?"

"We will get the results later today." I say.

Kyle looks at me. "Why didn't you call any of us?"

"Kyle, I am here with Cody and Landon, why would I call you all in Florida? What are you going to do about it down there?"

"Get in my car to bring you home."

"If you take me, I will report it as kidnapping." I say seriously.

"What is wrong with you?" He asks.

"Kyle, get back in your car and go home. I love you. You are like a brother to me but you are really nothing to me." I know what I just said hurt him. I know it would have been like a knife in the heart. We have a great relationship. We always have been close.

He looks at me and then at Cody. "Why would you bring her here?"

"I wanted her to see my home. I wanted to spend time with her and not be interrupted. I wanted to bring her away so that I can get to know personal things about her." He says and kisses me on the lips. He rubs his thumb against my cheek. He deepens the kiss. I wrap my arms around him.

Cody and I lay in his bed. I lay with my cheek on his shoulder. We are not sleeping. The television is on quietly. Cody looks at me. He runs his fingers through my hair and rubs his hand over my ribs. I wince a bit. "That still hurts?"

"Yes."

"Let me check it out." He says. "Becker said that its just bruised."

"Will we be able to leave when you need to? I heard him tell you that I shouldn't fly."

"We are going to be here for a week. Lets play it by ear and see what happens."

"Cody, do you think that I am ungrateful?"

"Ungrateful?" He asks.

"Yes. The way I spoke to Kyle. I am glad he was concerned. He has always loved me like I am his sister. I think I was his favorite when we were growing up. But when he demanded that I get in the car and that he was going to take me home. Do you think that I am ungrateful?"

"No. I think you sounded like a woman who knew that she was being bullied by her brother."

"He is going to tell Joanne and then she is going to treat me worse than she does now."

"Sweetheart, we will deal with that when we get home." He lays me back against the softness of the most comfortable sheets I have been in. "I am going to examine you." He says.

I smile at him. "Don't hurt me."

He kisses me. "I am not going to intentionally hurt you." He says. My body reacts to his softest touch. He smiles at me. "We are not doing that." He says and pushes his fingers into my ribs. I cry out. "I know it hurts. I am going to push harder. Take a deep breath."

"Don't hurt me." I say again.

He kisses me. "I am going to hurt you but I am not being mean."

I squirm.

Cody looks at me. "Crystal, let me do this."

I start to cry which is not my thing. I usually don't let anyone see me cry. I cover my face with my hands. The tears drip down the sides of my face.

"Crystal, are you in a lot of pain?"

"I have to sit up." I say.

He takes me in his arms and pulls me into his embrace. "Are you in a lot of pain?"

"No." I sob.

"Crystal, why are you crying?" He asks sincerely.

I push away from him and get off the bed. I go in the bathroom and close the door.

He walks over to the door. He knocks. "Crystal? What's going on?" He asks sweetly. "Can I come in?" He tries to open the door but its locked. "Crystal?"

He leaves the room. He looks at Paige who is sitting draped all over Landon. "Can you please go in there and talk to her? She has locked herself in the bathroom."

Paige jumps up. She slips on the tiled floor and Landon grabs her. She smiles at him. She slips her socks off and runs into Cody's room. "Tally, open the door." She says sweetly.

I unlock the door. She comes in and looks at me. She sits on the toilet so that we are eye to eye.

"You ok?" She asks.

"No."

"What's wrong?"

"My family sucks. I am upset that Kyle came and was so demanding. I am upset that he didn't call me. He is making me feel guilty."

"Hun, don't let him do that."

"That woman who hit me was so mean. I wish that the only pain I felt was in my ribs and my eye, but I feel sad. She said the meanest things to me."

Cody stands with Landon in the doorway listening.

"What did she say?" Paige asks.

"She said that Cody deserves so much better than my crippled ass." I sob.

Cody runs in the bathroom and takes me in his arms. He picks me up out of my wheelchair and holds me tight. Landon hugs me too. Paige cries. Cody talks quietly into my ear. "I don't want anyone else. I don't deserve you. You are so amazing. I am honored that you love me as much as you do."

His phone rings in his pocket. Landon looks at Cody and reaches in Cody's back pocket for the phone. His phone reads Beth. Landon looks at Cody. "Can I answer it?"

Cody nods his head. He sits me back in my wheelchair. He takes his phone from Landon and runs from the bathroom.

Landon wets a cloth and hands it to me. "We will give you time if you need it." He says. Landon gets on his knees and hugs me. He takes Paige's hand in his and they leave the bathroom.

I put the cloth to my face and wipe my tears away. I go into the room and pack up my stuff. I see Cody outside talking on the phone. I can tell that he is screaming at Beth. I take my phone off the nightstand. I call Kyle. He picks up on the first ring. "Can you bring me home?" I don't let him answer me. "I want you to know that I am really pissed off at you. I am mad that you think that I needed you to bring me home. When we get back to Florida, I am going to address somethings with the whole family and if all of you don't talk to me, I can live with that. I love Cody. You know that. You almost ruined my relationship like you did years ago with my prom date."

"I will bring you home." He says.

Landon and Paige are kissing on the couch. I have my stuff and I leave the house without them seeing me. I go down the ramp and push my wheelchair to the end of the long driveway. I wait for Kyle. When he pulls up, I get in his car. He puts my wheelchair in the car and gets in. We leave.

Chapter Sixteen

Cody stands on the grass yelling into his phone. "Beth, what the fuck is wrong with you? Who was the girl who you had punch Crystal in the face?"

"Her name is Claudia. She is my best friend." She laughs wickedly.

"Beth, how did you get my number?"

"It was in the bridal package files."

"No." He says. "How did you get my number?"

"Your cousin gave it to me. She thinks that you and I make a good couple."

"Beth!" He growls. "You and I are nothing. I am engaged—"

"Oh stop it. You are not engaged to that bitch!" She screeches

"I am engaged to her. I am going to marry her and spend the rest of my life with her."

"What does that fucking bitch have that I don't?"

"Me." He yells. "Beth, I am going to press charges against your friend and you. I am going to ruin you."

"Your mom even thinks that you are making a mistake." Beth says.

"My family loves her. My parents love that she brings out the best in me."

"I am the best for you."

"She brings the best out of me." Cody says. "If you call me again, I will press charges against you." He disconnects the phone. He runs in the bedroom and sees immediately that my stuff is gone. "Fuck!" He screams.

Landon and Paige run in his room. Landon notices that my things are gone. Paige runs from the room and outside.

"Crystal!" She yells.

Cody calls Kyle. Kyle answers on the first ring. "Bring her back!" He yells.

"She wants to go home."

"Kyle, you are my best fucking friend. Bring her back!"

"We are on the highway heading south."

"Kyle, when you get to Kentucky you fucking stop. I will fly there. Don't go further."

"Ok." Kyle agrees.

Cody runs in the house. "I need a ride to the airport."

Paige looks at him. "Take the car. They can't be that far ahead of you. Be safe." She says. "Its only forty minutes away. Go after her."

Landon walks in the room. "Go to the park, your ride is waiting for you."

Cody hugs his brother tight. "You called in a favor?"

"No, one of my clients has hot air balloons." Landon says.

"What?" Cody and Paige both ask at the same time.

Landon laughs. "My friend has a helicopter. He is going to fly you to the airport."

"Cody, she is going to need to drive home. She can't fly with cracked ribs. She does have a fracture in her cheek bone." Paige says.

"I know." He says.

Landon and Paige drive Cody to the park. He meets Landon's friend who owns the helicopter. Before Cody climbs in it, he looks at Landon. "Thank you. Can you please make sure that bear wearing the shirt gets packed up?"

"The bear is gone." Landon tells Cody.

Cody climbs in the helicopter and it takes off.

Kyle pulls off at the Ohio-Kentucky stop. I keep my gaze out the window. I am not paying attention. I hold the teddy bear that I sent to

Cody all those years back to my chest. I don't even notice that Kyle has stopped driving. He pulls the car into a parking lot.

"Are you going to talk to me?" He asks. "Dad is so mad at me. Your mom screamed at me. Brandon is livid with me. Your sisters are pissed off." He puts his hand on my hand. "I just wanted to protect you."

I look at him. "Where are we?" I ask wiping my eyes.

"I had to make a stop."

A helicopter circles a few times and then lands in an empty lot. Cody gets out of it and runs over to the car. He throws open the passenger door and takes me in his arms. We both cry.

"I thought I lost you." Cody says. He holds me tight in his arms. "I love you. I need you. I want you, forever!"

"I love you so much." I tell him.

Cody pulls away from me and looks at the teddy bear. "You are in Indian giver." He says.

I smile.

"No. You can't have beary, you gave him to me."

"To borrow." I say with a wide smile.

"Um no." Cody says.

I look at Cody and get serious for a moment. "Cody, you should get back to your house and pack it up. Kyle can take me home. I will see you in a few days."

"I am not letting you out of my sight." Cody says.

"Cody, you need to take care of things." I say.

"Crystal, we have legal issues to deal with in Indiana. We can't just leave yet. You can't just leave. We are pressing charges and making sure that they stand." Cody says. "We are all going to be here for you." He looks at Kyle. "Ky, will be here and anyone you want. If you want your friends or your sisters or—"

"Stew?" I ask quietly.

"Of course." Cody and Kyle say together.

The guy in the helicopter runs over, "I have to go back. I can take one of you with me."

Cody looks at Kyle. "Go ahead. I will drive back."

Kyle doesn't think twice about it. He kisses me on the cheek. "I love you."

"I love you too." I say to him. "I am so sorry for what I said yesterday."

Kyle looks at Cody. "Before I leave, can we talk a second?"

Cody stands me up and I hold on to the car before I sit in the passenger seat. Cody kisses me on the lips. "I will be right back."

Cody and Kyle walk out of ear shot. Actually everything is out of ear shot because of the sound of the helicopter. I sit in the car and watch them but I can't read lips well enough. I know they are talking about me because they both look at me at the same time. Kyle hugs Cody. Cody walks back to the car. He gets in the driver's seat and adjusts the seat.

"He told me that you said nothing to him." Cody says.

"I had nothing to say."

"Why?"

I look at him. I hold the teddy bear that I sent Cody in my arms. "Because I am really angry at him. They treat me like I am a baby and I am neglected in the middle. I got used to the fact that they were all busy with their lives and didn't interfere with mine. Kyle did interfere once before. He promised not to do it again."

"Tell me about it." Cody says. "And you can hold on to that teddy bear until we get home. Then I am taking her back."

"Her? Um no. It's a him."

"Now that I know its from you, it's a her."

I laugh.

"Tell me about Kyle interfering."

"I was in high school. I had a boyfriend and I really liked him. I didn't dream of being with him forever, but he asked me to prom and I was thrilled. Three days before prom he came to my mom's house and told me that he couldn't take me for fear of getting beaten up by not only Kyle but also the whole soccer and football teams."

"What did you do?"

"I went to prom anyway. He wasn't there. I had as much fun as I was going to have. I danced with my friends. I partied like I wanted to. I went home and my boyfriend was standing blocking my front door."

"What did you do?"

"I punched him in the balls. He fell into my mom's bougainvilleas."

"Ouch. They have thorns."

I laugh.

"I would have been more scared of you then of getting beaten up by Kyle. Kyle fights like a girl."

I laugh again.

"Talk to me. Tell me about your friends. Why did you go to school and not return?"

"My friends are great. I have a few of them that have been apart of my life since I was in kindergarten. I treasure them. They are like my chosen sisters. I love my sisters, but they would always gang up on me. They always thought that I got too much of my mom's time. I know that she and my dad had to dedicate a lot of time to make my life what it is now. My mom and dad were advocates for me. I remember my dad going to my school and yelling at my teacher in front of the whole class that she had some nerve not letting me go play on the playground with everyone else. From that day on, I was always included. My friends always played with me. They always made me feel so special. They never treated me differently."

"Are you still friends with them now?"

I look out the window.

"Crystal."

"I actually haven't spoken to the three of them in two years. They came into my bridal shop to get fitted for their dresses and I heard them talking to Beth. I don't know what its about her but people confide in her. I felt like I was stabbed in the back. My one friend was the bride. I didn't go to the wedding. I sent a gift in my absence."

"Crystal, tell me."

"Cody, I don't want to tell you."

"Why?"

"She returned my gift and everything was broken. She wrote me a note that the worst thing she did in her life was staying friends—" I choke on a sob.

Cody pulls the car over. He gets out of the car and hugs me. "She was wrong. You are the best person to know. I am sure she regrets that she ever said that to you. What did you get her?"

"I sent her a picture frame that she admired." I say. "I buried myself in work. I buried myself in knowing all your stats. That's what made me happy. I saw her a year after she was married. She came into my shop and she told me to my face that she would never see me again." I cry into his chest.

"When we go back to Florida we should see her."

"She left my shop and she drove her car into a cement pillar." I say. "She was three months pregnant."

"Oh my god, Crystal." Cody says.

"I went to her funeral. Her husband told me that I hurt her so much by not coming to the wedding." I wipe my tears. "I know he was hurting. It turned out that she left a note."

"What did the note say?"

"I never read the one that I got. I have it in a box, but I never opened it."

"I am sorry that happened. What was her name?"

"Gabriella." I say.

An hour and a half later, Cody pulls the car into the driveway of his house. He drove around longer so that we didn't have to return right away. When he parks the car, Landon and Kyle are standing outside waiting for us.

He gets out of the car. He walks over to the passenger side and opens the door. He takes me in his arms carefully so not to wake me up. He carries me up the steps. Kyle runs to the door and opens it for us.

Kyle opens his mouth to ask questions, Cody shakes his head. He walks right into his room and lays me in the middle of the bed.

Landon walks into the room with my wheelchair. He brings my bags in and Cody's teddy bear. "What did you talk about?"

Cody looks at Landon. He rubs his hands up and down my side.

"She told you about Gabriella?" Landon asks.

Cody looks at him with sadness in his eyes. "How do you know about her?"

"We were in school together. Not Gabriella and me, but—" he points at me. "She had been so excited about going to her best friend's wedding. She was excited that her friends were coming to get their dresses for the wedding at the Butterfly place. Rosa had sent her out for something and when she got back, her friends of many years were besties with Beth and talking shit about Crystal."

Cody kisses my lips.

Landon stands against the wall. "Crystal never let anyone see her cry. She always seems like everything is ok. That day in class when I made like I was cheating off her test, I was just trying to make her smile." He looks at Cody. "I swear, she ran out of that room. She hit that door so quickly and she was gone."

"Where did you find her?" Kyle asks.

"She was in the gym working out. It was like she was just on automatic. She was on the rowing machine and she never stopped. The cable snapped. The trainer ran over and got there before it injured her."

"What did she do?" Cody and Kyle ask together.

"She went into the locker room with such speed, everyone thought that she got hurt. I convinced them that I was her friend and I would check on her. When she saw me, she let me hold her while she cried." He looks at Cody. "It wasn't romantic."

"She told me that she loves you like a brother. She told me that you were very sweet to her. She didn't tell me the situation." Cody says. He kisses my cheek.

"She told me what happened. She cried her eyes out. Then when Gabriella returned the expensive gift that Crystal sent to her and it was shattered, Crystal was devastated. Gabriella went to her bridal shop and in front of a crowded store told Crystal off. Then she drove into a concrete support beam. She died on impact. I went with her to the funeral."

"She went to the funeral?" Kyle asks.

"What are the other two friends' names?" Cody asks.

"Amber and Heather." Kyle says. "The four of them were as thick as thieves growing up. They were so tight. Kelsey was jealous of their relationship. Honestly, Kelsey didn't make any grand effort to make her feel like she wanted her around." He looks at me sleeping. "I asked her if she went to the funeral and she told me that she didn't."

"She did." Landon says. "Gabriella's husband was mean to Crystal. Gabriella's mom and dad were glad to have her there. When it was all over, Crystal asked me if we could stay back a bit longer. She went over to where Gabriella's grave is and she spoke to her friend for almost an hour. I let her go alone. When she crumbled in tears, I brought her home." Landon wipes the tears out of his eyes. "The family welcomed everyone to come back to the house to gather. Gabriella's husband told her in front of a crowd of people that he didn't want her to come."

Paige walks into Cody's room. She wraps her arms around Landon. "She told me that the way you were there for her in a brotherly way meant the world to her. I know that she was devastated for a long time. It was like she stopped shining for awhile." She looks at Cody. "Then you cracked that grand slam and I swear it was like she was a bright light again. She was happy. One would think that she hit those grand slams. She spoke about it so much."

Cody kisses me again on the lips.

"We will see you in the morning." Kyle says. The three of them leave Cody's room.

My phone rings. I take it off the table and answer it without looking to see who is calling me. "Hello." I say cheerfully.

"Crystal, hi." Heather says.

"Heather?"

"Hi." She says.

"Hi?"

"How are you doing?"

"I am shocked that you are calling me." I say.

I hear her gasp. "I know, I have been a shitty friend. I am sorry that we lost touch."

"I am speechless. I don't know what you want."

"Jonathan said he saw you yesterday."

"Jonathan?"

"I am married to him. We have three children. A girl and twin sons."

"Congratulations." I say it dryly. "How did Jonathan see me? Where did he see me?"

"He flies commercial helicopters."

"Oh, you have to be fucking kidding me." I say. "Landon's pilot friend is Jonathan?" I laugh but not because I find any of this funny. "That's rich."

"I want to see you."

"Its good to want things."

"Listen—"

"No." I say.

"That is right, always be you. Someone pisses you off and you cut them off and out of your life."

"You didn't piss me off, you hurt me. You walked away." I defend myself.

"I wasn't calling to cause you any more troubles. I was calling to see if we could get together for lunch."

"Let me think about it."

"How long are you here?"

"At least a week." I admit.

"I will call you in a few days."

"Ok." I tell her. "What did you name your children?"

I hear her smile through the phone. "Courtney is five and the twins are three. We have Liam and Gabe."

"How wonderful." We hang up. I think about it. Gabriella is only gone five years. "Holy shit!" I say loudly.

Cody walks over. "Are you alright?" He asks kissing me on the lips.

"Heather and Jonathan were together before Gabriella died. Heather was pregnant." I scramble off the couch. I get in my wheelchair. I call my mom. "Is it ok if I go outside?" I ask Cody. I am not asking his permission, I am really asking him to help me out to the deck. There are steps leading to it.

"Yes." Cody says.

Kyle walks over, he picks me up in his arms and carries me to the deck. Cody brings my wheelchair. Kyle sits me in my wheelchair. He kisses me on the head and looks around making sure that there is plenty of room for me to pace because he knows that I am going to do that.

"We will leave the door open so we hear you when you are ready." Cody says.

"I will call you." I tell him.

"That makes sense." Cody and Kyle say smiling.

They walk in the house.

I call my mom. "Mom."

"Hi sweetheart." She says.

"Are you home?"

"I am."

"Can you go in my room and in the bottom of the closet is that white wedding box?"

"Yes." She says. I can hear her shuffling into my room. This makes me smile. I hear her open the closet door. "I will have to tell Stew to lube these doors."

I am caught off guard by her remark that I throw my head back and burst out laughing. I sober immediately.

"How are you doing?"

"I am sore really." I say.

"Ashley and Brandon came and showed us Facebook posts of you getting punched in the face."

"Yeah." I sigh.

"How are your ribs?"

"Cracked."

"Why did she do it?"

"She's friends with Beth." I say.

I hear Stew talking to mom. "I am going to the airport."

"Mom, give him the box. I need that box."

"Ok, sweetheart."

"Don't be mad that I asked for Stew."

"Sweetest, stop. Kyle told me whats been going on." She says.

"Of course he did." I look out at the skyline "When do they ever let me tell my own story?"

"You have to beat them to it." She says.

"Mom, did you ever see Heather after Gabriella got married?"

"How did this come up?"

"Heather called me."

"Out of the blue."

"Yes." I turn my wheelchair so that I can see in the house. Cody is standing talking to Kyle and Landon, Paige is sitting on the couch. "Did you hear anything from Heather after the wedding?"

"She moved in with them."

"What?"

"Heather and Gabriella lived together in school. When Gabriella got back from her honeymoon, she was so heart sick. She wanted to call you and clear things up with you."

"She sent me the gift I sent her shattered in a million pieces. I paid a lot of money for her gift. I planned on handing it to her on her wedding day."

"What happened?" Mom asks.

I tell her all about it. I don't hold back. I don't keep anything unsaid. When I finish, I am crying ugly tears.

"Sweetest, why didn't you tell us?"

"You and daddy were going to the wedding, I didn't want anything harsh said when I wasn't there. I didn't want her parents to know anything was wrong." I say through tears.

"Crystal, do you think that your absence went unnoticed? You four girls had been friends since kindergarten. Gabriella looked gorgeous but miserable. There were tears but not all of them were happy tears. Jonathan was happy for the both of them."

"Rosa and Beth had a plan and it backfired."

"I know all about that bitch Rosa."

"What do mean?"

"Sweetest, go enjoy your beautiful fiancé."

I smile and can't control my happiness. I am always happy when it comes to being with Cody. "Mom!"

"Crystal."

"I dreamt that I would be his."

"Well all that dreaming has paid off. When you get back to Florida, daddy and all of us want to treat you all to dinner."

"Mom!" I screech.

"What?"

"Don't call him daddy. He is not your daddy."

She laughs before she hangs up. "I love you." She doesn't allow me to answer her back.

Paige and I are in the kitchen. I cut the vegetables while she prepares the chicken. She is cutting it in strips. Landon walks in the kitchen. He kisses Paige on the cheek. She smiles and turns into him.

I look at the two of them. "Do you want me to give you some time?" I ask.

"You don't have to leave." Landon says.

I look at Landon. "How long have you been friends with Jonathan? I didn't know that when you went with me to my best friend's funeral that you knew her husband."

"Don't always think the worst of me." Landon says. He looks up at the ceiling.

Paige looks at him. "Tell her."

I look at Landon. I put the knife down on the table. I push away from the table. I try to leave the kitchen.

"Wait." Landon says. "I went with you to your friend's funeral because I thought you needed a friend. I didn't know Jonathan. I met him at the funeral." He scrubs his hands through his hair."You couldn't be dragged away from the grave. I waited and gave you space that I think you needed. Jonathan watched you crumble. We watched you and my heart broke. Jonathan wanted to go over and remove you personally. I threatened him. I told him that if he dared touch you, I would put him in the hospital." Landon sits at the table next to me. "Crystal, he told me that he needed legal advice. After I pointed him in the right direction, another lawyer handled his issues, he found me and wanted to know all about you."

"Me?"

"He wanted to know why you weren't at the wedding? You were supposed to be the maid of honor. He wanted to know what caused you to not show up but to send the most beautiful picture frame he had ever seen. He said that in the frame were pictures of him and her from when they started dating. He said that there were pictures of her bridal shower." He looks at me. "When she sent the frame back were the pictures with it?"

"Like confetti." I say.

"Johnathan told me that he wanted a copy of those pictures. He didn't have them. He said he came home from work and the frame was shattered. She packed it all up in a box." He says.

"I know. She mailed it to me." I look at him. "You know all about it."

"I do." Landon says.

"I don't think the worst of you." I say.

He looks at me. He takes me in his arms and hugs me. "I know you love me." He whispers in my ear.

"I do like a third brother." I hug him. "Did you know that Heather and him have three children together?"

"Yes."

"How long were they together?"

"Heather moved in with them right after they got back from their honey moon. The three of them had a threesome. They both got pregnant within a few months of each other."

Paige looks at me. "The truth is, Heather was always with Jonathan. They dated in college. She loved him. Then he met Gabriella and once they hooked up, they couldn't get enough of each other. Heather was heartbroken."

"I didn't know any of it. We went to different colleges. Kelsey and Kyle thought that I needed to make more friends. They said that I needed to be independent."

Landon's phone rings. He looks at it and walks out of the room after kissing me on the top of my head. He also kisses Paige on the lips.

I finish making the dinner by myself. I take the chicken that Paige cut into strips and put it in a marinade. I put it in a pan with the vegetables around it. The last I put on top is garlic cloves. I put it in the oven. I make a salad and other things for dinner as well.

Cody and Kyle get back to the house with Stew. When they walk in they are greeted with the smell of dinner. I baked brownies and cookies. I made a lot of things that I know Cody likes, but I also made things for everyone that is in the house with me.

Stew hugs me. "Hi." He says.

Kyle looks at me. "I need to talk to you for a moment." He says and takes my hand. He pulls me out of the kitchen. "Don't get upset but dad came too."

When my dad walks in the house, I rush to him and burst into tears. I try to pull myself together but I can't control the tears. He holds me tight and I wince but I don't want him to let me go. I want to be his baby girl again. I want to be a little girl in his arms and be surrounded by my dad's love.

We all sit down at the table for dinner. Everyone eats. My dinner was liked by everyone. There is none left for leftovers. After dinner, Landon and Paige load the dishwasher. We all sit around the den watching television. The whole time we sit with my family, Cody never lets go of my hand.

"Is there an ointment that you can put on your eye?" Stew asks.

"No." I say.

"When is she going to court?" Dad asks.

"Tuesday." Cody says.

We all watch my dad take his phone out of his pocket and look at the calendar. I feel my heart break. Why would he come if he can't stay? This is what I have asked myself my whole life since they divorced.

Kyle looks at him. "You told us that you can stay until next weekend."

Dad looks at all of us. "No. No. I am staying. I was just putting it in my calendar." He says. He looks at me. "I am staying."

Stew looks at me. "I am honored that you wanted me to come."

"I am so happy that you came." I say.

"I have that white box that you asked for." Stew says.

"Thank you."

Dad looks at me. "You wanted the wedding box?"

Everyone looks at me. "Its not a wedding box." It is a wedding box. "Its just something that I kept always."

"Why did you have me bring it?" Stew says.

"Gabriella left me a note. I never read it. I put it in the box."

"You are going to read it here?" Dad asks.

"Jonathan and Heather live up here." I say.

"You have got to be kidding me." Dad says.

I know exactly what he is thinking. I thought that same thing.

"Have you seen them?" Dad asks.

"No." I say.

Kyle looks at dad. "I told you that he was the helicopter pilot."

Later, Cody and I are sitting on Cody's bed. It is so comfortable. I sit with a pillow over my legs and the box is on top of it. Cody sits next to me. "Do you want me to give you some privacy?"

I shake my head. "No. I asked Stew to bring it so that I could read it with you."

"There is no rush, whenever you are ready." Cody says.

I open the white box. I take the lid off and lay it on the bed next to me. Cody looks in the box. I take the letter out. It is still in the envelope. I hand it to Cody.

"You want me to read it?" He asks.

"Yes." I say.

Crystal,

I am so mad at you. I can't get over it. Its been so long since we have spoken to each other. What happened to us? I am heartbroken that you think that I would ever bad mouth you to Beth. I don't know what you heard or what she told you, but I never spoke badly of you. You were my best friend. You knew all my secrets but one. I never told you that I had a crush on you. You were always there for me. So when I needed you to be there for me at my wedding, and you weren't, I felt abandoned by you. You told me that you felt abandoned by your dad leaving your mom and marrying Joanne. You said that you never wished that feeling on anyone, well that's exactly how you made me feel. I want to curse at you. I want to call you all the bad names that we promised each other we would never say to one another. I hate that you missed my wedding. I hate that you weren't there for me. I hate that I can't hate you. I hate Heather. She knew — she fucking knew how much I loved Jonathan. I know that you think that everything changed between us when I met Jonathan, but I am not sure that is the truth. I think that we were growing apart because we were growing up. Kelsey was happy that you and I didn't go to the same schools for college. The truth is, I needed time to get over you. You didn't do anything to lead me on or anything, but I found myself wanting to spend time with you.

I made the biggest mistake of my life. I let someone else into my bed. I have to be honest with you because I have always been honest with you. Heather and I have been fooling around with one another for a few years now. After I got married and got back from my honeymoon, I found myself truly sad. Heather came for a visit and told us that she was being kicked out of her house. She asked if she could stay with us for a few days. I agreed because I was in need of a friend. I know why I am sad, but I can't tell anyone. I am going to tell you, I was pregnant before I got married. I carried him for eight months and then there was problems. I lost him. We had a funeral for him and I am so mad that you weren't there. My mom and dad yelled at me and told me that I couldn't be mad at you because you didn't know about it. I didn't tell you. I wanted you to be there.

Crystal, I blame you for a lot of things that went wrong in my life. This is the last time that I will blame you. I came home from work early in hopes to catch my husband alone and tell him my good news. I am pregnant. I can tell that this one is going to be different. I feel so energized. I can't keep busy enough. But when I came home, I heard noises coming from my room. And oh my god! Heather was naked straddled on top of my husband. We had always had a threesome encounters, but it was always her and I that touched each other and I was the only one having sex with my husband. At least that's what I thought. I am so heart sick. I lost you and now I agree that its my fault. You didn't know. I saw you and I wanted to come over and hug you. I wanted to run to you and cry in your arms. I heard you on the radio and you sounded so happy. I can hear the love that you have for Cody Parker. It is beyond me why you would love anyone who goes by the nickname Lover Boy. That's not true. He is gorgeous.

I wish you love, my friend. Heather is pregnant. If we both have children now, what will people think. I have to tell you, that I love you. I love that you never stopped being friends with me. I know I was the weird one. You have shared so many wonderful moments with me. I will be leaving soon for another place. I have no love, but I take your love that you always shared with me with me. Good bye my friend. I love you. Go find your Lover Boy and make him yours, you deserve him. You deserve the world. Your dad abandoned you all those years ago, I know now that I am the one who abandoned you and I am doing it again. I believe in my heart of hearts that we will meet again. Until then, love as much as you do. Share your love, it's a gift."

All my love,

Gabs

I sob. I can't stop the tears. Cody holds me and cries with me.

We lay in bed and he sleeps. I lay next to him wide awake. I get out of bed and go into the kitchen for a drink. Kyle sits at the table with his laptop doing work. He looks at me. I look at him.
"You ok?" He asks. He holds his arms out to me.

Chapter Seventeen

"I read the note that she left for me." I say.

"She wrote you a note?"

"She did." I say into his chest. "She planned it. She drove into the wall on purpose."

"You knew that." Kyle says.

"I know but I hoped, I always hoped that it was wrong. She caught Heather and Jonathan in bed together."

"Crystal, Jonathan and Heather had been together a long time. They never stopped dating each other when he got together with Gabriella. When he got with her, she was pregnant already."

"How do you know that?" I ask pulling away from him.

"I can't tell you." He says.

"Was the baby yours? Is what I heard them talking about in my bridal shop true? She was getting fucked by my brother?" I look at him. "Please tell me it wasn't you."

"It wasn't me."

"Brandon?" I ask.

"Crystal, if I tell you—"

"They made it seem like they were all with you. Even Beth."

"I hate that bitch. I was never with Beth."

"Was Brandon?" I ask like I am a child.

My voice is low, I get mad at myself. It is late so I don't want to yell, but why didn't I ask it in a normal tone? I know why, I don't want to know if he did. I don't want to think differently of him. I know that he was always looking for a companion. He couldn't get enough attention. I never gave him the attention that he craved, but I wouldn't put it past my friends that they did. I loved my friends and they loved me, but when we grew old enough to notice boys, they did and changed which one they liked almost daily. I liked one or two but I didn't transition easily between them. I did date boys, but I didn't go through them like dirty tissues. My friends did. I didn't judge them, it was something that I knew from a very young age. It was the one conversation that I remember like it took place yesterday between my mother and myself.

She told me that she didn't care what my friends did. She wanted me to love people for who they were. She told me to love the one that I was with at the time that I was with them, but to know that not everything last forever. At the time, I thought it was the wisest of words that I had ever heard. Now I think differently because my mom was telling me not to be her. Not to use men. Not to go run from one bed to another. That's what she was doing. She told me that was what my friends were doing. I always thought that she knew best.

I did have boyfriends. When one ended, I took time to get over it. I reflected on what I learned from them to not do in the next relationship. I had one who told me that it wasn't me. He went on to tell me that he was nervous that he would break me if we had been intimate. He broke up with me and was with Amber four days later. They stayed together from middle school through high school. She stayed with him through college. They are supposed to be married soon.

I don't know that Amber was ever with anyone else. We were the best of friends. I think I was the most hurt by her picking Gabriella over me. Gabriella had turned time and time again on Amber. I stayed loyal and it meant nothing.

Kyle pokes my arm. I blink a few times and look at him. "Did you hear what I said?"

I shake my head. "No." I say.

"Crystal, you haven't zoned since you were young."

"I am sorry, what did you say?"

"Brandon did sleep with both Heather and Gabriella."

"Why? He was so popular. Bad at baseball but so popular, why couldn't he leave my friends alone?"

"They went after him." Kyle says.

"Did Amber?"

"Never." He looks at me. "What did the letter say?"

I leave the room and go back into Cody's bedroom. He is still sleeping soundly. I get the letter and return to the kitchen. I hand him the letter. I take the glass of water and drink the whole thing.

"Why is dad here?" I ask.

"He wanted to make sure that you are fine."

I look at Kyle. "Am I fine? Have I ever been fine? I might have said that I was fine, but why didn't anyone see that I was not fine at all?"

"I always made sure I knew what you were up to."

"I know. You cost me a prom date." I say.

"You know he was the wrong person for you."

"I knew that I didn't see him as my forever, but I would have liked to have had a prom date. I would have liked to have had a romantic dance."

"You didn't dance at prom?"

"Not with a boy." I tell him.

"Boys only had one thing on their minds."

"Girls equally had that same thought." I tell him with a smile. "Read the letter and then hide it so no one else sees it."

He takes me in his arms and hugs me. "Stay with me." He says.

I fill the glass with water again. I go sit on the couch and Kyle sits next to me. I sit with my legs straight in front of me and recline on the couch. I cover myself with a blanket. I watch television while he reads the letter.

Kyle reads my friend's letter in her beautiful handwriting. She had the best handwriting since we were young. I worked really hard to write with pretty penmanship and I think I mastered it, but I always thought that my writing never held weight next to Gabriella's.

I close my eyes while he reads. I listen to the movie that I have seen so many times I know it word for word and scene for scene. I hear Kyle gasp a few times.

When he finishes reading it, he reads it again. When he finishes it a second time, he touches my arm lightly.

I open my eyes and look at him. "You know that you didn't do anything wrong." He says it sweetly.

I don't say anything.

"Tally, tell me what you heard when you went back into the bridal shop."

"I don't remember." I say. I do remember it like it happened just yesterday.

"I don't believe you." He says.

"No." I tell him.

"Tell me."

"No. I have shed enough tears over them." I say. I get back in my wheelchair. "Good night." I say. I take the letter and bring it back into the room with me. I put it back in the box. I take things out of it and put the letter at the bottom of the box. I get back in bed with Cody.

I can't stop the dream that comes to me. I enter the bridal shop and Beth is standing with her back to me, but through the mirrors she knows that I am back. Plus when I open the door to the bridal shop, I swing the door open and maneuver my wheelchair through the door, but the door hits the frame. Beth stands with her hands on her hips and says loudly,

"So you know that we have all been with the brother. Are you even sure that the baby is Johnathan's?"

"Beth, I am going to marry him. I love him."

"You know, you are so lucky that Jonathan never met Crystal because if he had, she would have found a way to be with him." Beth says.

"She is a bit quiet, you always have to be aware of the quiet ones." Rosa says.

"She is my best friend." Gabriella says.

"Your best friend who talks shit about you." Beth says. "She told everyone that you are such a fucking loser and that she is glad that you both went to different schools because she felt bad that she has to pretend that she still likes you."

Heather looks at me and sees me, "Crystal, oh we didn't know you would be here."

"I work here, so why wouldn't I be here? Plus you are my friends and I expected you to be here to pick your dresses and let me know which dress you want me to wear."

"You won't need a dress to wear to my wedding. You aren't coming to it."

"What?" I ask. Tears pool in my eyes.

"You are no longer my friend. You bitch! Beth told us while you were gone that you tried hooking up with my fiancé."

"What are you talking about? Gab, I haven't met him. I wouldn't know him if he was standing next to me."

"Why couldn't you let me just have this time?" Gabriella asks. "This is your fault that my wedding will be shitty. You ruined my dress and had it shortened without me trying it on first."

"No. I never did that." I say.

"You were always jealous of my life. You can't come to my wedding. We can no longer be friends. I hate you." Gabriella says.

Beth smiles brightly. "She talks so much shit about all of you. She says that she never considered any of you her friends."

"That's not true." I say. I look at Beth. "Shut up!"

Rosa looks at me. "Go home. Take the rest of the day off."

I turn and leave with tears burning my eyes. "I love you all so much. We have been friends forever. You are my sisters in my heart." I tell my three friends. I leave the bridal shop with such sadness.

"You need to find someone else to be friends with." Gabriella yells after me.

In the morning, I stretch my body and feel Cody's hand on my stomach. He is still sleeping. I put my hand on his arm and turn into him. He opens his eyes. He smiles at me and kisses me on the lips.

"Good morning." I say. I put my hand on his shoulder.

"Good morning." He says. "She has court today."

"I know."

"We have to be there by ten."

I look at the clock on the nightstand. It reads seven-thirty. "Kiss me." I say. When he does, I relax against him. "Cody?"

"What?" He pulls back.

I close my eyes battling with the tears that are threatening to fall.

"I am yours. Do you hear me? I don't want anyone else. I have never wanted anyone more than you in my whole life." He tells me. "Open your eyes." He kisses me. "You have me. Trust me."

"Always." I say.

I get out of the shower and dry my hair. My hair is in waves around my shoulders. I pull half of it back. I put my makeup on before I leave the room. I go back into the bedroom and get dressed. I put on pants and a sweater top. I return to the bathroom and look at my blackened eye that I couldn't cover up with makeup. I don't do anything to make it stand out, it does that all on its own.

I leave the room and join Paige and the men in our lives. Dad looks at me for a long time. He doesn't say anything which both makes me feel sadness and nothing at all. This is his way. Stew smiles at me.

"Would you like something to eat?" Paige asks me.

"No." I say.

"You have to eat something." I hear from every male voice.

"A piece of toast." I say.

"You have to eat more than that." Dad says.

"Nope." I look at all of them. "We have to go soon."

Cody stands next to me. "Eat something." He says.

"I have an upset stomach, I can't eat. I will eat when its over."

We all go to the court house. Cody parks the car and gets my wheelchair for me. I get in it. He takes my hand. Kyle pushes my wheelchair. I hold Cody's hand tight. Paige walks next to Landon. My dad and Stew stand back and watch us for a moment.

"She is strong." Dad says.

"She usually doesn't let anything bother her. She looks defeated." Stew says. "She lost her job. She lost her shop. She lost her confidence. Someone told her that she isn't worthy of Cody's love."

"Whoever said that is a complete asshole." Kelsey says.

I hear her voice and I put my hands on my wheels to stop. Kyle looks at me. I see my sisters standing with my mom and even Joanne. Brandon is here too. My whole family.

Joanne hugs me first. She bends at the waist so that we are eye to eye. She looks at my blackened eye. She reaches her hand out and touches it lightly. She puts her fingers so lightly on my cheek, I feel like I am being kissed by angels.

"What are you all doing here?" I ask.

"Making sure that all this shit stops here." Kelsey says. She hugs me so tight I wince. "What's going on?"

"Cracked ribs." I say. I look at all of them. "How did you all get here?"

"Jonathan flew us here." Mom says.

"He paid for you all to come?" I ask a bit confused.

"No. He literally flew to Florida and flew us here to be with you." Mom says. She hugs me.

When Cody's family joins us, I feel my heart swell. Gianna hugs her brothers and then hugs me. Catalina hugs her sons and Sawyer does too.

We all go into the security check point. A woman officer looks at me. "Who did that to you?" She looks at Cody. "Did you do this?"

"He didn't do this." I say. "That's why we are here. The woman who hit me is having her day in court."

The police officer looks at me. "You are the one from the Baseball Café?" She asks.

"Yes." I say with confidence.

"Come right this way." She says. She looks at everyone standing around me. "Are they all with you?"

I smile. A face splitting smile that hurts my eye, but I don't care for the moment. "Yes." I say.

"You are one lucky girl."

"We are the lucky ones." Cody and my brothers say.

She ushers us down a long hallway. When we get to the end of the hall, she tells us to wait a moment. Jonathan and Heather walk down the hallway. The second that I see my friend since I was five years old, I can't hold back. I push my wheelchair as fast as I can to her and we embrace. She hugs me and cries.

Before we go in, I introduce everyone who doesn't know each other. I take Landon's hand. "Thank you." I say.

He kisses the top of my head.

Gianna stands back and looks at me. She walks over to Cody. "She isn't sitting up straight."

"She has cracked ribs." Cody tells her.

"What? Why?"

"She got shoved into a table."

"Who the hell would do that?" Gianna asks.

"Gia, why do you think we are here?" Cody asks her.

"I thought she was just punched in the face." She says.

"She was knocked pretty hard into the table she was at first, then she was punched in the face."

Becker and Stephanie walk over. They join all of us in the hallway. The doors open for the courtroom and they usher us all into the courtroom. The judge looks at the gallery of people. He looks at Claudia. Beth and Lee are sitting behind her.

Beth sees Cody and she stands up. She walks over.

"If you touch me, I will press charges." He says.

She backs away and then turns back quickly and slaps me across the face.

The police officer who walked us in, grabs Beth.

I hold my cheek. Stephanie walks over. She hands me a tissue from her purse. I look at her with questioning eyes. "You are bleeding." She says.

Cody, Kyle, Brandon, Becker, Landon and Jonathan all surround me. Stephanie takes a few tissues out of her purse and she dabs at my cheek.

The judge orders that Beth be led out of the court room. She makes her body limp and she is dragged out. Lee stands and walks to the back of the court room. Claudia looks at me and she grins. "Bitch." She says.

"Excuse me." The judge says. He looks at me. "Are you alright?"

I nod my head.

"I need you to say yes or no." He says in a very concerned tone.

When I open my mouth to answer, my lip splits open.

Stephanie dabs my lip.

"Do you need a moment?" The judge asks.

"No." I say. "I would like to just get this over with."

"If you need us to break for any reason, just let me know." He says. He looks at Claudia. "Can you explain why you assaulted this young woman?"

"She is a home wrecker." Claudia says all smug.

"Can you tell me whose home did she wreck? Are all these people that are around her people that you know?"

"My friend Beth was engaged to that man right there." She says and points to Landon and not Cody.

The judge looks at Landon. "Can you state your name for the record?"

"My name is Landon Parker." He says.

"No!" Claudia says. "Your name is Cody."

"Sir? Is your name Cody?"

"Your honor, my name is Landon Parker. I am a lawyer."

"No." She says. "You are a has been base ball play-er." She says with disgust.

"I never played baseball. Soccer and volleyball were my sports."

Claudia looks around. She looks at the judge. Then she looks at Kyle. "That's him. Cody Parker. That's the one that she stole from my friend."

The judge looks at Kyle. "Sir can you state your name for the record?"

"My name is Kyle Davidson-Steele." He says. "I can assure you that Crystal, didn't steal me away from anyone. She is my sister."

Claudia throws herself back in the chair that she is sitting in.

The judge looks around the room again. "Is there a Cody Parker in the courtroom?"

Cody steps up. "Yes. I am Cody Parker."

Claudia makes a gagging noise.

"Quiet." The judge says to her. He looks at me. "Do you know the woman who slapped you?"

"Yes." I say. "She and I used to own a bridal shop together in Central Florida."

The judge looks at me. He looks down at notes that he has in front of him. "Are you the owner of Madame Butterfly's Bridal Boutique?"

"I am one of the owners." I say.

"Can you state your name for the record?" He asks.

"My name is Crystal Steele."

"Have you ever had any troubles with these women before?"

"Not Claudia, but Beth yes. She fired me through a phone call saying that I broke protocol, we have a no dating guests rule."

"Did you date a guest?"

"I put together the guest list and I didn't see Cody Parker's name on any guest list. His name wasn't part of the wedding party guests."

"Did you know who he was before the wedding that you attended?"

"I didn't attend the wedding. I was the wedding planner. I was there to make sure that the bride and groom got everything that they wanted and more. I did know Cody Parker before we officially met at the wedding."

"How is that?" He asks. He looks at the bailiff, "can you help her to the witness stand?"

She walks over to me and holds open the gate that separates the gallery from the front of the courtroom. She points to the direction that she wants me to go, I do. There are three short steps leading up to the witness stand. She walks over to where she can talk privately to the judge.

Cody looks at the judge. "I mean no disrespect, but can I help my fiancée?"

The judge looks at Cody. "Yes. Thank you."

Cody walks over to me and scoops me in his arms. He steps up the steps and supports me on my feet while the chair swivels. He uses his hip to hold the chair still and waits for me to sit down. When I am adjusted in the chair, he returns to the gallery and takes a seat next to my brothers and Landon.

"I am sorry for the inconvenience." The judge says.

"Its fine." I say.

"You were telling everyone—" he looks at his bailiff. "Swear her in." He says.

She does and then the judge starts again.

"How is that you knew who Cody Parker was?"

"She didn't know who he was!" Claudia says.

"Continue." The judge says.

"Cody Parker played baseball and he was my ultimate favorite player. I went to college for sports commentating. I won a scholarship because Cody had a fabulous game." I look at him and smile. There is no containing my admiration I have for him. He smiles at me. "We actually met on a plane leaving from Indiana to Georgia. When he saw me checking into the resort where the wedding was being held, he kissed me. We have been together ever since."

The judge looks at me. "You know him well enough to decide that you want to be with him for the rest of your life?"

"Yes." I say.

"She needs to get over him and give him back to my friend." Claudia says.

The judge looks at me. "The woman who slapped you, do you want to press charges?"

"Yes." I say. "I didn't when she hit me in Florida after she fired me, but yes."

He looks at Cody. "Can you help her back to her wheelchair?"

Cody does. When he is just about to sit me in my wheelchair, Claudia pulls the wheelchair away. Landon runs over and holds my wheelchair as Cody sits me in it.

"Young lady, this is your trial. Your behavior towards a disabled person is abuse. That's a felony. What you are doing is against the law."

"What are you going to do about it?" She asks.

"I sentence you to sixty days without possibility of bond." The judge says and slams the gavel down.

She jumps up. "What?"

"I sentence you to sixty days without possibility of bond." He repeats. "Sixty days in a women's correction center." He looks at the bailiff. "Can you bring that other woman back in here?"

She gets Beth. Beth walks into the court room.

The judge looks at her. "I sentence you to sixty days without the possibility of bond in a women's correction center."

"I am sorry. What?" She asks.

He looks at the room at large, "do you all understand me?"

Everyone says yes.

"You bitch! You are getting me locked up! I can't go to work because you sold the building." Beth yells.

"Remove the two of them please. Case dismissed."

The two of them are taken from the room. Lee gets up and leaves the courtroom. He goes outside in the hallway and calls his sister. "They are going to jail for sixty days." He gets in the elevator and leaves.

The judge looks at Cody and me. He looks at everyone. "You can all go. You two stay for a moment." He says to Cody and me.

Our family and friends get up and leave the courtroom. Mom leaves us last. She looks at the two of us, "We will wait for you downstairs."

"Ok." I say.

"I am so proud of you." She tells me.

"Thank you."

"I love you."

"I love you too." I tell her.

She walks out and joins Stew.

The doors close and the judge leaves the bench where he sits and walks down the steps and joins us at a table. "I just want to tell you that you are a beautiful couple." He looks at me. "I heard you on the radio years ago giving the play-by-plays of Cody Parkers grand slam home runs. There was no denying the happiness in your voice when you announced that he was up at bat again. You called it. Ball one. Foul ball. Ball two. Strike. Ball three. You announced that he had a full count and then he hit the ball, everyone listening to you heard the smile that graced your face. I was so excited to hear the joy in your voice. I was sad too because my son was the pitcher in that game."

Cody looks at the judge. "Jay is your son?"

"Yes."

"Small world."

"Who is going to marry you?" He asks shocking us.

"Are you offering?" I ask him.

"I am offering. Not today, but when it happens, I would like to marry the two of you."

"We don't live here."

"I will fly to wherever it is you are holding your wedding." He smiles. "Jay was sad that he missed you. He had to fly to Florida for a job."

"We live in Florida." Cody says. "We are only here to close on my house. I am selling it."

"Cody, Jay told me that after that game, you treated him to dinner and you invited his younger twin sisters to join you. He told me that you were so nice and that you paid for everything." He looks at me. "I know all about you and your bridal shop. I know that you donate the used dresses to girls who can't afford them. My twins went into the shop and did an experiment for school. One of them is short and very thin, the other is taller and fuller. They said that when they walked into your store and they told you what they were looking for, you never thought twice about them being there. You helped each of them separately and gave them a lot of time to really know what they wanted."

"I remember the twins." I say. "They were so wonderful. I did find out about their project for school and when they came in with all the money for the dresses that they left with, they were surprised that I didn't take the money from them. They did come in to the shop over the summer and volunteered on their own, I truly enjoyed them. They were funny without even trying. The two of them bickered about everything but it never got nasty. It was just like being stuck in a day time soap opera all day long."

He laughs. "That sounds like my girls." He laughs again. "They were the ones who called me and told me to put the radio on. You paid tribute to Jay. When everyone else was saying to take him out and put in another pitcher, you gave everyone history on him. You said the nicest things about my son. We heard you on the radio announcing his next game where he pitched a no hitter. There was so much excitement in your voice for him. I want you to know that we were all grateful." He looks at the big clock on the wall. "I have other cases to hear." He writes his number down on a sheet of paper. "Allow me to take the two of you out for dinner before you go. My wife and girls would love to see you again."

We leave. Cody looks at me when we are tucked into the elevator just the two of us. "I want to hear you talk about me playing baseball."

I smile at him. "Cody, I know Kyle told you this, or I think that he did, but I wished I could have run those bases with you. I was so excited for you. I couldn't contain my happiness for days."

"Where have you been my whole life?"

"Waiting for you to find me." I say to him.

Everyone comes back to Cody's house. There isn't enough room for everyone to stay overnight with us at his house, but they all come back to the house to be with us. Cody looks around his house at everyone that is there. He smiles. "Thank you for all your support today. All of you being there meant so much to us."

"Cody, we wouldn't have been anywhere else." Stephanie says. She looks at me, "You have to learn how to fight back." She hugs me.

"What did the judge keep you for?" Ashley asks.

"We can't tell you." Cody and I say together.

Stew walks over and hugs me. "I am so proud of you." He says.

"Why?" I ask.

"You didn't crumble or even shed a tear."

"My heart was crying." I say.

He hugs me tight. I feel like he is my father. Stew has always made me feel like I was totally adored by him. He was always so fatherly. Not that I needed to be told what to do and when to do it. He saw that I was in need of fatherly love and he supported me every time he could.

Mom walks over. She throws her arms around Stew's neck. "Come talk to me." She says to him. My mom is always in need of being Stew's world. She wants him to see no one else but her.

Everyone stays until eight. My sisters and Brandon plan to leave first. They have a system that they planned to get everyone to follow them to the hotel.

Brandon takes my hand. He pulls me into the kitchen. When its just the two of us in there, he hugs me. "How are you doing?" He asks.

"I am fine." I say. "I am just tired. Its been a long day."

"We are going to leave. I think everyone will follow." He says.

"It means so much to me that you are all here."

"My mom arranged it. If Jonathan didn't fly down to get us, my mom was planning on what airline could get us to you as fast as possible. She saw the footage on the news about you getting punched in the face. Then she saw you being carried out of some building and she got on the phone with everyone she knew."

"I will have to thank her." I say.

"If you need anything from us, call. We are here until you leave." He hugs me. I try not to wince in his arms but I do. "What hurts more?"

"My ribs hurt a lot. My eye hurts. My split lip really hurts."

"Is this the first time that Beth hit you?"

"No. She hit me in the resort in Fort Lauderdale."

"I know. I am asking if she ever hit you before."

"Yes." I say.

"How many times?"

"Once before."

"Why?" Brandon asks.

"Can we talk about it tomorrow?"

"I am holding you to it."

"I will tell you and everyone tomorrow. I promise." We say goodbye.

In the morning, we get up early. I look at Cody and Kyle. "Can we go for a run?"

"Are you up for that?" Cody asks.

"Its not going to hurt my cheekbone. My ribs hurt when I move, but I have to move." I say.

"Do you want to stretch?" Kyle asks.

"I want to push myself as far as I can." I say.

"I think we need to stretch first." Kyle looks at me.

"We can stay around the neighborhood." I say.

"We will go to Becker's place." Cody says.

"Isn't it your place?" I ask Cody.

"Its his place really. I own it technically, but I am hardly here." Cody says.

We get to the training facility. There is a young girl at the front desk. She smiles brightly at Cody and Kyle. She doesn't recognize Cody as being the one who's name appears on her checks. She looks at us. "New people have to pay up front."

Becker walks over. He looks at the young girl. "Do you know who this is?"

She looks at him batting her eyelashes. "Should I?"

"If you want to work here."

"I don't know who he is." She admits.

"Where are you?" Becker asks her.

"CP training facility." She says.

"Who is CP?" The girl asks with a bit of annoyance.

Cody takes his driver's license out of his pocket and hands it to her. She takes it from him and studies it for a moment. Her eyes grow wide in their sockets.

She looks at all of us. "I am so sorry." She looks at Cody. She looks at Becker. "I am sorry." She says to him.

"Listen, we didn't come here to ruin your day. We came here to workout." Kyle says.

Becker tells her to go take a break. He tells her to google the boss so that she will never make this mistake again.

We go over to the rowing machines. They are in a line. There are a few of them that face each other. Becker walks over and gets the cable ready for me. Cody and Kyle get on their machines that they will be using.

Becker puts the timers on. He counts us off and we all start rowing. The timer is set for a half hour. If any of us stop sooner, it ends. If we don't stop, alarms will go off. He doesn't go far. He sits on a workout bench and watches us.

Stephanie walks over and sits behind him with her head on his shoulder. "Is this the right thing for her to do?"

"I didn't make her cables heavy." He says.

"Hun, you run the gym. You know that when you pull back at fast speed, it will engage the weight?"

"No, I restricted it."

They sit and watch us.

We row on our separate machines. We keep the same speed with each other. We row like we are all one unit. The pace is moderate.

We go ten solid minutes before I feel a sharp pain in my ribs. I don't stop going. I feel the pain sharper and sharper with every pull.

Stephanie looks at Becker. "This needs to stop. She's in pain."

"How do you know that?"

"She's only pulling with her left arm." She jumps up. She runs over and takes the cables from me. "Stop. Take a drink."

Cody and Kyle run over. Cody puts his hand on my side and pain shoots through my body. "Crystal are you ok?"

I try to catch my breath. When I do, I put my hands on my wheels and rush into the bathroom. I close the stall door and breathe deeply.

Cody walks in. "You ok?"

"Yes."

"Can I come in?" He asks.

I open the door.

He gets down on his knees. He puts his hands on my side. He pushes his palm into my side. "Does this hurt?" He asks.

"No." I say.

"Talk to me." He says.

"I am not a weak person."

"No one thinks that you are."

"Cody, I feel like my life is falling apart. I feel like the only thing that makes me happy is being with you."

He smiles.

"Cody, I feel lost."

"Why?" He asks.

I throw my arms around him and close my eyes. I just love being in his arms. I love the smell of him on top of the smell of sweat. "I have never been without a job. The lady said that she thinks it was right for me to get punched in the face because I am using you for your money."

"Crystal, every time we have done something, you have offered to pay the bill. Or you arranged to pay the bill before we ever sat down to do whatever we were doing. Who cares what people think?"

"I usually don't, but I don't want you to be unhappy."

"Crystal, since the day that I heard you mumble under your breath on the airplane that the woman was an idiot, you made me smile. I can tell you that I haven't smiled like that in a long long time. When I saw you in the resort, I couldn't hold back. I didn't want another second to pass by and not kiss the woman who changed my world by just the nice words you spoke." He kisses me.

I giggle against his lips.

He pulls back. "What are you giggling about?"

"If I was in my wheelchair in the plane, I would have approached her and punched her in the throat." I laugh. I throw my head back and laugh.

He tickles me so I laugh more. "Come on, lets go have lunch."

"Oh good, I am starving."

"Me too." He says and kisses my neck.

Cody and I sit at a table in the Baseball Café. We sit at a table by the window looking out over a beautiful body of water. There is a bridge. I look at the bridge. I look at Cody.

"Can we go on it?"

"Of course." He says.

"Is there some place that means the world to you that you want to go to?" I ask him.

"I will take you anywhere you want to go."

"I want to go somewhere that means a lot to you."

"Crystal, I want today to be about you. I think you need to be pampered. I think you need to know how much I love you."

"I don't doubt for a second that you love me." I tell him.

We finish our lunch. We get the bill it reads, the food was on them. Cody gets up from the table and walks over to the server. "I think this is wrong." He says.

"Is there a problem?"

"There is nothing on this."

"Yes sir, there is no mistake."

"Why?" He asks.

"Anytime that lady comes in here, the food is on us. My boss was so upset that she got hurt here in his restaurant."

Cody looks at her. "Do you know what happened?"

The host looks at him. "I saw you sitting with her. Didn't she tell you?"

He looks at me. "She doesn't like to tell a lot about her life."

"She was looking at a picture that my boss took off the wall. Let me go get it." She looks around and calls to another girl to come over and take her place. When the other host walks over, the one talking to Cody disappears. She comes back moments later with a poster size picture. She is holding it to her body so no one sees what the picture is of. She dismisses the other host. She turns the picture around and shows it to Cody.

"How do you have that?" He asks.

"My boss took the picture at a baseball game years ago."

"Can I talk to him?"

"Let me go get him." She says.

A guy walks over. He looks at Cody. "Can I help you?"

"Can I buy that picture?"

"I am going to tell you the same thing I told the young woman who asked the same question. No."

"A million dollars." Cody says.

"No." The man says.

"Well then can I get a copy of it?" Cody asks. He turns and looks at me. He sees the smile on my face. "Can I ask you, is that the young lady that wanted the picture?"

"No." The man says.

"If she asked you for it, would you give it to her?"

"Yes." He says. "When she was here with those other women, the one was taking a picture of her with this picture behind her."

"So someone took a picture of my wife with this behind her?"

"You are her husband?"

"Soon to be." Cody says.

"Ten bucks and an address where I can send it as a wedding gift."

"Can I ask you a question?" Cody says.

"Of course?"

"How do you have a picture of her in the stadium watching me hit that grand slam?"

"She was there."

"She was there?" Cody asks.

"I was there for the final game. No one knew it was your final game."

Cody turns and kisses me like he did in the resort in Fort Lauderdale. We hear people snapping pictures of us. I melt into his kiss. We stop kissing and smile at the owner and the host. I look at the picture of Cody smiling up into the stands, and me with my arms in the air screaming his name. I see the excitement all over my face and his face.

The owner leans into Cody. "After the play, she looked at the guys she was with and said to one, that she wanted to marry you."

I look at him. My cheeks burn with the blush that takes over my face. Cody looks at me. He looks back at the owner. "What else did she say?" Cody asks.

The owner looks at Cody and then at me. "She wanted to wait by the buses so that she could get a glimpse at you."

My cheeks burn more.

"I was there after the game." He says. He leaves us for a moment and comes back moments later. He hands Cody a box that is meant for leftover food. "Do not open it until you are alone." He says. He looks at me. "Does this lucky guy know that you bought all of his teddy bears with his jersey on it and you went to a children's hospital and you donated them to the children. Do you know that she held a gala and all the money raised went to your charity of choice?"

I look at him. "How do you know that?"

"My daughter was in the hospital here. She was so excited that she got a free bear from someone who came to visit her who also uses a wheelchair. She told my wife and I how you never stopped smiling. She said that when you talked to her about being in her wheelchair that you kept the conversation so light that she forgot for the rest of the day that she is in a wheelchair."

Cody looks at me. He kisses the top of my head. "I would like to pay for our lunch." Cody says.

"Do not insult me. Come back before you all leave. Its nice to have two real life heroes here."

"I am not a hero." I say.

"You were that day to my daughter. You were those days that you held those dances for the kids that wouldn't have been able to go to their proms. Every girl or boy who received a garment of clothing to wear to those dances free of charge from you, you are their hero."

The hostess looks at me. "Dad, you are embarrassing her. If her cheeks turn any redder she may pop."

I slip my hand in Cody's hand. He laces our fingers together. "Thank you for another delicious lunch." I say. I look at the bridge. "Is there an elevator or something that leads us to the bridge?"

"Oh that's right, you and your friends never made it to the bridge." He turns to the host. "Can you take them and show them where they have to go?"

"Yes." She says.

We leave the café holding hands. We get in the elevator and we can't stop kissing.

Chapter Eighteen

We are at the top of the bridge and I am shivering. Cody holds me in his arms. "Why are you shivering?"

"I thought that Kyle was the only one who has pictures of us— you running with your arms up in the air and me with my arms up in the air."

"Kyle has pictures of that?"

"Yes."

"Can I ask you a question?"

"Yes."

"Did I dream that you were holding my hand when I woke up from surgery?"

"Yes." I say. No, I was there. "I wish I was. I wish that I didn't wimp out."

"What?"

"I wimped out. I was there. Kyle was there. Stew told me that I could go in and hold your hand. I wish that I had."

"How did I get the bear from you?"

"Stew brought it for me."

"I asked him. He told me no."

"I begged him not to tell you." I say.

"Should we see what's in our box?"

"Yes."

Cody opens the box. There are pictures in it of me waiting at the gated area that day of the game. My smile can not be contained. There are pictures of the players coming out to greet the fans. There are serval pictures of Cody walking over to me and taking my hand. He smiles down at me, I smile up at him. There are a few of him hugging me.

"Did you really tell your brothers that you wanted to marry me?" Cody asks.

"Oh my god, yes." I say. I get all excited.

"Tell me about this wedding of ours."

"I dreamed of it every night. When I saw on the news that you were hurt, I cried. In my dreams Brandon walked with me and then Kyle Joined in. Then my dad joined us and last Stew. Brandon pushed one side of my wheelchair so that I could hold hands with my dad and Stew. Kyle pushed the other side. When we finally got to the end of the isle you are standing there and you took my hands in yours." I smile at him. "It was like I could feel you holding my hands."

"What else?"

"That's where it ended."

"I don't believe you." He says.

"The dress that I wanted to wear was discontinued and the one that I reserved at my bridal shop was died black and Beth wore it when she went to the charity event that you hosted. I tried calling the dress maker and asking him if he would make another dress for me. He told me that he was done with that style."

"Who is the designer?"

"Casper Peterson." I say.

"Is he still designing wedding dresses?"

"Yes, but they are not anything like the dress I dreamed of wearing for you."

Cody kisses me on the lips. It's a quick kiss. "Tell me about this dress."

"It was a heart shaped top with little capped sleeves and a mesh back that made it look like I was wearing nothing from the back."

"Maybe we can find him and tell him the importance of this dress."

"I never tried wedding dresses on, but that one. When I put it on, I felt like it was made for just me. It was the dress that I dreamed of." I smile at him. "When I tried the dress on, the television was on because the shop was closed for book keeping. I was wearing the dress and came out of the fitting room to show my sisters. They were showing images of your career on the television and I swooned."

"Why didn't you buy it and put it away?"

"I was superstitious about that. The thought that if I bought it and hung it in a closet, I would either lose it, or it would get ruined. I had it tucked away in the bridal shop. Rosa knew where it was hidden so that it wasn't on the racks. Then it was gone. Beth told me that she sold it to someone who requested that dress and it was the last one. I should have fired her that day."

"Wait, she worked for you?"

"Yes."

"Why did you give her the shop then?"

"She came to work with a lawyer who served me papers. I brought it to my lawyer and he said it was a takeover. Rosa had put in writing that Beth could buy me out. She did. But then I had to stay on and do the same job I was doing only as an assistant. She wanted to pay me less money."

"That better not have happened."

"No. I went to my lawyer and had him write in the contract when we agreed to her buying me out that I couldn't be paid less money. And there was a clause that I got ten percent of every wedding we booked. She was too stupid to see that. I think Lee brought it to her attention. She went to her lawyer and said that she wanted that changed. He said it was binding and already signed." I look out on the horizon. "I love that shop."

"I know you do." He stands behind me and puts his arms around me. "Do you want to move back to Orlando?"

"No."

"So what are we going to do?"

"I think maybe I could work there three days a week. I could take the train up to Orlando in the morning and come back in the afternoon."

"Would you want to do that?"

"I have always dreamed of doing it." I say honestly.

We walk around on the bridge. It is absolutely beautiful. The whole ambiance is romantic.

"Can I ask you a question?" I ask.

"Of course."

"Did you know that I was Kyle's sister when you paid my hospital bills?"

"No. I never knew you were Kyle's sister until we were in your guest house setting it up for you to live in it." Cody says with a wicked smile on his face.

"I know we just came from lunch, but I am so hungry." I say.

"Lets go get something to eat."

"Cody?"

"What?"

"I love you."

He takes me in his arms and holds me. We stay watching the sunset from the bridge. It is really beautiful. "What are you thinking?"

"My dad told me that if you listen carefully when watching the sunset, you can hear the hiss of the sun getting swallowed up by the water." I say.

"That's very sweet." Cody says. He tips my head back and looks at me. "You know he only said that to keep you quiet?"

"No." I say.

"Did you ever hear it?"

"At the beach."

"What?"

"Lightning struck just as the sun was setting and I heard the lightning hit the water. It was beautiful and scary at the same time. The lifeguard that ran out to see if I was ok told me that my wheelchair saved me from being electrocuted."

"Well I am so glad that didn't happen."

"Do you ever look up at the stars and wish on as many as you can see?"

"I did when I was young." He says.

"I still do" I say. I stand up and hold onto the bridge. I turn and wrap my arms around Cody. "I wished for you." I say.

He holds me in his arms. "Can you walk if you hold on to me?"

"Yes."

He steps back and we walk hand in hand. Not side by side. He walks backwards and holds my hands. I stand and reach for his shoulder. "Are you ok?"

"I need a little support." I smile.

"Do you need to sit?"

"Not yet."

He carries me back over by the bridge so I can hold onto the bridge and stand on my own. He stands close by me. He puts his hands on my sides. "Is this ok?"

"Yes."

"The physical therapist in me is planning so much to do with you."

I laugh.

"Don't make this dirty." He says smiling. He supports me with one arm around my waist and rubs his hand on my bruised ribs. "Does this hurt?"

"Yes." I say.

"What's on your mind?"

"I am thinking that Beth is going to get revenge for this."

"We will deal with that if it comes to that."

"I don't want to deal with her. I want my shop, I think I would be scared to go to Orlando and be there by myself. I never felt scared there before, but I think I would be scared that she will want revenge." I say.

"Crystal, we will deal with all of this. Maybe we can find you another location."

"I just don't want your dad to lose out on anything—"

"My dad knew what he was getting into."

"Cody, your parents treated me better than my own family have. I can't wait to be apart of your family."

"Crystal, you have to know that you brought them closer to me."

I wobble a bit. My legs start to shake. He lifts me in his arms. He sits me in my wheelchair and I pull him in for a much needed kiss. I love him so much.

Our families are still with us. They all are at Cody's house for dinner. When we got back to his house from our date, the driveway was full of cars. We didn't know what was going on until we went in the house.

Gianna and Lance have boxes all taped up. Cody looks at them. Gianna hugs him. "Don't be mad. We had a packing party. We didn't seal up all the boxes."

"Thank you." Cody says to her.

"Can I show you something?"

"Yes." He says.

She takes his hand. "We will be right back." She says. She takes Cody into one of the guest rooms. She opens a box that she has packed up. "Cody, did you know that you had this?" She asks.

She takes my press badge out of the box and also a t-shirt that has C. Steele-Parker on the back of it. She hands him a picture of him hugging me. It was at the game that I waited for him to come out and greet the fans. He holds me like there is no other woman on the planet. I have my arms around his neck and a bright smile on my face.

"Cody, how do you have this?"

He looks at his sister. "It wasn't a fucking dream." He says. He runs out of the room and runs over to me. "Come with me." He says.

"Cody, I am talking to your mom."

"She can wait, this can't." He pushes my wheelchair into the guest bedroom. Gianna attempts to leave. "Stay." He says to her.

"Cody, whats going on?" I ask.

"Show her what you found." He says to Gianna.

"Cody." She says his name so softly.

"Please show her."

Kyle and Lance walk in. "Everything ok?" They both ask together.

"Gianna, can you please show us what you found?"

Gianna looks at him, "I didn't think you would make a big deal about this." She says. "I just wanted to know if you knew you had it."

"This is a big deal. This proves that I didn't dream her up." Cody looks at me. "You were there? When I opened my eyes you were holding my hand to your lips." He looks at Kyle. "Did you bring her?"

Stew walks in the room. "I brought her. She didn't leave anything there. The shirt, the teddy bear and the picture of you hugging her at the game. I left that for you. I wanted you to meet my sweet girl. I wanted you to be together. You found each other. I am so glad."

Everyone leaves the room leaving Cody and me alone. I pick up my shirt and look at it. My cheeks burn with embarrassment. I look at the picture of him holding me in his arms. I still don't look at Cody.

He gets on his knees in front of me and wraps his arms around me. "I thought I dreamed this. I thought that I conjured you up."

I wrap my arms around him. "Cody, marry me. Lets do it now. Lets do it soon. Our families are here."

"What was it that you were saying against my hand when you held it to your lips?"

"I was begging god to let you be ok and be able to play again. I wanted to watch you play. I wanted to be at a game of yours and sit in the front row of the stadium where I had seen you come over and talk to the fans. I wanted you to come talk to me." I look at the picture. "Then you held me so tight in your arms. I never wanted you to let me go."

"I didn't want to let you go. I didn't know that Kyle was with you."

"Cody, I love you so much."

"I love you too." He pulls away and holds my shirt up. "What was this all about?"

"Brandon made it for me. It was my birthday present and then it was gone. I thought that I left it somewhere and couldn't find it anywhere."

"Why both of our names?"

"He saw the excitement when I watched you play. When I opened it up on my birthday, I burst into happy tears. I wore it for weeks. When you got mugged and hurt, I held that shirt so tight to my chest and hugged it. I prayed that you would be unharmed. I prayed that it wasn't career ending. I don't remember if I was wearing it when I came to see you. I just thought that I would stay in the hallway. You cried out in your sleep and Stew went to check on you. He pushed me in the room and he took your hand and put it in mine. It was so cold. I rubbed your hand and you never opened your eyes. You cried out in pain a lot. They upped the medications. You gripped my hand so hard."

"Did I hurt you?"

"No." I say. In reality I had to have my hand wrapped for weeks. He squeezed my hand so tight, he popped a blood vessel.

"Why do I get the feeling that I hurt you?"

"No." I say again.

"How long did you stay?"

"Two days."

"Did you sleep?"

"With my head on your side."

"I thought I was imagining a girl in my room. Were you comfortable?"

"It was a long time ago." I couldn't move my hand for weeks and my neck was kinked for days. Stew laughed at me. He said that I was pushing my wheelchair with a limp.

"Why did you stay two days?"

"You gripped my hand and didn't let it go. Stew brought me food and a book I read to you."

"What did you read?"

"Sense and Sensibility." I laugh.

"You find that funny?" He says.

"Well now I do." I approach the box and see my book. I lift it up and hold it up for him. I open the book and there inside is a paper that I wrote on. I take it out and read it. I put it back in the book quickly.

"What's that?" He asks taking the book from me. He opens it and flips through the book. He takes my note out and holds it.

I turn away from him and try to leave the room.

"What are you doing?"

"We have been in here a long time, my family probably thinks we are having sex." I say.

"Who cares. You are an adult. I am an adult." He holds the note in his fingers. He goes back on his knees. He reads my words out loud. "I can't believe I am sitting holding Cody Parker's hand. He is squeezing the life out of my hand. It hurts so bad, but I can't force myself to pull my hand out of his grip. He opened his eyes and looked right at me. I know he didn't see me. He must be so drugged. When he cries out, it makes me cry. God, I want to marry him. I love this man."

"I do love you. I feel like I always have." I throw myself at him. He catches me and I kiss him with everything I have in me.

He takes my hand in his hand and kisses it. I touch the scars on his shoulder. I kiss him again. We spent the whole day together and yet I feel like we have been away from each other too long.

A knock on the door stops us. We both hold each other and laugh uncontrollably. Sawyer walks in the room. He takes the shirt and holds it up. "Now it makes sense." He says. "I thought that a crazed fan sent it to you. You were being protected so that not just anyone could get to you. When they told your mom and I that there was a girl who had spent two days with you while you were in ICU, I demanded to know who. No one could tell me. I came to the hospital and saw the book, I read the note in the book. I saw the shirt. I saw the bear. I couldn't get that bear out of your grasp, but I put the other stuff in a box and packed it away. I saw the picture of you hugging a girl. We didn't know that it was your model girlfriend that set you up. We were told a fan attacked you. I thought that it was the fan that you were hugging in the picture." He looks at both of us. "Please don't be mad at me." He inhales sharply. "I was going to burn the book and the things that I found. Landon stopped me. He said that he would put it somewhere safe."

I look at both of them. "Landon knew about my crush on Cody. He never said anything?"

Cody looks at me. "He told me that I had an adoring fan who would move heaven and earth for me if she could. I never asked him what he meant by that. I should have done that."

"We are all waiting. Your moms made the most delicious Italian dinner for all of us. We are all leaving to go back tomorrow."

"I can't thank you all enough for coming to support me." I say.

"We welcome you with open arms — all of us — to our family." He says.

Cody hugs me.

"There was a commotion that took place at the hospital and the nurses said that the girl who was in with you wouldn't let anyone come in your room." Sawyer looks at me. "What happened?"

I look at him. "Someone was claiming to be Catalina."

"How did you know it wasn't her?' Sawyer asks.

"I had worked with Catalina at a charity event. She was the most beautiful woman I had ever seen in my whole life. She still is the most beautiful woman I have ever met in my life. The woman who showed up was cursing and yelling. She was overweight and unkempt. But the one thing that sent the red flags warning was that she didn't know Cody's name. She kept calling him Donavan."

They both look at each other.

"Donavan?" Cody asks.

"I don't doubt that the woman knows your family but how did she not know that Donavan passed away?" I say.

Cody hugs me again. "What don't you know?" He asks me.

"Landon told me about Donavan. I went with him to the gravesite."

"You went to the gravesite?" Sawyer asks.

"Yes."

"Why?" Cody asks. "Landon wasn't nice to you. Why would you do anything with him?"

"Cody." Sawyer says.

Landon walks back in the room. "What are you talking about?"

"She knows about Donavan?" Sawyer asks.

Landon looks at me. He looks at his brother and dad. "On Donavan's birthday I wanted to go to the cemetery and put balloons and flowers. I was giving a lecture and a few of my students had known about Donavan. When I left my lecture, I was emotional. I couldn't get away from people soon enough. Crystal was struggling with something. I helped her and she rolled over my foot."

I look at him. "That's not what happened." I say.

"You know that you ran over my foot. I was wearing flip flops."

"Why were you wearing flip flops when you were giving a lecture?" Cody asks.

"I didn't know that I was covering for a lecture." He looks at Cody. "It was the day." He blinks a few times. "It was the anniversary of the day—"

I reach out to him and he hugs me. I hug him while he cries. I rub his back. "Landon, everything that I know about what happened proves it was an accident."

"It should have been me." He says.

Cody drops on his knees and hugs the two of us. "Landon, don't say that."

"Landon, don't say that." Sawyer and I say together.

He cries on my shoulder like he did when we went to the cemetery. I hold him tight like I did that day that I went with him on the anniversary of Donavan's death. I rub my hands up and down his back.

Sawyer looks at me. "You saved my sons."

I put my head on Cody's shoulder as he is on his knees on the side of my wheelchair. I cry into his shoulder. He wraps his arms around me as I still hold Landon in a hug.

"What did you do?" Sawyer asks. "Landon came home a changed person."

"I didn't do anything." I say.

"She never left. She was pissed off mad at me but she never left." Landon says.

"She never left." Cody says repeating the words that Landon said.

I wrap my arms around Cody. "I love you." I tell him. "That woman creeped me out. They told me later that she had a knife with her."

"What did you do?" He says into my hair.

"I threw the blanket over your head and prayed that you wouldn't call out in your sleep. I pulled a cable on a machine. The machine started buzzing and everyone came running to make sure that you were ok. A nurse saw what I had done and she covered up for it, but they found that the lady had a knife. She was planning on cutting off Cody's fingers."

Catalina walks in the room. She sees her sons on their knees hugging me. "What's going on?"

Sawyer walks over to her and hugs her. He kisses her on the lips. "She knows about Donavan."

"I know." Catalina says. "I was at the cemetery when I saw Landon crying and his friend holding his hand. I got close to them without them knowing. Landon told her all about Donavan. He was sitting on a bench and Crystal was talking so softly to him that what he told her didn't sound like it was anything that could have been avoided." She looks at Landon. "Donavan was in no pain. He went so fast."

Landon cries harder. I wrap my arms around him again. "I didn't mean for him to get hurt let alone die." Landon wraps his arms around me holding me close to him as he sobs.

"Landon, you didn't do anything wrong. Sweetheart, it was an accident. You had him wear a helmet and protective clothing. Sweetheart, it was an accident."

"I held him in my arms and didn't get a chance to tell him I loved him."

"Landon, he knew." Catalina says. "Sweetheart." She says and pulls him to his feet. She wraps her arms around him. "Landon, forgive yourself. It was an accident."

"I shouldn't have taken him with me."

Stew walks in the room. "Is everything ok?" He asks. He knew about Donavan. He was the emergency room doctor. Landon was covered in Donavan's blood. Stew thought that Landon was hurt too. "Son, I told you then and I will tell you again. You tried to save him. He punctured his jugular. Landon, you did everything you could to try to save him."

I look at Stew. "The little boy you told mom about that night." I say.

Cody bursts into tears. He was there too with them. He was with Gianna. By the time they got to the accident site, Donavan was gone. They all held him in their arms. "He was the best of us."

"You are all wonderful. You all are the most amazing people. He was loved. All of you radiate love." I say holding Cody in my arms.

"You make me a better person." Cody says.

"I love you because of who you are. I don't make you better. You are fabulous just the way you are."

Catalina looks at all of us. "How did my sweet Donavan come up in conversation?"

"We were talking about Cody being in the hospital." Sawyer says.

Catalina looks at me. "You think that you don't bring out the best in us, well you are wrong. You do. You know us like we are your family. You are the most amazing woman that I know. The things that you have done to bring happiness to others is all you." Catalina sees the shirt with my name and their last name. She picks it up. She holds it and then looks at me.

Kyle walks into the room. "Is everything ok?" He looks at all of us. We all have tears in our eyes. Kyle puts his hand on Cody's shoulder. Kyle looks at Catalina holding my shirt up. He smiles. He looks at me. "I told you I didn't have it." He says.

I look at him and smile.

Catalina looks at me. "When did you do this?"

"She didn't do it. Brandon did it for her. When Cody had his best game, we were there. We were in the stands. Cody threw his arms up in the air as he ran the bases and Crystal threw her hands up in the air. She was so excited for him. He looked up in the stands and it seemed like he was looking right at her. He wasn't. He was looking for someone that he expected to be there. Crystal leaned into me and said that she wished that one day she would marry him." Kyle says.

I feel my skin burn with the blush that takes over my face. I smile and then hide my face in Cody's chest. He kisses my head.

Catalina looks at all of us. "Don't stay in here much longer. We have guests." She says and we all burst into a fit of laughter. "I am glad you all think I am funny." She says. She looks at me. "Cody, kiss her until her blush disappears." We all laugh again,

We sit around the table. Joanne looks across the table at me. She studies me. I never stop smiling and reaching out to Cody. I hold his hand. She watches her sons and how they interact with all of us. Kyle smiles at me when he talks to me. Brandon and Ashley never take their hands off each other. They don't get carried away touching each other but they do. They kiss every once in a while.

She notices that when the conversation transitions from one topic to another, I pay attention before I jump into the conversation. When my sisters talk, I back off. When Kyle and Brandon talk, I jump into their conversations and add details that pertain to the events. Joanne watches Cody. While everyone chats, he moves his hand from my hand to my arm. He puts his hand on my shoulder. He rubs my arm. He kisses me on the shoulder.

Dad looks at her. "Stop." He says quietly. "You are making them feel uncomfortable."

"Who?" She hisses in a whisper.

"All of them. My girls, our boys."

"Your girls don't respect me." She says a bit louder.

I look across the table at her. "You have been staring at me since we started eating. Am I doing something wrong?"

"You always get so bent out of shape."

"Is that what I am doing? I am getting bent out of shape?"

"I am not looking for an argument."

"We are not looking for any arguments with you." Kelsey says.

Trevor takes her hand.

Catalina looks at Joanna. "When you married Jack were you not aware that he came with three daughters?"

Joanne looks at Catalina. "I knew he came with three daughters."

"Can you tell me anything about any of them?" Catalina says it sweetly. Its said so sweetly, the hair on my arms prickle. It came across as a sweet fuck you to Joanna, but a fuck you none-the-less.

"I know that they don't like me." Joanna says.

"That is not true." Ashley and Kelsey say together.

I don't say anything.

"You say that they don't respect you. Do you respect them?" Stew asks.

Joanna looks at dad. "Jack, you never defend me."

"Why is it that we always have this same conversation?" I ask. I look right at her. "Can you answer Catalina's question? Do you know anything about any of us? And your sons for that matter?" Cody takes my fingers in his and laces them together. He knows how hard it is for me to be confrontational with people. I don't want my dad to be mad at me.

"Why are you always so hateful towards me?" She asks.

"Why are you always the victim?" Kyle asks her. "What can you tell us that you know about the five of us?"

She tries to leave the table.

"Sit down." Dad says sharply to her in a tone just louder than a whisper.

She looks at him. "Jack."

"I am sick of this. Our children are asking you to inform us about what you can share about them. What can you tell us about our children?"

"I am always being attacked." Joanna says.

"Excuse me." I say.

I push away from the table and go outside.

Cody follows me. "Whats going on?"

"She can say nice things about everyone of them, she can't say anything nice about me. Even when she is acting like she likes me, she is acting. My dad only sees her as some fucking angel. She is not." I put my hands over my face. "I do a lot of nice things and she can't name one thing. Not one fucking nice thing."

"Don't cover your face." Cody says and takes my wrists in his hands and lowers my hands away from my face. He then slides his hands into my hands.

"I don't know if my mom could even say something nice about me. But your parents who I just met can say the nicest things about me. They tell me things about myself that I forgot I did."

He smiles. "You do that to me." He says. "Its wicked creepy isn't it?"

I look at him and smile. "I love you."

Kelsey and Ashley walk outside. I look at them and then look away. Kelsey walks over and hugs me. "I am so proud of you!"

"I don't want to come between her and daddy." I say.

"We are adults. We can speak our minds and speak out for what we know is true." Kelsey says.

"She knows and can tell wonderful things about the two of you. She has pushed me away forever. And now that mom and her are friends, I feel like I have lost her too." I say. I look at my sisters. "I only know Cody's parents a short time, but they know details about my life that I am not sure any of you know. I am not sure that any of you care. I am just not sure. I am grateful that you all came to be supportive of me."

"I love you." Ashley says.

"You tolerate me." I say.

"That's not true." She says. "Brandon and I love you. I can tell you all the things that you have done. I am not sure that you can tell anything exciting about me."

I look at her. "I have seen every show you have ever been in. I have seen you on Broadway and off Broadway. I have seen you and Brandon in the most intimate scene on a stage ever. I was the only one in the audience who knew that moment you both shared was not an act. I know that you host a charity ball every year. I know that you do it for research on neurological causes." I look away. "I know that you and Brandon got an apartment that I can access. I know that when I stayed with the two of you, I felt like I was home."

Ashley looks at me. "Why didn't you let me know that you were there for my plays?"

"Where do you think the purple and yellow roses came from?" I ask her.

"They said a fan." She says.

"I am your biggest fan." I tell her.

"You saw the play that I was in with Brandon?"

"Every night. The rest of the audiences may not have noticed the change in the actor on stage with you for the sex scene but I did. When you moaned out every night, I wondered it it was the night that you were going to get pregnant."

She runs to me and hugs me. "We lost the baby." She says.

I hug her tighter. "I know. I was there."

She buries herself in my embrace. "You would have loved him. Why didn't you say anything?"

"I didn't know if you wanted me to." I run my hands over her shoulders. "I love you."

Kelsey stands watching us. "Can you give me details of my life?"

I look at her. "You danced in so many shows, I thought I was going to go broke flying to see you. When you twisted your ankle I sobbed so loud, I expected them to remove me from the audience. I was at the hospital waiting for you to come out, you never did. I stayed until a doctor came over and told me that you were gone. When I asked about your ankle, he smiled and said that you were fine. It just needed to be wrapped and iced for a few weeks. When I went back the next night to see you dance, they said that my tickets were not valid." I tell her. I look at her. "I stayed in the lobby and I watched the doctor come in and take my seat. I watched you kiss him when the show was over and you weren't even limping."

"You called me a bitch." She said.

"I didn't. I just said the word bitch." I say. "Then you moved into your apartment and I came to visit and found out that there was no elevator. I left you roses."

"I know you did." She says.

"I got on a plane to Orlando and never looked back."

Cody stands there. He watches us interact with one another. He says nothing.

"You pushed me away. I came home for Thanksgiving to spend with mom and found out that she was on a cruise. I called dad and Joanna told me that she didn't expect me and to make room for me was too—" I choke on the words. Emotions are thick in my throat. "Kyle must have heard her on the phone with me because he spent Thanksgiving with me."

Cody walks over and takes me in his arms. "You will never spend another holiday alone again." He says. He kisses me with so much passion.

My tears fall down my cheeks. I can't control them. When Cody pulls back a bit, I look at my sisters. "She told me I wasn't family and that she was grateful that I wasn't her daughter."

Cody lifts me in his arms. He looks at my dad who was standing by the French doors. Dad turns and goes back in the house. He walks over to Kyle. "I need to talk to you."

Kyle gets up from the table. He and dad walk into the kitchen. Dad wipes his face. Kyle looks at him. "Dad, is everything alright?"

"Did your mother actually say that she was grateful that she isn't Crystal's mother?" He says the words with a knot in his throat.

"She did."

"Why didn't I know about it?"

"Crystal begged me not to say anything to you. She didn't want to be the reason of harshness between you and mom."

"She must think that I am a monster." Dad says.

"She thinks that you live with a monster. She only thinks the best of you. She always has."

"All of you have kept this from me." Dad says.

"We wanted to tell you. So many times we wanted to come to you and tell you, she made us promise that your marriage wouldn't end because of her." Kyle says. "She always wanted you to have the best of everything and feel that love that you never felt being with Margie." Kyle runs his hand through his hair. "She blamed herself for your marriage falling apart. She knew how much money and time went into her hospital bills and her therapy sessions. When you left them for my mom, Tally told me that she had decided that day that she would take a back burner so that you can be happy."

Dad pounds his fists into the counter. "The five of you betrayed me."

"No we didn't. We protected her." Kyle says.

"You all kept her from me."

"No. We kept her from being abused by my mom."

"Does she talk to Margie often?"

"She did. Then mom and mom became friends. Stew shows up for everything for Tally."

Landon hears them talking. He walks into the kitchen. "She is so loyal. She is a true friend. She loves unconditionally until she is given a reason to be guarded. Her shield is happiness. She can pull off happiness even when her heart is breaking in a million pieces. Her smiles aren't always happy ones but only the people who truly know her know that about her. I know that I wronged her but when I asked her to go somewhere with me, she agreed no questions asked. And when I fell apart, she was there to just be there. To listen. To reassure me. To make me feel that I didn't have to face what I was facing alone."

Kyle looks at dad. "You are her father, you should know her better than anyone."

"I do know my daughters."

"Do you know that Kelsey had her removed from a theater of sold out tickets so that her boyfriend could be there?" Landon says. "It was the first time that I saw her cry. I think that she held those tears all the way from Boston."

"Boston?" Dad asks.

"That's where Kelsey was dancing. She had taken a bad fall and Crystal went and waited at the hospital. Kelsey went out a side door. Then she had the ushers tell her that her tickets were not valid. They didn't let her into the auditorium but they didn't make her leave. When the show was over, Kelsey and the doctor were in the lobby kissing. She left Crystal sitting in the lobby all night long. It was like they were strangers." Landon says.

"I am sad to hear that." Dad says.

"Are you really?" Brandon asks. "I don't want to make it like I am attacking you, but you stayed away and so did Kelsey. I was at that show for Kelsey. I heard the commotion about the ticket. I also heard the usher say that she hated that she lied to someone with a valid ticket. She was sad that she took the ticket from Crystal and ripped it in half."

"I am not sure how I can deal with this." Dad says.

"Don't let my mom abuse her anymore." Brandon says. "Call your daughters and ask them to spend time with you. They are all craving time with you." Brandon hugs dad. "We all are."

"Crystal has Stew." Dad says.

"He is not a replacement for you. She wants you. She has always wanted you. The difference is, Stew shows up, even when he is not invited. He shows up just to let her know that someone out there loves her. Margie used to do that, but than for some reason that stopped."

"I am sure that she feels abandoned." Dad says.

"That's just it, she doesn't. She is ok being by herself. She wants to be with all of you, all of us, but she is ok with being alone." Kyle says. "If she stays away, she can't get hurt."

Chapter Nineteen

Everyone flew home. Kyle flew home leaving his car for Cody, Landon and me to drive home. After days of packing all of Cody's stuff up and taping boxes closed, I was in so much pain. Cody wound up taking me to the hospital. While there, I had more x-rays done of my ribs and my cheek. It turned out that my cheek bone was fractured. And my ribs were fractured which we knew. The doctor said that I couldn't fly for at least three to four weeks. Another doctor who saw me in the hospital couldn't take his eyes off me. He wasn't flirting with me, he was trying to place who I was.

The doctor is the one who took my seat in Boston. Vinny. He looks at me and Cody. He recognizes Cody almost immediately.

"Mr. Parker. Its good to see you again." Vinny says.

"Its good to see you too."

"What brings you here?"

"My fiancé was injured a little more than a week ago. She is in a lot of pain. Her eye and cheek are getting worse everyday."

Vinny looks at me. "Where do I know you from?"

"Boston." I say.

"Boston?" He asks. He looks at his assistant in the office. She looks at him and is all flirty.

"Yes. Boston. I am Kelsey's sister."

"Oh my god, Kels, how is she? Is she still dancing?"

"She is great. She does still dance." I say.

"You live here now?"

"No." Cody says. "I have a house here and we are here packing it up. I am moving to Florida with Crystal."

"Crystal." Vinny says. "That's right. You are Crystal?" He walks closer to me and touches my cheek.

I see stars. Tears stream down my cheeks.

"Cody, can you stand behind her and hold her head still?" Vinny asks.

"Don't hurt me." I say.

"What happened to your cheek?" Vinny asks,

The assistant looks at Vinny like he is crazy. "You don't follow the news?"

Vinny looks at her. "What?"

"This is Crystal. She is the girl that got shoved into a table at Baseball Café and she got punched in the face by Cody's former girlfriend."

"Cody never dated that woman who punched me in the face." I say.

Vinny looks at Cody. Cody takes my head in his hands and holds my head. Vinny pushes on my nose and my cheek. My head falls back as my world goes black. Cody looks at Vinny. "Did you know that was going to happen?"

"I thought that it might." Vinny says. He examines my eye and my cheek. "Its going to look worse before it gets better. It is actually healing. She can't sleep on it."

"She sleeps on her left side." Cody says.

"Let me see about her ribs."

"She winces every time she moves a certain way. She cringes when she sleeps." Cody says. He looks at Vinny. "Did you really take her seat in Boston?"

"What?" Vinny asks.

"You went to see Kelsey dance a sold out show. They confiscated Crystal's ticket so that you can see Kelsey dance."

"I didn't know that happened." He looks at me. "She must think I am a prick."

"No. She thinks her sister is an asshole."

Vinny goes over the x-rays. "She can't fly for a month." He looks at Cody. "Take her home and let her rest. She needs to reframe from anything that will make her stretch for a week or so."

"No sex?"

"Just for a week. She needs to rest."

"Is she going to be ok?" Cody asks kissing the top of my head.

Vinny looks at him. "You know, I am sure that you know, when you kissed her in that resort at the wedding that you went to, you stopped time. The world gasped. Women passed out. You crushed dreams. But for her, you made her dream come true."

Cody looks at Vinny. "What does that mean?"

"When I went to see Kels dance, I went into the lobby to answer a phone call. I saw Crystal waiting. I didn't know about the ticket and I will address it with Kels, but she had her phone with her and she was watching the baseball game. You were playing. I don't think you had a hit at all in that game, but her watching you was like watching a child seeing Santa Claus or Mickey Mouse. I stood behind her. She radiated love for you."

"Awe. I hear that from a lot of people." He kisses my cheek.

"Make sure that she stays calm. Her bruising is going to get worst still."

"What can I do for her?"

"What you are doing."

"I love this girl." Cody says.

"Cody, there is no doubt that you love her." He looks at me. "I am going to wake her up so we can give her a MRI."

"Don't wake her up." Cody says.

"What?"

"She panics."

Vinny looks at Cody. "Can you carry her?"

"Yes." He says. He lifts me up in his arms. I am limp in his arms. Cody looks at Vinny. "She is limp."

"She's ok." Vinny says. He walks into the room where the MRI is. Cody lays me on the table. "You can hold her hand in case she wakes up." He puts the cage over my face to stop me from moving. He slides the table into place.

"Can we put a pillow under her knees? She can't lay flat. It freaks her out."

"Yes of course." The technician says.

Cody lifts my legs and they slide a pillow underneath my knees. Cody sits next to the machine and he takes my hand in his. "Please sleep through this."

Forty-five minutes later Cody lifts me back in his arms and carries me back into the room where my wheelchair is. My head drops back on his shoulder. Cody sits in a chair and holds me on his lap. He runs his fingers through my hair.

Vinny comes into the room. "Her cheek is healing. Its going to turn darker before it lightens up."

"I have had black eyes before." Cody says.

"I will send the reports to the courts. I think that they should serve more time. Each of them." He looks at the monitor on the wall. "Her ribs concern me."

"Why?"

"They are fractured."

"Yeah, we knew that."

"She needs to not move for three full days."

"Vinny, she is not going to stand for that."

"I know." He smiles at Cody. "Kels was the same way. I told her to stay off her ankle."

"So she was hurt?"

"She broke it." He looks at me. "Her ribs need to be wrapped. She needs to wear a back brace to keep her restricted."

"She's going to hate that."

Vinny laughs. "I bet she will." He looks away. "Does Kels have anyone in her life?"

"Trevor." Cody answers.

"Does she love him?"

"I am not around her enough to say either way. She avoids Crystal."

"Do you call her Tally?"

"No. I hate that they do."

"Its not anything meant out of malice. She was struggling in her stats class. She kept coming up with the same answer over and over and over again. Everything she did she couldn't get the right answer. Then Cody Parker did the unthinkable. I was in the room with Kelsey and Crystal was in the other room. The joining door was cracked open. It was so hard to have sex and be quiet when— never mind." Vinny says. "We heard her crying."

"Crying?"

"Cody, she was sobbing. She was clapping her hands and sobbing. We went running into the room and she was clapping her hands and the tears of joy flowed down her face. She had written on her paper that she was working on Crys Tally Parker. She told us that she wrote it just before you got up to bat. She told us that she always did. When she didn't do it you didn't hit so well."

Cody laughs. "That's one that no one ever told me."

"She was inspiring to listen to. She knows about almost everything. She can carry on conversations with young children, old people, and all in between. I didn't know that Kels had taken the seat away from her sister. Kels and I were dating. I proposed to her and two weeks later she freaked out and I never saw her again. I went to a gala in Orlando and didn't know that the gala was completely put together by Crystal. She did all the work. She made sure that there was nothing left out. The details were flawless."

"What gala?" Cody asks.

"Your mom was there. She is beautiful on television, but in person, she is stunning."

"What gala?" Cody asks.

"I really don't know what it was for. Hanging on a tripod was a picture of a girl that needed surgery. The surgery was expensive and every penny was covered by Crystal."

I open my eyes and look around the room. I hide my face in Cody's chest.

"Are you alright?" Cody asks against my temple.

"Why are we still here?" I ask.

"You passed out." Vinny says.

I put my fingertips to my cheek. "My cheek hurts so much."

"Its going to hurt. We did another MRI and you seem to be just bruised. You can put ice on it to keep the swelling at bay. Your ribs are fractured. You are going to have to wear a brace." Vinny says.

"No way." I say.

"Well then you have to be wrapped up."

"That's fine." I say.

Cody pushes my wheelchair out to the car. He puts the brakes on and lifts me into the car. He puts my wheelchair in the trunk. He gets in the car. He drives back to the house. "Are you hungry?"

"We have plenty of food to eat." I say.

Cody gets out of the car and opens the trunk. He takes my wheelchair in the house. He then comes back outside and lifts me out of the car. He carries me in the house.

Landon looks at Cody. "How did everything go?"

Cody sits me on the couch. I get comfortable and fall asleep.

"Did she have a CT scan or MRI?" Landon asks.

"Actually yes." He looks at me. "How do you know that?"

"They ware her out."

"She needs to be wrapped up for a week or two."

Landon puts his hand on my cheek . "Lets wrap her up."

"You will help me?"

"Yes." Landon walks over to his training workout bag. He takes out bandages. He walks back over to Cody. "We should let her sleep."

Cody and Landon walk into the kitchen and have something to eat. They then sit on the couches which will be staying behind and watch television. Landon flips through the stations and they find an old baseball game on. Cody is playing. From the angle of the cameras the stadium can be seen. Cody looks and finds me in the crowd holding a self made poster. He looks at Landon. "Can you make that bigger?"

Landon takes the remote from Cody and makes the image bigger. "What do you see?"

"Her." He sits on the edge of the couch. "I know what I did in the game, I want to watch her watching me."

Landon gets up. He walks over to a box. He bends and lifts it off the ground. Landon walks back over and gives it to Cody.

Cody looks at him. "What's this?"

"Kyle and Stew left this for you."

Cody opens the box. Inside the box are USB sticks. He stands and gets his laptop. He turns it on and sticks one into the computer.

"Welcome baseball fans to another start to what will hopefully be a successful baseball season." I smile at the camera and laugh. "A girl can dream." I smile again. "Well we are here to be just fans today and not call play-by-play shots of the game." I look into the camera and smile brightly. "This is going to be so hard, but I have taken another job." The National Anthem plays in the background. I put my hand over my heart. When it ends I look back at the camera. "We have to go in! The game is going to start. Annnd— Cody Parker is playing! Brandon, Kyle come on." I say.

Cody takes that one out after it fades to black. He puts another one in. I don't know that I am being recorded in this one. I fix my hair. I hold the sign up that reads, I Believe In Cody Parker! Its in glitter. Brandon is off camera but he talks to me. "Hey Tally." When he says the name, I smile almost immediately. "Tell me again how Tally came to be your nickname."

"Brandon, you know." I say.

"I know I know, but tell me again." He says.

In the background you hear the announcer saying. "Next at bat is our very own Cody Parker."

I scream with excitement. I hold the sign up. "Come on baby!" I say. "Crack it!" The hit is so loud. I throw my hands in the air. "GRAND SLAM HOME RUN!" I throw my hands up in the air. "Run!" I yell. "I love him. I am going to marry him one day." I say it softly. I look into the camera that I didn't know was recording me. "He looked up at the stands."

"I think he saw you." Kyle's voice is heard. "What did you say?"

I smile at him. "I want to marry him."

"Why?" Both Kyle and Brandon ask together.

"I love him."

The screen goes black. Cody plays it again. When it finishes a second time, he takes it out and puts another one in.

"Welcome to the stadium. I am Crystal Steele reporting for the last time. Cody Parker," I wipe my eyes free of tears that are brimming on my bottom eye lashes. "Cody Parker," I say again. "Was sadly injured. He was mugged while out with his girlfriend. I am going to watch the game, but it will not be the same. Best wishes go out to Cody Parker." I say. "I love him." I whisper.

We go into the stadium. We go into the gift shop. The camera zooms in on the shelf that I approach. It is filled with teddy bears wearing Cody Parker jerseys.

"How much are the teddy bears?" I ask.

You hear the store worker answer me. "For a hundred bucks you can have all of them. Cody Parker is a fucking loser."

I don't blink. I look at the guy. "Is this all of them?"

"Lady, we just got six boxes full."

"And I can have all of them for a hundred dollars?"

"Yep. No one wants them."

I thrust a hundred dollars at him. "I want all of them."

"What are you going to do with them? Burn them? They should be burned."

"Its my business what I am going to do with all of them." I say.

The screen goes black.

Cody looks at me sleeping with the teddy bear that I sent him in my arms. He looks at Landon. "Did you give her the teddy bear?"

Landon looks at him. "The teddy bear was on the couch where she left it before you both left."

"She bought all the teddy bears."

"I know." Landon says. "I helped her move them."

"What did she do with all of them?"

"She took four boxes to a children's hospital. She had a story book that went a long with it."

"What story book?"

Landon walks over to another box that Kyle left. He opens it. He comes back with a book. He hands it to Cody.

Cody takes the book and he opens it. He looks at Landon. "She wrote a book?"

"Apparently." Landon says.

"And she gave them out?"

"At a children's hospital event."

Cody opens the book and flips through the pages. They are animated drawings of events that happened. A fan in a wheelchair with a sign. A fan in the grandstands watching. The players on the field. Cody walking over to a crowd of people. Cody holding his hat up in the air waving at fans. Cody on third base running home. The words Grand Slam fills the next two pages. On the last page it's a picture of my sign. It reads You are a Super Star. Be like Cody Parker. Be kind for no other reason than to just be kind. In the bottom on the last page is a little tiny drawn post-it that reads I love you Cody Parker always and forever.

I stretch and try to roll over. I almost fall off the couch. Cody grabs me in his arms. I look at him and smile. "Hi."

"Hi." He says. "How many of these did you hand out?"

I look at the book that he is holding. "How do you have that?" I ask.

"Crystal, how many did you hand out?"

I shake my head. "I only had two of them made. I have one and Kyle had the other one."

"I heard that you handed them out at a children's hospital?"

"No." I say. "I showed the copy that I kept to the children that I visited. I didn't give any out to any children. I didn't have permission to distribute it."

He holds me in his arms. "Why do you love me?"

"Why wouldn't I love you?" I kiss him on the lips. I then stand holding on to him and put my hands on his shoulders before I wrap my arms around him. "I don't need a reason to love you, I just do. I always have. When you hugged me protecting me from that crazy fan after your game, I was glad that you were safe. I wanted you to hold me everyday forever."

Landon looks at Cody. "You told dad that the crazy fan didn't get close enough to you."

"I know what I told him."

"Why did you lie?"

"Crazy fans showed up at every game."

"The fan wasn't there to hurt Cody. He was a fan. He was there to hurt the girl who caught the foul ball ." I say.

"Crystal, you told me that you didn't get the ball." Landon says.

"I didn't. Kyle got it."

"That big lug didn't let you have the ball?" Cody asks.

"No. He caught it. He kept it." I say.

Cody takes his phone out of his pocket. He punches in Kyle's number. He puts the phone to his ear.

"Hey man, whats going on?" Kyle asks.

"Did you all get home safely?" Cody asks really caring.

"We did. I drove your parents home and Gianna. They never stopped talking about the two of you and how cute you are."

"Ky I have a question."

"Shoot."

"My last game that you all came to—"

Kyle starts laughing. "I knew you longer." He says.

"You didn't give it to her?"

"He teased me with it." I say smiling.

"You teased her with it?"

Kyle laughs into the phone. "Hell yes." He says. "I knew you longer."

"What the hell is that? A Twinkie defense?"

"I guess." Kyle says.

"What did you do with it?"

"Its on the shelf with the other foul balls I caught."

"You are a jerk." Cody teases him

"How is she?" Kyle asks with concern deep in his tone.

"I will call you later."

"Love her."

"I do."

"She loves you very much."

"Thank you for all that you left here."

"Did you see all of them?"

"No."

"They were numbered."

"What?" Cody asks.

"They were numbered." Kyle repeats.

Cody takes the one USB stick in his fingers. He looks for a number and sees that it does in fact have a number three on it. He takes the ones out that he already looked at them seeing that they are numbered one and two. He smiles. "I didn't know that they were numbered but I have watched them so far in order."

"Good." Kyle says. "Listen, I have to run. Be nice to my car."

"Run it into the ground?" Cody teases. "I will run it hard."

"I will hurt you."

"I love you." Cody says.

"I love you too." Kyle says.

Cody puts his phone on the coffee table.

"Should I be concerned?" I ask teasing him.

He sinks his teeth into me.

"Ouch!" I say. I stretch and something pulls in my side. "Oh my god, ouch!" I cry. "Oh it hurts so much. Ow! Ow! Ow!"

Cody sits me on the couch. "Let me check it out."

Tears stream down my cheeks.

Landon walks over. He puts his hands on my sides. "Where does it hurt?" He asks.

I just cry.

"Crystal, tell us where it hurts." Cody says.

"When I stretch my arms up it hurts so much." I say.

"Go take a hot shower. When you get out, we will wrap your ribs." Cody says.

I get in my wheelchair carefully and go into Cody's bedroom and get undressed. I get in the shower. Reaching my arms up to shampoo my hair hurts my ribs. The movement makes my breath catch. When I finish in the shower, I dry off and wrap myself in a towel. I move carefully and get in my wheelchair. I push my wheelchair into the room and then go back in the bathroom. I angle my wheelchair. I open the towel and look at my ribs. They are black and blue. Its dark purple in spots. I touch it and even when I touch it, there is immediate pain. Shooting pain.

Cody knocks on the door. "How are you doing?"

"I am ok." I say.

"Let me take a look." Cody says.

"Yeah, you can come in." I say. I cover my breasts with the towel.

He walks in and gets on his knees.

"Cody, you are going to hurt your knees."

"My knees are fine." He says. "Let me look." He moves the towel. "Wow, it looks worst than it did just a few hours ago."

"Did Vinny see me naked?"

"No." He says.

"He pushed on my cheek and I saw stars. My world went dark. How come he didn't wake me up right away?"

"He wanted to but I told him to wait. I told him that you freak out having an MRI." He kisses me. "Get dressed in something light. Land and I will wrap you up."

"Cody."

"What?"

"I love you."

"I love you too."

"Cody, I don't want you to think that I ever had a relationship with Landon."

"Crystal, the truth is he told me all about you and told me how much you disliked him. Then he told me about you going with him to the cemetery for the anniversary of Donny. He told me how you held him while he cried and you told him that you would always love him like a brother."

"He really screwed me over."

"He felt bad about it. He tried to make it right."

"I know he did." I say. "He did though, he couldn't get my grade changed back, but he showed up at the right time and got me out of a situation."

"Tell me about it."

"Please get off your knees." I say to him.

"You are going to be begging me to stay on my knees."

I laugh.

"Unfortunately we have to hold back on sex for a couple weeks."

I look at myself in the mirror. "I am sorry."

"No. I didn't realize I was hurting you." He says. "Get dressed. Land and I will wait for you."

"I think I need some assistance. It hurts when I raise my arms up."

"Show me what you want to wear."

We go into the bedroom. He lifts me out of my wheelchair and lays my naked body on the bed. He slides my panties up my legs so passionately and a pair of leggings. He slides them up to my waist. He puts his hands on my shoulders and pulls me to a sitting position. He cups my breasts in his hands and kisses my chest. He takes the sports bra and helps me into it. He sits me in my wheelchair.

I go in the bathroom and brush my hair. It hurts to stretch my arms up but I pull my hair into a ponytail. I leave the room and find the two of them sitting on the couch waiting for me. "I don't want to be a bother but I am starving." I say.

"That's not a bother. What do you want?" Landon asks.

"There is a lot of food in the refrigerator. I don't know. I like it all."

"Let me make you something." Landon says.

Cody looks at Landon. "You wrap better. I will get her something to eat." Cody kisses me on the lips. He then walks into the kitchen. He opens the refrigerator and takes the Dixie paper plates out of the drawer. He cuts a nice size piece of meatloaf. He puts mashed potatoes and veggies on the plate. He looks at me. "Do you want me to warm it?"

"No." I say.

"Oh my god, Crystal. You eat cold food too? Iced coffee and cold food?"

I laugh. "Don't make fun." I look at Landon. "Landon, please don't hurt me."

"I won't intentionally hurt you." He says. He pulls me to the edge of my seat. He gets on his knees in front of me. He takes the bandages and starts wrapping my ribs. "Is that too tight?"

"Its snug." I say.

"Snug is good." Landon says. "I am going to get you Advils. He puts his hands on my knees and pushes me back in my seat. He kisses the top of my head. He stands and walks into the bathroom to get Advil.

Cody walks over. He gives me the plate of food. He sits on the couch with a plate of his own. He warmed his up. We have dinner together. "This is the most delicious meatloaf." He says.

"Ashley made it. She knows it's my favorite."

"I will have to tell my mom. She will make it for you. You will love it."

"Cody, I want to go home."

"We are going home tomorrow." He says.

"Cody, what's in that box?"

"Nothing." He says.

We finish dinner. Landon comes back in with the Advil. I take it with water. We settle on the couch and watch television together. I fall asleep on the couch with my head on Cody's lap.

"Did you give her something?"

"Advil." Landon says.

"Regular Advil?"

"No." Landon smiles. "Advil PM." He says. "She needs to rest and she hates to rest. She takes care of everything. She takes care of every detail of things, but when it comes to her, she doesn't stop to care for herself. She wants to make everyone happy. She thinks that if she hides her pain she will be like everyone else."

"What was the situation that you got her out of?"

Landon shakes his head. "She needs to tell you."

"Tell me."

Landon gets up from the couch. "She was talking sports. She was talking baseball. This guy in school argued everything with her. You had an off day. You struck out every time you were up. You couldn't get your head in the game and she was defending you. He got a group of guys to surround her. She didn't fucking back down. She continued saying that you were great. She never backed down. They were getting closer and closer to her and I was getting nervous that they would hurt her. I tipped her wheelchair backwards and pulled her away. I thought she was going to yell at me. She looked at me and said that I took my sweet ass time to get to her. She made me laugh. She didn't know that I was your brother. I didn't tell her for a few more weeks."

"What was her reaction?"

"She smiled brightly. She looked at me and said, oh shit, we are going to be related."

"What?" Cody asks.

"She told me that she wanted to marry you."

"Why didn't you tell me?"

"We weren't talking. I had my head up my ass in grief over Donny. You had your career and I didn't want to burden you with anything. But I have to tell you, when she found out that I was your brother, she didn't act any differently. She would tell me things about you that I didn't know. It was like she was educating me on my own brother. And the way she spoke about you always caught me off guard."

"What would she say?" He asks. He looks at me sleeping.

"When she first started working for Rosa, she came to school late and she was annoyed. She turned on her radio channel that she listened to and you had just hit a single. You got on first base and then the next two guys struck out. She thought that you were remarkable for clapping your hands and cheering on the next two players. She looked at me when she said, you know no one does that for him. He does it for every guy that is up directly in front of him and the ones that follow him."

"What did you do?"

"I watched your next series of games closer and she was absolutely right. No one cheered you on." Landon looks at me sleeping and than back at Cody. "When she found out that you were hurt, oh my god, you would thank that someone had died. She cried. She was in classes and she wore sunglasses because her eyes were bloodshot. She couldn't stop the tears. She heard that you were in surgery and the next thing I knew she was gone."

"I woke up in the hospital and she was holding my hand. I thought I dreamed her up."

"Cody, you should have heard her talk about mom. I was watching mom's runway show that she was in. Crystal was sick. She had a cold. She was shivering and sweating at the same time. Her roommate was annoyed that she was sick. She never missed anything that she needed to do. Her classes. Her job. Whatever she was obligated to do, she didn't miss it. Then she got caught in the rain and she broke down crying. I ran over and helped her. I held an umbrella over her. She went back to her room and showered. She climbed in bed and she couldn't get out of bed for three days. Her roommate came running out to the RA."

"RA?" Cody asks.

"Resident advisor." Landon says.

"You did that?"

"I did it for two years. I got free housing." Landon says. "So I went into the room and she was so weak. I was just starting my physical therapy classes. I worked her legs. I made her soup. Then I put the television on to watch mom. She watched with me. She didn't know it was mom. I mean she knew Catalina Parker but Crystal didn't know that she was our mom. She looked at me and said that mom was the most beautiful woman she had ever seen. She closed her eyes but she continued talking that when she met Catalina Parker at a charity event she was mesmerized by mom's beauty."

"Wow. Sometimes I don't think that I am worthy of her."

"Cody, you are everything that she ever wanted."

The moving truck is finally delivered. The guys that come in three vehicles pack up all the boxes. The men that came with the trucks say that they will drive two of them but the third one needs a driver. We waited for the moving truck to come and load up all his house. Landon decides that he will drive the truck to Florida. We are going to stay together. Landon takes our luggage with him in the front of the truck. The two trucks leave ahead of us.

He sets out on the road an hour before we do. Before he left, he wrapped my ribs. He kisses me on the head and hugs Cody.

Cody puts my wheelchair in the car. We listen to music and chat the whole way. When we get to Georgia, Cody tells me that he can't drive another mile. I agree that we should stop for the night. Cody calls Landon who is now behind us. Landon agrees.

When we get to the hotel that we are staying in for the night. I go in first and get the room. When they join me in the lobby, Landon looks at me. Cody walks over to join us. The woman gives me the keys.

We enter the diner and have dinner. Cody orders iced coffee for me while I go to use the bathroom. Its after midnight when we find the room. There is two beds in the room. Landon looks at Cody.

"I will get my own room."

"Landon, there are two beds." I say.

"There are three of us."

"Cody and I will share one bed. He has been sleeping in my bed for months." I smile at the two of them. "I am going to marry him." I can't contain my happiness.

"Can we put the television on?" Landon asks.

"Yes." Cody and I say together.

I go into the bathroom and change into shorts and a shirt. I am still wearing my sports bra. When I get on the bed, Cody takes the bandages off. He rubs my back. I curl into him and fall asleep quickly.

Landon looks at me. He gets in the other bed and turns to face the television.

Cody stays awake for a while. He holds me in his arms.

I open my eyes, "What's wrong?"

"Nothing." Cody says.

"Cody, I love you." I reach my hand up and touch his scar. He winces from the touch. "Am I hurting you?"

"No." He says. "I told you, I never let anyone touch my scars." He kisses me. "I want you to touch every inch of me."

"Not tonight." Landon says.

The three of us burst into laughter. We laugh for a while.

"Landon, thanks for all that you do." I say.

He rolls over and looks at the two of us. "Paige is going to meet us tomorrow for breakfast." He looks at Cody. "Is that ok?"

"Of course it is. Is she here now?"

"She's staying with her aunt."

"She loves you." I say to Landon.

"How do you know that?" He asks.

"She looks at you the same way that I look at Cody."

"How's that?"

"She looks at you like there is no other man on the planet." I sit up. I put my hand lightly over Cody's scar. I look at Landon. "You are worth loving. You are kind. You are everything that she dreamed of." I look at Cody. "You are everything I ever wanted my whole life. When my friends growing up were dreaming of Prince Charming, I was dreaming of you."

He takes me in his arms and he hugs me. "You are everything that I ever dreamed of too. When I saw you on that plane, I wanted to keep you."

"I am yours." I tell him.

Chapter Twenty

I wake up in the morning and my ribs are already wrapped. Although it feels snug, I feel like my ribs are being hugged. It is so helpful. I get dressed and push my wheelchair down to the lobby. Paige is sitting at a table just off the diner having coffee.

I put my hand on her arm. She looks up and hugs me. "Hi." She says with excitement.

"Hi." I say to her. "It means so much to Landon that you drove up to meet us."

"My brother drove me. I am going to drive back with Land in the moving truck." She says.

"You look beautiful."

"You look like you are still in pain." She comments.

"I am."

"How's it going?"

"It hurts." I tell her.

A woman watches us from a neighboring table. She looks at my face. "Sweetheart, if you are in an abusive relationship, there are places you can go."

I smile at her. "I was involved in a bar fight." I say.

"What does the other girl look like?" She asks.

"Worse than this." I say.

"You know, no one has the right to hit someone with a disability." The woman says.

"She was jealous." Paige says.

"Why?" The woman asks.

"Because when everything is said and done, I am going to marry the guy." I smile.

Cody walks over with Landon. Cody kisses me on the lips like he always does. The woman watches us. She gasps. "I have to be honest, I would punch you in the throat." The woman says with a big grin on her face.

"Nice." Paige says to the lady.

Cody steps closer to me and deepens the kiss.

Landon hugs Paige. She fits perfectly against him. She wraps her arms around his neck. She kisses his lips.

Oscar walks over to us. He taps my arm. I look at him. He hugs me. I hug him. He steps back and looks at my face. "Why does it look worse then it did when we were in Indiana?"

"Vinny said it will look worse before it gets better." I say.

"Vinny?" He looks at all of us. "You went to Boston?"

"No. Vinny is in Indiana now."

"Does Kels know?"

"I don't know."

"Does Trevor know that Kels keeps in touch with Vinny?" Oscar asks.

"Oscar, what are you doing here?" I ask. Other than making me crazy with all these questions.

"I am visiting my grandpa. He heard from the management that you had checked into a room with two guys."

"Oscar, I am not sure that is anyone's business." Paige says. She is on the defense.

The lady looks at all of us. "Its seems that this guy cares deeply for you." She says pointing to Oscar.

I glare at him. "If only it was genuine." I say.

"Tally, I do love you."

"Don't call me Tally."

"But I gave you that nickname."

I glare at him again. "No. No you had nothing to do with my nickname." I say to him.

Oscar looks at Cody. "Do you know how she got the nickname?"

"The one that you gave her?" Cody asks. "I know how she got it."

"How did she get it?" Oscar asks.

"She was working on her statistics homework and she was stuck on a problem. She was watching me play baseball and she was writing her name on the top of the page. She wrote C-r-y-s and than she wrote Tally hyphen Parker. And she wrote on the paper that she was going to marry me."

I look at him. "How did you know that?"

"Do I ask you how you know all my secrets?" Cody asks with a big grin on his face. He kisses my lips.

"You do not." I say smiling against his lips.

"Everyone knows that you love each other, you don't have to show PDA." Oscar says. "You never did it when we dated."

I turn quickly and look at Oscar. "You never wanted anyone to know that you were dating me. You wanted it to be a secret. You hated holding hands. You hated everything."

"You didn't kiss me like that." He says.

"You hardly ever kissed me." I say. "You took credit for photos that Stew took. Why did you do that?"

"I took the same ones." He says.

I don't doubt that he did. He takes beautiful pictures. He always makes me look great in the images that he takes. I feel that he is jealous. But when he dated me, he didn't want anyone to know that we were together.

Cody looks at all of us. "We have to get on the road."

"I thought you were going to stay a few days here." Oscar says.

"Who told you that?" I ask.

"My grandpa."

"We have to get home." Cody says.

"What home do you have?" Oscar asks Cody.

"He lives with me. He's going to marry me." I say.

The lady that has been involving herself in our conversation looks at Cody. She looks down at me and then back up at Cody's very handsome face. I look at her and sense that she is going to say something shitty. I look at my friends.

"Excuse me a moment." I say. I push away from all of them. I go into the gift shop and look around.

The woman looks at Cody. "You make a beautiful couple. Don't allow anyone to pull you apart from one another. She knows your secrets, you know her secrets. That's amazing."

"Thank you for saying that." Cody looks around and doesn't see me anywhere.

Paige looks at him. She looks at the gift shop. "She went in there." Paige puts her hand on his arm. "She loves you. I have known her a long time. You know the thing that meant the most to her was when you paid for her hospital bills. She was so surprised. She had insurance, but when she went to pay the co-payment they told her that it was all covered. She investigated why it was all covered. That always meant the world to her."

"Thanks for saying that." He says.

Landon looks at Cody. "Go after her." He laces his fingers in Paige's fingers. He pulls her hand to his lips and kisses it. "Thank you for saying that."

"It's the truth. She loves everything about him. There isn't one thing that she doesn't like about him."

Cody walks into the gift shop. He walks behind me and hugs me. "You should have stayed. She said the nicest thing."

"I didn't want to hear anything negative. A lot of people like to point out why we shouldn't be together."

"I don't care what other people think. Its only important what you and I think and feel."

"Cody, I don't want to live one day without you in my life."

"I feel the same about you."

"I wish I knew you my whole life."

"I feel like I have known you my whole life. The things that you know. The things that you admire about me. The things that you want to know." He kisses my lips as he walks around me. "I want to take you one place before we leave Georgia."

"Of course." I say to him. "I trust you with my life."

Landon and Paige walk into the gift shop. "Nanny is coming." Landon says.

"Nanny's coming?" Cody asks.

"She heard from the grapevine that we are here. She wants to see us." Landon says.

I look at Landon. "I love Nanny." I smile at him.

"You know Nanny?" Paige asks.

"I met her at the cemetery when I went with Landon." I say. "She was so nice to me. Then she came to the bridal shop when Jillian was planning her wedding."

"Oh right." Cody says. "I forgot that you planned a whole menu for Nanny that wasn't paid for."

I smile at him. "It was paid for."

"Crystal, I know that you didn't take money from her for the different menu."

"Cody, she was wonderful."

"Crystal." He says.

A woman comes from behind the counter. She looks at me. "Crystal Belle Steele! Oh my goodness! As I live and breathe. You are in my shop."

I look at the screeching woman. "Aunt Ginny!" I say with excitement

"Why didn't you tell me that you were going to be here? Are you staying here?" Aunt Ginny asks.

"Yes." I say. "We leave today."

"Oh no. Rethink that." She says.

"I am not here by myself." I say.

She looks at Cody. "Cody Parker!" She says and hugs me first and then hugs him. "Its good to see you again."

"Its good to see you too." He says. He smiles at her.

"You know my Aunt Ginny?"

"I know your Aunt Ginny for a long time. She is Ky's Aunt Ginny too right?"

"She is." I say. "But she was mine first." I smile at her.

She hugs me again. "Don't be childish." She says hugging me tighter. "Does your dad know that you are here?"

"No."

She looks at my face. "Wow that looks awful." She says. She touches it with her fingertip lightly. I wince. "It hurts you still?"

"Its fractured." Cody says.

"How did that happen?" Aunt Ginny asks.

"I am sure that dad told you and Uncle Johnny. A woman who is friends with Beth saw me having lunch with friends in a café in Indiana. She shoved me into a table and then sucker punched me in the eye."

"What's the problem with Beth?"

"Well she fired me. I still own the building so I have closed the bridal shop. She can't work. Well she can but not in my shop."

Aunt Ginny smiles. "You should have fired that bitch years ago."

I smile back. The smile makes my face hurt. I get a jabbing pain in my cheek and my eye. Cody sees me wince as small as it is and puts his hand on the back of my head. He puts his other hand on my forehead. I relax against his touch.

"I am sorry." Aunt Ginny says.

A woman walks into the shop and looks at all of us. She looks at Cody and Landon. "Ginny, your sons came to visit you?" The woman asks.

"This is my niece and her boyfriend." Aunt Ginny says.

"Your niece?"

"This is my favorite niece. She lived with Johnny and me when she was in college."

I look at her. That's not exactly true. I did stay with my aunt and my uncle when work was being done on my apartment that I lived in. I stayed with them for about three weeks. They were so nice to me and each of them tried to convince me to stay with them until I finished college. She kisses the top of my head. "Let me get rid of this customer." She kisses my cheek.

"Ginny are you going to be able to join us for Pictionary and Jenga?"

"Next week." She says quickly. "My niece is here. I am going to visit with her and her friends." She looks at the four of us. "I will not take no for an answer."

"Well in that case." I say and smile. Cody is still supporting the back of my head. It hurts but not so much.

"You ok?" Aunt Ginny asks.

"I need some water." I say.

"Let me get you something." She says and walks over to the door. She opens it and gets four bottles of water for us. "Did you eat?"

"No. We just came down to the lobby to check out." Landon says. He looks at me. "She's turning white."

Cody walks in front of me. "You ok?"

"Maybe we wrapped her too tight." Landon says.

"I feel like I can't breathe." I say.

"Whats the problem?" Cody asks. He squats in front of me. He puts his hands on my midsection.

"It hurts. Cody, something's wrong. It feels like something is jabbing me." I take a deep breath and feel a surge of pain.

"Come on, we have to get you laying down." Cody says. He lifts me out of my wheelchair.

"Bring her to my house." Aunt Ginny says.

Landon gets my wheelchair and my purse.

A young girl walks into the shop. "Hi Aunt Ginny." She says.

"Hi sweetheart." She says to the employee who is not related to her. "Can you please make sure that nothing goes wrong? I have to leave for sometime."

She looks at me. "Oh my god, is that Crystal?"

"Yes."

"Go, I will cover until you get back." She says. She looks at Ginny. "You know that woman who punched her in the face was bragging about doing it before she did it. She was planning to just shove her into something and then walk away. Then she got a call from her friend Beth."

"How do you know that?" Paige asks.

"My sister works in the Baseball Café. She heard the conversation. Beth was screaming that Cody is her's and that Crystal was living up to her last name and stealing what is hers. Beth said that if she was there she would punch Crystal in the face. My sister said the next thing she knew, the woman dropped the phone and ran over and punched Crystal in the face." The employee says.

Paige hugs her. "Thanks for saying all of this. If you need any help, let me know, I will come back and help you." She leaves her phone number with the employee.

"You know, before you go, do you want to hear how nice she was to my sister and me?"

"Yes." Paige says.

"So we lived in Orlando. And we were looking for prom dresses. We didn't go shopping with my mom. We just went into the store because we were there and it was raining. She was so nice to me. She was nice to my sister. We were in awe of being surrounded by the most beautiful dresses we had ever seen in our lives. She didn't kick us out when we got loud and excited about one dress or another dress. She just watched us with a smile on her face. Beth stood back with a glare of annoyance on her face. She was pissed off mad that Crystal wouldn't kick us out. They exchanged words between the two of them. I don't know what was said because they talked so quietly between the two of them. Beth left the store angry. My sister and I continued to look at dresses."

The employee takes something that is sitting awkwardly on a shelf off the shelf and then puts it back on the shelf the way it should have been displayed. She looks at Paige. "Crystal said to the two of us to pick any dress that we wanted to try on. We looked at her like she was crazy. She told us to walk around and pick any dresses we wanted to try on. When we each picked one dress each that we loved and wanted to wear to prom, she showed us to a fitting room. We came out to model the dresses so that she could see them. When I came out, I put my arms up and smiled brightly. She took pictures for us on my phone and we sent it to my mom. My mom told us to take the dresses off immediately and not rip them because we couldn't afford dresses like that. She told us that she was going to take us to the GoodWill so that we could get second hand dresses. Crystal saw the sadness on our faces when we hung up the phone with my mom. We were so excited. We knew we didn't have a lot of money to spend on dresses, but she let us dream for a moment that they could be ours. We took the dresses off and carefully hung them back up. She asked what school we attended. We wrote the name of the school and the day that prom was going to happen on a paper. We left sad." She looks at Paige and smiles. "Do you know what she did?"

"What did she do?" Paige asks smiling. She knows what I did. She was with me when I delivered the dresses to the school for the two girls and the shoes that matched and the accessories. Paige knew that included purses for them and hair pieces that they could wear. I also included a gift card for each of them to have their makeup done for the prom and their hair too.

The girl looks at Paige. "She brought everything to the school for us. The dresses, the shoes, the purses, everything. She paid for our hair and nails to get done and our makeup too. She made the two of us and others feel like we were princesses that just won the lottery. When we graduated high school, she sent over dresses for us because we were the top two in our class. I graduated top of my class. I wore two of the most beautiful dresses I have ever had in my life. She showed up at the graduation and when they called our names, she yelled the loudest for us. She paid for my sister and I to go to school for a year. Room and board and everything for one year."

"Oh wow, I didn't know that she did that."

The girl smiles at Paige. "She lived in Indiana for a year."

"Yes I know." Paige says.

"While she was there, she would go check on my sister almost every week to make sure that my sister was doing ok without me. It was the first time that we were separated. My sister felt comfort in Crystal doing that."

"That's so sweet."

Cody heard every word that the girl had told Paige. He brought me back to the room and they unwrapped my ribs. When I closed my eyes and fell asleep, he told Aunt Ginny that he had to go get something. He went back into the gift shop to get something for me. He overheard the employee talking to Paige.

Paige turned and saw Cody standing there. She smiles at him. She walks over. "Did you know that she did stuff like that?"

"I had heard it a few times." Cody says to her. He looks at Paige, "I love her. I feel like a kid at Christmas and I am excited to spend the rest of my life with her. I love her. I want everyone to know that I love her."

"She loves you the same way."

"What can I give her?"

"Really?" Paige asks.

"Yes."

"Let her watch you play a game."

Cody looks at her.

"Cody, pull some of your friends together and give her a chance to watch you. Listen to her when you play. I know that you sense her love for you, but let her get all silly over you. Its adorable to watch. She loves you."

Paige looks at him. "She was watching you play one time in a sports bar and she was so excited for you she screamed so loud. She made everyone in that bar cheer for you. Even fans that were cheering for the other team were cheering your name because of her. When you hit that home run she had her glass in hand. She threw her hands up and her drink went all over her. But she never stopped smiling. She couldn't contain her happiness."

Aunt Ginny walks back into the shop. Cody looks at her. She looks at Paige and Cody. "She's sleeping. I have never seen my niece so happy." She shakes her head. "I can't say that. She was always the happiest girl on the planet when she was doing her sports commentator job. When you hit all those home runs it was like she won the lottery over and over. Her uncle and I loved listening to her do the play-by-plays. She was going to stay with us when she took that job. Then Rosa gave her the bridal shop. When she had shitty brides come in who were not nice, she would watch you play and even if you struck out which you did a few times." She looks at Cody and winks and smiles. "You aren't perfect, but you are perfect for that baby girl."

"Aunt Ginny, thank you so much for saying that. I would love to hear her calling the play-by-plays."

"Johnny has a bunch of them recorded."

I come into the gift shop. I hug Cody. He looks at me. "You feeling better?"

"I am. I can't sit in the car for a long time."

"Why didn't you tell us?" Landon asks.

"I didn't want to hold you back." I say to Cody. "I was the one who said I wanted to go home."

Cody kisses me on the forehead. "Baby, you have to tell me when you have had too much."

"I can't get enough of you. I want to be with you all the time." I say to him. "I am so lucky that you love me."

"I am the lucky one."

"When do you have to get the moving truck turned in?" I ask.

"Sometime next week." Cody and Landon say together.

Landon looks at me. "I can go ahead of you both and get the truck unloaded and returned if I have to."

"I don't want to hold you back." I say.

"Stop." Cody says. "You do not hold me back."

"Ginny!" A male voice booms. "Ginny! Why didn't you tell me my favorite niece is here?" Uncle Johnny says. He walks over to me and carefully takes me in his arms and hugs me. "I want to squeeze you but I know you are injured."

"How?" I ask.

"I keep in touch with that lovely guy Vinny." Uncle Johnny says.

"Did you tell that lovely guy Vinny that Kelsey is dating a lovely guy named Trevor?" I ask him.

"She is dating Trevor?" Aunt Ginny asks. "The guy who never showed up to take her to prom."

"He did show up." I say. "She went with someone else."

"That's not how your parents said it happened."

"Aunt Ginny, dad really liked Trevor and he was pushing him on Kelsey all those years ago. Trevor didn't like her dancing. He wanted her to do something different. I remember that she came in my room at mom's house and she was crying on my bed saying that she didn't know what to do. I told her that if I could have her life, and walk one day in her dancing shoes I would never have stop dancing a day in my life. She jumped off the bed and hugged me like she had never done before and never has again. She was happy to hear that I said that." I look at my aunt. She knows what Kelsey did when she was dancing in Boston and I flew there to watch her dance in all four shows that she was going to be in. I only saw one.

"Vinny loves your sister." Uncle Johnny says.

"Uncle Johnny, that's for Kelsey to work out. I am not going to interfere. They are both nice to me. I know that Trevor loves her. I know that Vinny loves her."

"Would you hate your sister if she loved both of them?" Aunt Ginny asks. She is a woman who is married and has a lover. They know about each other and the three of them have slept in bed together.

I look at her. "Its not my lifestyle but if it is what she wants, I will love her the same as I do today. She is my sister. I adore her."

"You don't think its weird that Ashley is with Brandon?"

"They love each other. We are not biological siblings. They are not breaking any laws loving each other. We lived with mom mostly. Kyle and Brandon were full time with dad and Joanna."

"Do you think that Kyle loves Kelsey?" Uncle Johnny asks.

"As a sister only." I say.

We sit and have lunch with my beloved aunt and uncle. Uncle Johnny takes Cody into his office. He shows the videos that he has of me doing Cody's play-by-plays. Cody watches the excitement that I express. He watches how all the other commentators react to my excitement. He watches how I watch him take his stance before he gears up to hit the ball. I talk low and not into the microphone.

"Can you rewind that back?" Cody asks. Uncle Johnny gives him the remote. Cody Rewinds it and turns up the volume. "What does she say?"

Uncle Johnny looks at Cody. "She said that you weren't feeling it. She said that you were going to strike out."

Cody looks at Uncle Johnny. "How did she know?"

"She studied you. She studied other players too, but for whatever reason she could call with precision what you were going to do."

Cody watches the game and sure enough he struck out. He watches more. He is up again and notices himself that he comes into the box with a different approach. He hears me say the same.

"Ok everyone, Cody Parker is up to bat again. He walks to the plate with confidence and a new approach." I say into the microphone. I push it away from my mouth. "Come on Cody, this one is yours baby." I look at the guy next to me. "I feel it, it's a home run." I say.

Cody watches himself hit a home run on the first hit and he sees my reaction. "She gives me goosebumps." Cody says to Uncle Johnny.

"Its funny that you say that."

"Why is that funny?"

Uncle Johnny turns the volume up. "Listen to her."

"How did you call it?" The guy next to me asks.

"Every time he has a great hit, I get goosebumps." I say. I smile as the guy next to me scoffs at me.

"Do you love her?" Uncle Johnny asks Cody.

"So much." Cody says.

"I feel that what you say is true. She feels the same for you."

"She knows details of my life that no one knows. She sees it all. She loves me even though I am flawed."

"Everyone is flawed." Uncle Johnny says. "Be good to her."

"I will."

"Does she talk about what she wants her wedding to be like?"

"We have spoken about it."

"And what do you think?"

"I think that I want her to have everything that she wants. I think that she deserves everything that she wants."

"All she wants is to get married on a baseball field. As long as you are the groom that she is walking to."

"A baseball field?" Cody asks. "I haven't heard that."

"That's what she has always dreamed of so that if she was marrying you, she would be able to merge what you both loved."

"How is she getting what she loves if she is getting married on a baseball field?"

"She is getting you." Uncle Johnny says.

Cody hugs Uncle Johnny tight. "Thank you." Cody sits back down in the chair and looks at Uncle Johnny. "Can I watch more?"

"You can watch all of them. I will make you copies." He says.

"Can I ask a question?"

"Of course you are family."

"Why does Jack let Joanna treat her so poorly?"

Johnny runs his fingers through his hair. " I am not sure why. I think at first he didn't want to interfere with how his girls were with his new wife. He knew there would be animosity. I don't think he expected the animosity to come from Joanna. Margie accepted the boys like they were her own sons. She always treated them with respect. Joanna I think is jealous of Crystal and all the attention that she needed. She required therapy until she was fifteen and then it stopped because she had plateaued. The team of therapist that worked with her said she wasn't going to get any better. But they still took her for two more years. When she graduated high school they didn't expect that she would go away to school. She did it all on her own. Margie had been dating one guy after another."

"I thought that she was always with Stew."

"Stew is a fixture because Crystal bonded with him. She told him that she was never letting him go."

"When Margie came to Crystal's house, she was nasty to her. I was sleeping on the couch but I was awaken at how Margie was talking to Crystal. When Crystal was on the phone with her mom, they laughed and she was so supportive."

"Margie was supportive of what?"

"Us together."

"Then what was going on at the house?"

"Margie was upset that Crystal purchased one of Jack's houses."

"I am not sure why she would even care."

"Why do you say that?"

"Because Ginny and I had her living with us for a few years. We moved to Georgia so that she had a home to come to when she took that job."

"Was she sad that she took over the bridal shop?"

"No."

"Did she want the job here in Georgia?"

"She did. But she loved the bridal shop. She saw more potential for her giving back."

"She did." Cody says.

"Is that a question or a statement?"

"It's a statement. She did. She gives back. She makes dreams come true."

"She told us that you do the same." Uncle Johnny says.

Cody finds me outside the hotel sitting by the pool. I am wearing a sports bra and shorts. Cody stands back and watches me. A young girl walks over. She smiles at me.

"Hi." I say to her.

"What happened to you?" The young girl asks.

A woman walks over. "Hey! Don't be rude?"

"It's a question." I say. I look at her. "I was born with a disability."

"I know someone who uses a wheelchair. He can't walk." She says.

"Was he born not being able to walk?"

"No." She says. "He was in a car accident."

I look at the woman with her. She nods her head. "Wow, I am sorry to hear that."

"I am really nice to him."

"I am sure that you are nice to everyone." I say.

She smiles a big bright smile. "I am not nice to my sisters and brothers."

"Well that's ok. I am not nice to my sisters and brothers all the time." I say smiling.

"Can you walk?" She asks.

"I have to hold on to something to walk. I don't have balance."

"What?" She asks.

"Ok, I can show you what I mean." I say. "Can you stand on one leg?"

She lifts her one foot off the ground. "Yes." She says.

"I can't do that." I say. "Ok, I am going to show you something else." I say. I take her hand. I look at her mom and she nods her head. "Ok, if I pull you to me, you are going to step forward so that you don't fall." I pull her lightly to me. She does step forward. "Ok, now if I push you backwards, you are going to step back to catch yourself so you don't fall backwards. I can't do that. If I was standing up and someone pushed me, I would fall."

The young girl hugs me. "You are so pretty."

"Thank you. You are pretty too." I tell her.

The young girl sees Cody watching us. "That really cute guy is watching you." She says.

I look at where she points. I look back at her and smile. "I am going to marry him."

"Really?" She asks with as much excitement that I feel just saying that I am going to marry him. She looks at her mom, "Do you think I will marry someone as good looking as him?"

"I think you have a long time." Her mom says.

"I am sure that you will meet someone wonderful. You just wait for him to find you." I say.

"How did he find you?"

"We flew on a plane together." I say. She smiles and then she and her mom walk away. I smile at Cody.

He walks over and kisses me. He puts his hands on my sides and I wrap my arms around his neck. He lifts me in his arms. "Can you swim?" He asks.

"Yes." I say.

He walks into the pool with me in his arms. "Its physical therapy time." He says with a beaming smile. He supports me.

"Cody, I can stand in the water." I tell him. I stand up and put my hands above my head.

Cody puts his hands on my sides again. He feels me wince a bit. "Just walk with me." He says. He walks backwards and I walk forward. I bend my knee just a bit and step with my right leg. I follow through with my left leg. I don't drag it but it doesn't bend as high as my right leg. We walk in the pool for a while.

Cody takes me in his arms and he floats on is back. "Don't swim, just hold on. I got you."

I hug him tightly. "That's what you said to me when that fan was going crazy after that game."

"What?"

"You told me to just hold you, you got me."

He stands up and holds me in his arms. He kisses me on the lips. I put my hands on his shoulders and jump in his arms.

"Wait. What's going on here?"

I look at him. "What?"

"What are you doing?"

"In the water, I can move freely." I say with a smile on my face.

"Stand for a moment." He says.

"Why?" I ask. I walk over to the wall and hold on to it.

"You ok?" He asks.

"I am. I just need to hold on for a moment."

"Did you over do it?"

"Cody, I am fine." I put my arm over my head and stretch.

"Don't over do it."

"I need to heal quickly."

"Why?" He asks walking over to me.

I put my hand on his shoulder. "I just need to heal quickly."

"Why?" He asks again.

I go under water and sit on the pool floor for sometime. Cody stands next to me and waits for me to surface. When I do, he lifts me in his arms and walks out of the pool. He walks into the lobby and then down the hall to our room. "What about my wheelchair?"

"I will get it." Landon says. He looks at Cody and sees the seriousness in his face. "Is everything alright?"

"Yes." Cody says.

Landon looks at me. "You ok?"

"Yes."

He kisses me on the head before he leaves the room. "I will get your wheelchair and then I am going to meet Paige for lunch. I think that we should all meet for lunch."

"We will." Cody says.

Chapter Twenty-one

Cody sits on the bed with me. We sit looking at each other. "Crystal, tell me what you meant by your comment." He says.

"Cody, I just need to get back to my life. I want to heal quickly so that I can be independent and find out what I need to do to go back to work. I am freaking out a bit about money." I say.

"I can help you pay for the house and stuff."

"The house is mine. I paid cash."

"You don't have to worry about anything."

"But I do. I own a bridal shop that isn't open. I have employees waiting for me to decide what to do."

"We will work it all out."

"What do your friends think of you dating me?"

"My friends think that I found the one." Cody says. "What do your friends think of me?"

"They think I made it up. They think that I paid someone to kiss me."

"What?"

"My close friends know about my crush on you."

"You have a crush on me?" Cody asks. He smiles.

"Just a little one." I say smiling.

"Tell me something."

"Sure."

"What is your dream wedding?"

I look at him and smile. "You were talking to Uncle Johnny."

"Is what he says true?"

"What did he say?"

"Oh no. I am not the one who is going to talk this out. Tell me what you think he said."

"Did he tell you that I dreamed of getting married on a baseball field?" I watch his face. "Its true. If I had the chance to meet you, date you, get kissed by you and marry you. My dream would come true to watch you play baseball and marry you on home plate because in my heart, when you kissed me I was home."

He gets on his knees in front of me. "Tell me about this wedding."

I smile at him. "Well you would have to work for it."

"What?" He asks.

"Oh yeah, you would have to hit a grand slam home run and when you run into home plate, I would be there waiting for you in a white dress and you would kiss me and we would say I do." I smile.

"You would really make me work for it?"

"It was a dream." I say.

"What did you tell me when you held my hand in the hospital?"

I look at him. "I told you a lot of things."

"Like what?"

"I don't remember all of it."

"It doesn't have to be exact." Cody says. He kisses my forehead. He holds me in his arms and pulls me on his lap. "Tell me."

"Well I sat holding your hand crying for hours. I prayed so hard that you would be ok. I prayed that—" I hide my face in his chest.

"What? Tell me."

"I prayed that we would meet somewhere wonderful and you would kiss me."

He kisses me deeply. "Before we go home, we have to make a stop." Cody says.

"Where?"

"It's a surprise."

"Can I guess?"

"No."

"Do you ever go to watch baseball games?" I ask him.

"I haven't, but if you want to, we will do that."

"I love baseball."

"I would be concerned that you would fall in love with another player."

"No chance for that if you are right next to me. Then I will have two things that I love more than anything." I say. I put my hand on his tattoo. He has more than one tattoo, but I put my hand on the one that says lover boy. I kiss it.

"This was the stupidest thing that I did." He says.

I look at him. "I love it."

"Would you get a tattoo?"

"I have two tattoos." I say

"What?" He asks. "I have seen you naked. Where are they?"

I pull my hair up and at the base of my neck is a tattoo of crossed bats and underneath says always his. Each bat has writing on it. It reads Cody on one and the other says Parker. He kisses it.

"When did you do that?"

I look at him. "When you got hurt."

"Where is the other one?"

I laugh.

"Why are you laughing?" He asks.

"When you kiss me, you kiss it every time."

"Its in your mouth?" He asks.

"No."

"Where?"

"Right here." I say an put my finger on the top of my shoulder.

He looks at it. He laughs. "I thought that this was a birthmark."

"No."

He looks at it. "Did that hurt?"

"You have no idea."

"It looks like it was very painful."

"It was worth it."

"When did you do this?"

"After you kissed me."

"After I kissed you?"

"After I got fired. I wanted something that would always make me remember the moment that I felt completely loved. I got the infinity sign and two hearts joined because in that moment I felt our two hearts were completely joined."

He brushes my hair away from my neck and he kisses the tattoo of the crossed bats. He runs his finger over the bats that read his name. He then runs his finger over the words always his.

I look at his chest and see that there is a tattoo that is new. I look at it. It reads my name in a heart over his heart. "Cody, when did you do this?"

"Crystal, I got it right after I kissed you."

I put my head on his chest. "I love you."

"I love you." He says. "Does anyone know that you have these two tattoos?"

"Brandon and Ashley."

"How do they know?"

"Their friend did this one." I say and touch the one on my shoulder. "The one on my neck, Stew went with me and he paid for it. I was just going to get the cross bats. Stew told the guy to write your name on the bats and always his underneath. I was so excited that he did that."

Cody kisses it again. I put my hand on his chest. He holds me against him. "I have never felt so loved in all my life. I know that women have loved me, but I have never felt love like I do when I am with you." He tells me.

"Cody, I wish you could see yourself from my eyes, you would see that what I see is—" he kisses me.

"You make me want to be better."

"You don't have to be better. You are the best." I get on my knees and put my hands on his shoulders for support. I kiss him with everything that is in me. "The best." I say again. I kiss the tattoo on his chest.

We say goodbye to my aunt and uncle. They convinced us to stay for a few days. It was great to just rest and relax. My aunt made all my favorite things to eat. They showered us in unconditional love. They welcomed Landon and Paige too.

When we left them, I left with tears streaming down my cheeks. They both promise to visit us soon. Uncle Johnny paid one of his guys to drive the moving truck down to Fort Lauderdale. Cody had told him about the surprise stop. Everyone knew about it but me.

Cody gets in the driver's seat and drives south to Florida. When we get to St. Augustine he pulls off the highway. He looks at me to see if I know what is going on. Paige is talking and I am involved in conversation with her. I am not paying attention to where Cody is going.

When he gets off I-95 he heads east to the beach. I look out the window. I know the area. I look at Cody. "Where are we going?"

"I have to pick something up for someone." He says.

"Cody, this is where Casper Peterson's shops are."

"How do you know that?" Landon asks.

"Because I have been here a lot." I say and feel like my face is going to burst from the smile that is on my face.

"Did you date him?" Paige asks.

"No." I say.

"Why?" She asks. "From the pictures I have seen of him, he is extremely handsome."

"I never dated him." I say. I say it more for Cody than for anyone else.

"We know that." Landon says.

Cody pulls into the parking lot. He gets out of the car and gets my wheelchair out. I get in it and Cody takes my hand. As we approach the store, I see my sisters and Emma. Lynn and Brittany are standing next to my mom.

I look at Cody. "What did you do?" I ask him. I smile brightly.

The double dark mahogany doors open. Christian Peterson, Casper's husband walks over to me and takes me in his arms. He walks behind my wheelchair and takes control of it pushing me into the shop. He walks back outside with me. "Hug your gorgeous guy." He says to me. He looks at Cody. "Kiss her like you did at that resort, so all of our knees go weak."

Cody hugs Christian. "Thanks for doing this." He looks at me. "It means the world to her."

"Casper and I would do anything for her. She has done so much for us."

Cody looks at him. "I look forward to hearing all about it."

"I will tell you, honey." He looks at Cody. "Can I get you anything? You can't see her for a while."

Landon hugs Christian. Casper walks outside. He looks like he could be a Christian Dior runway male model. Both Casper and Christian do. They are beautiful men. Casper hugs Cody. "I wouldn't have done this for anyone else. When you told me it was for her." He looks at me. "I would do anything for her."

I try to contain my happiness but I can't. I let out a scream of happiness. Cody hugs me and kisses me with all the passion that he did that first time he kissed me.

Casper looks at Cody. "I have what you asked for." He looks at me. "Now, you have to come with me.

I look at Cody. "I love you so much." I say.

"I love you." Cody says.

Christian looks at Cody, "I will meet you in fifteen minutes."

Cody looks at Christian. "Take your time."

We enter the shop and there are dresses all around at levels that I can see and reach everything. I feel like I am in heaven. I see the dress of my dreams right away and I burst into tears. Casper and Christian both hug me.

My mom and my sisters walk over. Ashley hugs me. "Why are you crying?"

"I am so happy." I say.

Casper walks over with Champaign and a plate of fruit. "The strangest thing happened." He says. He looks at me. He smiles. "I was a guest at a wedding a few months ago and I heard about a dress. The story of the dress kept reaching me. I heard it from many people. I didn't think that my dresses were anyone's dream come true."

I look at him. "You are joking. I have sold so many of your dresses. Plain white long, short, mid lengths along with your elaborate dresses. The beaded cocktail dresses were the ones that went the fastest. I couldn't keep them in the store."

"I heard that there was one lone dress." He says.

"There was one lone dress."

"Why didn't you tuck it away?" Mom asks.

"I think it would have been bad luck to buy the dress and let it hang in my closet unused. I tucked the dress away and one day it went missing." I say.

"Was it sold?" Kelsey asks.

"Beth took it knowing that I admired that dress since the day I hung it out. She had the dress died." I look at Casper. "The dress was stunning in white. It was magnificent dyed. I cried my eyes out over that dress for a long time."

"Why didn't you contact the designer and ask for another dress?" Mom asks.

I look at her and then look back at Casper. "I did a few times and I was given the same answer. The dress was no longer available and you—" I say to him. I look at my mom. "—and he wasn't making any more of them. Mr. Peterson was moving on to bigger and better runway pieces."

"I heard that the dress went around a few times." Casper says.

I look at the dresses that are all around me. One is more beautiful than the next one. There are no plain dresses to be seen. They all sparkle and look amazing.

"Tell me about my dresses and how they went from being worn by beautiful brides to being worn as prom and homecoming dresses." Casper says.

I look at him. I say nothing.

"I heard that my dresses went on a red carpet journey before they showed up at the most elegant proms and homecomings. Is that true?"

"That is true." I say softly.

The door bell chimes. Christian gets up and walks to the door. He lets Catalina and Gianna in. They walk over and hug me. Catalina walks over to Casper and hugs him. "Its good to see you again."

"You as well." He looks at Gianna. "I heard that you made everyone want my ballet line."

"Actually, I saw the dress being worn by one of the most beautiful women I have ever met in my life. I thought that if she looked fabulous in it, and the matching shoes, then I wanted it. I did dance in your dresses and I heard that the style sold out overnight."

Kelsey looks at me. "You wore the princess dress with the empire waist when you came to see me. You wore the ballet slippers to match. Oscar took the most beautiful pictures of you in that dress."

Casper leaves all of us for a moment. He comes back with a box. "This is for you." He hands me the box that is wrapped in the most beautiful wrapping. I gently open the box. I am glad that I don't have to rip it apart to open it. The lid just lifts off. It's a picture of me in Casper's dress. The dress that I wore was my favorite black dress. I wore it a lot of places. I hold up the picture and standing behind me watching me is Cody with a smile on his face.

I put the box on my lap and push my wheelchair out of the store. Cody is standing with my dad and Stew. He looks at me. "You can't be done already." He says.

"Look at this." I tell him.

"It's a beautiful box."

"Cody!" I say with a smile.

Sawyer walks over. "Are you done?" He asks me.

"No." I say smiling. I look at Cody. "Open the box please."

He takes the lid off the box and sees immediately what brought me outside in my moment of pure happiness. He looks at me. "When I met you that night at Gianna's dance recital you told me your name was Bella. You didn't say your name is Crystal."

"I didn't tell you my name. You never came close enough for us to talk. You never stopped watching me."

He looks at Stew, "Why didn't you tell me it was her?"

Dad looks at Cody. "What are you talking about?"

I hug him. "I am going to pick my wedding dress." I say.

"Go. Have fun."

"Are we on any time restriction?"

"Crystal, you take all the time you want and need. You know how long it takes to pick a dress."

I smile. "That's just it, I have already picked the dress that I am going to wear when I marry you."

He kisses me.

"Cody, I love you." I say to him.

"I love you too." He hugs me. "I am keeping this with me. Go have fun."

I turn in a circle. I then throw my arms in the air. "I am picking my wedding dress." I start to giggle and cry at the same time. Cody runs over and hugs me tight. "Cody, I can't wait to be yours."

"You have always been mine." Cody says. He kisses me again and again.

Casper comes outside. "Crystal, come. I have so much to show you. We have so much to discuss." He walks behind me and takes control of my wheelchair. He looks over his shoulder at Cody, "Christian will be coming out to get you all fitted in your suit."

"I am waiting for him." Cody says.

I go into the fitting room and I put the dress of my dreams on. I sit in front of the mirror just staring at myself. Casper walks in. He sticks his head through the white curtains that are so thick and heavy. He looks at me and gasps. I look at him.

"I have had runway models in my dresses but holy shit, you are stunning." Casper says. He looks at me again. "Don't move, I will be right back." He disappears and returns with Oscar. Christian walks in too. He looks at me and looks at Casper. "I know right." He says.

Oscar starts taking pictures of me. He doesn't stop for ten full minutes. He leaves and joins my family. He is all set up with his camera to capture their reactions.

Casper pushes me out of the fitting room and into the main gallery. There is an audible gasp from everyone in the room. Every woman in the room gets their phones and snaps pictures of me.

I look at Casper, "Can I try one more on?"

"Crystal, you can try all of them on." He says. "I set these dresses out for you to try on."

"Can I come back in a bit, I have to eat something?" I feel embarrassed asking him.

He looks at me. "Sweetie, lets go have lunch. I am opened for you. Plus I have a proposition for you."

I go in the fitting room and put my clothes back on. I join everyone in the gallery. I look at Casper. "I can't thank you enough."

"I am opening a store in Fort Lauderdale and I want you to run it just like you did the one in Orlando. I want my name as part as a brand that gives back and you can do that for me. You have done that for me already. I have seen my elaborate dresses on everyone big and small. I think that a midget wore my dress." He laughs and reaches his hand out to me squeezing my hand.

I laugh. "Where is my family and soon to be my extended family?"

"I want them to be surprised when you come down that isle and you are the most beautiful bride that anyone has ever seen and every woman will pray that she can look a quarter as stunning as you."

I look at Casper. "So the dress that I tried on is—"

"The jumping off point." He says.

I smile brightly. "I have a jumping off point?"

"Of course." He says. "I am going to do something that I have wanted to do for a long long time. You are going to wear every single dress." He says.

I laugh. "I only need one."

"I want you and Cody to model for my line."

"I am not a model." I say to him. "I sell the dresses."

Casper looks at me, "I have had models in my dresses and no one has ever looked as stunning as you did in my dress. And the look on your face when you were wearing it was so natural. The excitement in your eyes is genuine. The models are paid to smile like you do and they don't get the looks that you have naturally."

"You said me and Cody?"

"Yes."

"Casper, its bad luck for the groom to see the bride in her dress before the big day." I can't help the smile on my face.

"Well, much like your guests who saw you in a wedding dress today, he will see you in many, but not the one that you are going to marry him in."

"Casper, I can't keep him away from his obligations."

"You won't be keeping me from anything." Cody says from behind me. He walks around my wheelchair and kisses me. "Crystal, I am starving."

"I am starving too." I say.

"Hey you two keep it clean." Casper says.

We burst into laughter.

"Watch it." Casper says.

"I am really hungry." I say.

We go to a beautiful restaurant. When we enter the restaurant everyone that we know are at a long table. I look at Cody. I slip my hand in his hand and he walks over to the table. Casper and Christian join us at the table.

I see Oscar and Marcus standing with their cameras at the ready. Kammy is here too and she has her camera set on a tripod.

"What's going on?" I ask Cody.

"An engagement party." He says. He takes my left hand in his and slips the ring, that he picked out of my jewelry box, off my finger. He gets down on one knee and takes my hands in his hands. "Crystal Bella Steele, will you marry me?"

"I can't wait, yes." I say. I wrap my arms around his neck and hug him. I kiss him. "I love you."

"I love you too." He tells me. He slips the ring on my finger. The ring sparkles and my three friends and employees take pictures.

We sit among our family members. Music plays softly and I feel so loved. Joanna is seated next to dad and she seems happy. It concerns me that she will ruin it. I notice for the first time that Aunt Ginny and Uncle Johnny are sitting across the table from Joanna and dad. They never take their eyes off of Joanna. Joanna is holding dad's hand with their fingers twined together.

Mom and Stew are not sitting next to each other. For a moment it makes my heart ache. He sees the sadness in my eyes. He stands and walks around the table to where I am. He sits next to me and hugs me.

"We got into a disagreement. I am taking a break from her for a short time, but no matter what happens with me and her, you are my baby girl. I adore you and your sisters. You will never get rid of me."

I hug him tight. He hugs me and feels my ribs. I wince at his touch. "I love you, Stew."

"I know you do. I love you too."

"What did you disagree about?"

"Nope! Today we celebrate you. Oscar showed me the pictures of you in the wedding dress and oh," he puts his hand on his chest over his heart. "You are beautiful."

"That's not the right dress." Casper says. "That was just the first one she tried on."

"She looked stunning." Mom says.

"Crystal did look gorgeous." Joanna says.

I smile at her. "Thank you for saying that."

"I am not just saying it. Its true." She says.

Brandon hugs me. "I am so happy for you, sister."

"Thank you." I say.

Kyle stands up. "I would like to raise a toast to my sister and the love of her life. Cody, thank you for loving my sister as deeply as you do. Best wishes to both of you. May today be the starting point to a life that is filled with everything that you both want."

We have a wonderful meal. We sit and enjoy being with our blended family and our friends. I catch myself lost in thought. I stare at my new ring. It's the most beautiful thing I have ever seen. Cody puts his hand on my arm and I look up at him and smile.

"You ok?"

"I am." I say. "Why?"

"Your mom has been talking to you for the last five minutes." He says.

I look at her and embarrassing hives climb up my neck instantaneously from the stress I feel when my family is around me. "I am sorry." I say. "I was caught up in listening to everyone talking." And my new ring. Oh my god! Its amazing.

Catalina puts her hand on my hand. "Its not a big deal. Take a drink of water." She says.

I find peace from her calmness.

Mom looks at me. "I was just saying that I am overwhelmed with how beautiful you looked in that wedding dress." She says and smiles at me. "And I am so excited that you had me come and be with you."

"I wouldn't have done this without any of you." I say.

"Liar." Cody says in my ear and I smile at him.

"What's going on with your house?" Ashley asks.

"Trevor is working on it." Kelsey says.

"I appreciate it." I say.

"He is altering somethings to your house." Kelsey says.

"I heard that Vinny saw you in Indiana." Joanna says.

Kelsey looks at me. "Vinny?"

I look at Joanna. "He is the best at what he does and I needed to be seen by the best." I look at my sister. "I was going to talk to you privately."

"Did he ask about me?"

"He did." Cody and I say together.

She blushes. "We will talk later."

"I want to." I tell her.

"Did you tell Crystal the good news?" Ashley asks.

Kelsey looks at Ashley who just put her on the spot. "You know I didn't tell her."

"We can talk later." I tell her.

She smiles with excitement. "You have a new neighbor. Actually not right next door but across the street a few houses down. And, I will be dancing with Gianna in a showcase expo."

I smile at her. "Neighbors? You are going to live in my neighborhood?"

Kyle looks at me. "I moved two blocks away."

I can't contain myself, I smile and cheer with my excitement.

Joanna looks at me. "You are happy about this?"

"We talked about living close by each other our whole lives. I am thrilled." I say.

Everyone leaves. I hug my dad and my mom. I hug Stew. He gets into the truck to drive the moving truck down to Fort Lauderdale for Cody. He leaves his car with Landon. When the last car leaves with dad and Joanna, I want to wave and flick them off at the same time. I love my dad, but I want him to defend me. I want him to stop Joanna.

Cody holds me in his arms. "You are amazing."

"Why do you say that?"

"I think that you are so strong. How did you not launch yourself across the table to choke her?"

I smile. "I didn't think it would be lady like."

Casper looks at me. "That bitch will not be at any fittings that you have."

I smile bigger. "You can ban her from ever attending any events in my life, I will run your store in Fort Lauderdale." I say.

"I am holding you to it." He says.

We go to a hotel and check in for the night. When Cody and I are in the room together I sit in his lap.

"Tell me about the day." He says.

"I felt so pretty in the dress."

"Did you try on more than one?"

"No."

"No?"

"I didn't want to take it off." I say.

He smiles.

"Casper is going to hire us to model his new line."

"Hire who?"

"Us."

"You and me? Us?"

I smile at him. "Yes."

"Isn't it bad luck to see the bride in her dress before the wedding?"

"Casper said that I won't try the dress on that I am going to wear to our wedding until last and you won't be around. He will swap you for a model."

"Um no." He says.

I laugh and kiss him.

"Are you really excited about your siblings living in your neighborhood?"

"Our neighborhood." I say. "And I am. If your siblings wanted to live close by too that would be amazing."

"Landon would love that." Cody says. "Can I ask you a question?" He doesn't wait for me to answer him. "Are you ok with Kelsey being with both Trevor and Vinny?"

"Its her business not mine." I say honestly. "If each of them makes her feel loved, then why not."

"So when we get married will she have a plus one or a plus two?"

I laugh. "Apparently she can have whomever she wants because Casper just named himself our wedding planner. He is banning Joanna."

"You are going to allow that to happen?"

"She thought that she would get a rise out of me mentioning that Kelsey is going to be my neighbor. Our neighbor. Little did she know that nothing makes me happier. I want to be closer to my siblings."

He kisses me on the lips. "What if Landon moved into our neighborhood?"

"Landon and Gianna. That would be great if they did. I know that Gia has an amazing condo on the beach."

"How do you know that?"

"I didn't know that you were her brother. When I met her, we were doing a charity event together. Your mom was there too. After the charity event, everyone went to another event upstairs at the venue. There was no elevator. They said that the event was being held for the biggest contributor."

"Who was the biggest contributor?"

"I don't know." I say.

"Crystal." He says my name softly. "Who was the biggest contributor?"

"Your mom." I tell him.

"I now that's not true. My mom told me all about that charity event. She told me that there where so many wonderful contributions but there was a leading contributor. She didn't know your name. She told me all about the night. Don't hold back. Tell me."

"Gia found out about the event not being accessible and she invited me to her condo. Your mom went to the event. There was an award given for top contributor."

"I know."

"How do you know?"

"I was the one giving out the award." Cody says.

"No. Hemingway Society was hosting the charity."

"Crystal, I know who was hosting the charity its my charity."

I try to get away from him. He holds me tighter to him.

"Why Hemingway?"

"Why didn't you stay for the award?"

"I didn't contribute to get an award. It was something that I wanted to do."

"Why didn't they say that it was you?"

"Its something I want kept secret."

"Cody why Hemingway?"

"Hemingway Hospital was where Donny was taken. He was injured so badly when—" he closes his eyes. I put my hand on his chest. He puts his hand over my hand. "I should have been there. He wanted to go with me."

"Cody, it was an accident."

"I am jealous that you went to the gravesite with Landon."

"I will go with you."

"Will you?"

"Of course." He looks at me and kisses my lips. "Didn't you see the pictures of us all around the room at the event?"

"No."

"And you didn't know that Gia and my mom were related to me?"

"I didn't."

"Crystal—"

"Make love to me."

"I told Vinny I wouldn't until you were better."

"I am better."

"Its nice of you to want to distract me."

"Cody, please." I say.

He slides his hand between my legs. I immediately respond to his touch. He lays me flat on the bed and he spreads my legs because I can not do it myself. My body tenses a bit and my legs close. He lets the stiffness pass. When it does, he spreads my legs again. "I am not going to hurt you."

"I don't think you are."

"Just relax." He says.

"I am relaxed." I say. I cry out and he isn't even touching me.

He looks at me. "Are you ok?" He undresses me and I am completely turned on and into his movements.

"Oh God, Cody, please." I say.

He smiles as he takes my nipple between his lips. He puts his arm around my back and supports my movement so that I can arch my back. I cry out as he slips his fingers into me. My body shutters with an orgasm. He pushes his fingers deeper and stars blur my vision.

"Please!" I say gasping.

He kisses my lips. "I am going to move your legs." He says.

"O-k." I pant.

"Tell me if its too much."

"If it hurts, my legs will close on their own. I have no control." I tell him.

"Its ok." He says and kisses me again. He uses his legs to spread mine. He rubs himself up my body and down and then enters me in one quick movement. We both cry out together. "Crystal!" He calls out my name. "I need you." He says and pulls back and then pushes in. "I need you." He says.

"I am here. You ha-ve me." I say.

Our love making is the best. He makes me feel the most loved I have ever felt in my life. I have had intimate encounters but when he is inside me, I don't ever want it to end. I want to stay connected as long as we can. I want to be more for him.

He pulls back and out of me. He helps me sit. He smiles at me. "How are your ribs?"

"They are there." I say.

"I didn't hurt you?"

"No. you were very gentle."

"Are you hungry?"

"For you."

He smiles at me. "Tell me something."

"Anything."

"Tell me about Casper and why his dresses mean so much to you."

I cover myself with the sheet as I sit in the middle of the bed waiting for him to come back. But I talk to him. "He was in Rosa's shop one day and he was bringing in his collection. One was more beautiful than the next one. I wanted to put them all on. I wanted to stand on the pedestal and twirl around. The one dress that I wanted to own and wear for you, he saw me admiring it. He hung it in the office that I used to do my work in. There was a woman in the shop looking at dresses and when she put on his dress she looked stunning. The dress wasn't what she had planned to wear. It wasn't the dress of her dreams, but it was the best dress for her. He had a set price for his dresses and it was well over the budget that she had for a dress. We had dresses in her budget line, but none of them looked remotely close to his dress did on her."

"You paid the difference."

"No." I say. "She left the store with a dress. She had to come back for a fitting. I had her set up with a tailor to do all the measurements and pinning. When she came back for the final fitting, Casper's dress which fit her perfectly was in her garment bag."

"What did you do with the other dress?"

"I had it cut down the size for her niece who was in a wheelchair and loved the wedding dress that her aunt had tried on."

"Didn't the shop lose money?"

"No." I say. I flip my hair around my shoulders and wrap the sheet tighter around me. "Rosa never lost any money. I worked for what I wanted and that was to make brides happy. That woman wanted Casper's dress. He saw it. I knew he did. He came into the store three days after the bride had her final fitting and picked up the dresses. He wanted her to have it. He was going to discount it so she could afford it. I was in the fitting room trying on that one dress that I wanted so desperately. He was standing close enough to hear me talking to myself."

"What did you say to yourself?" He asks.

"I looked at myself in the mirrors and I had tears in my eyes. I looked up at the mirror on the ceiling and saw him watching me. I couldn't hide my smile."

"What did you say?" Cody asks again sitting back on the bed and taking me in his arms. "Did you say that you were in a Casper Peterson dress and that it must have been a sign from the heavens above because you wanted to marry Cody Parker. CP. How could that be more clear?" He says.

"Who told you?"

"Casper told me. Landon worked really hard to track him down for you. Landon wasn't taking no for an answer."

I snuggle into him. "Cody I love you."

"I love you too."

"Tell me about the dress that the lucky bride wore."

"When she opened the garment bag the day of her wedding she called the shop to say that she had the wrong dress. I intentionally directed the call to my cell phone so that Rosa and Beth didn't know what I had done. I paid for the dress for her."

"How much did it put you out?"

I put my face in his chest. "Ten thousand."

"I am sorry. What did you say?"

"I spent ten thousand. I paid cash for it. It was my job to deposit the money into the bank so Rosa never knew what I had done. Somehow Casper found out. I still don't know how he found out. Three days after that wedding, I was cleaning up the banquet hall that the wedding had happened at. A guy walked over to me and handed me an envelope full of money. Casper had a picture of me in his wedding dress inside with the money. He wrote in the card that he knew what I had done and he wanted to give me back the money for a good deed. He gave me twelve thousand dollars."

"Twelve?" Cody asks. "Cash?"

I look at him. "Yes. Why?"

"That's how much money showed up at a charity event that I hosted and we couldn't track where the money came from. Twelve thousand was our goal. I matched dollar for dollar raised . We raised so much money that night." He looks at me. "Why?"

"It was the right thing to do."

"Why do you say that?"

"It was on every sports network what you were doing for a charity event. Time after time when I heard them mention your name, they weren't nice. They didn't even know what you were supporting, but it didn't prevent them from talking shit about you. I heard over and over that you wouldn't meet your goals. One of them said that twelve thousand dollars was needed to meet the goal. I had it and I went to the venue and put it in the donation box. When the woman saw me do it, she asked if I wanted a receipt. I took the receipt from her and tore it up."

"Why?"

"I wanted you to succeed."

He kisses me. "How did you have that kind of money?"

Chapter Twenty-two

"I had won a settlement from the accident that I was in. I didn't have any medical expenses. My physical therapy bills were paid for too. So I had money. I wanted to do something good in the world and make a difference." I look at Cody. "The truth is, I want to open a venue and host weddings." I smile brightly. "I want it to have a batting cage and a baseball field near by."

"What?"

"Its my dream." I feel my cheeks burning with heat from embarrassment.

"Tell me your dream?"

"No!" I laugh.

He takes me in his arms and hugs me. He tickles me. "Tell me."

"I want to own a whole sports complex. A dance studio and stage."

"Why?"

"I want my sisters closer to me. I want to draw them in. Joanna has outdone herself in putting distance between us. My dad doesn't even see it. Its like he's blinded by her power."

"Do you reach out to your dad?"

"My dad tolerates me."

"Why do you say that?"

"Its just a feeling I have always had. I think Joanna is like a bumble bee and buzzes what a problem I am."

"Did you ever tell him how you feel?"

"No. I was the one who was hurt when I left for school and my mom was on a cruise with her boyfriend and my dad was coming, but then Joanna had a medical emergency."

"What medical emergency?"

"She had to have her nose corrected."

"What?"

"That's why Kyle was there. He held me while I cried my eyes out. Kelsey came too which was so nice of her. That's why I thought I owed it to her to be at all of her dances. Little did I know, she didn't want me there." I put my arms around Cody. "Thanks to you, I got caught up in your drama and I wanted to be there with you."

"My life has had drama. So much of it that my siblings and my parents never came to one game."

"Landon went to games."

"How do you know that?"

"I made him go with me. I didn't know he was your brother but it was the one thing that I could think of that would take his attention away from Donavan. He never said anything about you being his brother even when we were watching you. I would lose it every time I saw you. Landon always encouraged me. He would say that he always heard you were a nice guy."

Cody smiles. "I always tried to be a nice guy."

"Cody, you can't convince me that you aren't a nice person."

"You will go with me to the gravesite?"

"Yes."

"When are we going to model for Casper?"

"We are going to have brunch with him tomorrow."

"Brunch?" Cody asks.

"Yes." I laugh. "He isn't a morning person."

Cody laughs.

"What about your obligations?"

"I have no pressing obligations. I am the assistant coach and luckily there are more than one assistant." Cody looks at me. "Before you say that they would really learn more from me, the other assistants are former professional baseball players too." He smiles brightly. "NO!"

I laugh. "No what?"

"NO. You will not be meeting any of them."

"Oh come on, I have to meet your friends."

"No." he laughs and kisses my neck.

"Will your friends be at our wedding?"

"In the back. The very back." He says and smiles.

I smile too. "I want all of your friends to know that I picked you. I will pick you everyday and any day my whole life long."

He lays me back down and covers me with his body. We don't make love but just lay there. "So tell me again, you would pick me everyday?"

"God yes."

"Tell me why you would pick me?"

"I love you. When you kissed me, I didn't want to be anywhere else. I didn't want you to stop kissing me. I wanted to stay wrapped in you forever." I say.

He sits up and pulls me in his lap. I am still naked, I get on my knees in front of him. His legs are spread wide so I am between them. I put my hands on his shoulders and then let go for a brief moment.

Cody puts his hands on my sides. "Do what you want, I will support you." He says.

I put my hands on his shoulders. I lean back against his arms. I close my eyes and shake my head so my hair tickles his legs. I then touch my forehead to his forehead and kiss his lips. I put my hand on his chest.

"Crystal, I will support you. I am not going to let you fall."

I want to be closer to him. "Can you help me move my leg?" I ask in a whisper.

"Yes." He says. He puts his hand on my left leg and moves it closer to his body. "This good?"

"Yes. Thank you." I kiss his lips. I put my hand on the back of his neck and then I slide my other arm around his back. "Touch me." I say against his lips.

"You are in control." He says.

"Cody, please."

"I like the way you are making me feel. Keep going." He says.

"Can you move my leg over your leg?"

He lifts my leg carefully so not to knock me off what little balance I have. He slides his leg between mine. He brings his leg up between my legs so I am sitting on it.

I stop what I am doing. "Is that your bad knee?"

"No. Don't worry about me. Continue your assault." He smiles and kisses my lips quickly.

I lean back a little and take his hand in my hand. I run my fingers up his arm to the tattoo. I bend my head and kiss his tattoo. I put my hand on his side. He doesn't wince when I touch his scar. I kiss him and leave my hand on his side. I feel him tremble. I pull back.

"Crystal, don't stop."

I move my hand and he takes my hand softly in his hand and puts my hand back on his side. He leaves his hand on top of mine. I kiss him again. I kiss his chin and his throat. I kiss the scar on his shoulder.

"Crystal, don't stop." He says again. He puts his hand on my side. "I am going to move you a bit."

Before he can, I move my right leg on my own. He bends his other leg. "Cody, please." I say.

"Not yet. Continue what you are doing. No one has ever made me feel so loved in all my life."

I put my hands on his shoulders and I arch my back. I kiss his shoulder again. He is still holding my hand on his scar on his side. I lick my lips and kiss his scar again.

"Crystal." He says in a gasp.

In one quick movement Cody stands and moves to the bed. He sits with me on his legs like we were on the floor. Cody kisses me and holds me with supportive hands.

I rub my teeth on the scar before I kiss it again. He trembles under my touch again.

When he has had enough, he lays me back on the bed. He sits next to me and he runs his hand up my leg. Cody slides his hand under my back. He continues to move his hand up my leg. I tip my head back in the pillow and close my eyes. "Cody. I. Love. You. Please!" I cry out the last word.

"Crystal." He says against my lips. "Tell me what Tally means."

I try to talk, but my words catch in my throat when he enters me. "Co-dy!" I cry. Tears escape my eyes. They are not tears of joy. They are not tears of hurt or pain. They are tears of passion. I wrap my arms around him. "Can you help me bend my leg?"

"Yes." He says.

"Oh Cody! Deeper. Please!"

He pulls out like he always does when I beg for him to go deeper. He pushes in and then pulls back. The friction is more than satisfying. He bends my knee so my foot is on the bed. He holds my ankle so my leg doesn't move as he glides into me. He calls my name.

We hold each other. He releases my ankle and once my leg is flat on the bed our bodies tremble together. We pant for breath. We moan into each other. Our sweat mixes together. We each cry out. Our orgasms peak and he thrusts one more time. My pelvis on its own rises to meet his movement. He kisses me and I feel exhausted and exhilarated.

"Cody, I have to sit up." I say against his cheek.

He sits up and helps me sit up. "You ok?"

"I am better than ok." I say.

"I love you."

"I love you too."

Casper and Christian are standing on the sidewalk outside of Marina's Coastal restaurant. It is a fancy beach restaurant. It looks like it should be located in New England and not in north east Florida. When we go inside, it's the most beautiful place I have been in. It looks a lot like the resort where I met Cody.

A beautiful woman meets us at the entrance. She looks at Casper and Christian. "Welcome back." She says. She looks at Cody and flirts with him. I look at her and smile. She looks at me. Cody takes my hand in his hand and laces our fingers together. "Let me show you to your table."

Casper looks at me. "You ok?"

"I am fine." I say smiling. Inside I am sad. If I had the ability to wrap myself around him I would have resembled a koala.

Cody looks at me. "You ok?"

"I am fine." I say.

The host walks over with menus. She puts her hand on Cody's shoulder. Casper looks at the woman with annoyance. Christian looks around the table.

"Cody Parker as I live and breathe." The woman says. "Lover Boy, I can't believe you are here." She rubs his shoulder. Cody tenses under her hand.

Cody looks at her. "Please stop being inappropriate. You are making a fool out of yourself in front of my wife."

She looks at me. She sees the ring on my finger. She takes her hand away like she was bit by a snake. She steps away. "I am sorry."

I smile at Cody. I can't contain my smile. "I love you."

He leans closer to me and kisses me. It's the most romantic kiss I have ever experienced and he has kissed me with more passion that I never knew existed until him.

A woman walks over to the table. "Honey, don't ever let her go." She says to Cody. "You don't know what a gem you have."

I am dazed from the kiss. I look at her. "Rosa?"

She smiles at me. "Hello my darling."

"Cody, this is Rosa. Rosa, this is Cody. You know Casper. This is Christian."

She kisses me on the cheek. "I am so happy for you." She says.

"Thank you." I say. I look at Casper.

Christian looks at all of us. "Casp, I think we need to go somewhere else."

The woman who works in the restaurant looks at Christian. "I apologize for everything. Please feel free to move anywhere you want." She looks at me. "I am sorry."

Christian looks at her. "Is the atrium available?"

She looks at Christian. "Yes. I will get it ready for you."

"Thank you." Casper says.

She walks away quickly. She goes to the atrium and sets up the table for us. It's a private area. There are only three tables available. Christian has made it clear that it will only be us out there.

Christian and Casper go out there first. They tell us that we need to give them five minutes. They walk away hand in hand and shoulder to shoulder. They are beautiful to look at. They look like they just stepped out of the pages of Glamour Magazine. They are always so well put together.

We Join them in the atrium and I see Oscar and Marcus are out there. They both have their cameras aimed at us. They never stop snapping. Cody and I are natural as we approach the table. I hold his hand. Marcus goes behind us and snaps pictures of us from behind us.

Cody tips my wheelchair back and kisses me. I wrap my arms around him. Oscar snaps one after another. I know the sounds of his shutter going off. Marcus's shutter is quieter.

They leave the area and we have a beautiful brunch with Casper and Christian. We are not interrupted. Casper watches Cody and me. He watches to see how we act and react to each other. Casper tells stories about me.

"Crystal Bella Steele, took back dresses that were lightly used and gave them over to young people who could not afford them. But she got back a few dresses that should have gone from the event that they attended right to the garbage cans. One was shred so badly but the bodice was in good condition. She took a skirt that no one wanted that was going to be sent back to the designer. She stitched the bodice to that skirt and holy hell everyone wanted it. Women were rushing the store to get it."

"Who's skirt was it?" Cody asks.

"Mine." Christian says.

"It wasn't ugly." I say.

"It was until you paired it with that beautiful piece of junk that it became something wonderful."

"Christian, it wasn't you, the skirt was beautiful. It was a bad print."

"Bella, don't lie." Christian says.

"Tally." Casper says.

"Tally?" Cody asks.

Christian starts to laugh. "Everyone seated at this table has a C name." He takes his champagne and drains the glass. He laughs harder. "Crystal, you saved my fucking career and you don't take any credit for it."

"I can't take the credit. I didn't do anything."

"You repurposed my life."

"Tally, does lover boy know why they call you Tally?"

I know that nothing is meant to be mean at this table. I don't hide from them. I feel like I am floating on a cloud.

"Tell me about Tally." Cody says kissing the back of my hand.

"You know about Tally." I say to him.

"Tell me in your words." He says.

Christian smiles.

"In my own words." I say. "Well I was in Boston with Kelsey and Vinny. They were in the joining room to the room that I was staying in. They were having a sex fest. They were trying to be quiet about it, but I knew what they were doing. I had a stats class that I needed to submit my test. I but the baseball game on and—" I look at Cody. "You were on your game. I wrote on the top of my paper my name and while I was doing it you hit a home run. I couldn't contain my excitement. I wrote Crys Tally on my paper and Kelsey started calling me Tally. It didn't bother me. It made me feel like she was interested in my life."

Casper looks at the two of us. "So I want you both to model my next line. I have a men's line coming out and more bridal dresses. I will pay you for time. I want you to start tomorrow." He looks at me. "I have asked Ashely and Kelsey to model some of the dresses too." He looks at Cody. "Landon and Gianna are going to model too."

"Kyle? What about Kyle?" Cody asks. "He is my best friend and her brother."

"Who ever you want, but we are going to line you up as the bride and groom." Casper says. "Will this bother you?"

"No." We both say.

"Tomorrow its all about you two. Tomorrow there will be no one but the two of you."

I smile.

"I have done something with that ugly skirt and I think you are going to love it." Christian says.

"Don't put words in my mouth, I never said the skirt was ugly." I say.

"Why did you do it?"

"I wanted it. I wanted the skirt. I wanted to just see what it would look like together. I pinned it and my seamstress sewed it for me. She hung it and a woman walked in and said that she wanted it. Then another woman came in and she wanted it. I told them that I only had one and I was expecting more of them in. I took a picture of the new dress and sent it to the designer. I didn't know it was Christian." I say. "You supplied me with twelve of them. I couldn't keep them on my racks."

"I saw my dress at a benefit and I felt proud of my designs." Christian says.

"I want to pay for your wedding." Casper says.

"No." Cody and I say together.

"Cody, you did something for my niece that everyone else wouldn't have thought of. You didn't even think twice. I know what you did." Casper says. He looks at me. "And you, you did something for that same niece so that she didn't feel left out. I am paying for your wedding. The whole thing. There will be nothing missed. Whatever you want. I want you to go all out. I want you to have everything that you ever wanted. I want to give you what you give to your brides." Casper says.

"I have saved money for the wedding of my dreams." I say.

"Make it a nest egg." Casper says.

"Tell me about the wedding of your dreams." Christian says. "What color schemes do you want? How many bridesmaids? What are the details?"

I saw it all coming true when Cody kissed me in the lobby of the resort that we actually met at. When I was lost in Cody's kiss, I pictured the whole thing. I came into the lobby in my wedding gown and the train for the dress was attached to my wheelchair. Brandon and Kyle push my wheelchair together through the lobby to the atrium. Cody is waiting for me standing under an arch waiting for me.

Stew is standing smiling. My dad and Stew take my hands and walk me down the isle. When we get down the isle, Kyle and Brandon each stand on either side of me. They hold me up so that I am standing holding Cody's hands. Stew walks around the arch and he is the one who presides over our wedding.

When we exchange our vows, Cody Kisses me taking me in his arms. I wrap my arms around his neck and he lifts me and carries me down the isle. He carries me into the lobby and sits me on one of the beautiful benches. He then sits next to me and kisses me.

Cody looks at me. "You thought all of that when I kissed you."

"I saw my life flash in front of me and it was a great event. I never wanted that kiss to end." I say.

Cody kisses me.

"I need to do measurements for you Cody. I need to do that today so that I can plan for tomorrow." Casper says. "I will text both of you the location where I want you to show up tomorrow. I just ask that you tell no one."

"Of course." We both say together.

"What color schemes?" Christian asks again.

I look a Cody. "I didn't plan colors."

"What would be your idea for colors?" Cody asks.

"I think maybe different colors. Emerald green, sapphire blue, and ruby red." I say.

"Why the different colors?"

"Our sisters collectively look best in those colors."

Cody takes my hand in his hand and lifts it to his lips. He kisses the back of my hand. "You. We don't have to plan the colors of our wedding based on my sister and what color she looks best in." He kisses my hand again.

"What is your favorite color?" Christian asks me.

"I love the jewel tones. I would want red and white roses and carnations."

"What kind of cake?"

"Carrot." We both say together.

"How many tiers?"

"I am not sure." I say. I look at Cody. "What color do you want for our wedding?"

Cody smiles. "Lets see what we like when we see all the different styles and what we like best."

"I agree." I say. Cody puts his arm around me. I lean into him. "Its not just my wedding. If I have learned anything from planning as many weddings as I have, I want you to have equal say in our wedding."

"I want you to have everything that you want."

"Cody, its only half about me. The other half is you."

Cody looks at me. "I want you to have all that you want."

"I want you." I pull him closer and kiss him on the lips.

Cody goes off with Christian who takes his measurements. Christian lets Cody try on suits. He keeps Cody for a little more than two hours.

While Cody is with Christian, Casper takes me back to his bridal shop. We sit at a table together and he takes out his big binders. I smile. I think of all the brides that have come into my shop and how giddy they get when I would take out the binder. I react the same way.

Casper looks at me. "Show me what you like."

I look at him. I smile brightly. I open the binder and see pictures of me in the dress that I wore to show my family. I gasp. Tears gather in my eyes. I look at Casper. "Wow." I whisper.

"You are beautiful."

"Thank you."

"Does he know as much about you as you know about him?"

"He is learning about me."

"Crystal, you deserve to be happy. You have brought so much happiness to so many people."

"He does too." I say.

"I know he does. That's what I am saying. You both pay it forward. You both do so much to make others happy. You both have families that don't know the half of the things that you do."

"I know my parents and my sisters love me. I know that Kyle and Brandon love me. But Casper, I can tell you that I never felt so much love in my life until I joined Cody at his parents home. I felt like I entered a dream. I felt their love for each other, for Cody and for me the moment that I met them."

"Crystal, you brought them back their son. Cody has stayed away over the years."

"His brother Donavan died."

"I know. I was at the funeral." Casper says tenderly.

"I was there too." I say.

"I know sweet girl. I saw you there." He blinks tears away. "Donavan was my godson."

"I know you designed for Catalina."

"My Cat. She was always so nice to me. She was always welcoming to me and my lifestyle."

"Anyone who is not, is an asshole." I say.

"Not everyone loves me."

"Well they are missing out on knowing you and what greatness you bring to the world."

Casper gasps. "Where did you come from? Can I clone you and keep you around all the time."

I smile at him.

"Why do you do that?"

"Do what?" I ask.

"Build people up?"

I look away. "I want people to do that same thing for me. I want people to see my accomplishments and point them out some times." I blink my own tears away. "I want my family to be closer. My dad tolerates me. My mom is wonderful as long as it's a phone call. When it's in person, she gets snappy and has to point out things that I haven't done. And Joanna absolutely hates me." I wipe at the tears that brim. "Joanna would be happy if—" I can't finish what I am thinking.

"I saw how she treated you. I watched her act nice to you and then I saw her stab you in the back with her hypothetical knife. But I saw your siblings join you and surround you."

"They were good for a while. Kyle is the only one who is a hundred percent on my side. Brandon too. My sisters could give a shit. Kelsey is the worst. I know that I took up a lot of my parents time. I think that she sees her dance classes as something that would keep her out of my parents hairs. I would have traded places with her. She toe dances like no one else in the world. She is wonderful at it." I flip the book and look through it. Something on the page catches my eye. I smile.

"What do you like?" Casper asks.

I look at him. "Everything."

"You want a canopy?"

"I do."

"I will have to see what I can pull together. When are you going to get married?"

"I don't know. We haven't set a date."

"We will have to find out what the time frame is."

Cody walks over and tilts my head back. He kisses me on the lips. Casper clears his throat. Cody smiles against my lips.

"When do you want to get married?" Casper asks Cody.

Cody smiles. "Tomorrow, sunset."

"That's not funny." Casper says.

"I am not kidding. I want to marry her as soon as possible."

The front doors of the bridal shop open and two tall men walk through. They look at Cody and walk over. One of them runs his fingers through Cody's hair. "You never liked cutting your hair." He says.

Cody turns quickly and looks at the two men. "Rayf!" Cody says and hugs him. He looks at the other guy. "Marshall." Cody looks at them. "How are you here?"

"We got a call from Landon." Rayf says.

"What did he say?" Cody asks.

Rayf looks at me. "He told us that you met the woman of your dreams." Rayf again looks at me from head to toe. "I know you." He says.

Marshall smiles at Cody. "How is everything going?" He looks at me. He looks at Cody. "This is the girl that wouldn't let anyone come visit you in the hospital."

I don't ever feel like I should hide, but I try to hide behind Cody.

"It was remarkable that she stood her ground. She held your hand. That woman in the hallway called you Donavan." Marshall looks at me. "Crystal? Right?" He asks looking at me.

"Yes." I say.

"Crystal was at Donavan's funeral."

Cody looks at me.

I look at him. "I was there with Landon. We really missed the whole thing. He didn't want to go. He wanted to go. He didn't want to go. We went back and fourth about ten times. We finally went in. By the time we went over to the gravestone, no one was there." I hold Cody's hand. "Landon needed a friend."

Cody looks at me. "Landon told me all about it. I am not second guessing anything. When I say that I love you, I love you."

Casper looks at all of us. "I was there. What you did for Landon was amazing. He had told me what he did to you. He felt awful—"

"What did he do?" Rayf asks.

I shake my head. "He cheated off of my test. It was a big test. He was trying to make me laugh. I had just been dumped publicly by a guy that I dated for almost a year." I look at Cody. "He wasn't my forever, but I liked him."

"Crystal, you don't have to justify anything. My ex-girlfriend landed me in the hospital."

"What did Landon do?" Marshall asks.

"When the guy showed up anywhere I was, he tried to embarrass me. Landon never let it escalate." I look at Cody. "I never knew that Landon was your brother. I never knew that Gianna was your sister. And your mom, well, I have admired her forever for her elegance. I didn't know she was your mom."

"I know all this." Cody says.

"What did Land do?" Rayf asks.

"He beat the shit out of the guy. It took seven people to pull him off of the guy. After he regained himself, he hugged me tight. I felt like I was being hugged by Kyle."

"Kyle?" Rayf asks.

"Kyle who?" Marshall asks.

"Steele?" Rayf asks.

"Kyle is my brother. My dad adopted him and his brother after he married their mom."

"Jack is your dad?" Marshall asks.

"Yes." I say.

Rayf looks at me. "What did Landon do?"

"He was just there. I felt like I had family around when he was near. I was mad at him for a while. I had to go to another campus to take a stats class, but maybe he knew what he was doing." I look at Cody. "He knew how much I cared for you. He would go with me to baseball games. He would cheer me on while I was cheering for you. He always encouraged me. I think he was the one who had Gianna show up at my charity event with your mom. He never admitted to it, but I think he did."

Casper looks at me. "The way you held him when he needed it was truly beautiful to watch. He had told me what he had done. He was trying to make it up to you. But when he asked you to go with him you didn't hesitate. When you went with him and you held his hand or more dragged him in that cemetery, it was a nice thing that you did. I heard you tell him what he needed to hear over and over, it was an accident and he tried everything he could to save Donavan. You told him that day that God needed an angel." Casper gets up from the head of the table where he sits and he walks around the table and takes me in his arms. He kisses the top of my head. "What you did was so nice."

"What did she do?" Cody, Rayf, and Marshall ask.

I look at Casper. "How do you know that I did anything?"

"Why hide it?"

"I don't hide anything I do." I say.

"What did you do?" Cody asks.

"Donavan's angel." Casper says.

Cody looks at Casper. "My parents did that."

"No." Casper says.

Cody looks at me. "You did that?"

"I did." I say.

"Why? You didn't know him."

"I read about it. Then I read that he was your brother. You had done something for me without knowing me. I saw the angels when I was leaving the cemetery. I asked about them before I had known that he was your little brother. The stone was beautiful but I felt like it needed something special. I had told Landon that God needed and angel."

"Its beautiful." Cody says. "I never questioned it because I thought that my parents did it." He looks at me. "Are you the one who puts flowers for his birthday every year?"

I don't answer. "Don't be upset." I say.

"No." Cody says. He kisses me. He trembles against me. There is so much emotion in that kiss that we share in front of his friends. He holds me tightly against him. "I love you. You are so good to me and my family. You have done something for everyone of us. God, I don't deserve you."

"No, I have waited for you! I love you. I don't want anyone else. I want to marry you. I told you and I mean it from the bottom of my heart, I will pick you everyday. Cody!" I wrap my arms around him. "I love you. Only you."

Rayf looks at us. "Cody, I knew that you wanted her after that game we had. She was there to greet the players and there was a crazy fan. You held her tight. Then you talked about her in your sleep."

Cody looks at him. "What?"

"You did. We were on the bus heading to the resort and you fell asleep. You said, over and over, you just met the woman you wanted to marry." Marshall says.

"What did Landon tell both of you?" I ask.

"He told us that Cody was planning his wedding and as groomsmen, we needed to show up." Rayf says.

"Landon is picking my groomsmen?" Cody asks. "If that's true, where is Tate?"

A guy walks into the bridal shop. "Is there a wedding planner planning to get married to her favorite baseball player?" Tate asks.

I look at him and smile. "Asshole." I say quietly.

"You know Tate?" Cody asks.

"Kyle introduced us." Tate says. He looks at me and smiles brightly. "You kiss your boyfriend with that mouth?" He teases.

"I do." I say. I smile.

Tate looks at me and smiles. "How is Kyle?"

"He is doing well."

Cody spends the rest of the day with his friends. I spend the rest of the day with my Aunt Ginny. She takes me to a wheelchair accessible beach. She rents a beach wheelchair and we set off to walk the beach. The beach chair is motorized so it allows us to walk side by side on the sand.

My mom and my sisters come to meet me on the beach. Kelsey hugs me. Ashley hugs me too. Mom watches me. When Ashley puts her arms around me, I pull her on my lap and hug her tight.

Gianna and Catalina come down the beach. Catalina walks over and embraces me. I feel that motherly love. "Thank you." She says. She kisses the top of my head. "Thank you." She says again. "The second that we met you, we knew you were the right person for Cody." She kisses my hair again. "Thank you." She says again. She hugs me tighter. "What you did and continue to do for our family can never be repaid."

Mom looks at her. "What are you talking about?"

Catalina steps away and looks at all of us. "You don't even know how magnificent she is. You don't know of all the wonderful things she does." When I first met my future in-laws I said almost the same things about Cody to them. "It's a shame that Jack doesn't see his daughter the way that we see her." She looks at Kelsey. "What you did was pretty awful."

Kelsey looks at me. "You told people?"

"No." Catalina says. "She didn't have to. Gianna danced that night too. I was there and heard the commotion. I didn't realize that she was related to you until after the show."

Mom looks at Kelsey. "What did you do?"

"It doesn't matter." I say.

Kelsey looks at me. "I am sorry."

"I heard you moved into the neighborhood." I say.

"What neighborhood?" Mom asks.

"Gulfport." Kelsey says.

"You moved into Gulfport?" Mom asks.

I put my hand on the remote for the wheelchair. Before my mom starts yelling at Kelsey, I don't want to be part of it. Ashley comes running after me. Because the wheelchair is motorized, I am able to go faster than I can pushing myself. But realistically if I was in my wheelchair I was be stranded in the sand. Wheelchairs and sand don't go hand in hand. But the beach chair allows me to go completely on my own.

"Wait!" Ashley yells. "Don't make me run! I hate running." She says.

I turn the wheelchair and sand sprays her. She stops and laughs.

"Oh wait, you want to play it that way!" She yells. She picks sand up and tosses it at me.

I laugh. The sand is damp so it sticks to me.

Gianna runs over. She slips her shoe off her foot and puts her foot on my shoulder and then bends backwards putting her arms up. Ashley goes behind me and does a split on the frame of the wheelchair. She takes my hands and holds them.

Marcus walks over. "Can I?" He asks.

I look at him and smile.

He takes his camera out of his bag and starts taking pictures.

Kelsey stands with mom. "She never invites me to do stuff like that."

"She didn't ask them."

Cody stands on the pier with Landon, Rayf, Tate and Marshall. They are looking out on the horizon. They hear laughter and Cody turns. Landon puts his hand on his chest. Cody looks at him.
"Are you ok?"
"Its her dream." Landon says.
"What's her dream?" Tate asks.
"To be a dancer. Look at them." Landon says.

Kelsey comes running and she leaps in front of me. Marcus catches the shot of her in the air. She then does a split in the sand and takes my hand, Gianna does the same and takes my other hand. They both lean forward and I fall out of the wheelchair.
I lay in the sand laughing. Cody and Landon come running over. Cody picks me up in his arms. I hug him.
"You ok?" Cody asks.
"I am fine." I say. "Just sandy."
Gianna looks at me. "Crystal, I am so sorry."
"I am fine. I lost my center and there is no seatbelt in this wheelchair."
Kelsey looks at Gianna. "I have an idea." She looks at Ashley. "Come chat with us for a moment."
Cody turns and runs into the ocean with me. He holds me close to him as he runs deeper in the water. He then runs back.
Marcus stands snapping pictures of me. He looks at Kelsey. "What are you planning?"
"A dance that she can be in. Cody and the guys need to be in it too."
"You know that they are ball players."
"They won't need to dance. But will have to play baseball." She tells him her idea.
"Kelsey, that sounds remarkable." Marcus looks at her. "Why did you do it?

Chapter Twenty–three

I put on the last dress for the model shoot. Cody puts on the last suit. I look at myself in the mirror before I go to join Cody for another photo shoot. I feel so beautiful in this dress. It's the most beautiful dress that I have ever put on. Cody walks out of the fitting room that he is in. He looks at me.

"Oh my god, you look beautiful." He says.

I smile at him. "Cody, that's what you have said for the last nine dresses I have had on."

"You are beautiful." He says.

I smile again. "The way you look at me makes me feel beautiful."

Cody looks at me. "Will you go with me tomorrow?"

I look at him. "Yes. Of course."

He looks at me. "Crystal, are you worried that we are moving too fast?"

His words catch me off guard. I look at him and then away from him. I look at him again. I reach my hands out to him. "I have waited my whole life for this. If you think its too soon, we can wait, just as long as I don't have to be separated from you." I say the words with confidence that I always possessed. "Why do you say that? Are you feeling rushed?" I look at us in the mirrors around us. "This is overwhelming."

"Is it anything close to what you want?"

"This dress is gorgeous and I feel beautiful in it, but its not my wedding dress. Its not the one that feels like it's the right one."

Cody sits next to me. He hangs his head. I put my hand on his side.

"Cody, if you don't want to marry me—"

His head springs up. "I want to marry you. I don't want to do these photos any more. It's enough. I want our actual wedding photos to be authentic and if we keep posing how will we know that the actual photos are real?"

"If you think we are done, we are done." I say to him.

"I don't want to keep you from fulfilling your dream."

"Wearing ten wedding dresses is not my dream. My dream is to be by your side for the rest of my life."

Casper walks into the fitting rooms. "No! Go take them off. Both of you! We have what we need. We know, we are done."

Cody looks at Casper. "Let Marcus take a few of her in this dress. She looks like a fucking dream."

I smile.

"I won't be in the pictures with her. But this dress needs her to wear it and it needs to be photographed." Cody slips into the fitting room and changes his clothes.

Casper pushes my wheelchair out of the fitting rooms and into the staging area that is set up for the photo shoots. When he pushes me over to the area its all black curtains. I look around.

"Why the change?" I ask.

"We wanted you to stick out more. This is the last dress. This is supposed to be the one that makes the showcase." Casper says.

I smile and laugh. "Casper you said that about every dress I have had on."

"I mean it about this one." He says.

I reach out to touch the curtain.

"No" he says loudly. He positions me the way that he wants me. "Do not look behind you."

Marcus comes in front of me. He tilts my wheelchair a bit so that I am more angled. "Turn your body." Marcus tells me.

I hear rustling going on behind me, but I don't turn around. I know Cody is behind me, I can smell his cologne. Marcus doesn't have to tell me to smile bigger, I do it naturally.

Tate, Rayf and Marshall walk over and they are dressed in baseball uniforms. They each take a knee next to me. Then I see it. The baseball bats and gloves. Cody stands behind me and wraps his arm around me. The way he holds me with his one arm, Lover Boy is across my chest. I can't contain my smile.

When we are just about finished, Christian walks over. He smiles at me. "I have one more thing for you. Come with me." He blindfolds me.

"Christian, where are we going?"

"I don't want you to see what you are going to wear, I just need you to trust me." He says. He pushes my wheelchair into the fitting room and helps me get changed.

"Can I take the blindfold off?"

"No." He says. He helps me stand up. "Hold on to the railing."

I feel for the railing. "Christian, I feel like I am going to fall. You know what the number one thing you never do to someone who has no balance? Blindfold them." I say.

"You are in good hands." Kelsey says. She puts her hands on my waist. "Hold on my shoulders." She takes my hand and puts my hand on her shoulder. "Hold the railing." She says and puts my other hand on the railing. "Stand tall." She says.

I feel the material slide up my body. Christian zips the dress. He positions my wheelchair. "Sit down." He says.

"Can I take the blindfold off?"

"No." He says. He takes my foot and slips my shoe off. He puts a shoe on my foot. He then takes my other leg and slips the shoe off. He puts another shoe on my foot. "Put your hands in your lap." He says. I do. He pushes me out of the fitting room and into the staging room.

When we are back, I am still blindfolded. Everyone gasps when they see me. Christian takes the material of the dress and flares it out around the wheelchair. He takes my feet off the brackets, that my feet sit on so that I can get around, and puts my feet on the floor. He takes my right leg and holds it out straight in front of me.

Someone sits in front of me and my leg is put over that person's shoulder. Its not Cody. I can tell. It's a woman who is in front of me.

"Christian, can I take the blindfold off?" I ask.

"Not yet. We are almost done." He says. "Give me your right hand." I do. Someone stands next to me and holds my hand. "Ok, give me your left hand." Christian says. I do. "Raise your arm up." He says. "Ok good."

He steps behind me and takes the blindfold off. "Close your eyes." He says. Someone takes my left hand in her hand and I can feel her positioning herself. "Marcus, on your ready." Christian says.

"Ready." Marcus says.

"Crystal, open your eyes."

I do. I look at Kelsey standing on her toes next to me, she looks like a beautiful ballerina. In front of me is Ashley. My leg is over her shoulder. She looks like a ballerina too. On my right is Gianna. She is standing on one leg, with her other leg bent. Marcus keeps snapping pictures. I look down at myself and see that I am dressed like a ballerina too.

"Put your arms above your head." Marcus says to all of us. Everyone repositions. "Beautiful."

Ashley jumps up after a few more shots. "I have an idea for a shot." She says. She stands behind me and tips my wheelchair back. I throw my arms up to try to grab my wheels. Marcus captured the image that Ashley wanted. When I threw my hands up the dress flew up too. Ashley rights my wheelchair.

"I want one more." I say.

They all look at me. Marcus smiles. "I was waiting for you to call something."

I look at myself in the mirrors and realize that this is the dress that I put together. The skirt is shorter but it's a replica of the bodice and skirt that I put together.

Casper walks over. "Oh my god, if I was into women, you would be stripped out of that dress." He smiles.

I smile. "Thank you."

"Tell us what you want."

"Can I just show you?"

"Of course." He says.

I leave the area. They all stand there watching. I come back with pillows on my lap. They all watch me throw the pillows on the floor and then I get out of my wheelchair. I sit on the floor and arrange the pillows. I then lay back on the pillows.

Cody comes and lays next to me. His friends lay with us. Our sisters lay with us. Vinny walks in which is my surprise for my sister. Brandon and Kyle walk in. They all lay with me so that we make a big circle on the floor. Trevor walks in last and he lays next to Kelsey.

Marcus stands on a ladder looking down at us and takes many pictures. Oscar takes pictures too.

Everyone sits up. Cody helps me sit up. I look at Casper and Christian. "I have one more idea." I say. I side sit and hold my hands out to them both. They both make themselves comfortable on the pillows and I lean my shoulder against Casper.

Marcus agains snaps picture after picture. The last photos he snaps, is Cody lifting me off the ground and sitting me in my wheelchair. Cody kisses me.

Marcus looks at all of us. "Ok, I have work to do." He looks at Oscar. "Want me to do that too?"

"You can take it back to the studio for me. I will be there shortly."

I go back in the fitting room and get dressed in my clothes. Its been a whole day. Its been exhausting. Casper and Christian take all of us to dinner. Cody and Casper sit side by side chatting.

"When do you want to marry her?"

"Tomorrow." Cody says. "Last week. The day I met her."

"Tell me about how you met her."

Cody looks at him. "Everyone knows how I met her."

"Tell me. I don't think I heard it."

"We had random encounters." He says to Casper. "She told me that I helped her in a Target store. But we met on a flight together. A woman on the plane recognized me and at first flirted but she was sitting next to a guy who told her who I was and then she called me an asshole." Cody looks at me. "Crystal made a comment and I heard her. She looked at me and she smiled. I felt that smile in my heart. She fell asleep on the plane. The pilot asked me to watch out for her. She put her head against my arm and she slept. She held on to me. It was like she touched my heart."

"Then when did you kiss her?"

"Tyler, my cousin's idiot now husband, wouldn't stop teasing me about all that Lover Boy crap. He said I could have anyone I wanted. He was just about to bet me that I wouldn't kiss the next pretty girl I saw, when I saw her. I didn't want her to get away. She had held my arm so tightly during the flight in her sleep. I took her in my arms and crushed her lips with my mouth." He looks at me and then back at Casper. "I couldn't get enough of her. I wished that I could have just left with her and started our lives together that night."

I watch Cody. I can't take my eyes off of him. I don't want to. I watch him talking to his friends and to Casper. I smile so much, my cheeks hurt. Kelsey sits next to me. She puts her arm around me.

"Hi." I say.

"Hi."

"Whats going on?"

"I want to know something."

I look at her and smile. "What would that be?"

"Do you mind if I move into the neighborhood?"

"No." I say honestly.

"And does it bother you that I am in a relationship with two guys?"

I take her hand in my hand. "Does it make you happy?"

"More than you will ever know." She says. Then she smiles. "I am sure that Cody makes you feel as happy as I feel. The only difference, I need two men to make me feel that loved."

"Kelsey, I am not going to love you any less."

"You must really hate Vinny." She says.

"Vinny was the doctor who knocked me out and ultimately made me feel better. I don't know what he did, but he touched my cheek. I felt so much pain I passed out from the pain. When I woke up, I felt better." I smile at her. "He loves you. I saw it in the hospital. I saw it in the lobby when he kissed you. I wished that someone would kiss me like that."

"Cody did." She says.

"Cody did." I say. "I have never felt more loved in my life."

"I am so happy for you." Kelsey says. "Who do I bring as my plus one?"

"I am giving you a plus two."

"Where do you you want to get married?"

I get silly. "I want to marry Cody Parker in the lobby of the resort where he kissed me. I want to have our reception in the atrium. When he danced with me." I get silly again. "I never wanted to be out of his arms."

Cody walks over and kisses me. "We will have to go there and see what date works."

Kelsey looks at us. "Casper is the owner of the resort."

I look at her. "No way!" I say with shock. I look at Casper and smile.

Cody and I leave the next day to return to Fort Lauderdale. We go to my house and the moving trucks are waiting for us. They unload all the stuff from the trucks and arrange the furniture.

Cody looks at me. "My stuff doesn't need to be in your house."

I look at him. "Cody, this is a big house. And you and I are going to be married. Tomorrow we can go find out when."

Trevor walks in the house. "My designer will be here shortly to arrange the furniture."

Cody looks at him. "Thanks. We need to talk about what is going where."

Trevor looks at me. "I got your diagram."

I smile. "Follow it please."

Cody looks at me. "What diagram?"

"I will show you later. Right now we have to go have dinner with your parents. They expected us about a half hour ago." I turn and Cody takes my hand and turns me back. "Cody, we have to go." I say.

"I thought that we would be arranging the furniture ourselves." Cody says.

Trevor looks at Cody. "This is my treat." He looks at me and smiles. "I spoke to your sister. She told me what you said about your wedding. That is very nice of you." He takes me in his arms and hugs me. He looks out the front bay window and points to the house diagonally across the street. "That is where we are going to be." He kisses the top of my head. "She is lucky to have you for a sister. Ashley wasn't as welcoming about the situation."

I look at Trevor. "That's rich. She and Brandon are dating and have been for years. In some respects its incest. I mean I know he isn't our biological brother but we were raised like siblings. She won't have to change her last name." When I say that it makes me smile. I look at Cody. "Would you be willing to change your last name?" I say jokingly.

He looks at me seriously. "If you wanted me to and it would make you happy."

"I was just joking." I say. "I have already written my whole name out with Parker as my last name and I love it." I grin.

"Ok, you two go and my team and I will set up the place. Give us about three hours." Trevor says. He looks at both of us. "If its not ready, you two can sleep at my house."

I smile again. "Thank you. We do have a cute guest house."

"That's true." Trevor says. "The invitation stands."

Cody and I leave the house. We get into my car. I store my wheelchair in the topper. I pull out of the driveway and drive north on I-95.

Forty minutes later we arrive at Sawyer and Catalina's house. We made two stops on our way. We stopped to get flowers and we stopped to get something for dinner. I get out of the car and into my wheelchair. Cody gets the bags from our stops and hands them to me. We enter the house.

The house smells so good. Catalina greets us. "What did you do?" She asks.

"We stopped to get something for dinner." Cody says.

"Come in." She says to both of us.

As we walk through the hallway, I notice that the walls are adorn with new pictures. Pictures of Cody and me from the photo shoots. I look at the images. Cody looks at them too.

"How do you have these already?" Cody asks.

She smiles at both of us. "I have my ways."

The last one catches me completely off guard, it's the one of my sisters, Gianna and me. I am on my knees with my arms stretched out to Gianna. Ashley has her arm around me supporting me. Kelsey stands behind me with her foot on my shoulder. Her knee is bent and she has her arms arched over her head.

"Wow, that's beautiful." I say.

Gianna walks over and hugs me. "Hi." She says.

"Hi." I say.

She looks at Cody. "I need to talk to you for a moment."

"Sure." Cody says.

Catalina takes the bags from me. "Come with me." She says. We go into the kitchen. I help her take the food out of the containers. "I wanted to tell you that my niece is here for dinner."

I know that she is talking about Jillian and Tyler.

Catalina looks at me. "Is that a problem?"

I shake my head. "Of course not."

"She feels awful for all the trouble that she caused you."

"Catalina, its fine. It happened."

Jillian walks into the kitchen and hugs Catalina. She looks at me and smiles. "Its good to see you again."

"You too." I say.

"I want to say that the pictures of you and Cody are remarkable."

"Thank you."

Tyler joins us in the kitchen. "Hi Crystal. Its good to see you again."

"You too." I say.

Catalina looks around her extra large kitchen. "It feels tight in here." She says.

I look at her and smile.

Cody walks in the kitchen. "What's going on in here?"

"Cody, give me a chance." Jillian says. "We used to be so close."

"Us not being as close has nothing to do with Crystal." Cody says. "Its what you did. I can't help but think that you did it on purpose. You made sure that my mom and dad couldn't be there. You made sure that Landon and Gianna weren't going to be there. I can't help but think that you did that on purpose." He says to Jillian. "And you made sure that Tyler tried to bet me that I couldn't get any woman to kiss me."

I look at Cody. "I should thank Tyler."

"Beth was my wedding planner. She knew that Cody was going to be there." Jillian says.

"Jillian, Beth took the credit for being your wedding planner, but I was it from start to finish. Cody's name was not on any guest list." My cheek is still bruised. I can camouflage it with makeup but it's still a bit noticeable.

"Beth told me that she was overseeing all the details." Jillian says.

"I can tell you again, every detail, was not overseen by Beth." I laugh. "She barely worked. She liked taking the credit for it. She liked putting the money in her bank. Every note was hand written by me for all the details of your wedding. Beth told me that I had to go to Indiana to get something special for the wedding. When I got to Indiana, she texted me and told me that it was in Atlanta. When I was stuck in planes and in airports, she told me that I had to get to Fort Lauderdale." I look at Cody. "Were you that special gift?" I smile. I stand up holding on to the counter. I reach my hand out to him.

He takes me in his arms. "I was your gift."

"Oh my god, for sure." I say.

"You were my gift." Cody says.

Jillian stomps her foot.

I lean into Cody. "Is everything ok with Gianna?"

"She told me that she is dating one of my friends." Cody says.

"Is it Rayf?" I ask.

"How did you know that?" He asks.

"I suspected."

"Why do you say that?" He asks me.

"He looks at her the way that you look at me." I say to him.

He senses that my knees are going to buckle so he lifts me up to sit on the counter.

"Are you ok with that?" Jillian asks.

"Why you want to break them apart?" Cody asks.

I wrap my arms around Cody. "Be nice." I whisper in his ear.

Sawyer walks into the kitchen. He dips Catalina back and kisses her on the lips. When she stands next to him, she puts her hand delicately on his shoulder. She gestures at all of us. "There will be no bickering in front of Grammy."

"Of course." We all say.

Grammy walks in the kitchen and sits at the table. She looks at all of us. She narrows her eyes at Jillian. "Did you say what you were going to say to your cousin and his beautiful fiancé?"

Jillian turns into Tyler. "We should go. They are never going to let this go."

"Just say you are sorry." Tyler says.

"You too." She whines."

Landon walks into the kitchen. He walks over to the counter and lifts me off of it. He seats me in my wheelchair. He turns and takes Cody's hand and mine. "We have something to do."

Cody takes my hand. He looks at Landon. "Where are we going?"

Landon walks out the front door. He walks to the side of the house. When I see the baseball diamond set up, I smile and screech with excitement.

My siblings are all standing there. Kyle runs over and takes me in his arms. Brandon hugs me next. He kisses me on the forehead. "I love this excitement." He says.

Kyle looks at Cody. "This is how she always acted or reacted when she would go to the stadium.

Its not a real baseball game going on as there are not enough players to play, but Cody's friends and my brothers play baseball. Every time Cody is up to bat, I get excited. I scream for him.

Kyle stands on the field with Cody. "This is how she always reacted. Even when she was calling the play-by-plays, she would get so excited they would make her start over and over. They would rehearse with her. The guys sitting with her would say, next up Cody Parker. She would get all excited and do her little scream thing that she did. She would pull herself together and call the plays like she didn't have a favorite player."

"Ky, why didn't you ever tell me about your sister?" Cody asks.

Kyle looks at him. "You weren't ready to meet her when we were in school together." Kyle puts his hand on Cody's arm. "I don't mean anything bad by it."

"I am not taking it that way." Cody says. "Sometimes I was an asshole."

Kyle looks at me. "In that girl's eyes you never were. She would call them CP off days. Then she would laugh because she related it to her condition. When she wasn't into doing something when she was young, she would say she was having a CP off day. Then you came along and when you had bad plays—" Tyler ribs Cody. "You had some really crappy plays."

"You said that coach changed the way I played because of her notes?"

"Yes. She saw that you hung your arm and then your plays were really off. She knew when you were going to have a great hit and she knew when you weren't."

"How?" Cody asks.

"She paid attention." Rayf says. "My brother was in the box with her and he said that she would watch you come out of the dug out. She could tell the way you walked out if you were going to have a good play or not. My brother would pay attention to her observations and he would text the coach in the dugout."

Cody looks at me. "What did she think? Did she think I was on drugs or something?"

"Never." Rayf and Kyle say together.

"Others would say that, but she never did. Not one time did she think that you were doing drugs." Kyle says. "You know that game that you passed out at, she said that you must have been drugged."

Rayf looks at Kyle and Cody. "My brother heard her say that. He sent a text to the coaches and they had you tested. She was right. She was devastated that you passed out and left early."

Cody runs over to where I am. He takes me in his arms and hugs me. He kisses my lips over and over again. He hugs me.

"Cody, are you ok?" I ask.

"Oh baby, thank you."

"Thank you for what?"

"Knowing me."

I wrap my arms around him. "Cody, I don't want to wait too much longer to be your wife. I love you. I wanted you forever. I need you." I kiss his lips. "Make love to me." I say quietly against his lips.

He plays baseball and the last play he hits a home run. I throw my hands up in the air. "That's my Cody Parker!" I scream. I howl for him. I am so excited.

My sisters sit next to me. Brandon sits next to Ashley. She holds his hand. When the game is over, we go in the house and have dinner. We all stay and watch a movie together. After the movie is over, everyone slowly leaves.

Cody sits outside with his parents. He watches me. I stayed inside with my sisters. Gianna sits next to me.

Kelsey looks at me. "Are you happy to be going home?"

"The house looks great. Trevor worked hard on all the things that I wanted. I am so appreciative."

"He knows." Kelsey says. "He is happy that we are going to be neighbors."

"I am happy too." I say.

Ashley looks at me. "Are you ok with Brandon and I not living in the neighborhood?"

"Of course." I say. "It would be so weird if we all lived in the same neighborhood. I have to watch you and Brandon constantly touching each other. You both are a bit annoying." I say teasing her.

Gianna looks at me. She smiles. "You brought Cody back to us." She looks outside at Cody talking with their parents. "Did you ever go to the cemetery?"

"No. We are going tomorrow."

"I thought you were going before you got back." Gianna says.

"We were excited about the house." I say.

"So you came to spend the day with all of us?" Gianna asks.

"I want Cody to be surprised by the house." I smile.

Cody drives to the cemetery. He bounces his leg. I put my hand on his knee. He puts his hand on top of mine. "Thank you." He says.

I look at him. "You don't have to thank me."

He parks the car. He gets my wheelchair out of the car. When I am adjusted in it, he takes me in his arms. "I didn't go to the funeral." He says.

"Cody, Donavan knew how much he was loved." I rub my hands over his shoulders.

"I wasn't there when he needed me." Cody says. His words are full of emotions.

"Cody."

He pulls back. He looks me in the eyes. "Do you believe in guardian angels?"

"I do." I say. "I believe one led me to you."

He wraps his arms around me and holds me tight. "When I heard you cheering for me the other day when I was playing baseball, I somehow heard Donavan cheering along with you."

"Who's to say he wasn't?" I say.

"I don't want to go in." He says.

"Cody, whatever you want. Whenever you are ready. I am here with you. Or if you want to go alone, I will wait for you."

"Did you say the same thing to Landon?"

I laugh. "No. I was forceful with him."

Cody smiles.

"No one is judging you." I say to him.

"What if—"

"Cody, he knows that you are here. Even if you don't go to the gravestone. He knows that you are here." I put my hand on his chest. "He is here with you always. He is in your heart."

"Do you think he felt abandoned?"

"No. Landon held him in his arms. Gianna and you were there. Like I said, he knows that he was loved."

A groundsman walks over. "Hi can I help you find what you are looking for?"

Cody looks at him. "No. We know where to go." Cody says. "Thank you." He takes my hand and walks through the gates with me. He walks slowly to the back of the cemetery. Cody steps back.

I look at him. "Whats wrong?"

"Where did the tree come from?" He looks at me. "I was here just three months ago and that tree wasn't here."

"Maybe someone had it planted."

"That was his favorite tree." Cody says. "He loved my grandma's dwarf trees." He smiles. "He said he felt like a giant next to the trees."

I smile at him.

"Did you do this?"

"I didn't." I say.

"Crystal, you promise you didn't know about the tree?"

"I didn't know about the tree."

A woman walks over to us. She puts her arms around Cody. He turns quickly to see who it is. Grammy hugs him. "The angel needed a shade." She says.

Cody hugs her.

"You both make me so proud to be your grandma." Grammy says. She looks at me. "Can I ask you a question?"

"Of course." I say.

"How much out of your pocket money did you spend to make sure that I was a satisfied guest at my granddaughter's wedding?"

"Everything was paid for." I tell her.

"I know that's not true because when I asked my son and granddaughter they had no clue what I was talking about."

"Grammy, you were a guest at a wedding that I hosted, you were the guest of honor as far as I am concerned. You were the best guest." I look at Cody I smile. "You were the best guest at the wedding."

They both smile.

"I want to pay you what you spent out of pocket for me to be a guest at my granddaughter's wedding."

"No." I say. "It was my pleasure having you at the wedding. I wanted to make sure that you were the most comfortable to be there."

"Cody, talk sense into her."

Cody looks at Grammy. "She paid for Donny's angel."

Grammy looks at the two of us. "I was under the impression that your parents paid for the angel."

"No one knew where it came from and everyone thought that the others did it." Cody says. He puts his arms around me. "My angel is the one who paid for Donny's angel."

Grammy looks at me. "It must have cost you a fortune."

I shake my head. "No." I look at Cody. "I did it for you and Landon. I didn't know Donavan, but I wanted to do something nice for you and Landon. You paid my hospital bills and for me to have therapy. You didn't know who I was."

"You shouldn't have felt obligated to do this." Grammy says.

"I didn't feel obligated to do this. I wanted to do it just to do it. I came here with Landon the day of the funeral and I know how hard it was for him. When we were leaving, we walked past the angels. I came back to find out if they were for sale and when the lady told me that they were, I purchased one. The grounds keeper brought me back over here and asked where I wanted it placed." I look at them. "If you want it moved, feel free to move it."

"No one is moving it." Cody says. He takes me in his arms again. "What you did was so sweet."

Grammy looks at the two of us. "You both are meant for each other. I am so glad that you found each other." She looks at the dwarf tree. "Come see Donavan's tree." She takes Cody's hand. I give them time alone. I watch Grammy with her grandson and I smile.

Cody walks back over. "What are you doing?"

"You and your grandma need a moment. Go. I will wait for you."

He takes my hand. "We do this together." He laces his fingers with mine.

I look at him. "Can we plant some of the dwarf trees around our house? I want to feel like a giant." I say.

Cody drops to his knees and hugs me.

Grammy leaves us after a half hour. Cody sits with his back to the gravestone and talks to Donavan like he is talking to Landon.

"Hey little brother, I am sorry I haven't visited more often. I want you to meet Crystal. I am going to marry her. She is the one who bought this beautiful angel for you. You are right, she looks familiar because she came here years ago when you left us with Landon. She is my biggest fan. Again you are right, you were my biggest fan. I miss you, little one. We all do. You are never forgotten. Crystal and I will come back and visit more often. Grandma planted your dwarf tree for you. We are going to plant some for you by our house."

We stay a bit longer. Cody didn't want to come at first and now he finds it hard to leave. I hold his hand. "Cody, we will come back." I say.

"Did I keep you from doing something that you needed to do?"

"No." I say.

"Can I ask you a question?"

"Yes."

"Did you spend a lot of money making sure that Grammy was happy at Jill's wedding?"

"Cody, it was part of the package."

"I know that's not true."

"Cody, I am never going to tell how much anything cost. As far as anyone is concerned it was part of the wedding package."

"You went out of your way to know the details of the mushrooms and the wine that she drinks."

"When she is a guest at our wedding, I don't have to ask her for any details. I know them. I know that she was interested in dancing with her grandson. She wants her grandchildren to believe that you are her favorite." I put my hand on Donavan's gravestone. "Clearly this is not true. She made sure that you have your dwarf trees." I say. I kiss my hand and then place it back on the headstone.

Cody kisses me.

"Not in front of the child." I say.

He smiles against my lips. He takes my hand and we walk back to the car.

Chapter Twenty-four

We prepare the house for a party. Cody and I are hosting a party for our guests that are coming to our wedding. We didn't have a bridal shower because I have everything that I would ever want. Cody and I don't want to take advantage of anything. I didn't want one of my family members showing up with a toaster or a blender that I don't need nor want.

Our backyard is beautiful. I went to a nursery and found out about dwarf trees and I had them planted around the yard. Cody had gone out of town for a few days with Landon and Rayf and when he came back the trees were planted. I also had an angel statue put under one tree.

A crew of people are setting up tables in the yard. They are setting up a stage area. The catering company is due to come in a half hour.

Casper and Christian come over. When they walk in the house, the two of them gasp. Casper looks at me. "I have something for you."

"What else? You didn't let me see a bill for my wedding." I say.

"No. And don't ask."

"Is this how all wedding planners plan weddings? They pay for the weddings themselves?" Cody asks.

I smile at him. "When it's a special wedding and the bride is a princess."

Casper looks at me and smiles. "You truly are a princess." He looks at Cody. "And you Cody Parker are the prince of her dreams."

Christian looks at Cody and me. "Do you have your vows ready?"

"Yes." We both say.

"Give them to me." He says.

I enter our bedroom and get changed. Cody comes in the room. He sits on the bed and watches me change. I look at him and smile.

"I love the way you love me." He says.

"That's a song." I say.

"No its my truth."

I stand up holding on to the bed. "Can you zip me up?"

"Can I leave it unzipped?" He asks and kisses the back of my neck where I have the matching tattoo of his crossed bats. He slips his arm around my midsection. He holds me against his chest. He kisses my neck again. "I love you."

"I love you too." I put my hands back on the bed. "Zip my dress."

"Do I have to?"

"Cody, we have a house full of people." I say with a big grin on my face.

"What are you thinking?"

"Tomorrow, I will be your bride. I will be yours forever. You will be mine forever."

"Are you sure that you are ok waiting for the honeymoon?"

"Of course I am. You are going to be coaching professional upcoming baseball players and I get to watch you all the time." I say.

He zips my dress and I sit back in my wheelchair. He hugs me tight and kisses me deeply.

"If you wrinkle this dress, Casper might kill you." I say smiling against his lips.

"And you are sure that you want to go to Hawaii?"

"Cody, I would go anywhere with you. Everywhere with you."

A knock on our bedroom door makes the two of us laugh. Casper walks in the room. He looks at the two of us. "You look beautiful." Casper says.

"I feel beautiful in your dresses." I say smiling.

"I can't take the credit for this one. This one is Christian's. The line won't launch for another month, but we thought that he needed to show it off."

"We are having a rehearsal dinner in our backyard." I say.

"Not to fret, I have photographers that will get the dress from every angle." He smiles brightly. "Well the two of you from every angle." He looks at Cody. "If she didn't capture your heart, I would turn you." He laughs.

Cody smiles but he moves a step closer to me. I smile and pull him closer to me still so that I can kiss him.

"I barged in because I have a gift for the two of you. I wanted to give it to you privately. In addition to designing wedding dresses, I also dabble in memories."

We both look at him confused.

He hands a box to Cody. Cody sits on the bed and puts the box on his lap. He opens the box. In the box is a picture of Cody kissing me. In the corner watching us kiss is Donavan. He is smiling brightly at the two of us.

Cody looks at Casper and jumps off the bed. He runs to him and hugs him. "Thank you."

I look at the picture. I look at the little boy in the picture. "Wait! That's Donavan?" I ask.

Cody turns and looks at me. "That's my little brother."

"This is the little boy that danced with Gianna in one of her recitals." I say.

Cody walks over and squats next to me. "You saw them dance together?"

"Yes, because both my sisters were in that same show. He was the little boy that was handing out flowers at the end of the performance. He gave me a red rose." I leave them for a moment and enter the closet. I take out a shadowbox that has a playbill in it and the rose. It looks like it was just taken from the vine. On the playbill is Donavan's signature. It's a sloppy kids signature, but it reads clearly Donavan Parker. Also in the shadowbox is a picture of me hugging Donavan. I leave the closet and join them in the bedroom. "Look." I say. I hand it to Cody.

Cody looks at the picture of Donavan and me hugging. He sees me holding the rose in the picture. "Crystal!" Cody says with tears in his throat. "He told me that evening that he met the woman I should marry. He told me that he gave that woman a rose and his signed playbook that he wanted to keep."

I hug Cody. "He was so sweet and he was excited that I wanted to hug him because other people were there to see the older dancers. He hugged me so tight. He handed me that playbill and he signed it for me."

Cody leaves the room with the two pictures. He shows them to Landon first because Landon is standing by the couch. Paige and him are embracing each other. Landon looks at Cody.

"You ok?" Landon asks.

"Look." He says. He shows him the pictures.

Landon puts his hand to his chest. He looks at me. "You were the one that Donny talked about nonstop. He said you were the nicest fan. He said that he gave you his playbill and the rose and you gave him a candy bar, a hug and a small bear that he wanted from the gift shop."

"The bear in tap shoes?" Cody asks. He looks at me. "You bought that for him?"

"I paid for it." I say.

"You didn't have to do it"

"He was trying to steal it." I say with a smile. "He danced so beautiful with our sisters, I didn't want him to get into trouble. I paid for the bear. It wasn't expensive."

Catalina walks over. "What's going on over here? The guests of honor need to come join their guests." She looks at the shadowbox. "What is this?"

Cody hands it to her. She gasps. Cody hugs her. She hugs me.

"You were the one who bought him the tap dancing teddy bear." She looks at Cody and Landon. "When you pulled the string the bear actually tap danced."

I take Cody's hand. "He gave me his playbill and he signed it." I say. "He was incredible. I didn't realize that was Donavan."

"What was Donavan?" Gianna asks.

"Donavan?" Kelsey asks. "The little boy that danced with us. He was so remarkable." She looks around. "Whatever happened to him?"

Landon looks at her. "He died."

Kelsey puts her hand to her chest like Landon had just done moments before. "I am sorry to hear that. I didn't know." She looks at Gianna. "That's why you were missing from all those shows."

Gianna nods her head.

"I am sorry." Kelsey says again.

Gianna looks at the shadowbox. "Why do you have that? Why do you have the playbill?" She looks at Cody.

"Its mine." I say.

Gianna now looks at me. "What is it with you?" She asks. "You knew everyone of us and touched all of our lives." She looks at the picture of me hugging Donavan. "Wait!" She says. "Are you the one that bought him the tap dancing bear?"

"Yes."

"You bitch!" She says with laughter in her tone. "I promised to buy it for him. When I went to get it, it was gone. That night when I went to kiss him good night, he had it. He told me that a fan bought it for him."

"Crystal is the one who bought the angel for him."

Sawyer and dad walk over together. "Crystal, you bought the angel?" Sawyer asks.

"I did." I say.

"Why?" Dad asks.

"I did it for Landon."

Landon looks at me. "Why?"

"When I was with you at the cemetery we walked past the angels and you put your hand on one of them a few times. When you went to move the car, I found out about it. I didn't know that I had met Donavan, but I felt compelled to do it."

Mom walks over. She looks at all of us. She looks at me and stares for a moment. "Wow." She says. "You look stunning."

Stew walks in. "Look at my girl." Stew says.

I notice for the first time that dad doesn't get mad when Stew says that. For a moment I feel sad. I always wondered if I was Stew's daughter. He has always been a solid fixture in my life. But in my heart I want to be Crystal Bella Steele. My dad has pulled away from me over the years and I don't think that its all Joanna's fault.

Mom looks at me. "Are you alright?"

"I am." I say. I put my hand in Cody's hand. He laces his fingers with mine.

"We should go say hello to our friends." Cody says.

"Yes."

When we get outside, Cody pushes my wheelchair against a wall and stands in front of me. "Talk to me." He says.

"I am just thinking something that I don't know if I know it is true or something that my head is making up."

"What's that?" He asks.

"I think that Stew is my dad."

"Why do you think that?"

"I don't know. All I know is that my dad stepped away and Stew was always there. He was always— he is always here when I need someone. It just makes me think that maybe he is my dad. My sisters look like my dad. I don't look like him."

"Do you want to ask Stew?"

"Yes. No. Yes. Not today. Today its about us. Our wedding rehearsal." I kiss him. "Tomorrow, none of it will matter, I will be yours and part of a family that wants me to be part of my family."

"They want to be your family."

I put my finger on his lips. "All I want is you. All I want to be is yours. All I ever wanted was to be yours."

"All I ever wanted was to be yours. I feel like I have been searching my whole life for you. When you were closer than I thought being my best friend's sister."

Kyle clears his throat. We both look at him and smile. Everything that I just said to Cody about not caring about my family goes up in the air carried off by a gust of wind. Kyle looks at me and its like he knows what is coming.

He hugs me as Cody steps away but never lets go of my hand.

"Kyle, is Stew my dad?" I ask softly but they hear me.

"What do you think?" Kyle asks.

"Kyle just tell me. My dad is not my dad. Stew is my dad."

"Maybe your mom should tell you."

"Why did everyone wait to tell me? Why today? Why on the happiest day of my life? Why can't you all just let me be happy?" I look into Kyle's eyes. "Not you. I don't say it about you."

"Sweetheart, we all love you." He looks at me and tilts his head. "Not my mom." He smiles.

I laugh. "I love you Kyle."

"Tally! I love you." Kyle says.

"Is he?"

He hugs me.

"What's Stew's last name?" I ask.

"Steele." Stew says.

I look at him. "You and my dad are brothers?"

"Yes." Stew says.

"Am I your daughter?"

Kyle still holds me in a hug.

"Yes." Stew says.

"Are my sisters your daughters?"

"No."

"Is that why my dad ignores me?"

"Sweetheart, please." Stew says.

"So what Joanna said years ago was right?"

Kyle looks at me. Dad walks outside to hear me say that. They both say at the same time, "What did she say?"

"She said that Jack wasn't my dad. And she was annoyed that you had to pay for everything for me." I can't believe that I said it without crying.

"I love you." Dad says.

"Did everyone know but me?" I ask. "Why would Ashley bring me to this house and let me fall in love with it?"

Casper walks over. "What's going on?" He asks.

"Did you know?" I ask him.

"Know what?"

"Stew is my dad."

"No." Casper says. "Jack was at my shop telling me details for tomorrow that you can't go without."

"What?" I ask.

"Crystal, I asked your dad and Stew both to come to the bridal shop and tell me what was the number one thing that you wanted at your wedding and your dad told me."

"What did he tell you?"

"I can't tell you." Casper says.

All the guests that we invited fill my backyard and the tables that are set up. Everyone is enjoying the dinner. We walk around hand in hand greeting all of our guests.

When we get to Grammy, she looks at the two of us. She hands Cody a box. She looks at Cody. "Where are you living?"

"I live here."

"You live where?" She asks.

"This is Crystal's house. I live with Crystal."

"Do you have your own room?" She asks.

"Do I have my own room?" Cody asks.

"Don't tell me she makes you stay in the garage." She says joking.

"We share a bedroom." I say.

"Aren't you two too old for bunk beds."

Sawyer walks outside. "Mom, stop it." He says softly.

She turns to her son. "Did you know that Cody is sharing a bed with Crystal?"

"If they weren't sharing a bed, I would worry." Sawyer says. He reaches his hand out and puts it on my shoulder. "I heard what just happened. How are you?"

I look at him and smile. But really I feel sadness in my heart. I want to be something to Jack. I am glad to hear that I am Stew's daughter, but he came into my life when I was almost a teenager. My mom and him have an on-again-off-again relationship. Mostly they are off.

I go inside the house, everyone is outside. I change my clothes and put on pants and a sweater. Cody comes in the house and looks for me. When he finds me he holds me in his arms. He picks me up in his arms and holds me. Landon and Kyle come in the house and find us. They both hug the two of us. I cry earth shattering sobs. The three of them hold me. Kyle kisses the top of my head.

Ashley, Brandon and Kelsey walk in the house. They hear me crying and they come in the room. They hug us too.

Cody sits on the bed with me in his lap. Our siblings all sit around me. Gianna is the only one that doesn't join us. I have my head on Cody's chest and he rubs my back. Our siblings rub my back too. I close my eyes and the tears just run down my cheeks. Ashley wipes them away.

Cody talks softly and I feel the vibration in his chest when he talks to our collective siblings. "Events like this, will never happen again. Not for any of us. If anyone has big happy devastating news, no on will ever do this to her again. I will not allow it."

"We won't allow it either." Kyle says. He puts his hand on my arm. "I won't allow it." He kisses my head.

"Crystal, hear me, we won't allow anything like this to happen." Landon says.

There is a commotion going on outside. Kelsey gets off the bed and goes outside. Gianna is standing on a chair clapping her hands. Kelsey looks at her. Gianna looks at Kelsey and points to the chair next to her. Kelsey climbs up on the chair next to Gianna.

"Excuse me, can I get everyone's attention please?" Gianna says sharply to all the guests who are outside.

Everyone looks at Gianna.

She takes a deep breath and then says to everyone, "My dear friend is getting married. She is marrying my hero, my brother Cody. Today was to be the happiest day of their single lives before they join their hearts, their hands and their lives together. My friend who does the most wonderful things for people that she knows all the time to make their dreams come true would have prevented an event like what happened here today for anyone of her brides." She looks at my dad and Stew. "I am sure that you both love her. Tomorrow when she walks down the isle to my brother, to start the next chapter in their book of love. Tomorrow, I am asking you both to sit this one out and let the men in her life who have been supportive of her her whole life give her away on her journey to love and ultimate happiness. She deserves that."

Dad looks at her. "Who do you think you are?"

"Someone who loves her unconditionally." She looks at Kelsey and doesn't know what took place in my bedroom with all of the siblings but its like she was there with all of us. She laces her fingers again with Kelsey. "We the collective siblings will be walking her down the isle." She looks at Casper. "What you did for my friend and soon to be sister is beautiful. I appreciate all of this."

Kelsey looks at everyone. "Please enjoy the rest of your meals. The guests of honor will see you all tomorrow."

Mom looks at her. "You are kicking us all out?"

"Yes." She says.

Vinny and Trevor each walk over and stand on either side of Kelsey who is still standing on the chair and they add distance between Kelsey and mom. Vinny reaches his hand up to Kelsey. She takes his hand and steps down. Trevor sees her falling and grabs her around the waist. Vinny steadies her.

Rayf walks over and reaches both of his arms out for Gianna. She puts her hands on his broad shoulders and steps down. She hugs him. Rayf who I have known the least amount of time, takes the lead of my sister and Gianna. "Thank you all for coming to the rehearsal dinner." He says in a booming voice.

Vinny and Trevor walk our guests through the gates of the backyard to the street where their cars are parked. When they return to the backyard, its all cleaned up. The food has all been put into containers for storage. They find Kelsey sitting by herself in the backyard.

They both sit next to her. She reaches her hands out to each of them. Vinny, the more romantic of the two takes her hand to his lips and kisses it.

"You ok?" Trevor asks.

"Do you want to go to our home?" Vinny asks.

"No." She says.

"To which one?" Trevor asks.

She smiles a small smile. "Both."

"Talk to us." Vinny says.

"I knew my whole life that my dad wasn't Crystal's dad. They made me promise that I would never tell her."

"How did you know?" They both ask her together.

"My dad was off on a vacation and my mom was in bed with Uncle Stew." She says.

"Why was your dad on vacation without your mom and you? You were two when she was born. How do you remember?"

"I remember things that happened since my first birthday. I remember my first birthday. My parents had hired a clown. They thought that I would enjoy her. I hated every second that she was there. It was awful. I wasn't scared of her because she was dressed as a clown. I was scared of her height."

They both laugh at her.

"Don't laugh." She says.

"What about her height?" Vinny asks.

"She was a grown woman and she was literally six inches taller than I was. I was petrified that I wasn't going to grow." She says.

They both laugh again.

Trevor looks at Kelsey. "What do you remember about Crystal?"

She looks at Trevor. "Everything. She was created in a night of passion. My mom knew that my dad was having an affair. My mom was devastated. I was a little more than a year old and Uncle Stew came to visit. Uncle Stew is my dad's twin brother."

I open the back door to hear her say that. "I am sorry, what did you just say?"

The three of them nearly jump out of their skins. They all three stand up. Kelsey looks at me. "You never knew?"

"I never knew." I say.

"Uncle Stew's last name is Steele." She looks sad.

I look at her. "Cody and I are going to elope. We want you to be there. All three of you."

"What about mom?"

"My last conversation that I had with her was not one of encouragement towards my marriage. She told me that it doesn't always end up in a happily ever after. She told me that I jumped into this relationship too fast because I was swept off my feet by a kiss."

"Will Cody's family be there?"

I nod my head. "It would mean the world to me if you were there."

"You know dad and Uncle Stew love you."

"Kelsey, I need time." I look at her. "They don't even look like brothers."

"Not all twins look alike." She says.

"Why today?" I ask. "Why did the fact that dad is not my dad and Stew is my dad have to come out today?"

"I don't know." She says.

"Cody and I have talked about it and we are going to elope and go on our honeymoon. Then we will come back and have a big reception. Cody's grandma can't get the idea out of her head that he is really going to live with me. She doesn't want him to give up on his career."

"Wait a fucking minute." Trevor says. "Cody's grandmother? The woman that you spent a thousand dollars of your own money to make that woman feel like an honored guest at a wedding that you got fired from."

I look at him. "How do you know how much I spent?"

"That grandmother?" Trevor asks avoiding my question.

I look at Kelsey. "The day that I moved into the house. This house. Well the guest house really. Anyway, the day that I moved into the house, who sent me the flowers?"

"Daddy sent them to you."

"No wonder why Joanna never liked me. She knew that I wasn't—" the words catch in my throat. "She knew that I wasn't his daughter."

"That doesn't give her the right to treat you the way that she does." Brandon says. He hugs me. "Ashley and I are going to go."

"No." Cody says. "All of us are staying here. All of you are welcome to stay here. We want to leave for the chapel together."

My siblings, Cody's siblings and the both of us sit on the couches in the den of my house. We snuggle up with big fluffy blankets.

Kelsey smiles. "Remember doing this?" She asks all of us.

I nod my head. "You all were so mean making me watch The Goonies. I was scared to death of the bad people."

Brandon smiles. "You loved One Eye Willie."

"Everyone loved One Eye Willie." I say.

"Tell us about this wedding." Gianna says. "How is it going to work?"

Cody looks at everyone. "We are going to the chapel, we are going to get married. And then we are going to go for lunch with all of you. Mom and dad are going to join us. Margie and Stew can join us. Jack can come too."

"Will Casper and Christian be there?" Ashley asks.

"Yes." I say. "Casper is going to give me away."

"That's so sweet." Kelsey says.

I look at Gianna. "Where is Rayf?"

"He has to work tomorrow. He was going to join us for the reception tomorrow night."

"We are still going to have the reception. Casper paid for it."

"Cody, where is the chapel?"

I smile at Cody. Cody kisses me on the lips. "Its at the resort that we met at." He says.

"They have a chapel?" Landon asks.

"Yes." I say. "I went into the chapel at the resort when I first got there and lit a candle. Then I went to check in and that's when I met Cody." I smile.

"You went into the chapel and lit a candle?" Cody asks.

I smile. "Yes. But I had to blow out the candle that I lit first."

Gianna sits up straight on the couch. "What?"

"The candle that I wanted to light was lit. I blew it out and then I lit it." I say.

Gianna looks at Cody. "What candle?"

"The one in the middle." I say.

Cody kisses me on the lips. "You blew out my candle and then you relit it."

I smile at everyone.

"What time will the marriage take place?" Brandon asks.

"Two thirty." I say.

Kelsey looks at Brandon and Ashley. "When are you two getting married?"

Ashley looks at Kelsey and all of us. "Um we are married." She says.

I look at Kelsey and see her sadness. She gets up and kisses everyone on the cheek. "I will see you all tomorrow. Crystal, I will help you with your hair and makeup."

Trevor and Vinny go with her.

I look at Ashley. "When did you get married?"

"A year ago."

I look at Kyle, "were you there?"

"If I say yes, I am betraying you and Kelsey. If I say no I betrayed my brother and Ashley." Kyle says.

"Just answer the question." I say to him. I look at Ashley. "Did dad give you away?"

She looks at Brandon. Then she looks at me. "He was the best man."

"I would have been there if you would have told me about it." I say.

Brandon takes Ashley's hand in his. "We didn't have a big wedding. We didn't even know that it was going to happen. We were talking about getting married. The next thing we knew we were married."

"Is that why Joanna was more hostile towards me?"

"Its possible." Brandon says.

"Did she ever like me?"

"This is not a sad day. We are not going to talk about sad things." Kyle says. "The important thing is that we all love you."

There is a knock on the door. Cody gets up. He goes to the door and opens the door. Kelsey stands there. Cody hugs her.

"I am sorry. This is not about them. This is about you and my sister."

"Please come in." Cody says.

"Vinny got a phone call that he had to take and Trevor fell asleep."

"Vinny can come over anytime he wants. Trevor looked tired." Cody says to her.

"He is upset for Crystal." Kelsey says. "He is upset with me for not telling her what I knew."

Cody hugs her.

"I thought not telling her what I knew was keeping her protected. I knew Uncle Stew was Dad's twin my whole life. I don't know why Crystal and Ashley never knew or figured it out. Uncle Stew always just went by Stew. No last name. My mom's other boyfriends we knew by first and last names but Stew was always Stew. When I was three years old they gave me money to stop saying Uncle Stew."

Vinny walks up behind her. They finally walk into the house and join everyone again on the couches. An hour later we all fall asleep.

Cody carries me to bed. When he lays me in our bed, I wrap my arms around him and sleep soundly. "Cody, I love you."

"I love you too." He says.

In the morning I wake up first. I get out of bed and get into my wheelchair. I leave the bedroom where Cody sleeps soundly. I go in the kitchen and make myself a cup of coffee. Landon walks in the kitchen.

"I can make you one." I say.

"No. I have already had a cup." Landon says. "How are you?"

"I am excited about today."

"You look very beautiful." He says. "No sad eyes."

I look at him and smile. I had said the same thing to him years ago. I had told him that he looked handsome and although he was mourning his brother I told him that there were no sad eyes.

Landon puts his hand on top of my hand. "Can I ask you a question that I hope will not make you cry?"

I look at him and smile. "I might cry, but my day is going to end with me belonging to a family that wants me. You and your family have made me feel so loved."

"Me?" He asks.

"In your Landonish way."

"My Landonish way? Is that a thing?"

"It is a thing." I say.

Cody walks in the kitchen. He takes my ice coffee off the table and takes a big sip. He puts the cup back on the table. "What's a thing?"

Landon smiles. "She said that something was Landonish."

Cody kisses me. "Are you ready for today?"

"My whole life."

"How is it going to work? Who is going to walk you down the isle?" Landon asks.

"You and Kyle." Cody says.

"Who's your best man?"

"You and Kyle. Brandon, Rayf, and Vinny."

I smile at Cody. "That's very nice of you."

"It's a family thing." Cody says.

"What about Trevor?"

"We asked him and he said that he wants to just sit and watch." Cody says.

"What about on the bride's side?"

I look at him. "We are eloping. There is no one on my side."

"What about your sisters? My sister? Your friends?" Landon asks.

"This is a Landonish moment." I say.

"What time are you going over to the resort?" Cody asks me.

"I am going to head over there at ten."

"You look beautiful." Cody tells me.

Landon smiles. "I am pretty?"

"You are pretty." I say. "Are you sure you aren't a girl?"

He leaps up from his chair and rubs his knuckles on my head.

"Landon! What the hell are you doing to the bride?" Gianna asks.

"She will be a bride later, but right now she is bothering me." Landon says.

"You are being Landonish." I smile.

"Landonish?" Gianna asks. "Yes that fits him."

When I get to the resort where Cody and my life started its whirlwind love, there is a crowd of women standing outside. They are all holding parasols. When I see them, I smile brightly. Emma runs over and hugs me.

"Emmy, I love you." I say.

"Don't cry. There were be no tears today." She says. "You look beautiful."

Oscar walks over and hugs me. I hug him. "You are here!" I say.

"Where else would I be? The most beautiful bride is getting married today." Marcus says hugging tight. "No tears today unless they are happy tears."

Emma goes back and joins the line of women who are family and friends. She closes her parasol and everyone follows her direction. As I pass by each of them, they hug me and open their parasol making an arch for me to go under. This was something that I had mentioned to Emma when we would get lost in conversations about what we wanted in our lives. I didn't think she was listening to me when we were having this conversation.

When I enter the lobby, Kent and Pam are standing next to Casper and Christian. They all hug me. Kent takes my hand. "Hi. You know, you and your kissing have caused this place to flourish."

I look at him.

"Its true. Every woman that comes in this lobby wants to be met by her own version of Cody and wants to be kissed like he kissed you. Hell, I am waiting for my version of Cody to come kiss me the way that he kissed you." Kent says.

"Where are you taking me?" I ask.

"Its your wedding day princess. Let us get you ready for your prince." Kent is still holding my hand and takes me into the salon.

A guy comes over and takes a strand of my hair in his fingers. "Oh my goodness, Bella, lets get you ready for your beast." He smiles. "I am Zac. Let me get you blown out and styled." He sashays. He winks at Kent. He moves the chair and directs me how he wants me. He turns me away from the mirror. He takes the blow dryer and starts straightening my hair. When he was done with the blow dryer he takes the curler and makes big curls. He takes a comb with a long pick at the end and separates the curls. "Shake your head from side to side."

I do. "Can I look?" I ask.

"Not yet." Zac says. He clicks his fingers and like a genie a woman walks over with a box and hands it to Zac. He opens the box. "Close your eyes." I do. Zac starts putting makeup on my face.

"Can I look?" I ask with excitement in my tone.

"No."

"Now?" I ask.

"No." Zac says. "Stop or I will draw lightning bolts on your cheeks." I laugh. "No."

"Stop talking and moving." Zac says. He puts more makeup on my face. He puts his fingers on the side of my eye and pulls the skin to apply eyeliner. When he finishes he taps my forehead softly. "Open your eyes." Again when I follow his directions, he takes the mascara and applies it.

"Can I look now?" I ask.

"Almost ready." He says. He clicks his fingers again and the same woman walks over with my wedding dress. She pulls over the most beautiful Chinese privacy screen that I have ever seen. "Ok hands up." Zac says. He pulls the shirt over my head and then helps me with my dress. He covers the mirrors so I can't see myself yet and has me stand up so he can close up my dress. "Fucking Casper with all these fucking buttons."

I laugh. "It's a zipper."

He opens the dress up a bit and then finds the zipper. "Are you ok. I am going to take pictures of the back of your dress for you."

"I can stand for a minute."

"That's all I need." I hear Oscar's voice.

Marcus is the one who starts snapping away. He finishes quickly.

Zac removes the sheets that cover the mirror. When I see myself in the mirrors I gasp. I know my own beauty without being conceited, but I have never looked this beautiful. Marcus and Oscar start taking pictures of me. They are such experts that they capture the image of me alone in the mirror.

Casper walks in the salon and pulls the back of the dress up a bit so that I am comfortable when I sit. He fans the dress out when I adjust my legs. Zac squats in front of me and lifts my dress a bit. He slips my shoes off my feet and puts heals on me. He pulls the dress down and fans my hair around my shoulders. The last thing he does is attach the vail to my hair. Casper steps behind me and attaches the train to the back of my wheelchair like I wanted.

Marcus wipes tears out of his eyes. "You are the most beautiful bride I have ever fucking seen. And we have seen some beautiful brides. Crystal, its an honor to be able to capture you on your day."

I reach my hand out to him. "Thank you." I say. "I love you guys."

The Chinese screen is removed and a wall of mirrors fills with only me. I gasp again. "Oh my god! I have never looked this beautiful a day in my life."

Zac stands next to me. "Bella, I just accented your beauty. You are beautiful everyday. Your beauty radiates from your kindness. Its going to be an honor working with you."

I look at him.

Casper looks at me. "My wedding gift to you is making you my wedding planner for my biggest venue."

Now I look at Casper. "What are you talking about?"

"I wanted to open another bridal shop here and have you run it, but after a million meetings, we—" he points to everyone in the room. Zac, Kent, Pam, my photographers and the staff at the resort. "After a million meetings, we have decided that you are the best one and the only one that they would work with." He kisses the top of my head.

"If you ruin my creation, I will slap the shit out of you." Zac says.

I laugh.

"Do not laugh at him." Casper says. "I will fire his ass."

"Not today." I say.

"Come on Bella." Zac says. "Your beast waits for you."

"My lover boy." I say his nickname that I usually never say because its such a negative reminder for him of the life that he led. But its true. He is my lover boy.

"That boy has brought a lot of people to this resort in hopes of getting kissed like you shared with that beast." He looks at me. "I call him beast not as in insult."

"Zac, I know who you are. I am glad to see that you found your way but you were just as much a beast on the baseball field as my lover boy." I say.

"You know who I am?" Zac asks. He smiles. "Lets get you married. Before I fight you for him."

I laugh. I start giggling and can't stop.

Casper looks at me. "Pull yourself together." He says in a light tone.

"Do you know what he said about your dress?" I ask still giggling.

Casper looks at Zac. "I will stab you." He threatens lightheartedly.

I giggle more.

Zac smiles. He looks at me. "Its not too late to draw lightning fucking bolts on your cheeks."

I laugh uncontrollably.

Chapter Twenty-five

Cody stands looking at himself in the full length mirror. Landon puts his hand on his brother's shoulder. "What's the matter?" Landon asks.

"I am nervous." Cody says.

"Why?"

"What if she decides that I am not the right one for her?"

"Cody, stop thinking that you aren't worth it. You are. She loves you. She has loved you for so long. I know her love for you is true. The truest. Remember, she didn't know that your family was your family. She didn't know that I am your brother. I saw her love for you. Her passion for baseball was outrageous, she loved the game, but she loved watching you. You made her talents stand out. She was like a kid in a candy store and she couldn't get enough. When she finished her segments she would whisper to no one how much she loved you. She meant it then and she means it now."

Kyle walks over to Cody and hugs him. "For the love of god, my sister has waited her whole life for you. When you kissed her in the lobby of this very resort, you encompassed her in love that she has been craving her whole life."

Brandon walks in the room. "Oh my god, wait until you see her. She is breathtaking." He takes his phone out and shows Landon and Kyle.

"I want to see." Cody says.

"Oh no." Christian says. He looks at Brandon. "Don't make me hurt you."

Brandon smiles. Landon smiles too.

Kyle looks at Cody. "What are you worried about?"

"I have a reputation."

"My sister doesn't give a rats ass about your reputation. She loves you unconditionally. She has wanted to have you her whole life. Well as long as she knew who you were. Believe me, this is the day of her dreams."

Sawyer walks in the room. "I know you are technically eloping and we aren't supposed to be here, but we couldn't stay away if you paid us to. That girl is the most beautiful girl I have ever seen. There are brides and then there is her. She is breathtaking. I have seen some beautiful brides in my day at weddings that your mom and I have attended and they have been beautiful, but I will tell you one thing, not one of them compares to the way Crystal Bella Steele looks right now."

"Dad, what if I am not good enough?" He says.

Sawyer looks at everyone in the room. "Please leave us."

Everyone leaves the room. Brandon walks back in and hands Cody a picture that Oscar printed for him. "Just one thing before I leave. Look at the smile on her face, you are the only one that has made her smile so brightly. She shines when she talks about you. She radiates when you are near her. She can't wait to be your wife. Just look at that smile. You are the one who does that for her." He leaves the room and pushes the lock on the inside of the door before he leaves so that they can be left alone for as long as they need.

Sawyer sits on an ottoman and points to the other one for Cody to sit on. "Cody, you want to talk it out? I know that I have missed big moments in your life, but I think this is one of the biggest." He looks at the picture. Inside Emma's parasol is a picture of Cody. The smile on my face is genuine. "The smile on her face is for you. Look at the picture."

Cody takes the picture and looks at it. He sees that all my friends and family members are standing outside of the resort have parasols and each one has a different image of him. Emma's parasol has the picture of him holding me close to him after that baseball game I went to and there was a crazed fan.

"Son, she is the one who embarrassed your mom and me about all the wonderful things that we missed knowing about you. I have to apologize for that. A lot of it was because I was grieving. I know we all were. I didn't know that every time you hit a home run you had Donavan's bear in your pocket."

Cody looks at Sawyer. "How did you know that? No one knew that?"

"Someone did know it. She pointed it out to me when we sat watching your playback."

"Who?"

"Your mother."

Cody puts his elbows on his knees and puts his head in his hands. "I am sorry. I took it and had it with me from the day of the accident. I had to have him with me." Cody cries. "I loved him. I should have been there. I didn't know that he was going to get on the four-wheeler by himself. By the time Gianna and I got back, he was already lying on the ground and there was so much blood. Dad, Landon had so much blood on him, I thought that they were both bleeding. Landon wouldn't let him go. Landon wouldn't let me see if I could help. Donavan begged me to take him and I was going to come back and get him, but I wanted to open it up with Gianna."

Sawyer stands up, he crosses the distance between them and squats in front of Cody. He puts his hand on Cody's shoulder. "Cody, your brother knew that you all loved him. I am sorry again. I knew how much you, Landon and Gianna wanted to go. I should have let the three of you go. Your mom wanted a chance to have me all to herself. She had been traveling a lot and when she was home, I wasn't. I should have kept Donavan with us. I didn't realize—"

Cody throws himself on top of Sawyer and sobs. "I am sorry." Cody says.

"Stop. Stop. I have learned more about you, Landon and Gianna from Crystal than I ever knew on my own. I am your dad. I have failed."

"No." Cody says.

"Dry your eyes." Sawyer hugs him. "I didn't want to come in here and make you cry like your sweet soon to be wife did yesterday. My heart breaks for her."

"Dad, she thinks that I am perfect. I am far from it."

"She knows that you are not perfect. Cody, she sees the best in you and likes to point it out as much as she can. You do the same for her. She does that about all of my children. She did it too about Donavan. I feel that she is a blessing. She sees the good in everyone she knows."

"Dad, I always wanted to find someone that would love me for me. She loves me for me."

"So then what are you worried about?"

"She sees through me."

"She sees your heart and she wants her heart to beat with it."

"I don't know that I can give her enough love. I don't want to disappoint her."

"Cody, look at me."

Cody lifts his head.

"Just kiss her everyday. When you kiss her, she feels your love for her leave you and enter her. That's what she told your mom." He stands up and takes Cody's hand. "Your princess is waiting for you and she looks stunning."

"How did you see her?"

"She is waiting for you." Sawyer says. "She asked me to escort her down the isle."

"What?" Cody asks incredulously.

"She said that when she met me, the second that you introduced the two of us in the driveway of my house and I hugged her, she felt like she was being hugged by a dad who loved her."

"She's amazing."

"You are amazing."

He looks at himself in the mirror. "Its time I go wait for my bride."

Kyle and Brandon wait for me outside the room that I am waiting in for the time to pass until its ready. Kent walks over to them. He nods his head. Kyle knocks on the door. "Sweetheart, its time."

I screech. I open the door. Brandon saw me in my dress, but Kyle didn't. When the door opens, Kyle looks at me. He puts his hand to his chest and he smiles.

"Oh my god, you are the most beautiful bride." Kyle says.

"I told you she looks beautiful." Brandon says.

Kelsey walks in the room and picks the train up so that it doesn't drag on the floor until its time. As I always planned it in my dreams, Kyle stands on one side of my wheelchair and Brandon on the other. They each put their hand on the handles meant for a companion to push a wheelchair. Kelsey stands a distance behind as my train is six feet long.

We get to the doors of the chapel and they are closed so that no one can see me until its time. Violins play Vivaldi's Spring and the doors are opened. I see Cody standing at the alter waiting for me. All of his friends stand beside him. Jonathan, Becker, Todd, Bruce, Logan, Rayf, Vinny and Trevor all stand in line as groomsmen. The only two missing are the two walking me down the isle.

All of my friends are standing at the back of the chapel waiting for me. Monica is the surprise. She is holding a satin pillow in the shape of a heart. Kent and Zac hold the doors open and Zac gives the signal. My friends stand on either side of the isle. They are strategically staggered at the end of the pews.

I want to take control of my wheelchair and rush the isle to join hands with Cody, but the music playing softly by three violinists stops me from doing anything fast. My brothers push me down the isle. Ashley is the first one to join us and hands me a parasol to hold in front of myself. A beautiful Chinese print that matches the screen from earlier is in front of me so that Cody, can't see all of me. One by one, my friends step out of the pew that they were in and line the isle. Ten of our women friends lead the way down the isle. Once they get to the alter, they take their spots that they picked themselves.

Sawyer takes my hand and my brothers continue their descend down the isle. Kelsey finally lets the train fall into place and fans it out. Its narrow at the top to accommodate my wheelchair. Then it fans out. It was exactly what I had told Casper that I wanted.

Marcus stands taking pictures. When Kelsey takes the parasol from me and closes it handing it to Kent, everyone who sits in the pews gasps. They are all seated so that everyone can see me go down the isle. Kelsey takes her place as my Maid-of-Honor.

The alter doesn't have any steps to go up. Its just a small ramp and then a wooden stage area. Kelsey steps closer to me and changes the position of the train. Sawyer places my hands in Cody's hands. Kyle and Brandon join the line of men.

When I turn my head, I see that my mom, Stew, dad, and Joanna are all here. So are my aunt and uncle. Grammy is here too. All the guests that were supposed to come help us start our lives together are all here to see us do just that.

Trevor steps off the line and stands on the stage alter. He is the one that wanted more than anything to officiate our wedding. Monica stands next to him holding the pillow that have the two rings on it. They are tied down on the lace pillow with the most beautiful ribbon that matches the train.

Trevor opens the book that he has. He clears his throat. "Thank you all for coming to join Cody Parker and Crystal Bella Steele." He looks at the two of us. He puts his hand on Cody's shoulder and then on my shoulder. "Love is patient." He starts. He recites the Bible verse to us. When he finishes, he looks at Cody. "Cody Parker, do you take Crystal Bella Steele to be your wife? To have and hold from this day forward?"

Cody takes my hand in his hand and holds it to his lips. "I do."

"Crystal Steele, do you take Cody Parker to be your husband? To have and to hold from this day forward?"

I take Cody's hand and kiss it. I look into his eyes. "I do."

Monica steps forward and hands us each matching silver wedding bands. I take the one Monica hands me. I slip it on Cody's finger. Cody takes my right hand in his hand and slips the ring on my right hand as I am still wearing the diamond engagement ring. It sparkles.

"Now, we have reached the part that everyone has waited for, but I am sure something we have all seen them do a lot." The chapel fills with laughter. "Cody, you may kiss your bride."

He steps to the side of my wheelchair and takes me in his arms. He kisses me just like he did when he first kissed me. The kiss is warm and tender. The kiss is something that I will never get bored of. It's a kiss that will stay on my lips from this moment until forever.

Everyone cheers.

"I now pronounce you husband and wife." Trevor says.

We are moved on the wooden floor to the center of it. Amber takes Dillon's hand and they walked to the back of the chapel. They are followed by Heather and Jonathan. They are followed by Stephanie and Becket. Emma and Bruce come next. Lynn takes Todd's hand. Brittany takes Logan's hand and they walk side by side the four of them down the isle.

Lacey beams at Kyle. She leans against him and kisses his lips. She laces her fingers with Kyle's. Paige reaches her hand out to Landon. She laces her fingers with his. She presses her shoulder against Landon's. Gianna is the next one to enter the isle. Rayf puts his arm around her waist and she fits herself right under his arm. Kelsey is the last one. Vinny joins her in the isle on one side and Trevor joins them with Kelsey sandwiched between them.

Each couple lines either side of the isle. All the men hold baseball bats. The women hold the parasols up like bats. Violins again start playing softly Cannon in D. Cody takes my hand and we go down the isle. As we do our friends and family make and arch for us. We leave the chapel and they all follow after us.

Marcus and Oscar take endless pictures. We are ushered into the lobby. Trevor announces to the crowd of people that are standing around to see the bride and groom. "Please welcome for the first time, Mr. and Mrs. Cody Parker." He announces. Cheers come from everywhere. "Family and guests, please make your way to atrium two." He looks at the two of us with pride. "Congratulations." He looks at me. "Show him your something borrowed."

I smile at Trevor. Cody looks at me. I lean to the side and reach behind me. I pull out that dancing teddy bear that I bought for Donavan. I hand it to Cody. He wraps his arms around me and kisses me deeply.

"I love you." He says.

"I love you." I say.

Trevor looks at the two of us. "We are going to get everything set up. There is a half hour window for you to do your wedding pictures." He looks at me. "Thank you for welcoming me into your family and allowing me to officiate your wedding."

"We didn't want anyone else." I tell him.

"Atrium one is waiting for you for your wedding photos." He says.

"Where are you going?" I ask him.

"To wait with the other guests?"

"Trevor, you are going to be family when you marry my sister. You are part of our wedding party. You have to be in the pictures." I tell him.

Vinny kisses me on the cheek. "Congratulations."

"Thank you." I say.

"I am going to—"

"Join us for photos." I say. "You are part of the wedding party."

Mom walks over and hugs me. She hugs Cody and then she hugs me again. "I am so proud of you." She takes my hands in her hands. "I am sorry."

I shake my head. "We will do that conversation once Cody and I get back from our Honeymoon."

"Where are you going?" Mom asks.

"We are going to Washington state for five days and then Hawaii for thirteen days." Cody says.

"I am so happy for the two of you."

Joanna walks over. She taps me on the shoulder. "I have been to many weddings, you are one of the most beautiful brides I have ever seen. Thank you for having your dad and me." She kisses me on the cheek. "Congratulations." She says.

"Thank you." We say together.

Dad walks over next. He hugs Cody. He hugs me. "You look stunning."

"Thank you." I say.

Stew walks over and I have mixed emotions. I want him to take me in his arms and hug me like he has done my whole life, he has always been the one person that has been there for every milestone in my life. But I am compelled too to just close my eyes and make him just walk away. Stew is the reason why I was able to be with Cody before we ever officially met. Stew let me stay with Cody in the room for as long as I wanted. I can't fault Stew for not saying anything. I blame my mother fully for this.

He doesn't give me an option, he takes me in a hug like he has done so many times in my life. "I am so proud of you. My beautiful girl."

They all make their way to the atrium where the photos are going to be taken. The parents photos are done first. That includes Cody's Grammy. When we do the picture with her, she tries to stand between Cody and myself. Cody stands behind the frame of my wheelchair and puts his hand on my shoulder. Grammy stands next to me.

Once the last wedding party photograph is snapped, everyone leaves Cody and me alone with Marcus and Oscar.

Cody takes my hand and we walk over to the waterfall. Cody positions my wheelchair in front of the waterfall and kisses me. When Marcus gets all the images he wants, we move on to the next location. Cody picks me up out of my wheelchair and sits on a bench. We look at each other and put our foreheads together.

Marcus looks at Cody. "We want to capture one more. The two of you standing on the bridge."

I smile at Marcus.

"Don't look surprised. These are the same images that you would capture for brides that you plan for." He gives me a sign that reads Just Married. I hold it and he snaps photographs.

Cody stands and carries me to the bridge. He supports me while I find my balance in the heals. I can stand in them, but can not walk in them. I put my hands on the bridge to hold on and Cody stands behind me. He stands with his arms around me.

After we do these. We finally go to the gazebo where Cody and I danced together after his cousin's wedding. Cody and I stand together again.

He whispers in my ear. "What is your something blue?"

I smile at him. "The undergarments I am wearing."

"Really?" He asks.

"You will see later."

"What's your something new?"

"I have to sit." I say.

He lifts me in his arms and walks over to the bench and sits down. I am again on his lap. "What is your something new?"

I pull my hair away from my shoulder to reveal a blue infinity symbol with our names tattooed on my shoulder. "I love you." I tell him.

"I love you." He says back.

We finally make our way to the other atrium. When the doors are opened for us, we are welcome with the smell of sweet flowers and food. Everyone stands waiting for us to come in. Stew starts clapping his hands and everyone joins in. There is a table set up in the middle of the atrium underneath the dome. The glass that the dome is made out of sparkles and the sparkles shine all the way down to the floor. Rays of sunshine beam brightly. This place is beautiful.

A staff member walks over and removes the chair. "Congratulations." He says.

"Thank you." Cody and I say together.

The lunch is served not a moment too soon because everyone is starving. Grammy complains that she is so hungry. We have her favorite things for her to eat and drink just like I had for her at Jillian's wedding. She ate everything there happily. This time she complains about everything.

"We should have eloped in a far off land." Cody says,

I smile at him.

Landon sits next to Grammy, "I heard that these were all your favorite things that you wanted at Jillian's wedding."

"Well I had them there. I wanted something else." She says.

"Grandma, that's not how it works unless you pay for it."

"They didn't give me an option."

"You showed up." Landon says.

"To make sure that no one gets out of hand."

"Stop this." Landon says. "You told mom and dad how much you fell in love with her at Jillian's wedding."

"I did enjoy myself there." Grammy says.

"You will here too."

"I will try to enjoy myself."

Landon takes his champagne glass and raises it in the air. "To the bride and groom." Landon looks at us. "Cody! Kiss your bride."

The whole atrium erupts into cheers.

Casper brings the cake. I look at Emma. She smiles at me. I look at Cody and I can't contain my big smile. Cody looks at me.

"You had a cake of the baseball stadium made for me?" He asks.

"For us." I say and lean into him.

"That's not the cake that you picked."

"It is the cake that I picked. The design is for you."

He gets up and looks at it. He sees that no detail has been left out. The score board reads Cody Parker. There are eatable players on the bases and he is up to bat. Cody walks back and kisses me. "I don't deserve you."

I look at him."You deserve more."

"No. I am not trading you for anything."

"I am not trading you either. I love you." I wrap my arms around his neck. "You deserve me." I whisper in his ear. "I know all your secrets."

He kisses me again and again. "Its true. You know more than anyone I have ever met in my life."

"We need to cut the cake so that we can eat it and get the hell out of here."

He laughs.

"I need you. I am hungry."

He laughs again. "There is a lot of food here."

"What I want to have is not on the menu." I say.

"Everyone told me you are an angel. I believed it until now." He kisses my lips again. "Kyle warned me abut you."

I laugh.

My dad watches me and sees how happy I am. He walks over to mom and sits next to her. "When was the last time you saw her that happy."

Kyle sits with them. "The day that Kels and I took her to school. She put her earbud in her ear as she started the interview process. Cody was playing in his first professional game and she didn't want to miss a minute. She listened to the interviewer and asked questions. She interviewed well. Then it was the next person's time. Cody hit a home run and she smiled brightly and started doing play-by-plays. She was fucking amazing."

I look over at the three of them and without hearing what Kyle just said, I know what he said. My parents look at me like Cody's parents looked at him when I bragged about all his great plays. Only I know Kyle is talking about me."

Kelsey walks over and kisses Kyle on the top of his head. "You're talking about when we saw her smile and happy like that?"

"Yes." He says.

Mom looks at Kelsey. "Who are you going to marry? And when?"

Kelsey looks at mom. "I am dating two guys." She says honestly.

"I know. Which one will you marry?"

"I may not marry ever." She says. "I want to live happy." She looks at me and Cody. "I want to feel the way she feels right now. Look how happy she is."

Brandon takes champagne and clicks his knife on the glass. "Kiss! Kiss!" He says. He takes Ashley in his arms and kisses her. Kyle finds Lacey and kisses her. Vinny walks over and takes Kelsey in his arms and kisses her. Cody kisses me. Rayf kisses Gianna.

We take the cake knife and we each hold it. We cut the cake together. When we cut into the cake, cheers sound from a speaker somewhere like we are in a stadium.

"Crystal and Cody hold the cake knife together and they slice into the cake as they make their first move together as husband and wife. Now they are going to put the one piece they cut together on a plate. They each take a fork and dig it into the cake. Cody squats down a bit and they each raise the forks to each other's lips. Nicely, I might add." Landon announces. "They both look over at the younger, very handsome brother and — they glare." He says.

We all laugh.

He raises his glass in the air. "To my brother and his wife, my new sister. I love you both very much."

Christian walks over and cuts cake for all the guests. The staff hand cake to all the guests. Grammy takes a bite of her cake. "Carrot! Who the hell has a carrot wedding cake?"

Sawyer looks at her. "Carrot cake brought them together." He says smiling.

I look at my father-in-law. "Don't change my story around to make him an angel. He ate my carrot cake. He knew it wasn't his cake." I say smiling.

Cody kisses me. "It was meant for me."

"I would have shared a crumb." I laugh.

"It was too delicious to share." Cody says.

"I know. It was mine."

Landon smiles. "Kiss her!" He tells Cody.

Cody Parks the famous singer takes the stage. He plays the opening to Take Me Out To The Ball Game. Then he plays Because of You. He sings A Thousand Years next and we dance again. The first dance leads to us dancing for the whole set of songs.

Cody Parks starts playing Butterfly Kisses and Stew walks over to me. He takes me in his arms and dances with me. While Cody sings the song, Stew kisses my forehead. "I love you."

"I am not ready to talk. Don't make me cry on my wedding day."

"Will you ever forgive me?"

"Now is not the time to talk about this."

"Please. I have loved you from the time that I held you in the hospital the day you were born. I wasn't married to your mother, but I loved her like she was mine. You were conceived in love, little girl."

"Please stop." I say.

Dad walks over and Stew steps aside. Cody Parks plays on his guitar What A Wonderful World. Cody dances with his mother to that song. Dad stands on the side of my wheelchair and holds me as we sway to the music. "I never wanted you to find out like this." He says.

"Dad please. Not now."

When the song ends Kyle and Brandon walk over. The playlist that they planned starts playing Isn't She Lovely. Both of them get on their knees on either side of my wheelchair and they both dance with me. Kyle takes me in his arms. "I love you so much. I am so proud of the woman you are and I am extremely happy for you and Cody."

Cody walks over and takes my hand. "I need to dance with my wife."

I smile brightly. "I need to dance with my husband."

Cody holds me in his arms while we dance. "You look very serious."

"I am ok." I say.

"Crystal, I can read you like a book and I know that's not true."

"Cody, please. This is our wedding day. I want us to be happy. I can deal with my family crap when we get back from our honeymoon."

"Crystal, you made this so spectacular."

"Casper and Christian made this day happen."

"Not all of it. I know your touches when I see them. I am so grateful." Cody says.

Cody Parks takes the microphone and taps on it. "Hello! Hello!" He says excitedly. "My name is Cody Parks and I have been friends with Cody Parker, the groom, since we were four and a half years old. While I am not his best man, but I should have been at least considered. I have seen Cody through his whole life grow into the person that he is today, but the truth is, I was here in this very resort that my friend, who I share with Kyle, but only when Kyle lets him go for a while. Anyway, I was here that night that Cody Parker kissed Crystal Steele. It was like we were standing in the most magical place on earth and someone set off fireworks inside the lobby. They connected in an instant. The truth is, they have had encounters with each other before that kiss that was seen all over the world.

"My friend and I were in a store in Indiana. Crystal needed help reaching something and she looked at Cody and asked him to reach something for her. He did. Then he paid for her items." He looks at Cody and me. "Cody told me that he fell in love with the woman with pink hair in Target. Congratulations!"

Kyle takes the microphone next. "Thank you Cody." He says to Cody Parks. "Everyone here knows that I don't like to share Cody. He is my best friend. We have been friends since high school and we went to college together. My sister fell in love with Cody the moment she laid eyes on him. Much like Cody Parks was saying, they had encounters. Brief meetings in life. I never believed in fate until I saw these two keep finding each other. I too was here that night Cody kissed my sister, and sparks could be seen. Crystal was a commentator and would give the best play-by-plays for any sport that she covered, but her favorite sport was baseball and covering Cody's games was the ultimate cherry on the top of the ice cream. Cody had a lot of home runs which by themselves were exciting. Listening to the joy in my sister's voice when she narrated that her favorite Cody Parker hit a home run or her absolute favorite a grand slam home run, she couldn't contain her excitement. They both found the perfect match for each other. I love you both very much. Congratulations!"

Landon takes the microphone next. "Hi everyone. I have known Cody my whole life as I am his younger brother. I have known Crystal a long time as we went to college together. I first heard her voice on the radio talking sports. And much like Kyle said she couldn't contain her excitement when she was talking about Cody. I set out to meet the woman who spoke highly of my brother even when he had off days."

Cody nods his head at Landon. I smile at him.

"Crystal didn't know that Cody and I were brothers. She found that out much later. I know that my brother searched his whole life for the woman who matched his kindness, sees the good in him and sees past the façade that he wanted people to see. We had a loss in our lives, a big one. Crystal went with me and was so supportive of me. Her kindness was the one that my brother was searching for.

"Cody was, as most of you know, attacked and required surgery. I don't know how Crystal did it, but she found out where he was and she went and stayed with him in ICU. A crazed fan went to the hospital and claimed that she was there to see—" he chokes on Donavan's name. "Don-a-van Parker. The woman was very loud and Crystal threw the blanket over Cody and held his hand tightly protecting him. The woman had a knife. She kept him safe. Cody thought he made her up in his dreams. He told me that if he ever found her, he was never going to let her go." He looks at Cody and me. "Don't ever let anyone or anything come between the two of you. You are meant for each other. I love you both deeply. Congratulations."

Kelsey walks over to the stage area and she takes the microphone from Landon. "I am going to speak on behalf of my sister and myself. I am the older sister and Ashley is the youngest sister. We are so grateful and we feel blessed to have Crystal as our sister. She and Cody are very much a like. They like to do good things for people without getting anything in return. Sometimes a thank you is offered to each of them for what they do, but they don't do it for any other reason than to just give back. My sister, Crystal, has shown up for everyone in this room because she wanted to show support for whatever event you were doing. Ashley and I are dancers as well as Gianna, and Crystal has shown up for so many of our programs." She looks at me and smiles brightly. She looks at Cody and then finds Catalina and Sawyer. "I had the honor of dancing with a beloved angel Donavan. He was excited to find out that my sister was going to watch the show. After it was over, he went out in the lobby and found Crystal. She bought him something and he gave her his signed playbill. They have touched each and everyone's life who is in this room celebrating their union." She looks at me and smiles. "I want to be kissed by someone who loves me as much as Cody loves you. Congratulations! I am so happy for both of you." She gives the microphone back to Cody Parks.

Brandon walks over to the stage. "Hi everyone, I am not going to talk long. I know everyone is ready to say our goodbyes to the bride and groom. All of you have said everything about these two but I need to take credit for something." He walks over to me and hugs me. He walks back over to the stage area. "The truth is, I am no good at sports. I loved baseball but playing it was not in the cards for me. But Crystal knew that I knew the ins and outs of baseball, so she sat with me and really learned what she wanted to know. When she and I watched baseball games, we would do play-by-plays. I did it just to make sure she was getting the concepts. She picked it up quickly. She watched Cody play college baseball and knew when he was having an off day just watching him take the plate. Someone heard her positive criticism and told the coach. He brought it to Cody's attention and the rest is history. I have a love like the one that Crystal always wanted and found in Cody." He looks from Cody to me. "Love each other always. Congratulations. I love you very much. I am honored to be your brother, Crystal. And Cody, I am honored to call you family now." He raises his glass. "To the bride and groom!"

Everyone cheers.

We wind up staying a long time. We lose track of time. Everyone is having a great time. We dance. At the end of the night, the lights in the atrium dim and it looks like there are fireflies all in the plants. It looks so pretty. Then the lights go even dimmer and fireworks erupt overhead.

I lean against Cody. We watch the fireworks. Cody wraps his arms around me and I close my eyes for a brief moment. Before I know it, I don't remember watching another firework or if there were any more at all.

Chapter Twenty–six

I open my eyes to the sun shining brightly in the room. I sit up as fast as I can. My wedding dress is hanging on a hanger on the bathroom door. I look around the room. I am alone. I look at the clock on the wall.

"No! It can't be eleven. Oh my god! I slept through my wedding night!" I get in my wheelchair and get my clothes. I get dressed quickly. I look around. "Cody!" I am totally alone in the hotel room that we shared that first night we met.

I leave the room. I try not to run to the lobby but I can't help it. I feel tears burning my eyes. I rush into the lobby. Kent greets me. When he hugs me, I burst into tears.

"What? What is that for?" Kent says sweetly in my ear.

"Do you know where Cody is?" I ask through my tears.

"Crystal?" Cody asks from behind me.

I pull away from Kent and his warm embrace and look at Cody.

He runs over. "What's the matter?"

I hug him and put my head against his chest. Tears soak the front of his shirt.

"What?" He asks.

"I ruined our wedding night." I cry.

"You didn't ruin anything." Cody says. He gets on his knees next to me.

"I fell asleep."

"I know. You didn't ruin anything." He kisses me. "I heard from almost everyone who knows you that when you plan weddings, you work so hard to make everything perfect that you usually don't make it past the fireworks. You were telling me time and time again that you were tired. I should have listened to you."

"No. I was excited to get to the wedding night."

"The wedding night can be anytime. How are you?"

I put my arms around his neck. "Cody, I am so sorry."

"Stop." He says. "We have the rest of our lives together."

"I don't want to disappoint you."

"Crystal, you bring out the best in me. You don't disappoint me. You make me extremely happy. I have never been more happy than I have been since I met you." He kisses me. "Our lives started last night as husband and wife, I am so grateful that you came into my life."

"Cody, get off your knees."

"Before we leave for our honeymoon, we are going to have lunch with my family."

"Our family." I say. I smile brightly. "Lets do it." I look at him once he stands up. "Where were you?"

"I had to go deal with something before it got out of control."

I look at him. "Should we delay our honeymoon?"

"No way." He says.

"Is your team coming together nicely?"

"My team?" He asks.

"My wedding gift to you."

"What?"

"Well the whole team isn't your's but you are the head batting coach."

He steps back. "What did you do?"

"We can chat about it on the way to your parents'. My in-laws." I say with a big smile on my face. "Guess what?" I ask Cody.

"What?"

"I finally have a family that loves me."

I hear a gasp from behind me and I know that its my mother. I lift my chin as I turn around. My mother looks at me and I can tell that she has been crying. The red rims around her eyes are not from recent. She looks at me. "I hope that you are happy." She says.

"I have waited my whole life to feel the way I do right now." I say honestly.

"We would like to see you when you return from your honeymoon."

"We would love that." Cody says. He is glowing just as bright as I am.

Kent is the one to comment on the glow. "You are both shining brighter than the sunshine."

"My wife bought me a baseball team." Cody says.

Kent looks at me. "You bought your husband a baseball team?"

I smile brightly. "He is the batting coach for the professionals."

Mom looks at me. "You did this for him?"

I look at her. "He did this. He was the best batter in the MLB. I am so proud of him. I have always been proud of him and now he is mine." I take Cody's hand in mine. "He didn't need me to get the job for him that he has been gunning for. If some woman didn't have him beaten up, he would still be playing. She could have just broken up with him and let him live the life he was meant to have."

"Crystal, it was meant to be. You and me together. The things that you did for each one of my family members goes above and beyond anything that I could have done on a baseball field."

I shake my head.

Mom looks at me. "Why are you shaking your head?"

"Every time Cody hit a home run, single or grand slam." I smile when I say grand slam. "He would give his entire paycheck to charity. Or pay off someone's medical bills."

Kent smiles. "Its just two do-gooders that found each other." He smiles at the two of us. Then he gags. "So annoying." He says laughing.

We laugh.

"Mr. Parker, I wanted to let you know that your room will always be available for you and Crystal anytime you come back. It will not be used by anyone else and the renovations will start on it early next week." Kent says.

I look at Cody. "You purchased our room?"

"It means a lot to me." Cody says.

I smile brightly again. "I am so excited."

Mom wipes her eyes. Tears fall from the corners of her eyes. I look at her. I look at Cody. "Do I have time to talk to my mom?"

"Sweetheart, you don't have to ask." Cody says.

"I know we are going to see your family."

"Go talk to your mother." He says and kisses my forehead.

I kiss him on the lips. "Don't go far." I tell him.

"I will be chatting with Kent." Cody kisses me again. "Did you think that I left you?"

"I woke up and I was alone. I didn't know what to think." I say.

"Now that we are married, you are stuck with me forever."

"I am so grateful." I say.

Mom and I walk outside together and she sits under an umbrella. She sits rigid in the chair. I look at her.

"What's going on?" I ask her.

"No one is talking to me." She says.

"Why?"

"Stew is mad at me."

I roll my eyes. "You are both guilty of keeping major secrets. Why did you have an affair with him in the first place?"

"Jack thought that I trapped him when I got pregnant with Kelsey."

"Trapped him? You were married. What did he think was going to happen?"

She looks at me. "Would Cody think that you trapped him?"

"Are you crazy?" I ask her. "Cody would be elated. Don't compare me and Cody to you and Jack." I look at her and then look away. "Well he must have loved you enough to sleep with you again because you and he share Ashley."

"When Kelsey came along he wanted to stop with just her. He fell in love with her and didn't think he had the heart to love more than one child. He had met Joanna and they were dating. Stew came to visit and he and I always loved each other. I wanted to marry him."

"So why didn't you?"

"Stew and I fell in love. I got pregnant right away. We only slept together a few times. Stew came home and we had mind blowing sex. It was wonderful. I knew I was pregnant before Jack and I were back together. I kept it from him. I didn't keep it from Stew. Jack missed everyone of you girls being born. Stew was there for all three of you."

"Why are you telling me this now? I am leaving for my honeymoon."

"How did you know that Cody was the one that you wanted to spend the rest of your life with?"

"When I first met him, he held me in a hug and I never wanted him to let me go. From that point on, I wanted to marry him. We kept having run ins with each other. Every time I thought of him, I would smile brighter. I would hope to see him in a grocery store, or the mall, or in an air port."

"And what happened?"

"Every time I hoped and prayed to see him, I would. Then when I entered the lobby of this resort, I was checking in and I turned to leave the lobby and go to my room. Cody kissed me. I never wanted it to end. I wanted it so badly to last forever."

"I can tell you that I never felt that way about your — either Jack or Stew. I mean I loved them, but it wasn't like what you have with Cody. Its not like what Kelsey has with Trevor and the other guy."

I look at her. "Vinny." I say his name and glare at my mother. "You know his name. You were there that night that she danced in Boston."

My mother looks at me. "How did you know that?"

"I never missed a show for either of my sisters. Never. I moved mountains to get to see them perform. It meant the world to me to be there."

"How do you know that I was there?"

"I saw you with your lawyer friend. He was moving his hand up your dress the first night. The second, you saw me get removed from the theater and you hid behind him."

She ducks her head. "I am sorry."

"I vowed never to let anyone feel that way again. So on that note, I am going to find my husband and go get my honeymoon started."

"Stew wants to leave me."

"Mom! You have strung him along nearly thirty years. You don't commit. Its not them. Its you. Jack committed to Joanna. As much to my heart's contentment, when I thought he was my dad, he picked her and he is committed. Stew loves you. If he is moving on, he needs to. Everyone was hurt yesterday. That wasn't my intention. I love Jack and Stew. I love you too. The ones who always made me feel loved was Kyle and Brandon.

When I showed up to support them in whatever they were doing, they acknowledged me. They wanted me there."

"All I wanted to do was keep you protected."

"I will call you when we get to Seattle."

"I thought you were going to Hawaii."

"We have a five day layover in Seattle."

"Why?" She asks.

"Because that's where we are going to look for a home."

"You are moving across the country? I just got you back."

"You ignored me. I bother you."

She stands up from her chair and hugs me tight. "No. Never." She says.

"Mom, things will work out for you and Stew. They always do. He loves you."

"You hurt him."

"Not now." I say. I hug her. Then I leave her outside.

I find Cody right where he said he would be. He is leaning against the counter talking to Kent. I rush to him and put my arm around his waist. "Lets go have lunch with our family. I am starving." I say smiling.

Cody looks at me. "We have to delay our departure." He says.

"Tell me in the car."

"I will." He says. He looks at Kent. "We will see you later."

"Of course." Kent says. "If you need anything, please let me know. We will get you everything you need and want."

We leave the lobby and when we are outside, I look at Cody. "You said delay our departure. Is everything alright?"

"Jack is in the hospital." He says.

I look at Cody and then cover my face with my hands. "I was so mean to him and Stew yesterday and the days leading to our wedding. We have to go see him." I look up again and put my hands in my lap. "Please can we go?"

"Sweetheart, you don't have to ask. Of course we will go to the hospital to see Jack."

Tears flood my face. "Is he going to die?"

"Its not that serious, but we will go right now."

"What about your family?"

"They advise that we do this first. They understand."

"Did Joanne stab him?" I ask. I don't know why I blurted it out but the words are out of my mouth before I can stop them.

Cody smiles at me. "I am not sure." He says. "There was an accident. That's all I was told."

The valet attendant brings the car up to the front. I get in the front seat and Cody puts the wheelchair in the trunk. He gets in the car and drives to Boca Raton which is about a half hour drive on I-95. He gets off at the exit 45. He heads east to the hospital. Cody parks the car and we get out.

"Why Boca?" I ask.

"He was air lifted." Cody says.

"Air lifted?" I ask. "Oh my god, is he going to die?"

Brandon runs over and hugs me. "Thanks for coming."

"Of course. He's my dad."

The three of us walk into the lobby. Kelsey and Ashley are in there with Kyle. They all walk over and hug me.

"What happened?" I ask. "Have you seen him?"

"We have all seen him." Brandon says.

"Is it bad?" I ask. I reach for Cody's hand and he grabs it and holds my hand and steps closer to me.

"He was in an accident." Kelsey says.

"I need to see him." I say.

Kyle holds out his hand to me and I take it but I don't let go of Cody's hand. I look around the lobby and see that Vinny is there and Trevor are sitting next to Lacey. Everyone looks miserable. I see Joanna sitting by herself. When I pull my hand out of Kyle's grasp he looks at me.

"You ok?" He asks.

"Is she ok?"

He looks over at his mother and then back at me. "We aren't talking to her."

"Why?"

"We will let you read the police report." He says. He reaches for my hand again and takes my hand in both of his hands this time. "Come see him. He requires surgery and they were waiting until you came."

We walk down the hallway and the smells catch in my nose. The last time I was in the hospital it was to see Cody. Kyle walks down the hallway which seems to never end. When we turn the corner, Stew is walking out of a room. He looks sad. I look up at him and for the first time ever in my life, I see the resemblance of Jack and Stew.

I release both Cody and Kyle's hands and push my wheelchair as fast as I can to Stew. He holds me in his arms and I hug him.

"Is he going to die?" I ask. The words come out softly but he hears me.

"No baby girl. You remember what Cody looked like after he was attacked?"

"Yes." I say.

"Jack looks bruised. There are bandages covering wounds that were at one time bleeding, but he is not bleeding now. He is alert. He is waiting for you."

"Come with me." I say.

"Of course." He says.

I turn my wheelchair and hold my hand out again to Cody. When I look down the hall, I see Landon is standing there.

A nurse walks over. She is very sweet. "He is limited for guests. Only two at a time."

Cody kisses me on the lips. "I will be in the lobby waiting for you."

"Take me with you." I say.

He squats down. "Crystal, you can do this."

"I don't want to do it alone." I say.

Cody kisses my forehead. "Stew is going in with you. We are all here for you when you come out. Tell Jack how much he means to you. You told me how much I meant to you years ago and I was a stranger to you."

"I knew who you were." I say.

He kisses me again. "You need to do this."

Stew walks away from the two of us. He takes his phone out of his pocket and texts me.

Stew: Baby girl, go see him with Cody. I will come in. He has to have surgery and they are going to take him soon.

I look at my phone. Cody sees my phone. He stands and takes my hand. He opens the door to the room and we both go inside. My dad is hooked up to machines. There are tubes and wires running all over the place.

I gasp and he opens his eyes. He holds his hand out to me.

"Are you alright?" I ask.

He smiles at me. "I know I look bad, but I broke my leg."

I look at him. "Your leg?" I take his hand as Cody pushes me forward.

"Hi Jack." Cody says.

"Cody." Dad says.

"What happened?" I ask.

"Don't be mad at Joanna." Dad says. "She grabbed the wheel and we hit a tree."

"Why did she grab the wheel?" Cody and I ask together.

Dad looks at me. "We were arguing about you."

"Me?" I ask.

"I am sorry." He says. "I never meant for you to be hurt. I always loved you like you were mine and if I treated you differently, I didn't know I was doing it. I am sorry. I did know that Stew is your biological father, but I want you to know that we both love you equally. I was told today that you think that mommy and I divorced because of you and all the medical expenses. I want you to know that is not even a bit true. I would spend all my money on you. Stew did step in when I couldn't be there but its not because I didn't love you. We never wanted you to feel alone. What we all intended for you not to feel was the way you were feeling, I can't say sorry enough."

"Daddy, please." I say.

He smiles when I call him daddy.

"Let them fix your leg, we will be here when you come out."

He looks at both Cody and me. "No, you go on your honeymoon."

"We will both be miserable waiting to find out what is going on with you." Cody says.

"Thank you Cody. Thank you for loving my favorite girl."

"Thank you for bringing her to baseball games." Cody says.

A nurse walks into the room. "Mr. Steele, we are going to take you now."

He looks at the nurse. "I am ready." He says. He squeezes my hand. I do the same to his. "I love you."

"I love you too." I tell him.

The nurse looks at me. "There is a private room if you want to wait in there."

"Thank you, but my family is all in the lobby."

"You are a part of that family that is in the lobby?" She asks.

"Have they been embarrassing?" I ask.

"They have been concerned. And the lady that sits by herself she needs to be looked at but she won't leave that seat."

"I am sorry, what?"

"Your dad was having an attack of some kind. And she grabbed the wheel to avoid an accident with a truck that had merged into their lane."

I don't wait to hear anymore, I push my wheelchair as fast as I can to the lobby. I look at Joanna and notice that she looks dazed. The color in her face is pale. I position my wheelchair in front of her. I put my hand on her shoulder and her head drops forward on her chest. Stew runs over and takes her pulse. Kyle runs over and takes her in his arms. Stew runs into a room and Kyle follows carrying his mother. Brandon takes my hand and runs after Kyle and Stew. Ashley and Kelsey run after us as well.

Kyle lays her on the bed and a team of doctors and nurses come running in. They all start taking her vitals and put her on oxygen. Her eyes roll back. She tries to look around the room for something that she recognizes. Everyone is pushed away from her, but I don't move away. I take her hand and hold it firmly.

"Just breathe. You are going to be ok. Why didn't you tell any of us that you were — hurt?" I choke out the word hurt. "I am sorry we are all so awful. We didn't even notice."

She shakes her head. She squeezes my hand and then her grasp goes limp. I look at Stew. He looks at me.

"Keep talking to her. Nothing negative."

Cody walks in the room and stands behind me.

"Joanne, do you remember when you first met us and my mom was at work, dad was off on a job and I got sick at school. They called everyone on the contact list and couldn't get anyone to come get me. I begged them to call you. You weren't one of the contacts and they were nervous that I was calling a stranger. When you came to get me I had a fever. When I was getting in the car, you didn't know what to do, or maybe you were watching me do what I could do on my own. I am not sure, but when a lady came over and started yelling at you to help me, you looked at me and then lifted me with one arm in the car. You put my wheelchair in the car and it got stuck. You drove with the back opened. You got in the car and asked me a million questions of what I was feeling. I told you that I had a headache and my throat was sore. You asked me if I wanted ice cream." I smile recalling the memory. "You brought me to the fanciest ice cream place I had ever been to. My hair was messy and you French braided it within seconds. We went inside and you asked what my favorite kind of ice cream was. My mom didn't allow us to eat ice cream unless it was our birthdays so you went to the guy and told him that you wanted to try every flavor. You called me your daughter. We had like a hundred different ice creams. My throat felt better, but my head was spinning. When you brought me home we sat on the couch and watched Beauty and the Beast. You sang softly in my ear as I fell asleep on the couch."

"You never cried or anything. When I took you to the doctor the next morning, you had double ear infections and a throat infection." She looks at our hands. "I didn't ever think that it meant anything to you."

"It meant the world to me." I say. "My mom didn't let us eat ice cream and you let me eat it for lunch and then breakfast the next day. I know that my mom was mad that you let me eat ice cream, but she shouldn't have said what she did to you. You told me when we were at the doctor's office that you always wanted a daughter and you were glad that Jack came with three."

She sits up and her color returns. "You heard what your mom said to me?"

I nod my head. "I told her that she shouldn't have spoken to you like that. I was grounded for a week."

"I am sorry for that."

"I am not. She was wrong. You were nice."

"I stayed distant from all of you," she looks around the room. "I was mourning my first love." She looks at Kyle and Brandon. "Your dad was my world. When he slipped away it broke my heart. Jack came into my life and I know that it destroyed his marriage, but he woke me up from my darkness." She looks at me. "I am sorry."

"When you showed up for me at the resort after I had been fired and you were supportive of me, it meant the world to me. I know things run hot and cold for us, but you are always going to be in our lives. I want you in mine. You are going to be a grandma one day to my children. You have a lot of fun stories that need to be passed on."

She looks at me. "You remember the stories that I told you?"

"I think you made a few of them up about a girl who used a walker and she always did kind things for people. Then you made that little girl in your story walk on her tiptoes in a forest full of lions, wolves and some ugly creature that you couldn't remember the name of."

She laughs. Everyone laughs. Brandon looks at Joanna. "You feeling better?"

"I am light headed." She says.

"We are going to run some tests." Stew says.

Two hours later Cody and I leave the hospital with Landon. Dad is out of recovery and was admitted for observations. He and Joanna are in the same room. She was diagnosed with a concussion and whiplash. When they said that she could leave, she stood up and nearly face planted on the floor. Kyle and Cody grabbed her. We stayed until they fell asleep.

Cody, Landon and I go back to the resort. We go to our room and Landon sits on one bed. I get into the bed that I assume Cody and I shared on our wedding night that I slept through. The second that I lay back against the pillows, I close my eyes and fall asleep. I feel Cody get in the bed and put his arms around me.

We get up the next day, the three of us and we go back to the hospital. Dad is sitting up in the bed. Joanna is sleeping. She again looks pale. Kyle looks at me and nods his head to the door. The two of us leave the room. Cody is in the lobby with everyone else.

Kyle looks at me. "My mom is not doing well." He says.

I reach my hand up to his chest. "What's going on?"

"Well your dad had a panic attack while he was driving yesterday and my mom had a slight heart attack."

"What?" I ask.

"She has kept her health issues from us for years."

"What health issues?"

"Did you know that she needed to have a hysterectomy?"

"Of course not."

"She had her gallbladder removed. Did you know that?"

"No." I look back into the room. "Kyle, I don't know much about her. She kept me at arms length and didn't want to be close to me. The most that I talked to her was last night. The most she talked to me was the event that I mentioned last night." I rub my neck. "Why did dad have a panic attack?"

"He was thinking about you and is stressing that if you leave for your honeymoon, you won't return."

"I will return." I say. "Why wouldn't I return?"

"You stayed away for years."

"Ky, please. You and Brandon were the only two who cared about what I was doing. My mom does from a distance. She calls me on the phone and we have great conversations. In person, not so nice. Dad is not my dad. I am sorry that they are having issues. I am not going to miss going on my honeymoon with a man who loves me and I love him equally as much."

"I am not asking you to stop doing what you have planned. Just stay a few days."

"Can I ask you something?"

"Yes." Kyle says.

"Other than you who ever changed their plans or their lives for me?"

"I hear you, but my mom needs all of us. She may be really sick."

"She doesn't even like me." I say. "Kyle if I change my plans its only for you. In reality. I would do anything for you."

He kisses the top of my head.

"Cody has to agree. If Cody says that we leave tomorrow, I am gone."

"Agreed."

"Ky, don't guilt him."

"I would never do that."

I go into the lobby and find Cody. He stands up and walks over to me. "Are you alright?"

"Just hug me." I say.

He looks at Kyle. "Is everything ok?"

"My mom is sick."

"What can we do?" Cody asks.

"Just be here for me." Kyle says to his best friend and his favorite sister.

"You got it." Cody says.

I look at Kyle, "You just agreed."

Two weeks later, Cody and I board a private plane. The plane lands in Washington. We are still going to see the city for just a few days. We check into the resort that we are staying in. We go to the room and get settled. We go for dinner. We sit at an outdoor diner enjoying the sights.

When we wake up the next morning it's a day full of rain. We call the pilot who flew us to Washington and ask him if he is available to take us early to Hawaii. He tells us to give him a few hours. We go down to the lobby.

A lady walks over to us. "Cody?"

Cody turns around and looks at her. "Can I help you?"

"Cody, you don't remember me?" She asks.

"I am sorry, should I know who you are?"

She looks at me. "You are one lucky woman."

Cody is holding my hand and I feel him tense. I look at him. "I truly am." I say.

"My nephew is a real catch." She says.

Cody looks at her. "I am sorry but who are you?"

Before she can answer, a security guard walks over. He looks at Cody and me. "Please come with me Mr. and Mrs. Steele."

I look at him because he used my last name and not Cody's last name. I smile when I see that it's Christian. Casper walks into the lobby and looks at the two of us. "Mr. and Mrs. Steele your ride is here."

I smile at the two of them. We leave with them. The woman follows us.

"Cody?" She stomps her foot.

Christian puts his hand in the middle of Cody's back. "Keep walking sir." He says.

"Your mom never spoke about me?" She asks. "You are my nephew."

"What's my mom's name?" He asks never turning back to her.

"Carolina."

No one calls her Carolina. Everyone calls her Catalina. We don't say this to anyone. We keep walking.

"Cody! I want to talk to you about Donavan. How old is he now?"

Cody tenses again. I hold firmly to his hand. We keep walking.

"Cody!" She calls out. "How is Donavan?"

Christian puts his hand on Cody's shoulder. He leans in closer to Cody and asks, "who is Donavan?"

"My brother."

"We didn't meet a Donavan at your wedding. Why wasn't he there?"

"He passed away." Cody says. "If that is my mom's sister, she should know that."

We reach the SUV. Casper opens the door for us. Cody lifts me out of my wheelchair and gets into the SUV. Christian puts my wheelchair in the trunk.

She bangs on the door. "How is Landon and Gianna doing? How is Donavan? Why are you leaving? Your mother told me where to find you and told me to catch up with you. Please.

I look at Cody. I try to prevent myself from trembling with fear, but I fail miserably at it. "Who is she?"

"I am not sure."

"Why is she asking about Donavan?" I ask.

"I don't know." He looks at me. "Are you shaking?"

"When you got beat up and stabbed, I heard that the people who did it were asking you questions about Donavan. My ex didn't know who the hell they were talking about. Do you think she wants to hurt you?"

"Sweetheart, we are safe. The windows are shatter proof." Casper says.

He no sooner says it and she throws something hard at the window. It doesn't break like Casper says it won't but it still scares the hell out of me. I curl into Cody.

"We are safe." Casper says.

"Why aren't we leaving?" I ask.

"The police have surrounded the vehicle." Christian says.

"Cody." I whisper.

He holds me tight against him. He takes his phone out of his pocket and calls his mother. She answers immediately. He doesn't start the conversation off like he normally would. He doesn't ask her how she is doing, instead he blurts out. "Do you have a sister?"

"What?" She asks.

"Mom, do you have a sister?"

"No. You know I don't." She says.

"There is a woman here in Washington telling me that she is your sister. She is asking about Donavan. She threw something at the window of the vehicle that we are in."

"Are you safe?"

"Yes." He kisses the top of my head. "We are scared."

"Are you going to continue on to Hawaii?" She asks.

"I am not sure."

"Do a detour."

"Where to?"

"Go to Colorado. Daddy and I have the cabin. We had it renovated for Crystal. We were going to surprise you both when we went there in the summer. Go there now. The keys are—"

"I know where the keys are." He says. "We will do that. I will call you from there."

"I love you."

"I love you too. I love you both." She tells Sawyer what is happening.

"Mom, she said she knew you."

"Sweetheart, anyone who knows me knows not to talk about Donny."

"Should we come home?"

"No. Go on your honeymoon, but detour for your safety just in case she knows the travel plans."

We go to the airport and we fly to Denver Colorado. We are met by three guys who look familiar to me, but I can't place where I know them from. Cody never lets go of my hand. We go to the van and one of them opens the door to reveal a ramp that they lower for me. Cody pushes me into the van. They take us to a house that looks much like Sawyer and Catalina's house in Florida. It almost contrasts with the neighboring houses.

We get out of the van and I notice right away that there are no steps, there are two ramps leading up to the front door. I can't contain my happiness and excitement. I throw my arms up in the air. I turn to Cody. "They love me."

"We all love you." He says.

We go into the house and we are welcomed with flowers and balloons. There is a card on the table.

Congratulations! Welcome to your home away from home. This is yours as much as it is ours. Please stay as long as you want. Be safe. We are so happy for you. We love you.

Love, mom and dad

We walk around the house and we decide on not staying in the master bedroom. On the bed in there is one of Catalina's robes. We find a second bedroom and on that bed is rose pedals. On the side of the bed on an end table are two Champaign glasses. There is a note next to them that the Champaign can be found in the wine cellar.

Cody walks across the room and looks out the French doors. The view is spectacular. He turns to me and holds out his hand. I cross the room and take his hand. We go outside. Cody sits in a chair and I sit as close to him as possible. I kiss him.

Once we start kissing, we don't stop. Cody smiles against my lips. "We never had a wedding night."

I smile against his lips. "Cody, I have a question to ask you?"

He pulls back but keeps me embraced. "What's that?"

"Do you take Crystal Belle Steele to be your wife forever?"

"I do." He says. He looks into my eyes, "Crystal, do you take Cody Parker to be your husband from this day until forever?"

"Always, I do." I say.

He kisses me with a hunger that he always has.

"Cody." I say breathlessly. "Make love to me."

We go in the house and he lifts me onto the bed. He undresses me slowly. When he removes my shirt, he slides his hands over my stomach and my breasts before he reaches for the hem of the shirt and slides it up over my head. He cups my breasts over my bra. He unclamps my bra from the front hooks and slides the straps off my shoulders. He cups one of my breasts and lowers his head to the other one. He licks at my nipple. He takes my nipple into his mouth and sucks.

"Oh Cody, please." I say.

After his welcomed assault on my nipple, he straddles me. He moves backwards and touches my stomach again. This time instead of going up, he slides his hands down my legs. He takes my pants down but leaves my underwear on. He pushes them to the side and slips his fingers into me.

"Cody!" I moan. "Cody, please." I beg.

He pulls his fingers out and then pushes them back in.

"I need you inside me."

He lays on top of me and kisses me. "You were meant for me." He says.

"I wanted to be yours since I saw you play. You were in college with Kyle." I say to him.

"He told me that you took notes on my posture when I played. He told me that he showed them to the coach. The coach changed some things and we worked on it. I didn't know until later but I wish I had. You were meant to be mine." He says again. "I have never been loved by anyone like you love me."

"Make love to me."

He gets undressed quickly and again lays on top of me. He pushes inside me. "I wanted to make love to you on our wedding night, but you fell asleep. There was no waking you up. Anything I tried to do to wake you, I couldn't. Stew sat next to me and told me that when I was in the hospital you went days without sleeping. You stayed with me. And then when you left me you crashed and you slept for two solid days."

"He told you that?"

"He did."

"Did you think that I was going to sleep two days?"

"You could have slept a week, I would have waited."

"This is not how we planned to start our lives together."

"This was just a few days in the chapter. Its not how we started our lives together. We started our lives together in a Target store, at a baseball game when I held you in my arms. On an air plane where you told people off to protect me. Our lives started when you bought an angel for my brother. Our lives started when I heard your voice talking to me telling me stories about your life when I was in the hospital recovering from an attack. So your dad being in the hospital and dealing with Joanna is not going to ruin our journey into this marriage." He kisses me with so much passion that all of his kisses have.

We react to each other. I feel his heat. He feels my heat. "Cody, I am so happy that we found each other. I am so happy that you kissed me in that resort lobby. You made me believe that I was a princess in a fairytale and my dreams were coming true."

"You make me feel like we were meant to be together. You know so much about me and you love me for me, and not what I can do for you."

I bury my face in his chest. "I have loved you from the second I watched you wiggle your ass when you went up to bat. You blew a kiss at Kyle and he pretended to fall back and faint. I know it was meant for him, but in my heart it was meant for me."

Cody kisses me. "If I would have known you then, it would have been meant for you."

"Do you think you will play again?" I ask more seriously. I put my hand on his shoulder and my fingers fall into the scars.

He winces.

"Does it still hurt?" I ask. I try to move my hand but he covers my hand with his hand. "I don't want to hurt you."

"You are not hurting me. I never let anyone touch it."

I look into his eyes. "I touched it while you slept in the hospital."

"Your dad brought us together."

I smile when he mentions my dad. Stew. Only I didn't know then that Stew was my dad. But what he says is true. Stew did bring us together. My dad, Jack, brought us together too. I wanted to connect with him and know sports. Football made no sense to me, but baseball made me fall in love.

"What are you thinking?" Cody asks me.

"That both of them actually brought us together. Stew actually pushed me in the room that you were in and told me to talk to you. But Jack loved baseball and I loved him and wanted to have a bond that my sisters didn't have with him. Baseball was that bond."

He kisses me. "You just wanted to play with my bat and balls."

I laugh.

We finally make it to our Honeymoon destination. When we check into the resort we are escorted to the most beautiful room that has the most beautiful view. Once we get settled in the room, we decide to go for a swim. The concierge tells us where the best waterfalls are. He tells us that there is a spot that we can go in the night where the water glows and illuminates the waterfall.

Cody takes my hand and we walk the path that the concierge told us about. We see the waterfall. Cody lifts me into his arms and carries me into the water. Once in the water, I stand in front of him and hold on to him. I put my hands on his shoulders and lift myself into his arms. Cody kisses me. He walks closer to the waterfall. We feel the water splash on us. I again stand in front of him holding on to his biceps. I lean into him and kiss him.

Cody pulls back a bit. He has a look on his face that I recognize. It's the same look that he had after every home run he hit.

"Are you happy?" I ask him.

"Extremely." He says. He lifts me in his arms and spins a few times. He places me back in the water so that I can stand. "Are you happy?"

"I couldn't ask for more. I love you. You are my lover boy."

"I regretted getting that tattoo always, but now I am grateful that I have it."

"I am grateful to have you."

"Kiss me!"

"Always." I throw my arms around his neck and pull myself up on his body and kiss him.

♥

Six months later, I sit in a baseball stadium right in the front row, where I have always wanted to be. My family and friends, who have become my family, sit next to me. Cody walks out of the dugout, takes his hat off his head, raises his arm and waves at the crowd. He turns a few times until he finds where I am sitting, he runs over and kisses me. The Jumbotron flashes with the image of him kissing me. It reads under the picture of us Grand Slam Home Run. Under that it reads Congratulations

Mr. & Mrs. Parker. Fireworks go off and illuminate the stadium in pink and blue. The screen than reads Twins!

Cody steps back and looks at the screen. "Twins?" He asks loudly over the roar that takes over the stadium.

"It's a grand slam home run." I say. I can not contain my happiness.

He looks at me. "What does that mean?"

"Three boys and one girl!" I say.

He hugs me again and lifts me in his arms. He runs around the bases with me and when he gets to home plate, the whole team that he coaches lifts him up and me too.

"And to think—" the assistant coach says.

"What?" Cody asks him.

"It all started with a kiss." He looks at Cody. "We are going to get fined if we don't get this game started." The assistant coach looks at Cody again. "What do you recommend I look for in a woman?"

"One that loves you unconditionally." Cody says.

I look at him and smile. He kisses me with that passion that again all his kisses contain. "That's how I love you, unconditionally." I smile against his lips. "Just think, this all started with just one kiss."

Cody slips his hands behind my head and kisses me with the hunger and passion we have shared since that very first kiss. "With one kiss, you changed my life."

"With one kiss, you made all my dreams come true. I love you." I say hugging Cody.

He puts his hands behind my head and kisses me with all the passion he possesses. Every time he kisses me, I feel like my dreams have all come true.